Tony.
Thank you for all your
help over the years

Don't let your Tea Go Cold

GU00763202

Shannon and Rob Marshall

Shannon X Rob ☺

P.S. There are coppers
mentioned in this :-)

Don't let your Tea Go Cold

© Shannon and Rob Marshall 2009

Published by Blue Ocean Publishing

St John's Innovation Centre

Cambridge CB4 0WS

United Kingdom

www.blueoceanpublishing.biz

Typesetting by Norman Brownsword, Spitfire Design

A catalogue record for this book is available from the British Library.

ISBN 978-0-9556430-5-7

First published in the United Kingdom in 2009 by Blue Ocean Publishing.

Shannon and Rob Marshall

This is Shannon and Rob's first novel. They live in Chertsey, Surrey with teenagers and a small fluffy dog. Both keen walkers and adventurists, they also like tea.

For Our Children

William, Elizabeth, Lydia, Anabel & Rose

Chapter One

Please make the noise stop. I can't get the damn thing within striking distance. Please make it stop. My eyes won't open! They must be glued shut. Of course the sunlight will penetrate my eyeballs and burn a hole right through my skull if I open them, so probably best not. Smoking cigarettes and singing Cracklin' Rose hasn't done my throat the world of good either. I can smell my own breath, a mixture of beer, fags and something I'd rather not think about now. There's something stuck in my hair; hm'm – it feels cold and crusty. Oh God! My ear smells of tomato. All I have to do is keep perfectly still and I'll be fine. Beer is so deceiving; the pump said Smooth. That's it, I'm writing a letter as soon as I can function.

Dear Mr Beermaker, I feel it necessary to write to complain about the labelling of your beer under the Trade Description Act 1968. 'Smooth' should read, 'Smooth now, but just you wait until five hours later and you'll feel about as smooth as a hedgehog's arse'. I'll gladly accept a free crate as compensation from *yourselves* for making *me* feel so ... I think I'm going to vomit ... rough ... quite soon. Love and kisses, Den.

At least I'm in my own bed. I'm assuming that I'm in my own bed; I can't feel another body. It is definitely my bed, no sane woman would have asked me to stay last night unless they had a fetish about a drunken man doing strange things with food. I snogged Mandy. I didn't need to remember that right now, the barmaid from the Anchor; oh dear. No. I mean, no idea. She'll be out buying a wedding dress today. Last thing I'd picked up about Mandy was that she had pulled Brian; he was drunk and afterwards she followed him around for weeks like a shadow, she even tipped up at work and asked him what time he was going to be home for tea. He thought it was a one-night stand but she didn't, and forsaking all others she pledged to bug him for the rest of his life, Amen. Okay. It's eyes open time, right now, after three. On the other hand, if I just have five minutes more in bed I'll feel even better and then I'll get up straight away. I couldn't very well be rude and not say goodbye to Geoff after working with him for six years and – well, you know how it goes in the pub and the lads are drinking and you're really up for it, even if it's a …Thursday. Bugger! I should know better. I've got a fitness test – oh well done. I love pizza – I hope it's pizza, so why the hell didn't I eat the damn thing instead of going to sleep on it? Right. I'm awake and my eyes are open, though I can't say working to their full potential. I can just about make my way around the room without damaging myself. I need to find my sports kit.

Hangovers are a personal thing; I think of mine as a sort of in-lieu-of girlfriend, you know she's there just looking and letting you suffer. Sometimes she says, 'Had a few too many last night did we?' No, I've got a special tablet I take when I haven't had enough! I ask you, what sort of question is that? Some things in life mystify me. When I have a girlfriend who's feeling fragile in the morning, I'll take her a cup of tea, let her lie in bed, talk sympathetically to her, because that's what I would like in return. I know my present state of health was my own doing but there's no need to remind me about it for the next week. Peanuts wouldn't, she'd just take the piss for a couple of hours and try and take me for another pint … hm'm, enough.

Good boy. One leg in without rolling over on my arse. I'll have to build up to the trainers in a minute. I've now got less than ten minutes to dress myself and get to the gym. I've got a bed, two wardrobes, a bedside table, an ironing board and a bottle full of pennies in my room; I can't find my daps and I look like I've just got dressed from the leftovers box in the charity shop. Outside the door – who put them there? Bending down to tighten my laces isn't the easiest of manoeuvres. It feels now like the contents of my head are trying to escape through my ears, it must be the pizza keeping it in. To try and enumerate this thing in my head, I'm sure if I informed Norris McWhirter CBE I'd get an entry into the Guinness Book of Records. Do you remember Record Breakers when the kids used to ask Norris to spout off world records from memory? I can see Roy Castle saying,

'And what's your name?'

'Amy.'

'And how old are you Amy?'

'I'm ten and a half.'

'And what's your question for Norris, Amy?'

'Who had the biggest hangover ever?'

'Ahh! Good question Amy! That was Denis Yarwood after drinking ten pints of Smooth and lots and lots of flaming zambukas. This resulted in the world's worst hangover, lasting three weeks.'

Ouch! my hand. That's great! Now I've not only got a hangover that could put a bull elephant into a coma, half a ham and mushroom pizza attached to my face, and an assortment of clothes that make me look like a poorly dressed Big Issue seller, but my left hand has obviously been in contact with someone else. I can't remember hitting anyone last night. Mind you I can't remember going to the toilet either, ha ha. I'll check my wardrobe later. I'm never drinking like that again; it's been so long since I've allowed myself and as soon as I do, I take it too far. It was an excellent night however; the lads were in such an infectious mood, and leaving dos are always like that. I think the Indian restaurant thought that they were being invaded as we piled in. It's getting to be a tradition that the leaver has to stomach a Tindaloo before we hit the pubs and Geoff scoffed the lot and had a pudding; he's always been a greedy beggar. The funniest part of the night was when we did the seven dwarves with the new boy Dave. What we do is: one at a time, the old and bold go into a pub and order one pint and six halves, then yodel 'Heigh-Ho!' Six of the lads, including the new boy, march in on their knees singing the Dwarf Chorus, drink up their halves and march out again. It gives the locals a laugh. At the last pub, it's the new boy's turn; Dave orders the drinks and hollers 'Heigh-Ho' at the top of his voice while the rest of us run off to the next pub. Childish but amusing.

Now, I can normally run a mile and a half in under nine minutes on a good day I'll stand with the lads and have a fag before I do it, just to get them riled. Running is easy, especially this route. For the first half a mile I can bomb around the sports pitch and get a good head of steam going, controlling my breathing every four strides. The next half mile takes us down Queens Avenue to the traffic lights and right towards Camp. I pace myself on the middle bit as I like to have a strong finish; I'll let Colin within about ten metres of me. He'll be blowing but he won't give up or slow down. He's a diamond bloke, gutsy and determined and when most of the others have given up he'll be there, chugging away like a trusty steam engine. At thirty he gets extra time to finish the test, but I don't think I'll ever see the day he has to use it. So we turn and I'm off, leaving Colin swearing at me between breaths. The last half a mile is the worst; my lungs are working like a singular piston, forcing the air out as hard as I can and sucking in every last drop of precious oxygen to feed my tiring limbs, my legs are getting heavy and sweat drips into my eyes. I know by this stage that I'll be motoring through the gates and looking for the instructor waiting with his stopwatch. I'm always first.

Today however, considering my physical state, I come third in nine forty five. Disgusting. Colin is chuffed, and takes great pleasure in slapping me hard on the back, and makes some feeble joke about having to get a bus pass. Well, I'm in no state to react so I'll just retreat to my room and try and remember how I hurt my hand. He took me on the corner by the lights; it wasn't a flash of black skin and running shoes, he just plodded past. In fact he ran next to me for about fifteen metres and then accelerated slowly; good bloke, I'd do it to him. I sidle back to my accommodation with the rest. We all look rough and I'm trying to decide if I feel as bad as they look. Mick was the only guy who didn't attend last night, which was probably a very sensible idea, and he trots up to me.

'Wotcha Den, you look like shit.'

'Why thank you. I feel so much better now.'

'Colin beat you today.' I wonder if they give out prizes for stating the obvious.

'Yeah, better luck next time, eh?' I'm really not in the mood for conversation and I need to drink a couple of gallons of water as my back is aching like mad.

'Have you seen the News today Den?' He's bristling with excitement and I don't want to listen but he's got a captive audience now.

'Mick, I'm about to see the contents of my stomach. *(Pause.)* No, I haven't.'

'Oh.' I hate it when someone is dying to keep the conversation going; it's tiresome. I have to ask.

'No. Why?'

'It's getting tasty in Kosovo; great, eh?' He runs away after giving me a wink and I don't respond, I've got far more pressing matters on my mind at this particular juncture. I know what he means though. After all of this time training for it, then there's a chance that if things got out of hand we might actually go.

My room looks like Stomp had a gig in here last night. There are clothes everywhere, bits of pizza box lay strewn on the floor I must have been slightly confused about the opening system as it's in several pieces. I think I'll wash my sheets before attempting to get under my duvet. The pizza has gone hard, I'll need a toffee hammer if I'm going to get it off. I hate hand washing, but I don't want to be the one who blows up the washing machine. I know that you're not strictly supposed to put boots in but it didn't say anything about *not* putting them in,. I blame Hotpoint. The physical exercise and dehydration are making me feel ill. I'm getting flashbacks to the Anchor and kissing Mandy. It wasn't one of those friendly peck on the cheek kisses either, I'm going to have to see her. Mind you, that would make her think I enjoyed the snog; yes, I *did,* but don't want the aftermath. She went bonkers with Brian. The other thing is that the lads took the mickey out of him, including me! She's not unattractive; in fact, she's a fine looking filly, but right now I can't do the relationship thing. Maybe if I just don't go to the Anchor for the rest of my life she'll forget. I'll get one of the boys to tell her that I was run over by a lorry, or I am married and my wife is pregnant with octuplets, or I'm gay...

Hang on a minute. I hit Brian, I remember now. I don't understand why he got so anti over a kiss with his stalker. It must be *his* fault that I punched him. Serves him right. Hey, maybe I'm off the hook? Mandy will love the idea of being fought over and Boxing Brian will be the hero, except he hit the ground like a sack of spuds. I'm going to be sick in a minute. No – now.

So is my life is going to be like this for ever? Drinking, feeling hung-over. I can remember when it started, but the most frightening thing is that I can't see it finishing, I don't want to drink myself to death, that's for certain, but memory loss is a comfort. That slut Mandy said I must be insecure. What does she know? I feel lively and the lads like me, how does that make me unstable? I'm a successful soldier and that's all that matters, if it's one thing I dislike it's being judged. Some people just love to do that; they go around condemning anyone for what they do and how they act, I shouldn't be so ... assured, ha! Sometimes I feel like they all want a piece of me, like I'm a one-man entertainment system. 'Come on Den, get on the karaoke' or 'Fancy a game of cards tonight?' Can't they amuse themselves? I mean, what is there to be scared of? I could go anywhere, just me on my own; I could go away to Amsterdam or somewhere else. I'll go to America, New York, where no one knows me or asks if I'm all right. I'll play cards with the Yanks and take their cash and get myself loaded. And I'll come home Den, a sober guy with money. I'll find a girl that I can trust, if there is such a thing.

I didn't used to have to drink so much back then before the letter; a few pints and I'd be away with the fairies. It must have been the late night card schools that got me into whisky. I can feel my liver rotting; I wonder when I get cremated it would take a couple of weeks to put me out? I'm not a numpty and I know that these guys aren't my friends. I have enough people around me to keep me occupied. I'll use them if they want to hang around to see me get drunk and fight, then let them. I lost a lot of money last night but it's swings and roundabouts in this game. Don't count the cards on the table, just put your money down and hope. I've won more than I've lost I think, but the trouble with cards is that the notes get transferred so quickly. It matters not, I'll be up tonight for definite and this is the big one. I've been waiting for this for a long time, and if I play well I'll be back on top I know it. Speculate to accumulate, and if I have got my sums right I'll be walking away with about four grand in my pocket ... easy money.

Chapter Two

I joined up after successfully screwing up or getting thrown out of every low-life poorly paid excuse for work there was. Luton isn't the best place to find employment, unless you want to be stuck in Vauxhalls for the rest of your days, inserting a hundred and fifty screws into a hundred and fifty cars, in the same hole every day, all day. Sorry, but that's not my idea of a living. I found school a drag, apart from the social aspect and the sports. I wasn't one of those disruptive kids, but I just didn't see much point in the lessons. I know how to add up, take away and spell my name so why bother with the other complicated facts? I can remember my fifth birthday; why do I need to know about Thomas A Whatshisface and the Magna Carthorse? So after five years of intense boredom, mixed with some rugby and fine-tuning my chatting-up skills on Samantha Gardener, I left school with a tear in my eye and two CSEs: Biology Grade 3 and Art Grade 2. The only reason I attended biology lessons in the first place was to see Mrs Packard's stilettos. Those shoes got me through puberty and quite a lot of my early adult life, I'm sure they contributed to some rather unhealthy fantasies as well. But they did make her legs look amazing; from a thirteen-year-old boy's view a nice pair of calves can structure your whole opinion on how a woman should look.

Anyway, if I had been more streetwise I'd have followed Marcus (my brother) into the Police Force. Instead, I decided to get into a car that a couple of my mates had sort of borrowed without asking the owner and go for a drive on Dunstable Downs. It seemed like a great idea at the time, but when you see blue flashing lights in the mirror and there's the possibility of your older brother arresting you, all of the glory of being a first time car thief seems to fade quite quickly. But that night I discovered that

I could run, fast as well. The other two were nicked and received a fine and community service but they had the manners not to grass. Marc would have knocked my block off and Mum would have been devastated. The funny thing was that he told me about the arrest the next day. He wasn't in the car apparently, but the copper who made the arrest had to chase us for nearly a mile before giving up on me; he probably needed the exercise anyway.

So I considered that after the trauma of secondary education, I'd take a gap year. The year was intended to evolve my social skills and pre-marital communication with the fairer gender. Mum wasn't that pleased about my decision because in fact it became her sending me to the Job Centre once a week. However, it seemed like a pleasant way to ease myself into the rat race. I mean you jump into something head first, you're up for a fall, aren't you?

My first day of proper adult work was for Bill the Boardman, who funnily enough was actually called Bill. Well, it made me chuckle. I had to mix the paste and hold the ladders while he did the complicated task of sticking the posters up the right way; it's just like wallpapering but bigger. Anyway, after three weeks of standing in the rain watching Bill put up the bills, I asked if I could have a go.

'Naw there's umpteen mooar ta puttin' up bills than meets t' eye lad.'

He was from Yorkshire and moved to Luton years ago, God knows why; I loathed the place and intended to move as far away as possible as soon as I had some money. I detest and hate being called lad as well. My dad used to call me his lad before he left us. My mum brought up us two boys with no money, after he disappeared to Peterborough with his fat secretary.

I don't see him, my dad. The last time was when I was nine; he came to my birthday party and didn't bring a present. I suppose that sounds spoilt but at nine it's polite to get something from your parent. He left our family when I was five so my memories of him being around aren't that clear Marc says that he was a great guy, always laughing and mucking about with his lads. Dad's got his own business selling office furniture. He lives in a big house with a big car ... and a jumbo wife. It's not the fact that he's wealthy and married that makes me resentful; more that Mum works really hard, she's done the whole lot and has resigned herself to being alone while responsible for us. I wish she'd meet someone nice.

So Bill taught me the intricate and diverse skills of sticking paper to plywood. It took nearly half an hour before I managed to master the centuries-old tradition. I'll be able to pass it on to my kids one day, I thought ... *not.* He said 'T' onny reason 'e wor showin' uz wor 'cos 'e 'ed ta nip on into a 'ospital for eur small operation t' followin' week 'n 'e 'oped ah could 'andle t' job soloa for eur few days'.

Monday of week two and I'm on my own. I can mix and stick, my employability has vastly improved. They'll be showing me in the gallery during Vision On. Bill has left me two jobs, one in the Arndale Centre for Vauxhall and the other is opposite the Luton & Dunstable Hospital, but he hasn't said who for. Hey, this is sticking up posters for goodness' sake – not rocket science! Bill insists that it's imperative to scrape the old sign off before putting the new one up. This takes ages, and it removes most of the skin off my knuckles, so I think to myself 'he'll never know', and whack the first one up in half an hour; 'job's a good'un.' If I can get number two up in the same time I'll be back in the house by lunchtime; easy money.

The old hoarding outside the hospital is for Wall's Ice Cream. 'Just Lick it and Taste the Difference'. Hm'm, didn't sell it for me, I'm afraid. The covering advert sticks down with ease. I love my job. I stand back and look on like a proud father viewing my son in his new school uniform. ARSENAL MOTORS OF LUTON. With a picture of a BMW and a guy with a cheesy grin and poorly fitted wig looking over the top of the car with his thumbs up: ooh, please don't ever let me go into car sales, if that's what it does to you.

I got home at twelve. Mum did me some soup and I settled down to do a serious bit of TV watching. I had two Simpsons' tapes to get through this afternoon. While I'm making myself comfortable on the sofa she gave me some popcorn too. Bless her. I know she'll not tell any of my mates that she puts extra sugar on because that's the way her boy likes them. About two the phone goes and Mum calls me, 'It's someone called Bill for you darling. He sounds huffy and cantankerous, like he's incensed about something. He won't talk with me and he said it's urgent.'

Before I got to the phone I hadn't uttered a word; however, he could sense I was on the line.

'Raa' firstly, wha' t' bloody 'ell are ye doin' a' 'ome a' dis tahhm?'

'Erm . . '

'Gerr ye bloody sen daahn 'eear naw laddoa,'

'Where?'

'T' bloody 'ospital, t' L&D ye gormless lahl bugga, ward three.'

That short exchange didn't fill me with the utmost conviction things were okay; the operation must have gone wrong. I know what he wants: he needs me to work on my own for another week, bonus. So I toddle off to the hospital; it's two buses to get there and I arrive about an hour later. I pop into the Spar on the way, pick up some grapes and a paper for Bill. Mum says it's wise to get in your employer's good books. I hope he hasn't got piles!

Bill hasn't got piles, he's stood by the window when I get into the ward, there are four nurses with him, giggling, and one's quite a girl, lovely set of pins.

'Gerr o'a 'eear laddoa 'n tell uz what's rong wi' dis bloody picture then, 'n theur lot can gi'o'a bloody laffin' an' orl.'

I didn't click, looking through the window; his ward was opposite where I had been working earlier. There it was, my handiwork, looking less slick than it had three hours before. These billboard posters are made in tiles and grid numbered to be put up and match up the design, but if you don't scrape the old one off first then the glue tends not to stick and peel. ARSE ... JUST LICK IT AND TASTE THE DIFFERENCE. The bloke with the wig was still visible with his cheesy grin and his thumbs in the air. Well, what was I supposed to say? I think the tears streaming down my face did it for Bill; he was red in the face, but I thought that it might have been due to the op. He lunged at me with both hands outstretched like Homer going to strangle Bart. One of the nurses, the shapely one, seized Bill and sat him down declaring he must relax or he'll do himself a mischief. She was smiling and trying to be attentive to Bill, who was in the middle of an oration.

'Thars getten twoa bloody 'ours ta gerr 'a' gabble sorted art lad. Theur maungy idle, feckless villian.'

Unfortunately I missed the rest as I ran through the swing door out of the ward but I imagine there were half a dozen more expletives and claims that I had been born out of wedlock.

Bill let me go after that (he actually said, 'Thas sacked lad, ah nivva want ta see thy spotty fyass agin.') and docked me the cost of the poster out of my wages; £5.65 for a week's work. I could just about afford a packet of fags and some chips. I'll put the car on the back burner for the next few years then.

Well – they say every cloud and that; the nurse, Julie, came to see me as I was attempting to fix my misdemeanour. I didn't recognise her at first as she had her hair down and a leather jacket over her uniform. She must have been at least three years older than me so goodness knows why she wanted to chat; maybe it was because I made her laugh.

'Nice work!'

'Why thanks. How's Mr Happy?'

'Oh, I'm sure he'll be fine. He swears a lot doesn't he?'

'Yea, too bloody much'

Instant laughter, I'm on a winner.

'So what's your name, laddo?'

'Ha ha, very good. Den. What about you? Let me guess. Florence?'

Giggling, 'Julie.'

This was going well; not only was she giggling, she looked experienced. Okay Den me lad, let's go for the kill.

'So Julie, fancy a night out with a retired billboard boy?'

'I'd love one. When?'

Crumbs, that was quick. I'm not used to it being this easy; normally I need to do more groundwork before I get an acceptance.

'Erm . . . I dunno – tomorrow?'

'What time?'

She's not serious, no one does this to me. I spent three years trying to get a look at Samantha Gardener's knickers and this girl wants me to take hers off right now. Sod it, I'm game.

'Eight o'clock, by the Odeon in town.' I was made up, she can't resist me,. Ha! I'm not surprised either, what young, beautiful, stocking wearing nurse could? Bloody hell, I nearly fell off my ladder.

'Okay, see you there, bye. Oh, by the way, tight butt.'

No, she didn't really say that, did she? I must tell Marc. He'll be hopping, he's been trying to get together with a nurse from the L&D for what seems like an eternity. I take one trip and the girls are throwing themselves at my feet.

Marc is livid, but not in a nasty way. We get on pretty well as brothers; he's twenty, twenty-one in March. I can't remember if it's the fifteenth or sixteenth; never mind, I'm sure I'll get the subtle reminders for about six weeks before the big day. He was a nightmare after his eighteenth, telling me of the nights he'd be spending in the pub and how much more attractive women found eighteen year olds; ha, well that blew his theory out of the window didn't it? Pubs aren't that big a thing anyway. I've been getting served for about six months now and it's not my eighteenth birthday until November and I'm taking a nurse out tonight, so sorry Marcus (he hates being called that) but I think your baby bruv is doing rather well for himself. I have got a lot of time for Marc; as blokes go, he's all right, even being a copper. He joined as soon as he could and has just finished probation and spends all of his time juggling his shift system with his social life. I know that when he moans he doesn't mean it; the Police Force was his ambition since he left school and he's done well to get in. Mum and I went to his passing-out parade, which was mega, though Marc looked a twit in his uniform, because they had run out of hats in his size, so he had to wear this enormous helmet that came over his eyes and wobbled with every move of his head. He said that it was because his name started with the letter Y that he was always at the back of the queue; silly thing to say in front of his mates as they followed it up with loads of jokes about brains, etc. Mum wasn't too happy either but I thought it was hilarious until they pointed out the fact that we share a surname. Marc has been seeing Debbie for about three months. She works at the station as a typist; she's lovely. I don't know why he keeps going on about nurses.

So tonight's the night, except I haven't got two pennies to rub together. Ah, I'll sponge a tenner from Marc until I get another job, he'll be fine. So what are my choices then? It's tough taking women out; I mean, what do they like? The pub: but that costs money, pictures means more cash. A meal? Yeah right, I'm sure she'll be blown away by fish and chips from the Hatters fish shop.

Ice skating, too far to travel. Bowling? No, that's in Dunstable and I could only afford one game. Erm . . . come on Den, think, man. Sex, that's free. I'll just meet her by the picture house and say, 'Right – let's shag'. What a line! I'll write that one down for future dates. It's brilliant.

'Marc?'

'Yes, young man. What can I do for you?'

He always answers like that when I'm on the scrounge; it's a real power thing, but he's the one with the cash and the decent shirts, so I keep going.

'Could you do me a huge favour mate?'

I'm starting to feel queasy; I need his black shirt as well as some dosh.

'How much?'

'Twenty, please, I'll pay you back next week.'

'How? You're out of work.'

'I don't know yet, I might sell a kidney.'

'Nice one. You could sell the contents of your pants mate, they're completely redundant at the moment, ha ha,'

'Yes, ha ha.' Here we go, I'm a virgin; and thanks to Marc, all of his mates, my mates and every girl he has brought home knows. But money is power and my day will come, so I laugh and hold my ribs as if they are going to explode.

'Here's fifteen, that's all I've got.'

'Thanks Marc, you're a great brother.'

Damn, Den, you've gone too far now.

'Which one?'

'The black one.'

'You know what I'll do if you damage it, don't you?'

'Look, can I borrow the friggin' shirt or not?'

'Oi! Watch your language in the house, Mum will hear you. Yes. You can piss off now.'

That's the nearest we come to arguing, ever. I need another job, fast.

Chapter Three

7.45pm. I'm waiting outside the cinema in the bus stop. I look great: snazzy shirt, good pair of jeans and my best trainers. I borrowed Marc's aftershave on my way out of the door so I smell lush too. Debbie buys him aftershave, so if she likes it, Julie is bound to; well, that's my theory. I've got £18.50 left after buying some ciggies so that should be enough for a few drinks in the Swan. That's the only place I can get served at the moment. Mum went nostalgic on me tonight because this is my first real proper date. She started telling me how her and Dad met, which to be truthful I didn't want to hear but I played along to make her feel better. I can't understand how she could talk about him like he was a knight in shining armour after he abandoned her. Anyway; the story goes, Mum was working in the restaurant at Vauxhall; Dad had been spying on her for weeks. Then one day when he came for his lunch he asked her for a dance and the rest is history. That's the précised version of course but, as I said, the whole thing of standing there declaring, 'Ah that's lovely, Mum' is diplomatically challenging. So they got married and had two wonderful ... CONDOMS! Time check: 7.50. I'll need to be quick, so I rush over to the Arndale Shopping Centre; they always have late night shopping.

Alleluia. I'll go to church for the next month, I promise. Okay Den, what you're about to do is perfectly normal. People buy condoms every day. I'm being responsible and sensible. No one will laugh, so don't worry, and anyway who wants to know about my lark? So, I bowl into the shop, head down and full of determination, moving rapidly towards the counter. As I get nearer, I can make out the packets; it's just a case of choosing the nearest box and putting it next to the till. There's not even a queue so I'll be through and out of here in seconds. This couldn't be easier. My arm stretches out, and in my other hand is a five-pound note ready to thrust at the shopkeeper and make my escape.

'Hello Denis! How's your Mum?'

'Fine thanks Mrs McKinney, a packet of Lockets please. Thank you. 'Bye.'

'Say hi to your Mum won't you dear?'

Rats.

7.55. Back to the bus shelter. If I ever get elected to Prime Minister I'll make it a law of the land that none of Mum's friends are allowed to work in chemists.

8.05. I've been stood up. What will I tell Marc? I won't; I'll have a few pints in the Swan and tell him that she took me back to her place and we did it all night and she had stockings on. I'm gutted; my first chance to get it on and she blew me out. That's really rude. Come on Den; let's get you a pint.

'Oi SEXY!'

I can't see her, but it's Julie, I look up and down the street but there are no women about that look like her.

'Over here.'

Crikey, I didn't know nurses could drive!

'Are you getting in or do you fancy running behind?'

'You look nice.' Mum told me to say that. I get a small smile but not enough to fill me with certainty that she is still interested.

'So where are we off to then?' I'm not doing so well now with the chat; Julie has definitely got the upper hand. I feel like she should be taking me to school. She's dressed to kill, beige blouse, tight black skirt, dangly earrings, loads of makeup and she's got her hair up, but not the same as it was when she was in uniform. It's in a tight bun and shows off her lovely long neck. God, what's she going to do to me?

'There's a pub next to Whipsnade Zoo that the girls go to, got a fab menu.'

Oh no. She's calling the shots already. Marc warned me about this, take a firm hand. Don't get pushed around Den, tell her now – you haven't got enough money.

'Fine, great.' Div!

Julie is in the second year of her nursing course; she came to Luton from Leicester to study and wants to settle here when she qualifies. What's wrong with these people? Anyway, as well as being able to drive, she can eat like a horse too. One steak and chips later, followed by coffee and four pints and I'm down to my last three quid and I'm starving. It was sacrificing my own dinner or doing a runner from the pub. I'd thought about it and it's a long way home. We sat with two frenzied student nurses who chatted furiously about various patients they have had to treat this week. I managed to keep up with the conversation for a while, pitching in about Bill, who by the way had the snip; but I soon ran out of any decent conversation, and ended up sitting through stories of enemas and bedpan contents. Nightmare.

Julie had drunk three pints and I'd forgotten that she had the car so I was taken aback when at closing time she casually chucked me the keys and said, 'Come on Tiger – take me home.'

'But I ...'

'Don't worry. My dad pays for my insurance. It's fully comp.'

'No, I ... '

'I'll direct. Don't worry, I'm not that drunk.'

I've only driven a car twice; the first time was with Kev, a mate from school. He'd asked me to go fishing with him and his dad, saying it was a cracking day out and we'd have a laugh, so with nothing better to do I joined them. No one caught a thing, and I think his dad could tell by my face that I was moping; so instead of going straight home he let us both have a go with his Mini in the car park. It seemed easy enough once I could remember which pedal did what. The other time was reversing Marc's old Mark IV Cortina out of the drive after much insincerity about how crackin' it looked and what a cool car it was.

So the prospect of driving Julie's new Fiesta through Dunstable to Luton, about ten miles, was frankly alarming, but I couldn't lose face. What made me worse was that Julie's two mates had jumped in the back. A voice in my head started saying 'We're going to die'.

I started up and fished around in the dark for the gear stick. It wasn't like I remembered; this one had a bar at the top and buttons on it. There were only two pedals as well, – it doesn't take a lot to confuse me. This did.

'Haven't you driven an automatic before?'

'Erm . . . '

'Sorry – I should have said,' and with that she lent over and put the lever into what was, visibly, reverse. I slipped off the handbrake and with a torrent of girlie screams we shot back about fifteen feet before I could find the brake. By this stage I was getting annoyed with myself for not having the bottle to come clean with Julie. With three drunken women jibing at my driving skills, I rammed the car into drive and put my foot down, turning the wheel to head out of the car park and onto the main road. I have no idea how close I was going to the other cars; the only indication was the sharp intakes of breath from Julie. My turn to take control.

'Having fun, girls?'

No answer.

'So where do you want dropping off?'

I was trying to talk, drive, and listen to Julie's very quiet directions, and by the time we reached Dunstable I'd mastered the controls and started to enjoy myself.

'Here, please.' From the back seat of the car.

Julie: 'But you live ...'

'THIS WILL DO FINE.'

I pulled over near the kerb, and my two rear seat passengers shot out of the car, bade us a brief farewell, and were off into the night. We drove on, slower than before, and reached Julie's flat at 11.30; she only lived about a mile from my house in one of the better estates for this area. It was then it dawned on me that this could be it; I'm going to get invited in for coffee or whatever they say on telly. I don't like coffee. Julie tells me where to park the car and we get out, making sure that the doors are locked.

'Right. Thanks. See you tomorrow then.'

I can't believe it. I've paid out for a meal and driven this girl home and she's not going to bonk me, not even a kiss! That's it, she's dumped. I'm not going to be messed around. Marc was right and I'm going to tell her I don't really fancy her anyway. Just then she bent over and our lips met, briefly. Wow. I've kissed loads of girls before, well, three, if you include Auntie Dawn but not like this. Her hand crept around to the back of my head with her fingers slipping through my hair, making it feel like it was standing on end. That wasn't the only thing starting to stand on end either.

'Yeah ... see you tomorrow,' I feebly replied.

My first real girlfriend. I wasn't in love or anything like that, but we seemed to get on pretty well. The next night I came clean about the driving and my age but she didn't seem to mind. She started calling me her toy-boy, which I found quite endearing, and as a seventeen-year-old it's cool to be going out with a nurse who's got a car. My main concern was that after our third date, again in another pub, she still hadn't made a move; now if I were going to get laid I'd have to take the initiative. Saturday came and I was invited around for a meal, her flatmate was out, and I'd had time to properly prepare. I'd found a chemist in Dunstable and ensured that there was no one who knew my family working inside and dashed in.

I pitched up outside her place bang on time carrying a bottle of

Lambrusco and some flowers that I was advised to take by Kev. He knew things about women that I didn't. I rang the bell and looked through the frosted glass front door as she descended the stairs and opened up.

'Wow, you look great!' I exclaimed as she stood there in a little black number and made-up to the hilt with her hair swept back to fully expose her exquisite face. I felt a little underdressed, as I'd only put jeans on, and a shirt that I'd liberated from Marc without him noticing, that I'd poorly ironed.

She led me in and thanked me for the flowers with a kiss and I followed her up the stairs and along a narrow landing to the front room. I could see three doors leading off the landing; one to the front room where we were, and the others to the kitchen and bedroom, I assumed. The room was homely and girly with fluffy cushions on the sofa, where I perched, as she went to open the wine. She had a stereo in one corner and a telly in the other, with a small foldout table in the middle that she had laid for two, with a candle smouldering. There wasn't much else in the room apart from a huge beanbag and rug, but at least it was independent living.

Julie returned with a vase in one hand and two glasses of wine in the other. I jumped up to relieve her of the glasses while she found somewhere to place the arrangement of pink carnations. (Kev said that roses were too much like commitment; go for cheap and cheerful.)

'They're lovely. Thank you Den,'

'Oh, that's no problem. They weren't expensive.'

'You certainly have the patter, don't you young man, ha ha?'

I felt my face flush as I realised my faux pas.

'Are you ready to eat then?'

'Yep, can I do anything to help?'

She twisted to return to the kitchen and then looked at me over her shoulder with a grin on her face.

'No, I'll be fine, sit down. I'm very good with my hands,' and she winked and left the room. I must be getting it tonight; I mean why go to all of this trouble? I checked my pocket again to make sure I'd remembered to pick up the condoms and wondered if I should take them out of the box in readiness so as not to delay proceedings. Too late – she made an entrance with two steaming hot plates and sat down with me.

'Tuck in then, I hope you like curry?'

'Oh yea, love it, thanks.'

'Good, you should see what I have got for pudding.' I nearly choked as she giggled and lifted her glass to chink against mine. The liquid wobbled as I waved it around in partial terror and anticipation.

We had dinner, listened to music, chatted about parties, and what was on at the pictures. We drank nearly two bottles of wine, which made me relax. We'd kissed quite a lot that week so I had no fear of grabbing her during the evening for the occasional snog as we sat on the sofa. I braced myself and slipped a sweaty hand up under her dress ... with no resistance. Now I've seen a porn film and done the sex education stuff in school, but navigating your way around someone else's body for the first time is stressful. There are buttons and clips all over the place; it's like a defence system. By the time I'd undone her bra strap my fingers were aching and I'd broken into a sweat.

'Have you got anything with you?'

'What?'

'Have you got any ... you know?'

What is she on about? Got what? Money? Chocolate? Oh – yeah! Now sound calm.

'Yes. Hang on.'

Challenge number two as I ripped open the condom packet.

Julie stood up and let her dress and bra drop gently to the floor. I must have looked ludicrous sat on her sofa, pants around my knees, mouth open, wrestling with a bit of rubber. Oh my God! She's got stockings on!

They are strange things stockings: too long to be socks and too thin to keep legs warm, as I see it, but nevertheless a powerful weapon in male seduction. I wonder who ever thought of inventing such an item of underwear and more importantly wondering why I found them so erotic. Whoever did it was very clever, because they not only give a woman's legs the most remarkable look but at the top where the suspender attaches to is a definite indicator of how well a man is doing in his venture; the giggle band, as Marc calls it, because if you can manage to get your grubby hands past it you're laughing. A bloke must have thought up stockings, as tights are definitely a female idea. Tights are used when any sort of penetration into undergarments is to be thwarted; tights are the enemy of men throughout the world and should be banned. Ah, another thing to put on my list of things to do when I'm Prime Minister. The woman who deviously created them clearly also thought up the ghastly term 'gusset'. I mean if the sheer (pardon the pun) frustration of not having access wasn't enough, I'm not going to entertain the idea of going anywhere near a gusset. It sounds like something that could take my arm off! I'm also not sure where, in my limited, nay, nonexistent experience of things erotic, my infatuation with stockings came from; it maybe a gene thing that is passed from male to male. To find a stocking-clad lady is a rare thing, according to my brother. Girls only wear them on special occasions and take them off as soon as they can. He must have had quite a bit of experience as he knows a lot about them. I myself had only ever seen them in a magazine and it hadn't done that much for me. This must mean that I am not a leg man so why am I feeling so turned on looking at her in her stockings? From other information I have, in the olden days if a girl couldn't afford stockings she would cover her legs in coffee and draw a line up the back with an eye-liner. What on earth is that about? Surely the girl would be sussed immediately a man tried to shove his hand up her skirt, or if it started raining. I can imagine some wannabe stocking wearer stood in the pub on a rainy night trying to seduce blokes into wanting to see her legs, stood in a puddle of Nescafé. Dead giveaway. So my conclusion is that they are not for warmth or they would have been made from wool; they aren't for comfort (unless you count going to the lav but I don't want to think about that) so they must be purely for aesthetics. Right – now that's sorted let's get on with business.

My first go at putting a condom on wasn't going well. I didn't research this, and when it popped out of the packet and I could see that it wasn't going to pull on like a sock I was confused. The wine hadn't helped, as I stared haplessly at this rolled—up rubber all slippery and smelly.

'Shall I help?' Julie bent over and took the johnny from me and smiled.

My mouth had dried. Am I the only person in the world who doesn't know how to have sex? Not only was I going to get the full Monty, she was going to touch me ... blimey, I wasn't expecting this. I don't think I'll ever know what happened to me in the next ten seconds; my head was spinning; I had no peripheral vision. There was a fully grown woman grappling with me, wanting to ...

'BEEP, BEEP, BEEP, OVERLOAD, DANGER ... YOU ARE ABOUT TO ENTER UNKNOWN TERRITORY, SYSTEM OVERLOAD ... RELEASE PRESSURE ...RELEASING SYSTEM PRESSURE NOW...'

And it was all over ... She hadn't even got the condom on.

'Oh, is that it then?' Yea, thanks for the support Julie.

'This your first time Den?' A question every man ever asked

has denied.

'No, I'm just a bit ... well, you know'

'A bit what?' She didn't sound very pleased; I don't know why *she* was looking so disappointed. She stood looking down at me waiting for an answer that never came as I pulled my trousers up.

'Look, you'd better go.'

And after five days and twelve hours of having my first girlfriend, I was walking home in the rain, still a virgin and very pissed off.

Chapter Four

Julie was a learning curve. Those five days probably prejudiced the way I behaved with girls as if they were an alien species and not the opposite gender. I spent a while regarding girlfriends as diverse experiments; each had their own characteristics that I could exploit; their reactions when I was annoyed or frustrated at the lack of decent work or life in Luton; but inherently they were all the same; someone to have fun with, not get too close to and certainly not to do anything preposterous like fall in love. The longest I ever managed to stay with a girl for was about five weeks. Janet Sobey. She had the best legs I'd ever seen. I dumped her for not picking up my snooker cue from the repair shop,. She had the biggest set of brothers I've ever had to run away from. I had formed a good relationship with Kev; we were similar. Neither of us could hold down a job for any respectable amount of time. Nothing seemed that inspirational. It made us feel like we had found our own special vocation in life: being unemployed.

Young men between the ages of seventeen and twenty-five have no real place in society; too young to have a decent opinion and nothing to say when we did open our mouths. Kev and I hung out in the snooker club, had crappy jobs and annoyed our parents. Even guys who had got jobs in a bank or for an estate agent were considered blokes who were waiting to mature into successful businessmen and grow into suits that fitted them properly. Kev's dad had tried to get him to go to college, without success; and my Mum badgered me about joining the Police like Marc, who was married to Debbie and had a little baby called Callum. They moved into a two-bedroomed house in Lewsey Farm it's like Beirut, only more violent. However, Marc was moving forward and I was standing still. We were nonetheless close but I found it increasingly harder to compare our lives. When he would tell me about his latest, dangerous and exciting course, I'd be telling him about the highest break I'd made that week.

Then Kev did something I'll never forgive him for; it was against our ideals. He landed a job on the conveyor belt at Vauxhalls. All of a sudden he had money to spend. I'd go to his social club with him and drink the beer that he'd buy me. We tried to carry on as we had been before but as with Marc, our conversation became strained and tiresome and we grew apart.

Anyhow, once a year the L&D Hospital have a carnival, so I thought I'd go along and see what was happening. I'd bumped into Julie last year with her doctor boyfriend and had a laugh about our hot date. During the arena display these blokes appeared on motorbikes; they were top, jumping through hoops of fire and standing on each other's shoulders. After they had driven off standing in a pyramid, I took a walk around to look at their bikes and chat to the lads. I had no idea that the White Helmets were anything to do with the Army; they were cool guys, with loads of women chatting to them. What a job! I suppose I was pretty much sold on the idea of being a soldier after talking to them. I'd have money, somewhere to live, a motorbike, and more women than I could shake a stick at and most importantly out of Luton!

The local Army Careers Office in Luton is opposite the cinema and I'd gazed into the window a few times. The posters were intrepid and stimulating, showing young men camouflaged up and running with rifles, smoke billowing from the explosion behind them, boys with toys (and money). It was right up my street. The blokes on the motorbikes were on a poster as well, jumping through fire. So I took the plunge and walked in, half expecting someone to start bawling and shouting at me. I was amazed to find everyone was as nice as pie and just wanted a chat about where I lived and did I see The Hatters win on Saturday?

They were positive, friendly guys.

'So what's your name mate?' the big bloke in uniform behind the desk enquired 'My name is Sergeant Neil, call me Roger if you like. Have you got a job in mind then Den?'

'Yeah, I quite like the guys who ride those motorbikes.' I pointed to the picture in the window.

'Oh, right. The best thing about us is we recruit the best blokes from around here, so you'll probably meet up with someone you know. Do you like football?'

'Yeah, but I would prefer to ride the bikes.'

'Well, let's see how you fare with the tests first. You can sort the bike stuff out once you're in.' I was chuffed to nuts; 'What a helpful man', I thought.

One of the things that surprised me about the Army recruitment process was taking tests, like at school. I imagined loads of running and seeing how fit you are; but for the first two visits I sat behind a computer answering random questions and judging the trajectory of a bouncing ball. It was nothing like I expected. The older-looking bloke, who took me through the process, told me that if I were good enough then I could join the same Regiment as him, which I thought was a clever move, as I'd already have an ally. We got on well, Sergeant Neil and me; he told me that the Guards were the best infantry Regiment in the British Army.

Then I had some medical checks and was sent away for two days to a proper Army Camp for my final interview and a running assessment. The running was great; I beat the instructor to the finish and he was not pleased, calling me a smart arse and said never to try that trick again, which I thought was a strange thing to say as I'd probably never see him for a second time. Anyway I returned to the recruiting office in Luton a hero; my Sergeant thought I was wonderful and said I'd make a fine infantry soldier.

Early one Thursday morning I reported to the Army Careers Office to be sworn in. Mum came and we were seated in the front of the office by the window with four other sets of parents and youths. We were called into a room all together where an officer (so I was told) explained that what we were about to do was swear elegance to the Queen, her heirs and commanders. He then proceeded to give us £5 each and requested us sign a document; he said that this was like getting the Queen's shilling but inflation had taken its toll, and laughed. Frankly I didn't have a clue what he was on about but stuffed the money into my pocket and signed the form. To this day I have no idea of the significance of signing that line. I can remember him saying that I would serve wherever the government required me but not a lot else. Should he have mentioned that you're just about to change your life, whether you last five minutes or fifty years I might have questioned him?. But I didn't; I put my mark down and had my hand shaken vigorously and my back slapped to the accompaniment of 'Welcome on board, we're very proud of you.' 'Welcome on board?' I thought. The Navy recruiting office was next door.

22 May 1994: 24955796 Private Yarwood stepped onto the platform of Brookwood Station to be met by the biggest, ugliest bloke I had ever seen; this guy was immense and seemed to have muscles on his eyelids.

'Pirbright!' he barked, as I strolled towards him with my case in one hand and a copy of the *Sun* in the other.

'Yep.'

' "Yep"? You sound like a dog. Get on the white minibus and tuck your bloody shirt in.'

Crumbs, who's popped his balloon?

Basic Training, as it's called, isn't actually basic from the point of view of a total military ignoramus; it would be better titled Quite Complicated And Intense Training, as there is so much information to take in. The fitness part was my only reprieve; whereas the other lads in my Platoon hated the gym work and the running, I loved getting out of uniform and jogging around the countryside. I enjoyed the mucking around with the guns as well, but I was waiting for the day we were given our Triumph 750 Tiger motorbikes. This is where the pre-job investigation and research would have come in handy, and where Sergeant Neil could have been more honest, as there isn't actually a lot of call for motorbike riders in the Coldstream Guards. The White Helmets are part of the Royal Corps of Signals! I shared my room with ten others, all of whom were going into the Guards, but different Battalions depending where they came from. Jock and Mack were going to the Scots Guards, Tony and me into the Coldstream; there were three guys from Cardiff going into the Welsh Guards and three scousers going into the Irish Guards? Beats me, and I didn't ask why.

After ten weeks of thrashing around Pirbright, getting shouted at for all manner of reasons, ironing my clothes, or kit as it's called, marching to one place, turning around and marching back again, it was my passing-out parade. Mum, Marc, Debbie (who is pregnant again) and little Callum came. I'd invited Kev, but he said that he couldn't get the time off work; sod him then. It was a brilliant day; I did my parade and was awarded a prize for the best recruit at PT (Physical Training). I've never been awarded anything in my life before. They gave me a statue of a soldier in his sports kit, and it was the best thing I'd ever seen. Callum was very impressed; he's nearly two, and brought his Action Man doll with him to show me. He's a cute lad and understandably loves his Uncle Den, I mean who wouldn't? Mum cried, of course, but managed to control herself in front of my training staff, thank goodness. We had a couple of drinks in the bar and then squeezed into Marc's car and went home for two weeks' leave. On the way home Mum said something odd. She's a great mum but I don't think she realises what she says.

'Your dad would have been proud of you.'

Chapter Five

I shared a room at Pirbright with ten other blokes. Tony came from Leagrave, which is about five miles from where I live, and he must be the only Luton Town fan I have ever met. He wasn't as fit as me but he could do the marching stuff well, so we mucked in and helped each other out. The thing about Tony was that he looked smart in anything; the uniform the Army issues only fits a few sizes and he was one of them. Our Corporal used to be on my back about the way I dressed. 'Yarwood, you'd look scruffy naked' ended up being one of his favourite phrases.

We were talking about going on leave before getting posted to our Battalion in Winchester. I'd arranged to meet up with Tony for a few beers in a pub called The Highwayman not far from the town centre so we could go to a club after. I had cash to spend and two weeks in which to charm as many girls as I could with my tales of military daring and ... well ... bullshit really.

A lad's night out is exactly what it means; beer, curry, club, punch up and pull if you're lucky, so when Tony waltzes into the pub with a bird in tow I was none too chuffed.

'Hiya. How's it going?'

'What's with the girl?' Whispering.

'Don't mate, she's getting binned later.'

'Do I get an introduction then?'

'Oh yeah, sorry. Den, this is Kerry.'

Kerry is a neat-looking girl; short but well formed. I suppose you wouldn't say stunningly beautiful but worth a second look. She's got mousy-brown shoulder length hair in a ponytail and a little nose that turns up slightly at the end; she's dressed in a denim miniskirt with crazy striped tights and a black T-shirt.

'Hi Den, Tony's told me about you.'

'Oh dear, so you'll be wanting me to leave then?'

She giggles.

Tony is a laugh, usually; he's always got something to say for himself and a story to tell, but as the night wears on he goes quiet, and I end up talking to his girlfriend instead. We head into town to hit the club; it's gone eleven, and I haven't managed to chat to one girl yet. Tony is looking decidedly worse for drink. He's hanging off Kerry's arm and talking gibberish about how hard life is as a soldier ... hm'm. I thought we left that sort of carry-on until two in the morning when all that's left to pull are the fat and the desperate.

'Is Tony gonna to be all right Kirsty?'

'Kerry.'

'What?'

'My name is Kerry, not Kirsty.'

'Sorry Kirsty.'

'He'll be fine, I'll put him in the corner and we can go and have a boogie.'

'Oh.'

'Don't you fancy a dance?'

'It's not that, Kelly.'

'KERRY.'

'Sorry, Kerry it's just ...'

'Yeah, I know I'm cramping your big night out with silly bugger here aren't I?'

'No, of course not. Sure we'll have a dance.'

'Tell you what: I'll help you get laid!'

'I can't do that, he's a mate.'

'Not with *me* stupid, I'll go and tell some random bird in the toilets what a stud you are and how I can't handle you, and hey presto! You'll have your strides around your ankles before you know it. Come on, it'll be a laugh.'

'Are you serious?'

'Course I'm serious. Are you scared or something?'

'No.'

'Well then, let's go, Stuuuud.'

I'm intrigued now. Kerry is inaudibly wild. I can see why Tony is going out with her, and she's exceptional. So we put Tony right next to the speaker with his head leaning against it. The music is that loud that it makes his spiked hair shake with the beat of the bass, and we make our way towards the dance floor. Now I'll let you in on a secret here: I dance like I'm having a fit. I don't know how girls make it look easy. I do the moves, try and copy every one else but my feet get stuck and I just end up wiggling my arse and flailing my arms. I remember knocking some bird over once and making her cry. It was a complete accident but Mr. Punchy her boyfriend took offence and I ended up getting unceremoniously launched out of the door.

So Kerry and I dance for a couple of numbers until she winks at me and tilts her head sideways in the direction of a stunning brunette with the most enormous assets I've ever seen, who's heading towards the ladies' toilets. I nod my head and mouth 'Yes' as she turns and follows the poor unsuspecting girl into the lavatories. Ha, little does she know, John Wayne Bobbet II is in the building and waiting to fulfil her every fantasy! I'm leaning casually against the cigarette machine, trying my best to look enticing and this girl emerges. She must be buzzing with anticipation because she scans the dance floor. I've got this stripy shirt on – very distinguishable – and it doesn't take long for her to spot me. Kerry must have done an outstanding job. An acknowledging signal and she's making a beeline. She can't wait, she's going to be getting a dose of Doctor Den's pleasure potion before she knows it!

'You Den?'

'Yeah.' I'm brimming with self-confidence now … you lucky lass.

'It's true isn't it?'

Bloody hell Kerry! You star.

'Yeah.' I'm as casual as you like.

'Shame, it's always the good-looking ones.' She's off to talk to her mates. They're looking over sympathetically, and winking. Kerry returns to me, smirking, her eyes sparkling.

'So what the f… .'

'Sorry Den, I couldn't resist it. I was going to set you up but the words came out all wrong.' By now Kerry has got the giggles; her hair shakes with her head and she's got her hand over her mouth.

'Go on then.'

'Well I sort of said that you were my gay cousin and …'

'WHAT!'

'That you – ha ha ha – sorry but it must have come out wrong. It was so funny,'

'Yeah, for you. They think I'm an effing uphill gardener.' I was starting to see how amusing it must have looked. Kerry has tears in her eyes and is laughing uncontrollably and it is infectious. I'm guffawing too, as she points to Tony who is slumped on the floor with two bouncers towering over him looking as if he was about to get the big heave-ho.

'Come on sweetie,' she says, 'let's get him out of here.'

I had to decant Tony in and out of the taxi with the help of his traitorous girlfriend. They were both staying with his mum, so after dragging and pushing the dead weight of a drunk body as quietly as we could up his mum's stairs, I bid them goodnight and walked home. I'll catch up with Tony on Tuesday when we returned to the barracks; we could talk in the car.

Chapter Six

Tony was an hour late already when I answered a knock at the door. We were meant to report to Battalion Headquarters before mid-day and it was now ten thirty. As I walked to my car I could see someone rummaging around in the boot. It was Tony's girlfriend loading an enormous suitcase.

'I *did* tell you we were giving her a lift. You remember? She's starting her Management course at university.' Tony said sheepishly by way of explanation.

I remembered a conversation from earlier in the week and I'd obviously agreed, so I couldn't complain.

'Where to?'

'She's at Winchester, just up the road from the Camp.'

We walked to the car.

'Hi Karen.'

'KERRY.'

'Oh yeah. Sorry, Kerry. Bring enough makeup?'

'What?'

'Or have you managed to pack the entire contents of your house?'

'Oh, Ha ha – a girl needs her clothes you know.'

Once Tony had crammed his small bag in the car there wasn't enough room to fit a spent match inside. I'd passed my driving test first time before I signed up and bought Marc's old Mini Metro from him for five hundred quid. I know they're not the best cars to pull but it got me from A to B. To say it wasn't particularly spacious would have been an understatement, and seeing as I'd forgotten that I was to have an extra passenger, I'd loaded it to leave the front seat free for Tony. Now the boot was full with Kerry's suitcase jammed against the roof and the back seats had my uniform laid across them with Tony's bags dumped on top. This gave Kerry enough room to slide over the bags and crawl in with her head jammed against the roof. She was wearing another pair of bizarre tights and looked like we'd just dragged her off the streets. I had to speed to get down the M3 to drop Kerry off and then get to Camp. By the time we'd navigated around the M25 she'd fallen asleep and started snoring. For a girl she could make some noise. I could hear her over the noise of the engine. Tony was looking embarrassed as we went on, and after trying to wake her up for the third time. He announced.

'I'm not spending the rest of my life listening to a wart-hog impersonator.'

'Come on mate, she's a good girl, you could do much worse.'

'Well, *I'd* like to have a go at doing much worse.'

I left the conversation at that. Tony was taking a dive. He was self-centred and I wasn't really sure if I liked him as much as I did when we were at work. He'd started seeing Kerry before we joined up, after meeting her at a Job Centre. They had each decided to do something radical, as neither had any direction in life. Kerry chose to go to university with the ambition of being a social worker – then; but she has subsequently changed her mind; and Tony wanted to join the Army, to travel the world and be somebody. He'd talk about Kerry a lot but not in an affectionate way, more of the-bird-I-shag way, which I accepted while I didn't know her. I pulled up outside the halls of residence and as if the noise of the car engine stopping was an alarm clock, Kerry awoke and prised herself out of the back seat. Tony was sitting there looking indignant and ignoring her. I started wrestling her suitcase out of the boot; it landed on the shingle and left a scar in the stones.

'Thanks sweetie.' She gave me a small peck on the cheek.

Tony hadn't uttered a word; she walked around to his door and poked her head through the window.

'Do I get a k-'?

'You're chucked.'

'What ...?'

'You heard me. Come on Den. Let's go.'

'You can't chuck me for no reason. What have I done...?'

'Look, you're dumped. Comprendo? Cheerio. Come on Den, we'll be late.'

I felt awkward standing there watching. She didn't cry, she looked confused and lost for words. I felt sorry for her and angry with Tony, not because he chucked her, but simply because it was a shite way of doing business.

'Look, Kerry,' I said, 'I'll have a word with him. It's the new job and that.'

'Don't bother. If he wants to be a loser, let him.'

And with that she grabbed the handle of the case and started dragging it across the forecourt towards the front door.

'Come on Den, we need to be there in ten minutes.'

'That was a crapulence thing to do, mate.' I didn't actually feel like calling him mate, I felt like giving him a clout but I was going to have to work with him for the foreseeable so I just got in the car and drove. Ten minutes of silence is bloody hard to keep up. I was relieved to see the Barrack gates.

I showed the guy on the gate my joining instructions and he looked at us and sneered, 'B Company, eh? You'll have fun!'

Once I'd got a pass for my car and been instructed where to park, we reported to the guardroom, which is a building near the entrance to the Camp. One of the soldiers from the guardroom took us to B Company lines and made us stand outside the Sergeant Major's office.

I heard his gravelly, booming voice behind me before spinning around to see the Sergeant Major glaring down at the back of my head.

'HAIRCUT!'

'What?'

'WHAT? You'll be calling the bloody Queen Liz next!'

Sergeant Major Flaherty isn't the sort of man to be ignored easily; he was six foot four with a Desperate Dan style chin and one eyebrow stretching across his forehead that shaded his piercing brown eyes. I think that when the Army promote people to the rank of Sergeant Major they look for the type of blokes normally seen on BBC's Crimewatch UK – those who are being hunted for mass murder with their bare hands.

'IN!'

He is clearly a man of few words. We march to his desk and halt; it astonishes me how he can make me feel rattled by saying so little to me, or in his case, at me. Then he lectures on how to behave while we are in *his* Company and how B Company were the best in the Battalion at football, rugby, basketball and – well – everything, it seemed. He did say something, which interested me about the cross-country team, running; my escape: I'll log that for later. The Company Clerk, who had been tasked to show us around the Camp showed Tony and me to the cookhouse for lunch. The restaurant was full to the brim of guys in different kit, some wearing drill uniform and others dressed in what I can only describe as a fancy-dress-Yeti suit. They wore regular combat trousers and jackets but sewn into their profile were strips of ripped material to give the effect of a bush I suppose; they looked hot and uncomfortable.

'Guilly suits Den,' Tony whispered and indicated in their direction. I returned a blank look. 'Sniper suits, cool eh?'

I was impressed, they didn't look like the other Guardsman, they appeared wild and mysterious, and I'd never imagined meeting a sniper. We ate lunch on a table to ourselves, feeling like the main attraction. Lads wandered past and glared down at us;

it felt like the first day at senior school all over again. After lunch we were given a tour of the facilities, starting with the accommodation and guardroom that we'd already seen, and then the gymnasium and swimming pool, finishing with the bar. It was rather exciting until we were shown back to the Company Offices to meet our Platoon staff and shown our new sections. I was amazed to find out that the men I had seen in the cookhouse were in my Company; they had been chosen to attend a sniper course and were preparing for it. I transferred my bags from my car into my room and was told to come to work in the morning at eight a.m. dressed in combat gear; it was only three in the afternoon. I'm not used to having time to myself in a work environment as the training regiment was so structured, so I put my running kit on and ventured out to find myself a route around Camp.

Life in a working infantry Company was different from training. There was the rifle stuff and marching but generally once my working day had finished my time was my own. After two weeks I was managing to keep myself out of trouble and fitting in with the other lads in 2 Platoon; things seemed pretty good. My Platoon Commander, Lieutenant Graves, passed out of his training from Sandhurst only six months ago and seemed to be right up himself. He was a well-spoken, pompous git who can't be much older than me and has more in common with the students I've seen downtown than his troops. Lance Sergeant Chant runs my Platoon and said that Lt. Graves is only there to sign paperwork. He's been in the Army twelve years and seems to have done everything; he even had a go at SAS selection but failed with an injury. I've got lots of respect for Chanty even though he rules us with a rod of iron. The third most important man in my world was our section Commander, Corporal Dave Tupp. He also comes from Luton (I'm beginning to wonder if there's a housing estate I haven't visited or maybe Luton's suddenly à la mode, and people lie about coming from Bedfordshire) and is one of the most ambitious men I'd ever met. Dave wanted to be a Sergeant next year and after five years he was doing well. I think he's the best Corporal in our Company; he's fit, fair and firm and sometimes that's all that's needed to be a good boss.

On the first day of my new job I'd met them all and had a series of interviews, the longest with Lance Sergeant Chant, who told me that we were going to Belfast in the summer for a six-month tour of duty at a place called Fort Whiterock. This meant I would earn a medal. I'd been told this when I left Pirbright. Our Battalion's rotation meant that we were due a tour this year and I loved the thought of going to somewhere dangerous. The Battalion had already started training a month previously and for the next three months we would be practising street patrol skills and learning about gathering information on the IRA and other terrorist groups, so I had a bit of catching up to do. Yes, cool start.

Chapter Seven

Tony was sent to 3 Platoon; the same Company, but we wouldn't be working side-by-side any more; it's similar to being in another house at school. I saw him during the day but when we were firing on the range, his Platoon would be doing car-searching drills or vice versa, and there was inter-Platoon rivalry; so I tended not to mix with him and stick to my own group even though our rooms were in the same barrack block. Maybe it would be good to get some distance from each other. I was surprised to get a room to myself; I thought that, like training I would be sharing again. Mum said that it sounded lovely when I'd called her but the truth was that my residence was a tad under-furnished. One Army bed with sagging springs and a half-inch thick mattress, a bin and a built-in wardrobe. The other lads who had been in the Battalion much longer than I had turned their rooms into impressive bachelor pads; they had their own telly, video and stereo, and some had a fridge. Nearly everyone apart from the NIGs (or New In Green boys) had a quilt as well.

I had a label: a NIG, which, I learnt, is opposed to a SWEAT (Soldier With Experience and Training), but it wasn't the most degrading of the new terms. One of 2 platoon's men had the unfortunate title of MONG, Man Of No Grounding, which essentially meant he was nauseating. The other thing that took me by surprise was that I didn't have to address everyone by their rank, only people above the rank of Sergeant. The Lance Corporals and Corporals told us that we could call them by their first names; it was a strange new world to me.

Winchester is a good place to meet a girl; the university enrols lots of women who are up for a laugh as well as gaining degrees. Having only one military Camp in the town means that the soldiers aren't everywhere like in a garrison town; but the disadvantage to this is that everyone knows the lads from Camp. This was alien to me, and it seemed like a lot of the blokes couldn't function outside of the Army environment. I loved the work and the guys were great, but I didn't want to spend all my waking hours with them. It was pack mentality; everyone from 3 Platoon would hang around and drink together as would each other Platoon, choosing to go to the same pubs and bars each night. Normally there will be a pair who have drunk too much and are singing inappropriate songs. Soldiers always get the blame for starting fights, regardless, and some pubs and clubs won't admit them. Women don't go for that. Occasionally when I didn't want to go out with a group of rowdy squaddies I'd take myself off to the Lord Nelson, where I stood a fair chance on my own. It was quiet there and an Army-free pub where the students went to drink. They aren't as brainless as I'd thought they were! The other attractions were that it was a free house and thus sold different beers to the other pubs, and the jukebox had decent music on it. It was only one room, and the bar was a half circle shape with bar-chairs; and on the outer walls they had built slight nooks with a comfy settle against the window and stools around small tables.

So I went out for a quiet couple of pints and see if I could spy some eye candy. I propped myself in the corner of the bar on one of the tall stools, set my fags down and happily tapped my foot along with the music. For a wee-day the Nelson always filled up, especially on a Thursday night, when there was either karaoke or a disco, but tonight it had a mix of regulars and the Uni lot. Men played darts on an ageing board with no oche; a line was drawn on the floor with a piece of chalk to indicate where to stand and take aim from. At intervals it would need to be re-drawn as it was rubbed out by their feet. People watching was becoming a pleasant pastime.

I was halfway through my second pint when someone tapped me on the shoulder and said, 'Hi sweetie!'

'Karen, I mean, Kelly!'

'Hi Dan!' she sarcastically replied with an 'I know you can't remember' smile on her face.

'Fancy a drink?'

'Yeah, pint of cider, please.' she said, 'How are you?'

I was in the mood for a chat so once I'd been served we sat down in the corner of the pub in an alcove and I lit a cigarette.

'That'll stunt your growth young man,' she said as she reached over and pulled a fag out of my packet.

'You started when you were three then!'

'Cheeky! But close ...'

I must have looked distracted; I was desperately trying to recall her name.

'Look if you can't remember my first name please call me Petra.'

'PET...?'

'Its like the Blue Peter dog, my mum liked it. Good job my dad registered me at birth or it would have been my Christian name.'

'Right! Would you like a bone with your drink?'

'Awright smarty-pants. How's Tony?'

I don't think the question meant, 'Have you seen Tony because I can't live without him?'; more the 'Have you seen that prat you are loosely associated with?' It was not a good topic for conversation. I told her that we'd sort of grown apart. I asked her how her course was going.

'Yeah, fine,' I don't think she wanted to talk about that either. So we chatted and drank a few pints, and drank and chatted. I'd told her that I was out on the pull tonight and that I was going to Northern Ireland. She told me about the different people on the Campus and the various freshman adventures. She described the college boys being immature and just after a shag. We got on like a house on fire and before I knew it the barman was calling time. Slightly the worse for wear we staggered down the street to the chip shop.

'Where are we going?' I blurted out between mouthfuls.

'Back to my place. I've got some vodka and there's bound to be a party somewhere.'

'Hey, why were you out on your own tonight? Solitary drinking at your age ... tut tut.'

'Look who's talking, the social pariah! I was meant to be meeting someone.'

'What – a bloke? Looks like you're left with your gay cousin!'

'No silly, I didn't mean that I ...'

'Come on then, let's party and I'll promise not to kiss any guys.'

I'm not in the habit of wandering around women's accommodation late at night (more's the pity) and I was relieved to find Kerry's room not far from the door on the ground floor, thinking it would be easy to escape, unnoticed. She had the same size lodgings as I had in my room at Camp, single bed, a chair in the corner, wardrobe and a bedside table. The difference was the amount of clothes she had left scattered around the place and the pile of makeup on her bedside table looking like a child's discarded play session. There were more bits and pieces to paint and draw with than the average decorator used. She fished around inside her wardrobe while I sat on her bed looking through one of her course folders titled, 'Exploration of the Economic, Political, Social and Environmental Aspects of This Burgeoning Global Activity'.

'Shouldn't this say, 'Answers to the Meaning of Life'? I asked as she ventured deeper into the recesses of the clothes Tardis, ignoring my comment.

She pulled the bottle out of the cupboard and staggered back, tripped and landed on her back next to me with a 'Ta-Daa,' like a magician pulling a rabbit out of a hat. The lid spun off and rolled across the floor and she took a big swig, closed her eyes and shuddered.

'No Pepsi I'm afraid.'

''S'okay,' I could hear myself slurring, and took a big gulp from the bottle.

'PEANUTS!'

'Sorry, no nuts either, you'll have to make do with vodka.'

'No I meant, I'll call you Peanuts,'

'What *are* you on about? *You're nuts.*' I could see her eyes rolling as she spoke, trying to focus on my face but not being able to fix.

'Well, I can't remember your name and I don't want to sound like John Noakes or whatever you said so I'll call you Peanuts.'

'You've lost me now sweetie. Give me a fag and stop twittering.'

'KP as in peanuts. Get it?'

I turned to look at her. She was snoring; from wide-awake to instant slumber; just add Den's voice, I thought. Before slipping out, I pulled a piece of paper out of the folder that I'd been reading and wrote with one of her makeup pencils.

To Peanuts

Nelson sat pm, bring your mates. I'll bring you a bloke, a straight one.

Den

Chapter Eight

Dave Tupp split us into groups of four for training. I had a Lance Corporal in charge of my team called Eddie Davis. He thought he was ultra intelligent and the rest of us were morons, and he'd always be asking the obvious, like:

'Has everyone got their rifles?'

Come on we're blinkin' soldiers! I felt like saying, 'Oh, corking idea Eddie! Thanks! Good job you were here!' He had joined the Junior Army at sixteen and been promoted to LCpl at nineteen. He had more military experience than me, but it was difficult to take orders from him at times despite this, because he was so supercilious.

Lofty and Mick, the other two lads in my team, had joined the Battalion from training last year and had spent the last six months doing guard shift; they were keen to get away from the guardroom. This was a breath of fresh air for them. I liked Lofty as soon as I'd met him; he was always in town drinking and could pull any girl. His looks weren't his best asset; I think the ladies used to go for his height; he's six foot two. The best chat-up line I've heard from him was: 'Walk up to a stunning girl in a pub, tap her on the shoulder and say 'Hi! Oh sorry. I thought you were someone else, you're far better looking than her. Can I get you a drink?'

I tried it once and got the response 'No. Now go and find the other girl and hope to hell she isn't wearing her glasses!'

Impertinent mare, I'm not that bad looking. Oh well, it's her loss.

Mick is quiet and doesn't drink. It makes him unpredictable. Once he's had a beer, and I mean one beer, his mood changes. In fact if he stood too near a wine gum he'd either be trying to punch someone or declaring his affections, so I think he prefers to stay off it. Sensible lad; I can get on with him but he's a pedestrian.

We practised two types of patrolling: foot and mobile. The foot patrols are hard work because we carry so much kit, including a rifle, body armour, baton guns to fire plastic bullets and various other bits of equipment to stop and detect bombs. When out on a footsie the route is mapped out for a three-hour patrol and there are different tasks to carry out, like searching wasteland for guns or explosives and seeing if specific people are on the patch. To practise this we went to a place in Folkestone called Tin City that is purpose built. Lads from another unit act as the local population; some are terrorists and others shopkeepers, pub landlords, etc. Our days are peppered with incidents like shootings and bomb blasts. We learn the ability to information-gather too. Mobile patrols are brilliant. Lofty and I stand in an armoured Land Rover with our heads poking out of a sunroof, and it is called being top cover, zooming around estates and reacting to incidents. Eddie sits in the front passenger seat as commander and Mick drives. The instructor told us that an armoured Land Rover is more liable to be hit by a terrorist in a vehicle as it's a big target; however I feel safer when going at speed. Being taller gives a greater field of vision, which I like. When we've finished our practice patrols, we watch ourselves on the CCTV video link; it's the best part of the day as we get to see anyone who's made a mistake. On the Wednesday we were sent to a mortar bomb attack and our job was to seal off the area. Mick had taken up a fire position by a house and one of the instructors with a video camera had been talking to him; he'd zoomed in on Mick's face so that we could hear what was being said.

Instructor: 'What's going on then?'

Mick: 'I'm on a cordon as there's been a mortar attack and we're restricting access into this area.'

Good answer Mick I thought.

Instructor: 'What type of mortar have they used, do you think?'

Mick: 'Probably a Mark ten.'

Instructor: 'What do they look like?'

Mick: 'They're made from gas containers, about four foot long, you can't miss them.'

Instructor: 'Well done sunshine.'

And with that he panned the camera back to reveal Mick squatting with his arse resting on a Mark ten mortar. It might have been the laughter that set the Sergeant Major off; he flew into a rage about checking the area before taking up a fire position and how many soldiers had lost lives and limbs because being unaware of their situation. Good lesson learnt and we spent the rest of the week ribbing Mick about it. I suppose making a mistake like that in training, the worst that happens is the lads taking the proverbial and a bollocking from the Sergeant Major.

The week flew by and by Friday night when we got back to Barracks we were exhausted. I needed to wash my kit and get some sleep. Lofty took a different direction, dumped his stuff in his room and went straight downtown for a few beers. As he left he tried to encourage me out too. I couldn't do that to myself; I certainly didn't have any energy for chatting up girls or anything else. I told him I'd take him out to meet some Uni girls on Saturday night to make it up to him. I slept like a baby and managed to get my personal paperwork out of the way by mid-morning on Saturday; and I went for a run in the afternoon.

By half past seven on Saturday night I was suited and booted and knocking on Lofty's door.

'What are you doing in there big boy?'

Silence…

'OI, Lofty!'

Nothing … One more knock and I pushed the door open to find

Lofty lying naked on his bed, personal stereo blasting out Meatloaf, a copy of Mayfair in one hand and the most enormous cock I've ever seen in the other (not that I look at other blokes' private parts, it's just that this thing was ... oh you know what I mean). He noticed me come in, casually took off his earphones and said

'Well I can't go on the pull with a loaded weapon can I? I'll be out in ten.'

Give the lad his due, ten minutes later and we were heading for town; he was in great spirits. I'm not surprised; if I was hung like something that passed the finishing post at Aintree I'd be happy too. We stopped at the God in the Wall to get some cash and arrived in the Nelson at just gone eight. The place was nearly empty; just Lofty, me, the barman and some bloke who looked like he'd had a great day at the bookies propping himself against the bar.

'Cor thanks for the invite mate!' Lofty said, as he pretended to push people out of the way and made a pathetic attempt to look as if he was squeezing his way to the bar.

'Two pints of bitter please barman, when you've got time of course!'

'Ay up mate they'll be here in a minute.'

Nine o'clock and the pub had started to fill up but no sign of Peanuts and her mates. Lofty nudged me as the door opened and three girls walked in.

'I'll take the one on the left, you get the one on the right, and the one in the middle can take the pictures.'

He had a lovely way with words, so we headed to intercept them as the reached the bar. My one (as designated by Lofty) had shoulder length blonde hair, about five foot four and very slim; she had a cream strapless top and a tight blue skirt with tassels hanging from the bottom of it. I was on a mission. Lofty had accosted the smallest of the three girls and towered over her. She was peachy and her face lit up when he spoke to her.

'Hi ladies. Lofty Coleman, fearless warrior and defender of the faith. Can I buy you delicious girls a drink?'

I could feel myself cringe; I looked at the girls who'd started giggling. If I had said that they would have walked straight out of the door, but they said Yes, and the small dark one was gazing up at Lofty like he was some sort of demigod.

'Er, hi – I'm Den, what's your name?' I'm pretty good at chatting up women, but his outrageous advances had completely thrown me so it took me some time to compose myself again. You have to be assertive with women, though not too cocky or they just think you're after one thing; well. You *are* after one thing but chatting them up as a preliminary warm-up before is amusing, as I love the chase.

'Jenny, they are squaddies!'

By now the third girl had realised that she wasn't going to get a look-in so she'd glowered at her friends and sat down in the corner alcove that I'd been chatting to Peanuts in the previous week.

'Yes, I'm afraid so Jenny. I take it that you don't like soldiers then?'

'Oh yes, I like a man in uniform, it's just that you're always after one thing,'

Sussed. Drat. Think cool as a cucumber.

'Only for world peace, saving the rainforest and keeping Britain tidy, so yes, I'm afraid you're right.'

Laughter, bingo! Den, sometimes I think you are a genius. I mean how many other men could pull that one out of the bag? So I took Jenny to another one of the small-seated booths to continue the seduction. Lofty had his girl perched on one of the bar stools and whatever he was saying had the girl in fits; it's great to watch a professional at work. If she only knew what he had in his shorts she'd run a mile.

Jenny worked in a hairdressers in town and had lived in the area all of her life. Her Saturday night out was the big event of the week; she liked to go to discos and parties and she hadn't had a boyfriend for ages. Her mates had told her not to go out with soldiers but she'd never actually chatted to one before. Things were looking up. She had been sharing a flat with Fiona, the girl talking to Lofty. Jenny had had a bust-up with her parents and walked out; she'd stayed with her older sister for a while but felt like she'd outstayed her welcome. Fiona, who Jenny works with, was struggling with her rent so, what do you know? Two problems solved at once. The other girl, Odette, had started work at the shop two weeks previously as an apprentice and tonight she'd invited herself along, so Jenny and Fiona didn't think twice about dumping her for two blokes.

I hadn't noticed Peanuts until she'd walked right up to me and stood so she was looking down onto our table. She had a pint of cider in one hand and a cigarette in the other. She was obviously out on the pull, wearing a tight black T-shirt and tartan miniskirt and had another pair of by now legendary stripy tights.

'Hi sweetie!'

'Hiya Peanuts! How's it going?' I felt like saying, 'Get lost Peanuts, I'm busy.' Instead I blurted out, 'Party tonight or what?'

'Of course, would I let you down? So you're coming?'

'Yeah, can I bring Jenny?' looking across the table.

'If you like. How do you do, Jenny?'

'This is Peanuts,' I said, 'she's a mate.'

'Yes that's right, I'm Peanuts ... a mate,' and she walked off towards her friends at the bar.

'What's up with her?' Jenny asked as she sat back down.

I didn't understand what had just happened there and it made me feel uncomfortable, so I said I'd get some more drinks and headed in her direction. As I approached, she was standing with her friends, chatting.

'I've brought a mate with me: Lofty, he's over there talking to the girl in the black top.'

'Okay, fine.'

'What time are we leaving then?'

'When they chuck us out.'

'Great, could you give me a shout?'

Brilliant I thought, everything's sorted then. I bought a pint and a white wine and made my way back to Jenny.

Chapter Nine

A bloke from behind the bar collected our empty glasses and took the full ashtray from our table. Jenny talked; I wasn't exactly unentertained by her conversation – just tired of her continuous drone. I knew the complete workings of her hairdressing salon; in fact I had enough information to start my own business. Peanuts was talking to her mates; she'd glanced across a few times and we'd made eye contact but she hadn't smiled. Suddenly she appeared at the table like Mr Ben's shopkeeper, hands on her hips and fag hanging precariously out of her mouth.

'Coming?'

'No. It's just the way I'm sitting but the night's still young, ha ha!'

My humour is lost on some people. I should have auditioned for the stage; I'd be a big star. Instead Jenny and I jump up, grab our coats and follow her out of the pub. Lofty and Fiona were nowhere in sight. Jenny said that she had seen them leave earlier; it made no difference to me though I did feel guilty that I'd left Peanuts out on a limb, though we're not going out together or anything so I ignored it.

The party was in one of the large first floor rooms; well, two rooms actually, one room had been cleared of furniture for dancing and had a stereo system with a few dim lights set up. Plastic chairs that had been borrowed from the canteen were scattered around. The other room was full of alcohol; crates of beer in one corner and a decorator's table by the window with bottles of wine and spirits on it; the room stank of sweaty bodies and blow. I didn't do a head count but there must have been at least one hundred and fifty people milling around. Most of them were scruffy, with ripped jeans or combat trousers and tee shirts with SAVE THE WHALE or GREENPEACE on them; loads of gothic girls and a couple of blokes in dinner jackets, string vests and cords wearing trainers that looked like they had been dragged out of the bin. I felt out of place as I pulled Jenny behind me in the direction of the beer stack. Peanuts had latched onto one of the guys in a tux; by the time I reached her, she was drinking a can of bitter, and she threw me a four pack of beer.

'Mad isn't it?'

'Yeah.' I had to shout to be heard over the sound of 'The Smiths,' playing full blast and I split the beer, handed one to Jenny and put the other two cans in my pockets while I struggled with mine.

'This is Marcus,' she shouted.

'Same name as my brother, nice one,' I replied as I stuck out my hand to shake his. He was tall and lanky with dark shoulder length unwashed hair and an angular face. He was trying to grow one of those pathetic goatee beards that looked like a piece of fine fur was stuck on his chin, surrounded by red spots.

'Yeah, interesting.' In two words, he had refused my hand and he looked at me as if I were the scum of the earth. I instantly despised the spindly weirdo.

I felt Jenny tugging on my shirt and I looked around. Her eyes were glazed and she had a smirk on her face; her hand came up and between her index and forefinger was a spliff, billowing its acrid, sweet smoke into my face.

'Want some?'

'Don't be ridiculous. I mean, no thanks,' and I pushed her arm away.

'Okay Den, let's put a smile on your face another way.' She put her beer on the table, grabbed my wrist and started pushing past people towards the door. We went up the corridor and Jenny pulled on the door handles as we walked.

'What the bloody hell are you ...?'

'It's all right, no one followed us, and they won't even notice we're gone.'

'But what ...?'

'Here we are.' She dragged me into the dimly lit room; it was obviously a guy's room as there were posters of Kim Wilde on the wall. She put the lock on the door and turned around, leaning back on one leg and lowering her head to look at me through her fringe.

'Come on then, soldier boy. Let's party!'

I don't need prompting after a proposition has been made, especially after a few drinks, but I stood there like a schoolboy as she approached me. Jenny grabbed and kissed me quite deliberately, one hand keeping her grip on my collar and the other sliding down my shirt until she found the first button of my jeans. My head was whizzing, I was in someone else's room, with a girl I hardly knew and I was horny. I could feel her tongue moving in my mouth, pushing against mine, running over my teeth, it was firm and purposeful, unrelenting. The distraction of the kiss had allowed Jenny to unbutton my trousers. I was hard and pushing against the material; the feeling of release made me want her soft fingers around me. I slipped my hand under her blouse and cupped her breast, moving my thumb gently over her, and felt her harden against the soft silky bra as my other hand crept down to meet the clip on the side of her skirt. I needed her, right now.

She drew back her head and released me from the kiss to look me in the eyes. She had an expression of control in her face, her eyes bright and excited, and pupils like saucers with a hint of devilish enjoyment in them. I could hear the noise of people chatting and laughing over thumping bass music. I wondered whose room this was. Would the door rattle with the noise of the owner returning? I didn't give a damn.

I felt her hand stop me fumbling with her clip, her other hand resting on my chest as she bent her knees and lowered her head.

Further down she went until she was kneeling below me, still looking. Her hand was around me again, moving slowly up and down as she opened her mouth. I shuddered as I felt the warmness of her lips encompassing me. I closed my eyes with a sharp intake of breath.

As I looked down at her again she started sucking; it was divine and dirty, sensual but outrageous; the more I watched her head bobbing, the more I could feel my excitement building. All of my senses working overtime, I could hear every noise, the party, the music; I could smell her perfume and see me disappear into her wanton mouth. As I felt myself grow nearer climax, I could hear Lofty's voice in my head.

'Describe your worst blowjob: wicked!'

Not now Lofty. Please be out of my head. I was nearly there and she knew it. As her head and mouth moved closer to me I pushed my hips forward, my legs weakened. I was there, exploding into her mouth and I didn't care, any tension I had released. The hair on the back of my head stood up and I could feel a tingle in the small of my back; my legs shook as Jenny pulled away smiling and licking her lips.

'Good?'

What was I meant to say?

'Not really, pretty crap actually; I think you should practise more.'

Jenny stood up, kissed me tenderly and took my hand.

'Come on big boy, we're missing the party,'

Jenny unlocked the door and scanned the corridor as I pulled up my trousers and fastened them.

'All clear,' she announced as she put her hand behind her back beckoning me.

We walked back and got ourselves two glasses of wine. It was nearly one in the morning and the partygoers had thinned.

Peanuts was leaning against the wall with the guy in the tux leaning one hand over her shoulder so that she was cornered. His head was lowered as he talked to her and a bottle of lager swung in his other hand.

We wandered into the dance room where Oasis was playing. How apt, I thought. The other tux was lolloping around the room with some goth girl; they were swinging their arms and frankly looked sissy. More bohemian students were sitting on the plastic chairs in groups, chatting. They seemed so miserable; it's a party for goodness' sake. I walked over to the stereo where the records and tapes lay scattered on the floor and started picking through them.

'Ah, that's more like it,' I exclaimed as I picked a record from the pile. It took me a while to familiarise myself with the machine, and the speakers made a scratching sound as I tore the needle away to shouts of 'Oi! What ya doin'?'

I cranked the volume up and waited for Parklife to start blasting out.

'Come on, let's talk to Peanuts, she's a good laugh,' I shouted at Jenny as we headed out.

'Really? She was doing a good impersonation of a miserable cow, last time I saw her,' Jenny retorted. Jenny was right, Peanuts wasn't laughing any more.

I could see her shaking her head and mouthing; as I moved towards them I could see Marcus looking at her frustrated with a furrowed brow; he held the bottle in his hand but his knuckles had turned white.

'Leave them to it,' Jenny said as she pulled at my arm. 'She'll be fine, Den. Let's have a dance.'

As I turned to tell her to shut up I heard the smashing of glass and a girl scream. My focus went straight back to Peanuts, Marcus was gripping her just beneath the shoulder holding her upper arm tightly so that the flesh was white. His other hand was raised behind his head, palm open and ready to strike.

'Is that the way you want it? You fuckin' tease.'

That's all I needed to react, my fist was formed before I'd taken two paces. As my right foot fell to the floor, my left hand was racing towards its target. He was taller than me so my arm had time to gain momentum and he had time to move out of the way … but he didn't. Marcus was so engrossed in the verbal attack that the punch knocked him clean out; his head jarred backwards and at the same time his knees buckled and he released his grip on her shoulder. He fell straight down; crumbling like a demolished building, his raised hand behind his head, and blood pouring from his nose. His long, matted hair covered most of his face and the pathetic attempt at a beard was bloody from his right nostril. Peanuts was sobbing and fell forward into my arms.

'Sorry,' she blabbed as she stepped over him. Marcus's friend, who was dressed identically, appeared like a petrified penguin. He had his arms stretched out in front of him with his hands facing palms forward. He edged towards us, guilt and fear etched into his face.

'Leave him mate, there's no need for trouble. He's really sorry,'

Was this guy psychic or what? How did he know if his mate was sorry? Did they have had an agreement before they went out this evening, if they made total pricks out of themselves later? 'Now if either one of us gets hammered, insults a girl and gets dropped by some guy, the other one's got to come and say he's sorry … deal?'

Peanuts had her face buried in my neck and I could feel her tears dripping from her eyes onto my shoulder; she was shaking. I wasn't in a hurry to let her go.

'Excuse me but what's going on here?'

Jenny had witnessed everything and was stood facing me with

her hands on her hips.

'Nothing. She's a mate, that's all,'

'You're supposed to be here with me.'

I know I had cemented my relationship with Jenny in the dorm down the corridor, but Peanuts was my friend, and in my book mates come before girls.

'Look Jenny, didn't you see what happened? She was in trouble.'

'Well, she's not now, so leave her alone, we're going home.'

Home! What the hell was she on about? I didn't follow.

'Let me take her to her room, she's upset' I said, rapidly losing patience. I could feel the adrenalin pumping around my body and by now the few people left had gathered around to see what was happening.

'No. You're coming back with me, let her friends sort her out.'

This was becoming intolerable, I've never been owned by anyone and I take enough orders during the day from the ranks, I certainly wasn't going to stand for getting bossed around in my own time.

'No, I'm taking Peanuts to her room.'

'Screw you.' Jenny turned and strutted out of the room, knocking into the table and spilling wine over the floor. It wasn't as if we'd been going out together for months. By the way she'd assumed possession I took a lucky escape there.

'You all right?' I bent my head to speak to Peanuts through her sobs as we walked down the stairs to the ground floor.

'Sorry Den.'

'Don't be sorry, he deserved that.'

'No, about Jenny.' She looked up at me with red eyes and mascara tracing a line down her cheek.

'Oh her! She's a certifiable. Never mind about her, let's get you sorted.'

I sat her on the bed and got her a glass of water. She'd stopped crying and was fumbling in her bag.

'Fag?' I held an open packet towards her.

'Thanks, mind reader.' She lit up and fell backwards onto the bed blowing a big billowing cloud into the air.

'You're a really good bloke Den,' she said as she lay there.

'Anything for a mate. Look, I need to go, all that hero stuff has worn me out.'

'You can stay here if you like.' She had pulled herself up and was leaning on her elbows looking at me through a fog of cigarette smoke.

'Nah, it's okay thanks, it won't take me long to walk back. I'll be down the Nelly on Saturday if you want to buy me a pint for saving your life. I'm away next week doing riot training, so I'll see you.'

Peanuts sank back.

'Take it easy.'

'By the way,' I said and she looked at me expectantly.

'Love the tights.'

Chapter Ten

Our Company arrived at Longmoor Training Camp early on Monday morning; everyone was looking forward to starting the riot training. Dave Tupp had been before, and he was telling us all about it. We listened to him recount some of the peculiarities of the week ahead like: How does a riot distinguish itself? This was one of the Army's labels for civil disorder in the way they categorise trouble in Ireland. I've seen what I thought were riots on telly with a couple of hundred people throwing stones and bottles at soldiers but apparently this is classed as only minor agro. A riot needs three hundred people or more. I mean, who's going to be counting rioters when it's raining rocks?

We started our training in our usual team patrols and were given a scenario by the instructors; it went like this: over the past few weeks the Army, the terrorists and the civilian population have not been getting on together. I'm not politically opinionated but I think that I catch the drift. There's been small road traffic accident involving an armoured Land Rover and a civilian Ford Sierra. The occupants of the car are injured (they are known terrorists) and nothing has been done to compensate the owner of the vehicle. Running in parallel to this, the political situation has deteriorated and tension within the local housing estates is high. The local police force is accused of over-reaction and have beaten up a local teenager over a minor theft incident.

So it begins. We were ordered to patrol first gathering information but carefully. The lads from A Company had been briefed to give us as hard a time as possible as they were standing in as the local population; they had alias names to make things more realistic. A policeman from the Royal Ulster Constabulary had come across from Belfast to advise and help with our training. The intention was that the situation would reach boiling point and a riot would break out. I was looking forward to this.

My first time on the streets was a footsie or foot patrol; Eddie Davis, Lance Corporal, took my team to a house with the policeman to serve a warrant. There are three teams working together so there's always support if one of the teams gets into trouble. The two other teams walk around the surrounding houses while we took up fire positions at the warrant house to protect the policeman; it seemed simple enough. I had to carry the heaviest bit of bomb detection kit for that day so by the time I had walked/run the mile or so to the house, my shoulders and back were aching and I'd broken into a sweat. Eddie told me to get into position by a wall surrounding the property; Lofty was at the gable end of a row of terrace houses and Mick was across the road. We had to look out for possible attacks on the copper while Eddie accompanied him to the door.

While the policeman spoke to the man at the door (he was renowned for fighting downtown and thought of as a bit of a Nutter as a real life soldier); his supposed wife (one of the female clerks) came out and started having a go at me. She was ranting and raving about trampling her flowerbed. This girl must have been about five foot max, weighing in at two stone wet through, but she had a mouth like the Mersey tunnel and was using language that I could only just keep up with. As she shouted at me, doors along the street started to open and the local populace came out for a look, bloody rent-a-crowd! I was trying to get a word in edgeways but it was nigh-on impossible. I thought if I stand up I could impose myself more. I'd been crouched down on my haunches for five minutes, but as I stretched upwards, I lost my balance. Unfortunately, this was the exact same moment that she decided to finger-poke me in the chest. With the weight of the equipment her small prod sent me staggering backwards over a two-foot surround wall. I could see the rooftops racing past and then clear sky as I crashed into the pavement. 'A' Company howled with laughter as Eddie ran around to try and haul me to my feet. The policeman stood there with a wry smile on his face, talking into his radio to call for back-up. What was meant to be the start of hostilities turned into a circus act.

We extracted our patrol and went back to Barracks where Sergeant Major Flaherty was waiting for us; we unloaded our rifles and filed into his temporary office.

'Great start, lads. Well done! If that had happened in the Province you'd have been bricked to death.' He'd started calmly, which took me by surprise as I've only ever heard him shout before.

'Corporal Davies.'

'Sir.'

And then it came out ...

'What was that? Rehearsal for panto? We don't pay stunt men so you can keep your film star good looks Titch. 'A' Company wet their pants after your performance today and I'm not best pleased with you hotshots.' While he was saying this he was spitting fire and napalm was issuing from his ears.

'WHAT THE FUCK DID YOU THINK YOU WERE FUCKING DOING'...breath... 'FUCKING "A" FUCKING COMPANY ARE ALL LAUGHING THEIR BOLLOCKS OFF OVER YOU...' breath 'AND YOUR BUNCH OF CRONIES.' It went on for what seemed like hours; this was a dressing-down to end all very long lectures, where the object of criticism can't get a word in. I could see the veins on the Sergeant Major's neck expanding as his head went redder and redder. All I'd done was fall over, for goodness' sake; it gave everyone a laugh but no harm was done, and this wasn't all Eddie's fault.

'Excuse me Sir.'

'WHAT, YARWOOD?'

'I lost my balance, it's not the crime of the century.'

Sometimes I should be grateful that I'm not the one in trouble and no matter what my conscience says, keep my trap shut. It reminded me of a story Lance Sergeant Chant told us on the coach on the way down to Folkestone. There was a sparrow flying over Essex and the weather was freezing. It was so cold that his wings froze. He was near to death from hypothermia and he plummeted to the ground. The lucky bird landed in the middle of a freshly laid cowpat. The heat from the manure defrosted him and he survived certain death. The sparrow was so happy at his good fortune he began to sing. On the other side of the field, the farm cat heard the beautiful song and went to investigate. She located the cowpat, saw the sparrow, and ate him.

The morals of the story are:

'Not everyone who shits on you is necessarily your enemy.'

'Not everyone who digs you out of the shit is necessarily your friend.'

Most importantly, 'if you're in manure; but happy, keep your gob shut.'

Unfortunately for me I'd remembered this too late, and by the time I'd realised my mistake, I found myself on my fourth lap out of fifty of the Camp perimeter, holding my rifle above my head.

'A' Company had also been given a dressing-down about the incident from their Sergeant Major for laughing at us, so the tension between the riot-training soldiers and the soldiers in the community became strained. It wasn't going to be play-acting any more; there was pride and professionalism at stake and nobody wanted to lose any more face in front of the NCOs. 'A' and 'B' Company haven't got on since one of our lads beat up a Corporal in a pub and put him in hospital three months ago. Neither

Company was about to enter mediation. It was going to make life more interesting anyhow.

Day two: I was on the Quick Reaction Force (QRF) and sat in the Barracks waiting for an incident to happen. When we got a call, we'd jump into our Land Rover and speed to support whomever needed some help. After three hours of sitting in a cold room wearing our equipment we were getting decidedly narked. Because there are two vehicles involved in the QRF, 3 Platoon manned the second team with us and Tony was in the other vehicle. We sat there and chatted. The more I talked to him the more I disliked him. He had no idea that I'd seen Peanuts since he'd given her the push, and he told me that he had been two-timing her with another girl and he preferred the other one. Sure it was fine to have two birds on the go at the same time; but once you've finished the relationship there's no need to go telling everyone that the dumped are frigid. Tony obviously didn't get to know her or rather didn't bother about knowing her, and had used her. To be honest I felt hacked off at the way he was talking about Peanuts; I'd liked her in the few times we'd met. Prat, I thought.

The conversation petered out, and by lunchtime everyone had started loosening his or her kit, undoing the bulletproof jackets, unfastening belts, etc. because it was uncomfortable. We had to go to lunch in pairs, just in case something went off, so I went first with Lofty and two guys from 3 Platoon. Eddie, Mick and the others went as soon as we had returned. Then the alarm sounded and we were scrambled. Well, to the Land Rover, with no driver or commander. Lofty and I got in the back anyway, shut the doors and we prepared ourselves. Mick was the first out of the cookhouse, jumping in the driver's seat with a pasty hanging out of his mouth and kit swinging. He started the vehicle before he'd sat down, gathering the loose items and stuffing them into the door with one hand as he took huge bites from the pasty in his other. Eddie came round the corner in much the same state, except he was attempting to talk into his radio at the same time as get into the vehicle. Small flakes of pastry flew out of his mouth as he responded to messages and he'd dribbled onto his hand microphone, his helmet at a jaunty angle and his rifle swung from its sling around his neck clanking onto the side of the Land Rover.

'You'll get indigestion.'

'Shut up Lofty,' Eddie responded and showered us in a volcano of crust, 'I'm trying to talk to Zero.'

'And did your mother not tell you not to talk with your mouth full?'

'You'll have a mouthful of fist if you don't zip it.'

We were smiling in the back as the vehicle lurched forward, sending us flying into each other. Eddie had thrown his food out of the window and was shouting directions to Mick, who was still chewing.

'Gower Street, turn right off Crumlin, down to the end and stop before you get to the last house.'

There was a muffled response and Eddie turned to tell us what was going on. I've got used to listening to information given at a rapid speed now; it's always abbreviated and there are few chances for questions. The team commanders had far too much on their minds to worry about us; we were responsible for thinking on our feet and I certainly didn't want to give Eddie any more to think about than he had already.

'Right. Listen in; there's been a shooting onto a footsie in Gower Street, two blokes down and rent-a-crowd are out in force. We're going to clear an ICP (Incident Control Point). If the civvies get arsey, don't wait for me to tell you to put plastic down. Den, get the baton gun ready.'

The baton gun used to be known as the plastic bullet gun and is used to disperse crowds of people when the situation is getting out of control. We had been issued with blank rounds to simulate it being fired, which means the gun just makes a loud bang. I loaded one into the gun and pushed my rifle onto my back and out of the way. This was only training but I could feel the adrenalin pumping through my body regardless. I looked across at Lofty; his eyes were as wide as saucers and he had a manic grin on his face. Our Land Rover was joined by 3 Platoon's and as we left the barracks and turned left onto the street, Lofty and I stood up to take our positions as top cover. I was facing to the right and back while Lofty's responsibility was left and front. I could see Tony poke his head out of the rear vehicle with his partner to assume identical positions. Mick tore through the streets with complete disregard for other road users; we had to get to the location as soon as we could but in the back of my mind I was thinking it would be more preferable to reach the location without having an accident. I held on ... to my breath and the side of the Land Rover.

The civvies were out in numbers as we closed in on the location; they had started shouting and throwing bottles at our vehicle. I could hear Eddie's voice, now a tone higher and more animatedly talking to Zero (Headquarters) about the situation on the radio.

'Hello Zero this is Foxtrot two two. Minor agro already started ... ICP location full of civvies. Do you want me to still locate ICP here? Over.'

It seemed like a sensible question to me. The ICP or Incident Control Point is always set up near the site of a shooting or bomb and it's the place where the necessary agencies gather, before going to the site. It allows the person in charge, the most senior rank on location, to brief everyone. Bit difficult, I thought, when rent-a-mob are chucking the local architecture at you!

'Bollocks. We're going to have to clear it.' Zero had obviously given their answer.

Eddie had his head twisted around to shout to us as Mick pulled up near to the curb.

'Lofty, pull your visor down, you twit,.' he shouted, as we pushed and pulled ourselves and our equipment out of the Land Rover to face a crowd of about thirty people. A tirade of noise, mostly verbal abuse, was pitched at us, and a hailstorm of potatoes. For training purposes we throw spuds at each other; funny it sounds, but if one manages to catch you in the right place you certainly know about it.

Mick and the driver of the 3 Platoon vehicle stayed close to look after any kit inside the Land Rovers, while the rest of the two teams (that means six of us) make a barrier with body length Perspex shields, and try to either disperse or push the crowd back. Everyone in our team is very aware of the location of the others, so there's no need to keep looking around to see where Lofty is. The only time I'll need to react is if someone trips or gets knocked down and then we protect them until they can recover. Eddie was telling me to fire at specific people in the crowd; I'd load up and push the baton gun through the shields, take aim and fire. Then one of the instructors would tap a member of the crowd on the shoulder and they would either lie down or run off. It was skill; for those few moments, I was the law and I was controlling them. I could make them do what I wanted, as they avoided my aim. Some more lads from 3 Platoon had been sent to help us; they joined the human barricade and fired more baton guns. Eddie was behind me with his head down, taking more instructions on the radio. My estimation of him had risen as he was talking, giving us instructions and making decisions whilst being hit by missiles and holding a shield. I wondered for a second if I could be as calm as he was if I were in his shoes.

'Lofty and you there,' he said pointing to one of the bigger guys from 3 Platoon. 'You're gonna be a snatch squad with me, get your kit ready.'

We had practised snatch squad routine at our own Barracks at Winchester. Three men go out from behind the shield barricade and pick up individuals injured by a baton gun round. Lofty was the biz at this because of his height. As he threw his rifle into the Land Rover and picked up a truncheon, he looked at me with eyes like a wild man. The three of them would bring back a downed civilian and hand them over to the police, who would arrest them. It looked like we would have a successful afternoon.

The instructors had brought in more of 'A' Company to bolster the crowd, increasing to about seventy to eighty people hurling spuds in our direction. Eddie pointed out my target and told the snatch squad to standby. Eddie had his rifle ready to cover the runners or retrievers who only carried a baton or truncheon, because they had to move fast and aggressively. All three risked becoming a focus of attention. I fired and they were off, pushing through the shields and sprinting towards the fallen civilian. Lofty has no running gait, his arms and legs flailed but he's fast. In no time the guy was unceremoniously lifted by any item of clothing available and frog-marched back to the shields, which opened and shut like automatic doors; you could nearly hear the hydraulics. I was reloading the baton gun as they arrived with their trophy; it was the same bloke from the day before, the local Nutter. Lofty had dropped him on the floor and was panting to try and catch his breath. He lifted the visor on his helmet, as it had steamed up. As he pushed the plastic upwards the bloke from 'A' Company launched his fist straight into Lofty's face. Lofty lashed out with his baton but missed the Nutter's head and lost his balance. He toppled on top of the Nutter and pinned him down with his weight. Eddie hadn't noticed the fracas behind him and had given me another target; I fired again. Eddie with only the 3 Platoon lad raced off; a second later Lofty pushed through the shields. In the chaos of the fight the two men had exchanged enough blows to become unaware of their situation. Lofty, hearing my baton gunfire again, instinctively ran with the snatch squad, and hadn't noticed that attached to his leg was the 'A' Company soldier. As they passed between the shields a couple of well-aimed kicks from the human barricade managed to release the Nutter's grip on Lofty's leg. Lofty lumbered away and picked up another rioter, returning back to the safety of the shields. As he passed the now stranded 'A' Company soldier, Lofty raised his arm and hit him on the head with his baton. The unofficial but highly important inter-company score, now one_one. A hail of cheers went up as the big man returned, bloody faced and extremely satisfied with his work.

The situation continued for another half an hour, and I could feel and see the strain people were under; my back was dripping wet with sweat and looking at the men on the shields, they looked exhausted. The situation seemed to have become a standoff. The crowd would throw a volley of missiles; we would fire baton rounds and send snatch squads out. Eddie, Lofty and the 3 Platoon guy must have been out to pick up about fifteen people. I was starting to wonder how long they could sustain the running back and forth. I could see the instructors shouting at the crowd; they split into two groups and started backing away. The distance was now too far for the snatch squads to run, and the crowd fragmented into the side streets and gunnels behind houses. If this were in the Province they would have done enough to destroy any forensic evidence and given the terrorists time to escape. We'd had this explained in the classroom and to see it demonstrated made it clear how simple and effective their tactics were. It was very realistic and suddenly terrifying to think that there would be a chance I'd be doing this for real in two months. My first proper practice dealing with a minor agro situation was coming to a close, and in the short space of time it had taken, from dismounting the vehicles to being in the chaos of it, I felt proud that I hadn't let anyone down.

'Mount up.' Eddie had to scream, his voice rasping after shouting for so long. We ran to our respective vehicles, throwing shields and batons into the back before squeezing inside. The crowd had done their job. Headquarters might have thought that to keep us out there would have just incited more agro and left us open to more attacks. So we'd been given the order to get back to Camp.

'Have fun boys?' Mick looked like he'd just turned up for work; composed and clean, he calmly got in behind the steering-wheel and started the engine.

Eddie climbed into the passenger seat, talking into his microphone between laboured breaths. I was glad to be part of his team. It was the first test and I felt we'd worked well together.

'Home James! Tea and medals when we get back. Eh ... what!' Eddie minced in an affected voice. He patted Mick on the back and sat bolt upright in his seat.

I looked over at Lofty, who at the moment was my idol. His combat jacket was ripped at the shoulder and his helmet covered in smashed potato. Through a dried bloody smile I could see he'd lost a tooth in the fight, his bright blue eyes the only thing that resembled Lofty any more.

'I'm gonna knock that wanker's head off when I see him downtown,' he said, grinning, as we stood up for the drive back to barracks.

Chapter Eleven

We had two days left of riot training before returning to Winchester at the weekend. The last day was reserved for cleaning up Longmoor Camp and packing our trucks. Tomorrow was the big one, and intelligence reports were coming in that there was going to be a terrorist funeral in the morning. We had been briefed that regular patrols were cancelled and that our Company was going to monitor the funeral procession from strategic points. If there was any trouble during the morning's ceremony we were to move back to Camp and prepare for a riot situation.

I loved every minute and wished that I could do more of this sort of training. All the chat between the lads was of the day before and Lofty's victory over the Nutter. Even the Sergeant Major had said a muffled 'Well done,' as he passed us in the cookhouse. In order to be ready for our return to Winchester, Lance Sergeant Chant had ordered a kit inspection that evening to see if any items had been lost or damaged during the last two days. He said that on our return to Camp we could get anything that had been damaged exchanged for new stuff. Lofty, Mick and I put our kit on our beds, laying out spare trousers, shirts, and socks. It was a part of the job I'd started to dislike; at my age I could look after my own things. The room smelt sweaty from the dirty clothing. My combat jacket smelled of cordite from firing the baton gun and I'd torn the knee of my trousers. Lofty laid out his jacket; it had a rip along the seam of the shoulder probably caused by the fighting. This was after two days of training and we'd damaged loads of gear; goodness knows what we'd be like after six months of this.

Lofty rummaged through his civilian holdall where he kept his wash kit and some books. He was looking for a pair of gloves that he'd managed to split and that needed swapping. He brought out a brown envelope and tossed it onto my bed.

'I meant to ask you last week mate, could you do the honours with these?'

I picked up the envelope; it felt like it contained two or possibly three letters. On the front in biro was written

'In The Event Of Me Snuffing It'

I looked blankly at the envelope and then back to Lofty.

'Sorry Lofty. You've lost me, do you want me to post this or what?'

'No! They're my death letters ... you know what I mean.'

'*No.* What are you on about?'

Mick was folding up an army issue towel and keeping quiet. Lofty glanced at him and then me.

'Don't you two know what death letters are?'

Silence.

'Loads of the blokes do it ... Look, if I get shot or blown up, well, however it happens – if I snuff it, you open the envelope and post the letters inside. They've got stamps on them.'

'What are they? Invites to the funeral or bills you haven't paid!'

'Don't take the piss Mick. I'm serious, ask Eddie, I bet he does them.'

I looked down at the envelope again.

'So you're saying if you die, you send a letter to your nearest and dearest telling them you're dead? They'd know anyway wouldn't they?'

Lofty sat down, 'Inside there are three letters, one to my mum and dad, one to my sister and one to Fiona ...'

'The girl from the Nelson?'

'Yeah ...We're getting on really well, she told me that you'd been binned by whatsername. Anyway, it tells them how I feel about ...'

'Getting shot! *Dear Mum and Dad, I've been shot and it bloody hurts, love and kisses Lofty.*'

'Fuck off Mick I'm serious. It explains how I feel, sort of a goodbye, telling them the stuff I don't say.'

I'd never heard him like this before; he was reflective and mature. Completely out of character, he continued.

'There was this soldier in the seventies who wrote a poem called something like Don't Stand For Me And Cry. I can't remember how it goes now but it's about not wanting his family to mourn him for ever and get on with their life.'

'So what's your poem then? Don't eat yellow snow, ha ha!'

'Mick, just get lost if you're not interested. It's nothing to do with you anyway.'

I felt caught in the middle while Lofty and Mick went at each other. We were working closer than we ever would at Camp; and Mick, who normally wouldn't say boo to a goose was getting really goby and Lofty had gone all deep and meaningful on me. I always thought of him as the big man who bowls along without a care in the world, shagging women and drinking near fatal amounts of alcohol, but I could see for a moment someone's son; responsible and sensitive. Mick grabbed his shower stuff from his bed and walked out.

I looked at the letters and wondered whom I'd write to or even if I'd write to anyone. Mum would be devastated if I died; I don't think she'd appreciate a letter from her dead son landing on the doormat a couple of days later. Marc would think it was bad taste; he'd probably say that I was tempting fate. I felt confused. Lofty asking me to be the bringer of bad news, even though I'd be anonymous. It would be my choice if they received news that may upset them more than they needed. I wouldn't know where to begin or how to start such a letter. Dear Mum, if you receive this letter I'm dead. No I can't do that, it's horrible and would she read it? Would she just throw it in the bin? She might keep it in her handbag and show her friends, The Letter From The Dead. I love my family, everyone, I assume, loves their family and I wouldn't want to hurt mine. When I joined the Army, Marc and Mum told me to take care and when I said I was going to Ireland, Mum's face dropped and she gave me a hug. They know that this is a dangerous job and I'm sure they're not ignorant of the fact that soldiers die on the streets of Belfast. So why should I write a stupid letter saying that I love them? I'll tell Mum next time I see her, she knows I love her.

I busied myself with my kit, composition of the letters swirling around in my head. I could write to Dad out of spite and say something like: *If you'd got to know me I might not have joined the Army and died.* Not even my resentment of him could make me do such a thing; I don't even know where he lives!

Lance Sergeant Chant came into the room at nine that evening; he had Corporal Dave Tupp with him, carrying a notebook. We'd been sharing a three-man room while Eddie had his own bunk, a single room, as he was a Lance Corporal. Lofty called it Eddie's Wanking Chariot and every time we passed he'd knock on the door and shout,

'Never function on automatic mate!'

They inspected and took notes on the damaged kit that needed exchanging; Lance Sergeant Chant was in a good mood because of our earlier success on the streets.

'Big one tomorrow lads, we get to kick some more 'A' Company arse.' He spoke as if the rivalry between the Companies had reached new heights. 'If you get a chance to sort out that idiot Topple again Lofty, make sure you get the first punch in this time, I don't want to be picking up any more of your teeth!'

And with that he held out his hand with Lofty's missing molar in it. So Lofty had a name now. Topple. The inspection over, we got ourselves ready for the morning, re-packed our kit and went to bed.

Wednesday began with the Company On Parade in the main square of the barracks. The Sergeant Major gave us a talk on not giving up and showing weaknesses. He'd been to Ireland on several tours, and relayed the perils of looking weak on the baseline, which is the name for the human barricade we put up. When he'd finished, one of the instructors standing to the side of the Company covertly threw a lit petrol bomb in front of us. The heat was instantaneous and black smoke billowed up from the fire. I was in the front rank and had to shield my face from the heat; as the flames died down he stepped to the front of the Company.

'Petrol ... flamin' nasty stuff, and we'll be using it on you today.'

What? WHAT! They want to throw real petrol bombs at me! Buckets of blood, whatever next! I looked at Mick whose mouth had fallen open in disbelief.

'Well what did you expect, gentlemen? Did you think we'd let you go out there not knowing what it was like to be petrol bombed?'

I don't know why I hadn't thought of it before. We had seen lots of video footage of riots and petrol bombs but it hadn't occurred to me that we'd need training on how to deal with them. I felt slightly guileless. After the last two days I'd lulled myself into a false sense of security thinking I knew everything there was to know about riots. What an idiot.

The instructors showed us how to hold the six-foot shield so that the fire from a petrol bomb would be deflected away from our body and by interlinking the shields in a line the theory was that everyone would be protected. If one came over the top of the baseline then there was a man watching, holding a fire extinguisher to put you out. We had one of the new soldiers in the Battalion doing this; he was too young at seventeen to go with us to Ireland but was allowed to do the training. Everyone kept telling him not to worry if any of the vehicles set alight, just look out for the guys. He must have been terrified as he kept getting threats like: 'If I burn mate I'm going to stick that extinguisher somewhere it will need surgically removing.'

I was picked with another three equally dubious Privates to line up and show everyone how easy it was to deal with a lit petrol bomb; this was the first time in the training I felt like panicking. This was a real Molotov cocktail and I'm the target. We interlinked shields, and waited.

'Don't forget lads, lower your heads so that the visor stops you getting a face full of smoke.'

'Oh, many thanks,' I thought. 'How about you stand here and get horribly burnt and inhale poisonous fumes?

I held the shield as tightly to my body as I could; my hand was hurting from the grip. I looked forward and saw the instructor lighting the bomb. He threw it overarm with a downward motion so that it hit the ground about a foot in front of the shields. The bottle made a popping sound. I closed my eyes and braced myself … nothing. The force of the impact had extinguished the flame at the fuse and petrol splashed onto our shields.

'It's okay lads. I've got some more. Stay where you are.'

Oh goodie! I thought you'd only brought one with you, hurry up then, I'm getting cold! Too late. He'd lit the second bomb and it was flying through the air, not as near as the first one but close enough so that when it fractured on the floor, the contents ignited the first one as well. The fire was intense and the heat punctured through the protection of the shields; my arm felt like a boil in the bag.

'Hold the line lads. Don't move the shields or you'll get burnt.'

The stench of petrol mixed with heated tarmac and plastic was overwhelming. I tried to keep my head down but my desire to breathe clean air was too much. I could feel the guy next to me leaning on me more forcefully than he should have; as I looked across, I could see he'd vomited in his helmet, the visor covered in puke. I had to breathe – I couldn't wait any longer. The flames were subsiding slightly so I lifted my head and gulped for air as tears streamed down my cheeks. Hot toxic stinging fog poured into my mouth and down my throat, as the first lungful was rejected; my natural reaction was to gasp for more air. The second lungful left me reeling in agony, I was in a fit of coughing and couldn't stop, bodily fluids left all my facial orifices at once, tears, snot, phlegm everywhere. My eyes were closed and I stood still, waiting for the pain to pass.

'Good lads,' I finally heard. 'That's how you do it troops, nothing to it, eh?'

The instructor came behind the rabble of coughing, spluttering men and slapped us on the back. I'm still not sure if it was congratulatory or just to give us a hand coughing up the remaining smoke.

'What was that like Den?' Lofty enquired, looking surprisingly concerned.

'Oh, piece of cake mate… no problem.'

With the unanticipated extra training extinguished, we were given a briefing from Lance Sergeant Chant about how this morning's duties would happen. Our team, with the support of another quartet from 3 Platoon, were to encamp ourselves at a road junction on the funeral route, observing the procession and reporting to Headquarters if we saw any known terrorists. The other teams had similar duties elsewhere on the route. There were a further two teams in vehicles, driving around the vicinity.

Everything was to be in place by ten o'clock. Our briefing finished at nine, and Eddie told us to be ready to leave on foot in half an hour. The mock village is only a mile long. At one end our Camp is located, and a small cemetery at the other; three streets run parallel to each other dissected by a single road of shops and a pub running north to south. Our junction was on the corner of the shops and the central street. It was here that most of the civilian population gather so I felt that I was going to be in the thick of it again. If trouble started, which I was fairly certain it would, we were to run back to Camp and start putting our riot kit on. Sounded like a good plan, and it was Mick's turn to carry the heavy kit today.

We left the barracks on the dot of nine-thirty and walked to our destination in patrol formation. This means that four people walk in two lines but staggered so that you're never next to someone; the theory is that if a bomb goes off the explosion doesn't catch anyone else. Not a nice thought but practical. Lofty would lead on the left-hand side of the street and behind was Eddie on the right. Me behind Lofty and Mick at the rear following Eddie. I had the job of walking backwards so that I made sure Mick was all right and not getting left behind. I'd watch out for him stopping and I'd stop and he would tell me when I needed to catch up with the others and I'd turn and run until I'd regained the distance. In the early stages of training I'd keep tripping over or lagging behind but over the weeks I'd become accustomed to the others' moves and signals and we could cover any amount of distance easily with no fuss or mistakes. From leaving the gates it only took us fifteen minutes to arrive at our junction; the streets were unusually empty; even as we approached the shops I could hear distorted voices from Eddie's radio but none of the usual abuse from the civilians.

'Go home ya Brits,' they'd normally shout as we passed, or 'Up the Ra,' which was short for 'Up the IRA,' I'd learned. But this morning, nothing.

In silence we took up our fire positions, next to walls and in the gardens of houses. I checked my watch; ten minutes past ten. Lance Sergeant Chant and his team of four were on the mobile patrol and as he reached us in his Land Rover, the door swung open and he leaned out.

'The procession's just left the house and it's heading towards you. No trouble lads; just get back to Camp if they start. They'll be here in five minutes, about eighty in the cortège. See ya.'

He drove off and all was quiet again. My stomach had butterflies in it, partly from the petrol bomb training and partly because I didn't know how long we were going to be working. It's always the not knowing that does it to me. I could hear sounds now, a car horn in the distance. It made me jump and look around; voices shouting in unison from the next street filled me with anticipation. Even knowing that it's an exercise didn't stop me feeling that I was in danger, an enemy in someone else's country. We had plenty of our soldiers on the streets but we were still in the minority and it made me feel vulnerable, no longer in control. I just had to face this situation and do my best not to get hurt. Gordon Bennett, Den – it's only training, don't flap.

Only seconds left to wait before they came into view. I could hear their shouts clearly. It sounded like thousands of people but my imagination was getting the better of me. This was unlike any funeral I'd witnessed before, mourners protesting and threatening. The first person around the corner was our Padre from Camp in Winchester. He participated to put some reality into the occasion. Next was the hearse, closely followed by the grieving widow and the cortège. It all looked very dramatic, everyone was serious and the atmosphere was tense.

'Brits out, Brits out!'

I felt the scrutinising eyes of the procession as I knelt in my fire position, I felt minor and inconsequential but not weak. Eddie was standing looking watchful and wary; I could see the other teams in position further along the road. My senses were working in overdrive, my eyes scanning faces, my ears hearing every shout. I smelt the perfume of the widow as she passed. I'm so focused and alert.

Nothing. They passed by. I could see the last few people turning right at the end of the street, walking slowly with their heads down. One of 3 Platoon's Corporals stood on the corner where the cortège turned; he's relaxed and walking around in the road.

'Okay lads. Let's get back then,' Eddie announces, and steps into the street too.

We follow him, still scanning. Suddenly there's a shout. I look up; I see the 3 Platoon Corporal doubled over holding his head in his hands. There are potatoes raining down on him from behind the corner house and he's caught in the open with nowhere to run. A loud cheer goes up from the crowd as more missiles are hurled, this time flooring the guy. His team run to assist, one man firing a baton gun and the other two dragging him towards us.

Eddie's radio erupts into a torrent of shouted instruction and we instinctively break into a sprint, no build up, full speed ahead toward the downed man. Mick attempts to put a round in the baton gun as he runs but drops it. It bounces down the road making a clanking sound; he bends down to pick it up but kicks it further away from his grasp. I load my baton gun and push my rifle under my arm out of the way. Loading the baton gun and running simultaneously had made me misjudge my location, and I had run into the middle of the road in nearly the exact spot where the Corporal had been standing. The crowd had spread out across the street; I couldn't see how deep the crowd was but it seemed much greater than before. They stood together shouting abuse and waving fingers. I raised the baton gun. I could see the instructors mingling with the crowd, giving orders, and then the missiles started. They flew into the air, spinning down and crashed at my feet, hitting my helmet and body. I fired. It took more missiles to make me aware of how vulnerable my position was.

'Get off the road!' Lofty shouted as he hid behind a wall. Mick, who was leaning against the gable end house, stepped into the street and raised his baton gun. The crowd were ushered back as he fired and there was a lull in the throwing. I ran back to the safety of the houses.

'Hello Zero? This is Bravo two two. Do you want us to move back now? Over.' Eddie scowled at me as he talked into his radio.

'Come on,' he shouted, not bothering to look out for us as he ran back in the direction of the Camp. I wasn't in any position to criticise his leadership, as I'd put us in a stupidly dangerous situation.

Our riot kit was laid out on the forecourt of the Camp as we ran through the gates. The Sergeant Major was waiting for us dressed and ready to go with his helmet and visor on, carrying a truncheon.

'Get kitted up, lads!' he sounded nearly jubilant. 'Been waiting for this all week. I want to be first in a snatch squad. How many did you lift on Tuesday? Fifteen?'

It's funny how one man's confidence can affect others so quickly. We put our riot kit on with renewed enthusiasm, soldiers poured in through the gates, panting and smiling equipping themselves with various items of kit. I was on the baseline so I grabbed a six-foot shield. Mick was going to be in the snatch squad with the Sergeant Major and Lofty. Just then, Lance Sergeant Chant's vehicle came back from its patrol covered in debris and he jumped out grinning like a Cheshire cat.

'Lofty, I've seen Topple. He's wearing a red top, black jeans and white trainers, you know the score.'

I was excited but I couldn't really understand the euphoric atmosphere, I thought that this couldn't happen when it's real life, in Northern Ireland surely? I didn't have long to contemplate the point, as we were ordered into groups, told where to stand in formation and who to listen to. A Saxon appeared at the Camp gates driven by a Royal Logistic Corps driver – a large-armoured troop carrier, used in riots as they have grilles on the windows and won't catch fire. It would give us more mobility on the baseline. We could have four men on each side with interlinking shields. We could block a whole street, and move backwards and forwards but with only eight men in the line. I felt more protected with this thing next to me.

The Sergeant Major told us to standby to move; he opened the back doors of the Saxon and shouted to the driver to keep it slow and not to run any of our guys over or he'd be for it.

'Move out.'

And we rolled off, shuffling next to the vehicle with our shields by our sides until we needed them. Behind us followed the snatch squads and baton gunners. They were trotting and looked like American football players with their visors down and helmets on. The last men to follow were the firemen and the Officer-In-Charge of 'B' Company, Major Bell. He'd not been seen during any of the training so far and wanted to join in now? RHIP (rank has its privileges) is the answer to that.

We moved through the village in three segments, dividing our force between the three streets. The plan was to contain any violent protests or rioting and then to push the crowd back towards the cemetery where they would have to disperse. Major Bell had passed a message that the Royal Ulster Constabulary

Police had been watching the funeral procession too and the angry crowds were now heading toward the Camp. The RUC reported that the crowd were aggrieved that the Army had been watching them so closely and they intended to cause as much damage as possible to the estate.

My group had the middle street. As we moved forward I could smell the distinctive chemical stench of burning car tyres and hear the dull shouts of an angry mob ahead. They appeared from nowhere, unlikely as it sounds. Crowds of people began to fill the street from behind houses and out of alleyways.

'Baseline', was called from someone behind us. We fanned out and linked shields. Debris started falling from the sky, the instructors must have re-supplied, as the shower was relentless. These were much bigger potatoes, which I found amusing; they must keep the baking spuds for the big riots! I even managed to pull a small smile to myself thinking about telling Peanuts or Mum. Mum would probably say it was a waste of food. 'There are children in Africa would be glad for some of those.' Well, tell them to come and get them quick before they do me some damage.

The first petrol bomb was delivered without anyone spotting it being thrown; it smashed into the shield next to mine and ignited in a spectacular flash of orange and yellow against the plastic. We had been briefed that morning to shout, 'Petrol,' if anyone spotted one being lit or thrown. The fireman raced forward and pointed his extinguisher at the shields; a hand grabbed his collar and pulled him backwards nearly causing his feet to lose traction with the ground.

'Only the lads, right, forget about the shields. Only the lads, now calm down.' Sergeant Major Flaherty spoke sternly.

'Sorry, Sir.' The soldier backed off brandishing the extinguisher as if it were a weapon.

'Petrol! Petrol!' A shout from the other side of the vehicle and then the smash of glass. This one must have been thrown against the Saxon as the flames licked the underside of the vehicle and spewed out at ankle height next to me. I could hear the fireman unleashing his extinguisher on the soldier who was stood next to the vehicle opposite me.

'Fuck, fire! FIRE! My bloody leg's on fire!' I'd felt the heat before looking down in horror and seeing my trouser leg burning from my boot to my knee. It felt like minutes before the freezing foam hit and snubbed the flames. I looked down to see how much damage had been done to my skin and amazingly the material of my trousers was still intact, only scorched. I was shaking, my helmet rattling on my head. I felt a sharp slap on my shoulder.

'Good lad. Yarwood, isn't it?' The Sergeant Major must have asked Lofty who I was; the only other time he'd spoken to me at length was to give me a dressing-down.

'Yes, Sir,' I felt privileged that someone with so much experience had praised me.

More petrol came and more missiles; the shouting was getting louder and the crowd were gaining in confidence but, of course they would, we'd done nothing but stand here for ten minutes and take a battering.

'Baton gunners ready.' At last, I thought. The Sergeant Major pointed out the first target. As the shot rang out the two huge men burst through the shields followed closely by Mick, his rifle pointing at the crowd, who had become too assertive and were only twenty feet away. As Lofty and the Sergeant Major reached the individual who had been told to lie on the floor I could see that he was tiny. He must have been the smallest man in 'A' Company! The two giants lifted him clear off the ground; as they ran back his legs kicked out comically. The snatched midget turned his head towards the Sergeant Major and spat on his visor. Simultaneously they let go of the soldier as the shields opened, sending him flying through the air before landing on his knees behind the baseline with a scream of pain.

'One down. Fifteen more to beat the record,' the Sergeant Major said as he wiped away the phlegm from his field of view. The retrieved soldier looked sheepish as he realised that he'd spat on the Sergeant Major of 'B' Company. He picked himself off the ground, holding an injured knee, and ran back towards the mob to inform them who was running the snatch squad.

Three men from a different squad relayed from the other side of the Saxon, snatching another, and then our side went out, alternating. Back and forth they went; each time the Sergeant Major shouted the tally. He sounded more resolute as he and Lofty dumped each live body behind us. Lofty looked sweaty, and as he passed he jokingly muttered something about wanting to go home.

Major Bell was shouting through a loud hailer instructing us to advance and push the crowd back. I heard the vehicle's engine rev and suddenly it lurched forward, taking us with it. We shuffled along with the Saxon, taking direct hits from the mob. The fragments on the ground were causing me to trip. I pushed the bottom edge of the shield along the road with my foot; potatoes and glass were getting trapped under the plastic. The opposite flank seemed to be having the same trouble keeping the shields together. The instructors in the gathering might have anticipated this as two petrol bombs sailed though the air, smashing into the unstable barricades we were trying to maintain. No one had shouted a warning, or if they did, it went unheard, and flames engulfed the three soldiers next to me. The crowd roared and I could hear the screams of the men from underneath their visors. Our single fireman was busy on the opposite side of the vehicle. The screaming and shouting was deafening. My efforts seemed futile. All of a sudden and none too soon streams of foam mushroom over us, making me cough. The Sergeant Major and Lofty had grabbed fire extinguishers and doused the burning troops.

'Right, I'm mad now.' The Sergeant Major threw down his extinguisher and picked up his truncheon, slapping it into his palm. The fire had forced us to stop temporarily. 'A' Company knew that we had received a good thrashing and it was our turn to obtain some revenge. The baton gunners were set new targets, and a volley of shots rang out; six men ran towards the mob, people scattered. An instructor had made two unlucky men rest in the road; Lofty headed straight for Topple, even though he was on the far side of the Saxon and should have been the duty of the other team. As Lofty and co. approached, Topple hid his face with his forearm. The two men hoisted him to his feet and started to run back to the baseline. Lofty held his truncheon between his victim's legs so that Topple danced on tiptoe, his lips tight and his eyes round. They moved swiftly, pushing the man ever faster. The shields didn't open. Topple crashed face first into the plastic, Lofty lowered his truncheon and let him slide to the ground.

'Oh! I am sorry, mate. I hope you're not hurt?' Lofty enquired in the most unconvincing way, shrugged his shoulders and walked casually around to the back of the shields where the others stood laughing.

'That's sixteen. Brilliant lads!' Sergeant Major Flaherty beamed despite his blackened face. He stepped towards the barricade ready to go out again. The mobs were retreating in the direction of the cemetery. The Saxon roared, indicating us to walk on. Our progress was gradual but we kept moving; every few paces the baton gunners would fire a round, but no more lifting of protestors. It was necessary to clear the crowd now. As the missiles became sporadic I could see people moving away, some limping, and I recognised a few who'd been picked up by the snatch squad. Topple was walking away with his head down, his nose was dripping blood; defiantly he raised two fingers before walking out of view. I rummaged in my pocket and pulled out my watch; it was twelve-thirty, and we'd been at this for over two hours. I started to feel drained. My eyes were heavy and stinging, my arm that held the shield was numb and my back ached. As the last of the crowd departed the vehicle stopped and a whistle sounded. This signalled that the exercise was finished. Just like that. I could have dropped to the ground and slept where I fell.

Chapter Twelve

After hastily dumping my kit on my bed, I sat down and opened my post. Lance Sergeant Chant handed out our letters like presents when we had arrived back in Winchester. I had two: one from Mum and a bank statement. Mum had written to notify me that Debbie had her second ultrasound scan and all was well with the baby. She also asked if I was coming home before I went to Ireland. I promised myself that I'd phone her in the morning after I'd organised myself and washed my clothes.

We'd arrived back at nine o'clock after a final long day at Longmoor. Major Bell was so pleased with us, he had declared Monday morning off work. Mick, Lofty and Eddie agreed that they were going out as soon as we had got back in but I was wornout from the week and had loads of personal admin to do. I busied myself cleaning my boots and sorting piles of laundry; it had gone ten and there was a knock on the door. Mick poked his head into my room; he'd had a shower and put on some smart clothes.

'Come on Den. We're going in a minute if you want to change your mind?'

The last time I'd gone out with Mick, he stood on a table singing 'Two Little Boys,' the Rolf Harris ditty. That isn't a crime, but we had only been out an hour and the landlord told us to get rid of him, stating he was bad for business. I got the short straw and ended up taking him back to Camp.

'No thanks mate. I'm not up for it,' I said, but actually thought 'no thanks mate, you're a pain in the ass when you're drunk, let Lofty take you home this time'.

'Ok see ya, Billy-no-mates, ha ha,' and with that he closed the door. I could hear him shouting for Lofty as he walked away. I'd put another wash in, have a shower and get into bed. I must have been asleep before my head hit the pillow as the next thing I knew there was light streaming through the window.

Saturday mornings had become a routine that I loved, a bit of solitary. My entire kit was clean and I had time to go running; it felt good. As I ran out of Winchester along the canal I thought of the past week and the riot training, how intense it had been, and wondered if I'd be facing that sort of stuff regularly in Ireland. Marc and Mum would be curious I suppose and no doubt fret once I'd explained. I thought about Lofty's death letters and how Mum would react. Would I write one? What was the purpose? I couldn't settle that debate so I planned what to wear tonight into town instead. I ran for an hour and as I sauntered through Camp I saw Lofty walking back to the accommodation. It looked like he'd just come in from the night before.

'Hi mate, what gives?'

'Don't shout Den.'

'I wasn't!'

'Ok just shut up and let me enjoy this hangover then.'

'How's Fiona?'

'Dumped.'

'Why? You said that you two were getting on really well.'

'No. *I* was getting on with her ... *she* was getting on with anyone in trousers.'

'Oh. So you had a good night then?'

'No. Crap. I got drunk and woke up in the park, I'm sodding freezing.'

He shook his head and looked down at the ground. I apologised and ran to my room; there wasn't a lot I could say to him. I couldn't really guess how he felt so I thought it was best just to leave him for the time being.

Once I'd showered I rang Mum. She was delighted to hear from me and I her, it seemed like ages since we'd spoken. One of the things I love about Mum was that she never spends too long on the phone; she'd rather cram in as much information as she could in a few sentences and say her goodbyes. The call went like this:

'Hi Mum! It's Den. How are you?'

'Oh Denis! Thanks for calling. I'm fine and so are Marcus and Debbie, she's doing really well with the pregnancy and little Callum is coming on so fast. He's been asking for you. Are we going to see you soon? How's the training going? When do you fly to Ireland? Are you keeping well? I broke your Messerschmitt, sorry, but the others are fine, it had fallen on the floor, but I've got all the pieces ...'

'Mum.'

'Yes dear?'

'Can I come for lunch on Sunday?'

'Of course Denis! I'll see if Marcus and Debbie will come over with little Callum. Oh, it will be lovely to see you, do you want beef? I'll make a crumble and I'll buy you another model to make up for the one I stood on, would you like another Messerschmitt or something else? Oh, I need some flour, I'll have to pop to the shops this afternoon, or I might ask Marcus to bring some ...'

'Mum.'

'Yes dear?'

'I'll see you at about eleven, don't worry about the plane, I just want to see you all, that would be lovely.'

'Eleven dear, that's lovely, drive safely now. Ta-ra!'

As a boy I was bought an Airfix kit by one of my aunties for Christmas. I must have been about nine. We didn't get loads of presents for Christmas; one main present and a few small ones from relatives. This particular year Mum had given me an Evel Knievel stunt cycle. Just wind up the gyro-energizing handle on the side to get the motorbike to whizz off and perform jumps and stunts. When it reached a certain momentum the bike and rider sped off a ramp, but the only hitch with it was that the handle passed so close to the floor that by Boxing Day my knuckles were red raw. So I was forced into opening my other gifts; socks, new pyjamas, a game of Ker-Plunk and a model aircraft kit. It was a Spitfire. I'd never seen one before. I remember opening the box and pulling out the first piece of grey framework. It looked beautiful. There were perfectly constructed pieces linked together by the plastic mesh, each one a tiny mechanical miracle. Wheels, hydraulic rams, cockpit windows and propellers, tiny wing mounted guns and a small pilot dressed in his flight suit and goggles, ready to fight the Third Reich. The instructions showed how to construct the plane in stages, starting with the fuselage, then the wings, engine, propeller, wheels and rams and finally the authentic RAF stickers that came on a white piece of paper along with the instructions. Whoever had sent me such a wonderful gift had sellotaped two tins of model paint and a paintbrush to the side of the box, British racing green and brown. The next three days I beavered away, gluing it together, painting it and attaching a piece of cotton from mum's sewing box onto the top of the plane, which I tied to my lampshade. That plane was magnificent. And that's what Mum had meant by breaking my Messerschmitt. In my room at home I had thirty-two airplanes, four helicopters, two tanks and a half finished frigate, which I didn't find that interesting. Those models took up most of my spare time from the age of nine until ... well, until I joined the Army actually. I thought that I'd be wiser to keep that hobby to myself; not that I considered it to be wet or anything, it was that I couldn't really take them with me and had nowhere else to store them and well, the other blokes might think I was a bit ... wet.

The Nelson was busy when I walked in at eight-thirty. I pushed my way to the bar and ordered myself a pint of Smooth. Peanuts was stood on a chair waving frantically, I could just see her above the heads of the customers. I started my careful sideways shuffle through the crowd, excusing myself every couple of steps and holding my precious pint at head height to ensure its safe carriage to my destination. I arrived after much body swerving at the window table to greet Peanuts and found her sat with seven student friends. Well, they were either students or a group of travelling exhibitionists dressed in what I can only refer to as curious clothes.

'Hey you guys! This is Den, a mate of mine.'

They looked me up and down; it seemed like I was being assessed. I'm not sure if I passed but they made a gap for me around the table and I sat down.

'Den, this is Lucy, Adrian, Melanie, Jayne, Damon, Joanne, Eleanor and Sarah. They're drama students at King Alfred's.'

'That'll explain it then,' I blurted out.

'What?'

I quickly learnt the two things not to do in the company of students. Number one:

'Erm, would anyone like a drink?'

The two blokes said they'd like a pint of lager and the girls wanted pints of cider except for Melanie, a tangled-hair ursine looking girl who was dressed in a multi-coloured caftan and wore Dr Martens boots; she asked for a gin and orange. I waited for a few seconds for the guys to jump up and volunteer to help me with the drinks ... then headed to the bar alone. The trip back from the bar was testing while I held a tray full of drinks; the lager splashed, making the pint pots move like bumper cars; but triumphantly I placed the tray with its cargo on the table. Peanuts grabbed her pint, winked at me and took a huge slurp. The others were extraordinary; in unison they lifted their drinks without even a 'thank you', just a small smile here and there. Like drinking with a main drain. Second mistake. I opened a packet of fags and gave one to Peanuts; unfortunately, I caught her neighbour's glance and ended up offering cigarettes around the table. Everyone took one and lit up. I was amazed to see lighters emerging from their pockets; no one had placed their packet on the table, and in fact I assumed that no one smoked! They began chatting between themselves again about their course work and who would get an audition and who was doing the most outrageous project this year. I was lost and slightly put out. Peanuts was completely absorbed in the exchange and I sat supping my pint quietly. Melanie, the girl in the caftan, spoke in a deep plummy tone, very posh and precise. She unexpectedly turned to me.

'One does apologise but I've forgotten your name, one is Melanie.'

'Den.'

'Soh what doh you doh Den?'

'Pardon?'

'At King Alfred's. Which course aaare you ohn?'

'Oh sorry I'm not, ha, no I'm not a student. I'm in the Army.'

At last I've broken into the conversation, even if it was with the undomesticated woman of Winchester, holding her cigarette like Joan Collins and blowing the smoke high into the air.

'Well, I say – oh...lovely!'

And that was it; she turned away disinterestedly and rejoined the main conversation, my answer thrown away like an odd sock. To be quite honest, I felt unworthy and this unsettled me.

'Guess who's doing Richaaard the jiffy this yeaaar?'

Sitting and listening to people chat when you're socially excluded is thirsty work. I'd downed my pint; I deliberately placed my empty pint pot on the table. It wasn't an 'Oi I've Finished And It's Not My Round,' placement; more of a 'Hello, it's polite in the Western world to buy a drink for those who've gone before thee,' placement. One of the lads stood up and left the table nearly immediately, heading for the bar to replenish our glasses, I thought. He came back minutes later with *his* pint of lager and sat down. I'm missing something here. As the others took their turns to taunt me I sat in despair, thirsty despair, until a time where I couldn't take any more punishment and retreated to the bar to get myself a pint. By then I had realised that I had been used, raped for drinks. On my return the conversation had changed to the worst makeup job they'd seen this year. Peanuts was in full flow; I'm pretty sure she isn't a drama student but she clearly knew her subject matter. She didn't even look at me when she helped herself to another of my fags without asking. I put the nearly empty packet in my jacket pocket. The guy who'd been to the bar on his own, Damon, shifted his seat and leaned across the table.

'Den, that's right isn't it? What are you reading?'

For the second time I explained that I wasn't in college.

'How do you know her?' He asked pointing at Kerry.

'Oh, I met Peanuts in Luton; she was going out with a mate of mine,'

'Peanuts? Are you related?'

'No, just a friend.'

'I'm terribly sorry but what's with the pet-name?'

'Its just, well ...'

'It was my nickname in Luton.' Thank goodness for that, it was the first thing she'd said of any use all night and I was pleased that she'd been sharp enough to dig me out of the hole I was excavating. Damon was looking puzzled at us; he didn't seem to get it.

'My dear old dad was in the Army too actually. He flew helicopters Captain Hill, have you heard of him?'

He must have noticed my half smile as I took another mouthful of beer, Damon Hill ha ha, poor boy; at least his dad had a sense of humour.

'No. I'm sorry I don't know him, why, was he famous?' I suppose sarcasm isn't the most endearing way to reply but repetition was making me rude.

'Not to my knowledge, he served in Northern Ireland, I recall.' Ah, the old needle in a haystack sketch, now that makes all the difference. I should be able to narrow it down to at least ten thousand soldiers to select from.

'I'm sorry mate but I've never heard of him.' More beer was in order; this time I sorted myself out and bought a whisky chaser to accompany my pint. When I sat down, Damon looked ready and primed for the next round of questioning. I didn't dislike him and talking about the Army is interesting to non-military people, but I was out for a laugh. I think the fact that I was being ignored on the whole, and a couple of pints to warm me up, had put me in a reckless mood.

'When did you attend Sandhurst? I know someone there at the moment and he says it's really tough. Absolutely top hole – I have to say.'

'I'm not an Officer, I'm a Guardsman.'

'What do you guard, Den?' He had a smile on his face, touché.

'Sponging students like yourself, the brains of Britain.'

Damon burst out laughing, far too loud to warrant praise for my pathetic joke, but it made me feel like I'd made an opening for myself and I didn't quite feel so much of an outsider any more. More beer I think; consequently, I'm off to the bar for further refreshments, feeling much brighter.

To my dismay, when I returned Damon had gone, so I'm plunged back into Coventry, listening to amusing student tales of how people corpsed in productions. I can't see the point of these drama students; what do they do after this? They can't all become celebrated actors and actresses. What jobs do you see advertised with the must-have drama degree or whatever they get? **'Situation Vacant:** Plumber, full time. Salary negotiable. Must be an undergraduate and wear blue stockings. Ability to recite the entire works of Shakespeare desirable. Experience not essential.' I'm being disparaging; everyone has a place in life, I mean even I found a decent job. Another beer while I ponder this sociological conundrum, and a chaser for medicinal purposes. Peanuts joins me at the bar, puts her glass down to be filled and tips out the contents of her pockets onto a beer mat. Loose change spills everywhere, a lipstick, lighter and a condom.

'Oops! Sorry, you never know, eh?'

She nudges me and winks, putting the offending article back into her pocket.

'You having a good time sweetie?'

'Yeah blinding thanks,' I lie.

'Jayne's having a party in her room later, are you up for it?'

'Na, sorry mate I'm going to see Mum in the morning.' I'm already half pissed and I'm looking forward to a lie-in tomorrow morning, but I'm defo not going to another student party tonight.

'Aw, come on Den.' Peanuts lays her head on my shoulder and looks at me with puppy dog eyes, 'It won't be the same without you.'

Damn, the flattery nearly breaks my defence but I really don't want to listen to any more of the rubbish her illuminated acquaintances are spouting. She offers me a fag, and as my fresh pint is placed on the counter, Peanuts pulls a tenner out from nowhere and presents it to the barman.

'Please Den, we'll have a laugh.'

No, no, no, definitely not.

'Look, I'll ring you.'

'But you haven't got my number.'

I beckoned to the barman and asked him for a pen, took my wallet out and found an old receipt.

Chapter Thirteen

The drive back to Winchester on Sunday evening was slow; there were queues on the way back until my exit on the M3. When the traffic is like that it is really annoying, or will induce a headache. Luckily for me I had other things to think about than the journey, so the tap-dancing-brake-pedal-pusher in front of me didn't wind me up. Mum had made the most lovely roast dinner with Yorkshire puddings, a real treat. Marc and Debbie arrived with Callum, and we chatted about my tour to Northern Ireland and how they wouldn't have to buy me a present, as I'd be away for my birthday and miss the birth of number two. It had been a fair day.

I turned into the Camp at ten o'clock and parked my car on the main square; I had intended to go straight to bed but with having no work until tomorrow lunchtime I decided to head to the Nelly for a beer instead. I would just make last orders. For a Sunday evening the bar was busy. I recognised a few students from Peanuts' university but no one I knew well enough to talk to, not that I was bothered. Seeing Mum and everyone this afternoon had made me reflect on those letters that Lofty wrote again. Marc had told me to keep my head down as I was leaving the house and it made me hark back; I couldn't find a solution. Why was it troubling me so much? It's not as if I *had* to write to anyone, I have made an Army Will, so there's no use elaborating. Would they speculate how I viewed the tour? Do I need to remind my family how I feel about them? I felt perplexed by the whole thing, so I made up my mind. No Den, it's a pointless idea, I'm not going to do it. I had two pints and walked back to Camp. I tried to imagine myself on the streets of Belfast, walking with my rifle at the ready. Checking cars and talking to the locals, it's an emotive thought to be responsible for a rifle and ammunition, and whether to shoot or not. We have been given yellow cards listing the rules to abide by when opening fire on a terrorist, I'd memorised it. Soldiers have been locked up for not adhering to the Rules of Engagement. I invented different scenarios in my head on the way back and lay awake thinking. It was a while before I got to sleep.

Lance Sergeant Chant stood in front of the Platoon reading out the flight list. There were four departures over a fortnight scheduled for leaving Camp and then a final flight date for those individuals responsible for closing down the barracks for our six months away and that was my birthday. I had resigned myself to the fact that I would be sober on my birthday even before I heard my name. Lofty's name came after mine so at least I wouldn't be on my own; he looked at me with a big toothy smile. That gave us three weeks' training before we go.

'Right lads, has anyone got any questions about when you're flying? Everyone will take four days' leave before their respective flight so get your leave applications in as soon as possible.'

'What are you doing for your leave Den?' Lofty asked as he scrawled on his application.

'No idea mate, I don't fancy going home, might just bum around here, what about you?'

'Fancy going away? It's the last chance to get inebriated and laid for a while.'

'Where? It's November.'

'Dunno ... Ibiza?'

'I don't want to go too far, how about Brighton?'

'I'm not going to Brighton Den. Use your bloomin' imagination!'

'Okay then ... where could we go that would guarantee us a shag and loads of cheap beer?'

'Blackpool!'

We sat considering our options while we wrote our leave

passes; Lofty kept looking up at the sky for inspiration and scratching his chin with his thumb and forefinger. Now I believe that great minds think alike. We looked at each other and jinxed ourselves.

'Amsterdam!'

It was genius. We decided to go to the travel agents that afternoon and book it; neither of us had been anywhere; I'd never been abroad. The Army were responsible for my passport application; I've not needed one before: no money. We'd have to get ourselves organised with currency and maybe a guidebook. We would fly, as the boat would take too long. I wasn't so shirty about missing a birthday night out. Things were not looking as cursed as they had been.

The woman in the travel agents looked at us over her glasses when we said where we wanted to go. I felt she had prejudged us and I was feeling incredibly guilty although I wasn't sure why.

'Okay gents,' she sounded sarcastic and knowing.

'Two return tickets are available departing LHR to Schiphol airport. You have to stay a Saturday night and there can be no amendments or alterations to the flights. Would you like me to book a hotel? Double or twin?'

We sat in the Nelly planning our trip. Four nights in the city, how many women we could pull? We hadn't bought a guidebook yet and it wasn't uppermost in our minds. Lofty suggested we have a wager. I shook his hand when we agreed ten pounds to the winner, production of a pair of knickers as evidence of the dirty deed.

'Ten pounds eh, you boys?'

'Hi Peanuts! What are you doing in here?'

'I'm stalking you.' She smiled and bent down to glare in my face trying to look scary.

'So tell me all about it. Where are you going?'

Again in unison we answered.

'I'm somewhat envious. Well, be careful you two, someone might take advantage.' You don't say things like that in front of Lofty.

'I bloody hope so, ha ha.'

'Right then, who wants another drink?' Peanuts clapped her hands as she spoke.

'Won the pools have we?' It wasn't like her to have money.

'Two beers then.' She returned with the beer, her pint of cider and some crisps. The pub had filled up by eight o'clock and my head was spinning. The conversation consisted of mindless drivel concerning any subject that cropped up. We were beginning to attract attention to ourselves as our volume rose; then Peanuts held her finger to her mouth to quieten us. SHHHHHHHHHHH!

'Whosh, tha' starin' at ush?' She slurred and pointed blatantly at a group of lads at the bar.

'I dunno' Lofty spun around on his stool, nearly knocking over the empty pint pots that had built up on the table. He squinted his eyes and tried to focus on the three or so lads who I began to loosely recognise.

'Topple.' He got up immediately and pulled his shirt straight, squared his shoulders and staggered across to where they stood. I followed knowing that if he were given the chance, Lofty would start a fight. As he drew up to the group, Topple moved forward too; he'd put his drink down and had his hands by his side with his fists clenched. I'd started to sober up.

'Wass goin' on?' I could feel Peanuts behind me.

'Go an' sit down. Now.'

'Oh Den what's ...?

'SIT DOWN.' Amazingly, she obeyed and returned to the table.

'You knocked my friggin' tooth out, ya friggin' tosser.' That's right Lofty, get off the fence and say what you mean. Topple looked at the drunken giant; he was smaller than Lofty by a couple of inches but his face was fixed and he looked ready to kick off.

'Well ya can't get any uglier can ya?' As he spoke he swayed from side to side.

'Watcha gonna do about it then, big boy?'

I've seen lots of fights in my time. Normal etiquette is to have a few words with the challenger and then launch an unsuspecting attack in the region of the chin or nose using a well-clenched fist. Surprise is the best ploy, not allowing your opponent see what's going to happen. Lofty, however, was so drunk that he was pulling his arm back slowly, his tongue hanging out of his mouth and one eye closed as if to make sure his aim was accurate. A tortoise would have had enough time to sidestep his punch. He might have posted him a letter saying, 'here it comes mate.' As Lofty's arm came closer, Topple ducked to avoid the flimsy fist but as he did so his backside pushed against the bar, sending him off balance temporarily, and uncontrollably reaching forward trying to regain his poise. He had no control over his direction, speed or stopping. Topple was heading towards our table. Staggering and trying to control himself, he outstretched his arms to break his fall. Peanuts sat in her chair looking as if she was going to catch him. Topple tripped on the carpet and fell forwards. There was a loud crack. He slumped over her like a rag doll, arms swinging and head on her shoulder; his legs were at full stretch behind him.

'Oh! He's charming but I'm sorry lads he's not my type!'

I burst into laughter, as did the two blokes with Topple. He was lying between Peanuts' legs looking like he'd fallen asleep on the job. Lofty was confused but triumphant; he'd seen Topple fall over but hadn't seen how he'd got there. He walked – well, to be honest – swaggered over to where the startled couple were still in full embrace, placed his hands on his hips and asked

"Ad enough then?'

Peanuts looked down at Topple and then at Lofty.

'Crikey Lofty, I can't believe out of ten thousand sperm, *he was* the fastest!' She started to giggle and try and push Topple off her.

'Well that'll teach 'im.' Lofty was far too pleased with himself to grasp it.

'Come on, I don't mind getting hit on but I like my men to be conscious.'

Andy, the barman who we'd got to know during our frequent visits, had now appeared by our side; he had his hands in his pockets and was smiling.

'Gents, I think it's time to take sleeping beauty home and as much as it hurts me to say, you lot aren't getting served any more today, no hard feelings eh?'

'Chips?'

'Why not? Our usual? I'm buying.'

We linked arms and walked the few hundred feet to the takeaway. Once we'd bought our chips we sat on a bench and ate them in silence.

'That was great,' she said as she finished her paper.

'What? The fight? I've seen better.'

'No the chips, you wally! Den?'

'H'm.' I was filling my face and speaking through a mouthful, hunger ruled over my manners.

'Dennn?'

'Yes?'

'Can I write to you in Belfast?'

'Yeah, if you like.'

'You know I really like you Den.'

'I like you too Peanuts, but I've got to get back to Camp, I'm busting for a leak.'

My head was starting to throb and I needed to sleep.

'Right, I'm off. See you on the weekend. Are you going to be all right getting home?'

'Yes, sure. I'll be fine. Goodnight darling Den.' She stood up, smiled and walked into the night.

Chapter Fourteen

Two weeks of constant shooting are enough to put anyone off guns for life, I'd expect. We'd shot at every type of target the Army could think of and I was getting more accurate with my rifle; even the moving targets weren't a problem. I'll give our superiors their due, they could think up some elaborate measures to keep us busy. On the last day we had a march and shoot competition, which involved running with all of our kit on for eight miles and then shooting at small metal plates which tipped over when hit. If a team knocked over all the targets and had ammo to spare, extra points were awarded; these were added to points gained from running the fastest time over the eight miles, and a score was given. Our team of four came third out of eleven and Eddie was pleased; he even offered to buy us a beer! Meanwhile the first two flights left for Northern Ireland without any problems. Lance Sergeant Chant had been updating us on the flight list every day as some individuals had to swap places to replace the soldiers we were relieving. We only had a week before our holiday and I'd started packing already. Lofty said that he'd throw a few things in a bag later and asked if I'd taken out shares in Durex yet and booked my liver transplant. I missed going to the pub at the weekend, as Lance Sergeant Chant had to put three of us on duty at short notice. C'est la vie! I'm pretty sure that's French!

On the Monday, I was sitting in my room after lunch reading a tourist guide that I'd picked up in town, when the door was violently thrown open and nearly came off its hinges.

'I'm friggin' flying tomorrow!' Lofty stood in the doorway, panting and red-faced.

'Bloody Chant said I've got to be ready to go at four o'clock in the bloody morning ... bastards.'

I didn't have the inclination or momentum to interrupt his rant; he was going into logorrhoea. Think, Den.

'We're gonna miss Amsterdam, Den. He said it was tough luck and Operations came first.'

'Loft ...'

'Bastards, we can't bloody go now,'

'Hang on a ...'

'Bloody paid for it now ... bastards. Sod it – I'm going AWOL.'

'LOFTY shut up!'

He was stomping around the room with his hands shoved deep into his pockets and a fag hanging out of his mouth.

'Are you sure he meant *you* mate?'

'Yes. I'm bloody sure!'

There was no talking to him. He paced around and walked out of my room cursing, I could hear his door slam shut seconds later. As I thought about it I felt myself getting despondent. We'd paid a lot of money for this and I didn't get any insurance; the woman had even asked twice. *I* could still go but I'd need to view the flight list to see who was left in Camp. I tapped on Lofty's door and waited.

'WHAT!' A muffled shout came from behind the door.

'It's Den, I've got an idea.'

'What?'

'Well, can I come in and I'll tell you'

The door opened and Lofty stood there in a pair of tracksuit bottoms, holding a bottle of beer.

'This had better be good.'

'Look mate, I can't do anything about the holiday and you, but if I found someone else to go, I could get some of your money back.'

'Oh thanks a lot mate! No, you go and bloody enjoy yourself mate, send me a postcard.'

'Look Lofty do you want your money back or not?'

'S'pose.' I'd never seen him sulk before, it wasn't like him and he looked egocentric.

'I'll ask one of the other lads to go, paying full costs of course, and we can go away when we get back, and I'll recce the women for you!'

'Yeah ... whatever.'

I thought that was the best response I could expect for now so I left him stood in a pile of Army kit swigging at his bottle and mumbling about how poxy the job was and how they don't do this at Sainsbury's. Lance Sergeant Chant let me look at the amended flight list; there would be no further changes, as it was too late. I wasn't bothered about changes, just finding someone from the Company who could string a sentence together and whom I thought I could share a room with for four nights without strangling. The only possible candidate was a guy called Guy Parker, who I'd been on the baseline with during training and who'd made a couple of funny comments. He was in 4 Platoon so I walked over to their accommodation to find his room. It was raining so I slung my coat over my shoulders and ran for it, hoping not to get too wet.

I knocked on his door. 'Guy!'

'It's open.' As I pushed the door I was faced by a wall of Marillion posters; they took up every available inch of wall space. His stereo was blaring a track by them and oh my God, he was wearing the T-shirt.

'Greetings Den, want a beer?'

Oh shit he likes me, but this sad and lonely Marillion fan, who had obviously been shunned by the rest of humanity, was now trying to intoxicate me with the intention of seduction into listening to more of the heavy metal being spewed from the machine in the corner. If he trapped me I'd become addicted too, and buy vinyl records with absurdly decorated covers, wear black T-shirts and call everybody 'man.' If I invited him to Amsterdam he'd be playing that awful din every day. Worse than that I'd be associated with the Marillion cronies – agh, a shiver went down my spine.

So what do I say now? 'Erm ... can I borrow some sugar?' Bloody hell, quickly retreat and don't be rude; it's not his fault that he has absolutely hideous taste.

'I ... was ... wondering ... if ... I ... could ... borrow one of your ...albums?' You've done it now Den, he'll be on to you like a rash. At least I didn't ask him to come on holiday.

'Yeah, man, which one?' Oh great, I don't even know the names of any of their songs, let alone an album title.

'The latest one?' My voice pitching slightly higher at the end of the question must have been a giveaway.

'Vinyl or tape mate?'

'Vinyl, please,' Den – just shut up and run. You don't even have a turntable!

'Don't scratch it man.'

'Right. Thanks. Bye.' And I made good my escape. I need to get my finger out and think of someone else. Everyone I got on with from work was leaving for Belfast in the next couple of days. Maybe if I'd kept in touch with Kev from home I could have asked him. I walked back to my block in the rain and put the record on my shelf. I'm a soldier who can adapt, overcome and improvise. I make decisions on my own and I can assemble a B52 bomber and paint it in four days ... and decided that the only thing to do was take radical action so I went to the pub.

Andy the barman asked after the other guys, as he knew we were leaving. He said that when we return in April that he'd have a party for us, which I knew was a way of regaining his regular trade, but it was an amiable idea.

'Oh that girl with the funny tights was in here asking for you on Saturday night.'

'You mean Peanuts, you're a mastermind Andy!'

I rummaged through my wallet and found the scrap of paper that she'd scribbled her number on.

'Can I borrow your phone Andy?'

'Yes Squire! Come through and you can watch the telly as well if you like,' I was far too distracted to listen to him properly.

'No thanks. I just want to make a call.'

'Goodness me and we pay you to defend our country?'

The phone rang for ages. Mind you we have a public phone in the block and I've learnt to ignore incoming calls too. The first week I was in Camp, the phone rang and I picked it up, only to find it was Lance Sergeant Chant.

'Ah good lad Yarwood, get your kit on, you're on guard this weekend.'

A steep learning curve. But students don't do duties so pick the effing phone up.

'Yeah?' A male voice sort of answered. I mean, how rude, it might be important!

'I need to speak to Peanuts.'

'And I'm Charlie Brown, what's happening Snoopy?' And the phone made a dull dial tone.

'Lippy squirt.' Lesson learnt. I dialled again and the phone was answered nearly immediately. This time I engaged brain.

'Hi. Could I speak to Kerry please?' I thought it best to speak before the customary greeting.

'Yeah,' it answered; but this time a female voice, and there was still no phone protocol. I could hear Peanuts' voice as she came towards the phone asking who it was. The other girl just said it was some bloke.

'Hi, Carl?'

'Who? No, it's Den,'

'Hi Sweetie! Long time no see, what happened to you?'

'Who's Carl?'

'Oh just some guy I met on Saturday. Why? Jealous are we?'

I felt foolish because I wasn't jealous. I don't know why I asked the question actually.

'No, sorry, nosey devil aren't I? Forget that. I wanted to ask you something,'

'Oh yes? Sounds ominous, let me guess ...'

'Stop it. Look, Lofty can't go to Amsterdam because he's flying to Belfast in the morning, and I've got this spare ticket, I know that you would probably need more time than this but I couldn't th ...'

'For goodness' sake man spit it out.'

'Well the thing is he's trying to get his money back and it's a twin room so it would mean that ...'

'Denis!'

'Don't call me that – you sound like my Mum.'

'Do you want me to come to Amsterdam with you?'

'Erm, look I know it's short notice and I won't mind if you say no ...'

'I'd love to, when do we fly?'

'Monday at eight ... WHAT?'

'Yes Den I'll come, how much does Lofty need for his ticket?'

'Oh Monday at eight o'clock from Heathrow, we can chat about money later, can you get the time off then?'

'I'll make sure I'm sick or something.'

'So you've got a passport and everything then?'

'No Den I intended to smuggle myself across borders posing as your daughter.'

'Sorry, I'm just relieved that's sorted, brilliant.'

'Thanks Den. Meet me in the Nelly tomorrow and we can talk

about it,'

'Can't do tomorrow, sorry. I'm giving the lads a hand with the baggage for Belfast.'

'Okay, Wednesday then?'

'Yep. Great, see you then.'

I hung up and had another pint.

Chapter Fifteen

I wanted to catch a taxi across town to the hotel but Peanuts insisted that the bussing it would be cheaper and more fun. The bus terminal was busy and the signs were confusing. Peanuts had a large suitcase with her, one of those canvas looking ones with dark flowery patterns on it, she must have borrowed it from her Gran. I on the other hand had my grip that I could sling over my shoulder and it contained enough clothes for the four nights so that I wouldn't have to do any washing. I also had my wash bag, swimming trunks (through force of habit from going on holiday with mum to Morecambe for years). Do I sound smug as a superior holiday packer? That's just a defence mechanism because I was still bewildered by the culture change that had occurred during our crossing of the North Sea. I felt relieved to be away from the battalion for a few days; even though I enjoyed the training schedule, it was soothing to relax in the thought that my days weren't going to be structured; it was a little like being unemployed again.

'Over here, I think I've found it,' Peanuts called as she waved her hand, pointing to a bus with 'Centrum' displayed on the front. I paid for our tickets and we took our seats.

'So where are we staying, Den?' I proudly took out the hotel booking papers from my jacket pocket and swished them around like a magic wand. The wallet was dog-eared because of me constantly opening it to look at the tickets every chance I had last week. I pulled out the voucher and read it.

'De Looier.'

'Sounds lovely, what's the hotel called?'

'Erm, De Looier.' My tourist guide that I had unfortunately left in my room on my bedside table had stated how easy it was to find your way around the city. It didn't look that big a place so finding one hotel shouldn't be a drama. Having said that I didn't mean to leave it behind. I looked up at Peanuts who was now reading her own guidebook; she was tracing her finger across the page.

'Ok we need to get to Derde Looiersdwars Straat 75, so we'll jump off in the city centre and walk across; Ja?'

'Oh, Ja indeed, whatever that means.' She'd bought her own tourist guide. I was appalled, how dare she take over this holiday and find me the right bus and know where to get off and say bloody, 'Ja'! I wonder what Ja means? I might as well broach the tricky subject of sleeping arrangements to even out the power struggle that was developing.

'Peanuts, you realise that we booked a twin room don't you?'

'Yes sweetie, are you worried I'll peep at your Y-fronts? Don't be silly Den, we'll be just fine. can we book in as Mr and Mrs Smith for a laugh, ha ha?'

'Ha, yes very funny – actually you are Mr Coleman this week, so ha, ha!'

'Unlikely. They'll think you're sharing with a transvestite won't they, Ja?' That girl has an answer for everything. Nevertheless be grateful for small mercies – I could have been travelling with marillion man.

'What is this Ja then?'

'It's yes Den, in Dutch surprisingly enough.' Oh great; she knows the lingo as well.

'I hope this place has got an en-suite,' she said as she studied her book, turning it to orientate the map. I grasped the carry handle on her suitcase as she wandered down the street. I didn't mean to be carrying both of the bags, I watched her walk away oblivious to my struggle, and she even had the audacity to look in some shop windows. She stopped outside what looked like an ordinary town house with twee net curtains and a big black front door with a brass bell button right in the middle of it.

'Ah, Ons hotel!'

'What?'

'The hotel Den, this is it.'

'Doesn't look like a hotel to me, are you sure?' But she'd already rung the bell and was looking through one of the downstairs windows. A small stout man opened the door wearing a white shirt and waistcoat that barely covered his stomach; he didn't look particularly friendly and looked at us up and down.

'Are you sure this is it?' I whispered out of the corner of my mouth.

'Shh Den. Goede Avond hebben wij hier geboekt een reserve bij dit hotel.'

'Ya, excuse me, I'm so sorry. Again? A room for two, ya?' Ah ha, she's not that good I thought, smiling to myself.

'Oh! You speak English, lovely; we're reserved under Yarwood and Coleman,'

'Oh ya, no problem. Welcome.' The man showed us to our room on the first floor. He gave us a key and another for the front door, told us not to make too much noise when we came in and wished us a pleasant stay.

'Right then, I'll get ready,' Peanuts had flung open her case and was dragging clothes out and laying them out She'd brought enough clothes to dress the cast of a soap opera.

'I need a lie down,' as I reclined back, my arms outstretched and feet hanging from the end of the bed.

'Oh come on Den we've only got four days. Let's hit the town, give me ten minutes to put slap on,' She was right, what was I going to do, go to bed for a couple of days? No, this was the big break from work. Peanuts had put some clothes under her arm and carried her makeup bag into the bathroom, shutting the door behind her. It gave me an opportunity to change too, I found a good pair of jeans and took my old ones off hastily, and crikey I *did* have Y-fronts on, how sad.

The signposts in Amsterdam meant nothing to me I'm not sure how the Dutch manage, everything was written in gobbledegook. We relied on the map and the directions from the hotel man to find the pub he had recommended. As we rounded the corner I could see the neon lights 'Paradiso' with tables and chairs strewn across the pavement.

'This isn't a pub!' I exclaimed in dismay.

'No, everyone drinks in cafés here, it's chic. They're just like pubs and you can get ...'

'Come on then, I'll get them in, you grab a table, what do you want?' It was too cold to sit outside so we found a table by the window. 'In fact, no I'll choose us something.' Okay Den, let's test your language skills on the locals then.

'Halloooo, can I 'ave deux bières por favor?'

'Which ones man?' The guy was a Yank; how strange, I've not met a Dutchman who speaks Dutch yet. I pointed at the nearest beer tap and waited. The frothy beer tasted sweet and took an age to pour so I ordered another before I sat down.

'Shall we eat? I'm starving.'

'Good idea.' I went back to the bar and collected two menus.

'Mm'm I think I'll have pasta and a salad.'

'Oh God you're a lentil case aren't you?'

'I beg your pardon.'

'A salad assassin, veggie,'

'Oh no, don't be silly, I like a bit of meat,' She was in an incredibly daft mood.

'Good, I'm having a steak.'

The food was delicious; we decided to stay here for the evening as the bar was filling up. I bought a bottle of wine and then

Peanuts insisted it was her turn for the drinks and we'd split the bill. 'We'll go Dutch!' she said as she laughed and went to the bar. I was enjoying myself; we stared out of the window and watched the people go by, making comments on their dress sense and lack of it, inventing imaginary characters for the stranger ones.

'Oh Den, look those trousers! They should be made illegal, I'm certain they used to be a torture method in Japan or somewhere.'

'We have got bylaws in England against them, I'm sure.'

We got progressively sillier, laughing at anyone and everyone who walked by or into the café.

'I'm just off to the little boys' room, back in a min.'

As I returned from the lavatory I ordered another beer and waited until it was poured. The feeling of being in a foreign country was getting me more keyed up, along with the effects of the alcohol. Peanuts was turning out to be a good replacement for Lofty. We laughed together and she had what I think of as a lad's sense of humour about her. Certainly the ribbing of the locals was getting to be a hoot. This time we decided to make up fictitious conversations between couples as we watched them amble around.

Guy 'Zo Ingrid, do yoo wunt to 'ave zex vis me later?'

Girl 'Oh ya Berni but zis time can vee not use ze chicken?'

I was howling with laughter as Peanuts went on, making up a story of them swinging from chandeliers in costumes. The music was getting louder in parallel with the volume of chatting around us as the café filled to what seemed capacity. Another couple sat down at our table, holding hands and whispering into each other's ears. Everyone in the place seemed to be having just a fine time, laughing and exchanging conversation. Peanuts got up and went to read a chalkboard that seemed to be of much interest to a lot of the crowd. She examined the notice and then headed for the bar.

'Not more food?' I asked, as she sat down smiling.

'No, just a little something for me. She had a packet of cigarette papers and what looked like an OXO cube in her hand. I watched as she took out a small scruffy packet of rolling tobacco from her pocket and started licking the papers and sticking them together. Once she'd constructed the large fag she took the cube and opened it, sprinkling some of its contents on the tobacco before sealing it with a swift but careful rolling action.

'Peanuts, what is that?' I knew very well what it was before she lit the end and sat back in her chair, letting the heavy smoke drift from her nostrils.

'Just a smidge of Red Leb, babe, it's great.'

'That's fuckin' dope!' My voice had risen without warning like my mum when she was telling me off after not listening.

'Shh Den, it's cool over here, the café sells it and you smoke here.'

'Its not fuckin' cool, its fuckin' drugs.' I was near shouting now and people were starting to stare.

'Chill out Den, what's up with you?'

'Nothing's up with me you stupid cow. You're the one taking the drugs, put it out.'

'Don't talk to me like that, I've done it before.'

The couple next to us put their drinks down and stood up to leave. I looked around and I could see that nearly everyone was smoking joints. It felt like I was the only one in the room that wasn't participating. Had they noticed that I was abstaining?

'I don't believe it, you've lost your senses.' I'd lowered my voice now.

'Don't bloody judge *me*; it's only hash for God sakes, Den. We are in Amsterdam aren't we?'

'Yeah we may be, but I still think you've got a screw loose, a bit of dope leads to a bit of something else and the next time, you'll be sticking needles in your arm.'

'Den, you're being childish.' She was starting to grin which made me more infuriated. I can't touch drugs even if I'd wanted to, which I didn't, and she was flaunting this in my face and smiling. I was excluded from the pathetic activity going on around me, segregated because I was normal. Oh this wasn't good, we were having such a super night and now she'd gone and ruined our evening by smoking drugs. I invited her and she was abusing my kindness knowing that once we were over here she could just go and do what she liked.

'Put it out Peanuts.'

'No I won't put it out, just shut up won't you?'

'If you don't put it out I'm leaving.'

'Den, you're being ridiculous now.' She was getting stoned as I watched her, nodding her head to the music and smiling at some guys who were stood next to our table, also high on drugs.

'You selfish bitch.' I stood up, leaving my drink and pushed past her table, bumping into people and slamming the door behind me. She'd made no effort to stop me as I walked away.

I was in a foul mood. I walked into a bar near our hotel that I'd spotted earlier. The girl behind the bar served me my beer and I perched on a stool and took out a fag. Her arm came over to me with a lighter at the ready. She smiled as I took my first drag but I couldn't respond, as my mind was busy reconstructing the argument with Peanuts in the Paradiso.

'You having a good time?' She spoke English with a lovely accent.

'No.' I felt terribly rude, it wasn't her fault.

'Oh sorry for you, that's too bad.'

I needed to calm down, it was my holiday and I certainly wasn't going to let Peanuts spoil it for me. I thought that I should try and enjoy myself before going back to the room. It was quite strange to be approached by a girl; it hadn't happened to me for a while and I felt flattered. She opened the bar hatch and took the stool next to mine, lighting her own cigarette on the way. She was willowy, blonde with sharp cheekbones and huge eyes. I introduced myself and she said her name was Helene. She was a welcome distraction and I felt myself cheering up again. I needed a plan for the next couple of days. The evenings would be simple; go find a bar (not Paradiso) and drink heartily. But the days were unfilled and left the potential to be wandering around Amsterdam spending money on souvenirs. That thought didn't enthral me as I see souvenir buying as an old person's hobby. Helene was going to be my source of information.

'What is there to do around here during the day?'

'Oh there's lots for seeing, the floating flower market or the Palace, then there's the Oude Kerk, which is the oldest church in the city.'

I must have looked clueless as she stopped talking mid-flow.

'Well you could always go to De Walletjes if that's your thang'

'Sorry – the what?'

'The red light district.'

Crumbs! I must look desperate or gormless if she thinks that I'm over here for ... well, I was coming over here for ... but that was with Lofty. I wonder how much it ... no Den you've never paid for it and you're not going to start now ... but I was on holiday and ... no, maybe Helene would ... No. I think I need to go to bed.

'Thanks, I think I'll try the Palace.' My reply was transparent but an easy way to finish the conversation so I said that I'd pop in for a beer the next day and thanked her.

I'm in bed waiting for the door to open, half worried, half annoyed at Peanuts for tainting everything. I imagine her stumbling in with a bloke in tow which would set me off again as I'm not lying here pretending to be asleep and listening to her get knobbed. She might still be at the bar, she might have got into trouble. She's doing my head in, that's what she's doing. I wish I'd never brought her along. I'd have been better off with marillion man. No. Be rational Den, she's a grown woman and knows how to handle herself, I think, like at the party when that idiot tried to … Oh bloody hell I should go and see if she's all right I suppose. It wouldn't sound good if she was to get herself into a situation and people found out I was sulking at the time. I got out of bed, only wearing my pants when I heard the latch on the door turn, so I dived back under the covers and lay as still as I could. I could hear Peanuts staggering around the room; she knocked over something on the chest of drawers by the door and I heard loose change spilling onto the floor. Then the toilet door opened and closed and opened again, I lay, not moving. She'd go straight to bed and we could sort this out in the morning. Her body weight made the bed sag on one side as she sat on the edge with a sigh. Her hand tapping clumsily on my shoulder.

'Dennnn?'

More tapping and her head came down to mine; I could smell the drink on her and the strange fags she'd been smoking.

'Dennn, I'm really sorry Den,' She wasn't crying, just a whiney voice like a child who was apologising after eating the chocolate biscuits. I'm not going to answer; she'll go away in a minute.

'Dennn, I won't do it again … I feel sick.' Shit, please go to the lavatory, I'd have to get up then if she vommed on me; maybe it's just a trick.

It wasn't a trick. She missed my bed thankfully as she struggled to make it into the bathroom. I didn't even look, I just lay there listening to her retching and thinking 'it serves you right'. But no – she was back and this time with breath from hell, trying to wake me to apologise. I thought if she wasn't careful she'd have the wallpaper off!

'Dennn, I've been sick … I'm really sorry.' This was getting impossible now; I was awake, angry and I could smell sick. That's it, she's getting told to go to ... I felt her head slump over my waist and an arm appeared around my neck, not affectionately, just drunkenly. She was away with the fairies, trapping me to my bed. I rolled over and she fell onto the floor and into the puddle near the door.

My stages of anger go as follows:

Mildly angry: I get slightly defensive and make my view known as to why I'm angry.

Pissed off: I go quiet and am liable to shout at anyone who upsets me.

Very Pissed off: Liable to fight, shout, swear and be uncompromising.

Raging: Animated and unpredictable telling anyone and everyone what they are doing wrong, much swearing and insulting.

Fuckety fucking fuckety bloody raging bull fucking angry: Unable to talk, develop a tick, rub my hands together and not trusted near sharp objects.

I stood over her, rubbing my hands together, thinking of how I could get her into her own bed without pulling her head off, which at this particular moment in time *was* an option. I hoisted her from under her armpits to a sitting position and lifted her onto the bed. She was a complete dead weight and her head swung from side to side. I let her go and watched her topple onto her pillow; she was snoring before I had a chance to pull a blanket over her shoulder. Thankful that she was safe and asleep and not bugging me any more, I stepped back and felt cold liquid force its way between my toes.

'Thanks Peanuts, it's been a truly wonderful experience,' I said, as I headed for the sink to clean my foot.

'Ya, no probs,' she mumbled, still asleep.

I'd left the hotel at six. My last-minute packing had worked out well, I thought, as I ran through the streets. It felt good to get some fresh air in my lungs after a night of beer and fags. The manager looked bemused as I jogged away. Girls must have strange dreams. Sleeping Pukey had snored all night and even started to talk about not wanting to go to school. (Mine consist of naked women.) I ran down the canal for a couple of miles, using the lamp posts to light my way and sprint between, avoiding passers-by in the darkness of the morning. For the first time I was enjoying just looking at the locals and seeing their day-to-day routine. Soon I'd be spending my days dressed in body armour and walking down hostile streets. It seemed a million miles away from what I was doing now, so very peaceful.

Peanuts was propped on the end of her bed when I returned, with her head in her hands, wearing the same clothes as the night before. We didn't speak and I took my clothes with me into the shower. I was determined not get into the 'what happened the night before' chat, and I hoped that she was in a fit state, and maybe we should go for an explore around the sights. My plan for the day seemed more appealing after seeing the city whilst running. We swapped places in the bathroom and I sorted my clothes out from the night before. She emerged with a towel around her head and one wrapped around her body; her eyes were red and puffy as if she'd been crying.

'Look, I'm going for a walk around town and to get something to eat, are you coming?'

'Yeah, sounds good, I'll tidy up. Will you wait for me?' I would have been pointless to start lecturing her about the dope now; it looked like she didn't need me adding to her obvious hangover so I went and waited in the lobby.

We bought breakfast and walked through the city, looking at shops and in the market. The day passed me by and I felt calmer and less stressed from the night before. Peanuts and I had exchanged pleasantries but not got into anything that could be described as a conversation. She looked at her watch as we walked along the canal towards the place I'd seen the traders that morning.

'Den, I need to lie down, would you mind if I went back to the hotel?' She did look tired and we'd walked for most of the day, only sitting down for a sandwich.

'Yeah, sure ... I'll see you later.'

'What are you going to do?'

'I don't know. I'll find something.' She made eye contact briefly with a sorry expression and made off in the direction of the hotel,; it was late afternoon. What was I going to do with myself indeed?

Helene greeted me with a smile and a beer; the bar was empty again and I felt like a sad daytime loner as I took a barstool.

'The weather is very mild, yes?'

'Sorry, Helene. Yeah, I was thinking about something else. Yeah, it's quite warm for November.'

Helene and I chatted for a couple of hours and I had a few more beers and bade her farewell, thinking that I'd go and wake Peanuts up and we could go out and get some dinner as a way of clearing the air. I felt as if last night should be forgotten; however. I was in the right about the drugs. But I wasn't helping things by not forgiving her and getting on with the holiday. We were still friends, and friends have arguments don't they? I didn't dislike her for what she'd done, just disagreed with it she is her own person after all and she can do what she likes. I've got no ties over her. When I get back I'll make up with her and we can get on and have some fun. She was asleep when I returned to the room, so I took to the comfort of my bed too. We would sort it out in the morning.

I could smell tea before I'd opened my eyes. By my bed holding a steaming cup stood Peanuts.

'I asked the man downstairs if I could make one, I didn't know if you took sugar' There wasn't any tea-making stuff in the room so she'd made the effort to go and get a brew. I was grateful and thought it was a great start to the day. Peanuts gave me a smile as I took the cup from her.

'Thanks, yes, no sugar is right.'

'Den, I'm sorry about the other night, I didn't mean to upset you and if it's any consolation I felt terrible all day yesterday,' she apologised.

'Yeah, well, maybe I overreacted, so I'm sorry too, this tea is lovely,' I'm not one to hold grudges and was feeling much happier that we'd actually spoken to each other properly.

'So what shall we do today then?' Again I had no plan.

'Well seeing as you took me on the bus-less city tour yesterday I thought I'd treat you.'

'Oh! Okay, so what's on the agenda then?'

'Well how about we go and see The Night Watchman?'

'Who?'

'Not who silly, it's by Rembrandt, at the Rijksmuseum.'

'Oh!' I must have had my blank look on.

'Art, Den. It's an oil painting.'

'You want to take me to see a picture?'

'It's probably the most important work in Europe. I've always wanted to see it,'

'Why? What's so special about it?' Me and art are quite a distance apart, in fact I've never even considered art before, it's has no place in my world but if she thought it was worth going to see then I'd give it a go. It was better than any suggestion I'd had that day; in fact it was the only suggestion so far.

'It's caused quite a controversy over the years. It's been attacked and slashed.'

'Crikey! What ... has it got bound naked women in it or

something?' She shot me a look that made me feel like I was on thin ice and it's cracking.

'Den, you must have seen a painting you've liked?'

'No, not really, it's only an old way of taking a photo.'

She rolled her eyes. 'You're incredible! Art can tell stories, capture a moment in time, and be a historical record. I bet you can name an artist but you can't name a photographer.'

'That's not the point Peanuts, it's not that important to me. If I want to look at pictures I'll buy a book, I don't have to go to a museum.'

'Go on then, name me an artist,'

'Rembrandt.'

'No, I said that already!'

'All right then ... Mozart.'

'He's a composer! Really, think about ninja turtles.'

'I know, Lowry!'

'See? I knew you'd know one,'

'He did the matchstick men song. Okay I'll go and see it with you but I don't see the point.' I finished my tea, picked up some clothes and headed into the bathroom for a wash and a shave. Peanuts had got me thinking now, don't get me wrong, I'm not totally ignorant to it, I heard about the Mona Lisa and I do know that Lowry painted the matchstick men but it was never an influence in my life so I didn't need to study it or anything. However, I wasn't going to shun the idea of seeing something she considered to be important, like a painting, a photograph of its era, and probably just a picture of some random guy who happened to be hanging around at the time; no one memorable. So I'll go and show willing. It will give me something to refer back to when she appreciates that it's only a picture. It dawned on me that it was the first time I'd ever talked to someone about this posh-persons subject. Art wasn't for the likes of me, who it may well be wasted on. That thin-ice feeling came back. As I came out of the bathroom she was sat reading her map.

'So what do you do when you go to these art museums then?'

'Well normally I go to galleries, like the Tate, but you don't actually *do* anything, you see the artist's interpretation and their style, compare their work to others and let the paintings say something to you.'

'What? they talk as well?' I knew this would get her going.

We caught a bus across town; it was a lovely sunny winter's day. The museum was busy and we had to queue for a while before we could get in. We found the picture eventually after an age of looking. It was bigger than I imagined and not of only one person but a crowd in a scene. It was quite interesting; the picture had been attacked a few times by protesters for whatever reason; the last time some bloke threw acid over it. Why bother? The repairs to the canvas took months, plus during the War it had been hidden away in an underground bunker. I still didn't really understand the importance of it but the history was quite impressive. Peanuts took great interest in the work displayed, looking long and hard at each picture, sometimes smiling and standing back to view it. We spent the morning and most of the afternoon in the museum and decided to walk back and have a meal on the way.

'So what did you think then?'

'Yes, very good – ... big, isn't it?'

'Apart from its size?'

'No, it was good, I liked the history behind it and it must have taken a lot of work to repair it after it was slashed.'

'Fantastic that it's still around, really. Did you like the darkness?'

'Well ... erm ... oh look shall we eat here?' I was out of my depth.

Peanuts looked exasperated. She'd tried her best to enlighten me but all I wanted now was some food and a beer. I'd had a worthy afternoon, doing something new that I probably won't repeat. I'm not revealing to the lads that I went to Amsterdam and looked at art.

'Are you looking forward to going away?' Peanuts asked as I poured the wine.

'Yeah, it's exciting; I'm not too sure what it's going to be like though. We've done loads of training. Some of the lads said that it gets dragging at times.'

'You're gonna miss Christmas and New Year?'

'Yep but we don't do a lot for Christmas really, Mum does the dinner and the only one out of the family who gets decent presents any more is Callum; he got Scalextric last year. Marc and me and him played it all day. What are you doing?'

'Oh I dunno, go home I suppose, unless I get invited somewhere. I quite fancy New Year in Scotland, Hogmanay in Edinburgh sounds like fun.' I was learning more about Peanuts all of the time; she wanted to know everything about the tour and the flights and threats. She's intelligent, far more than I, and it crossed my mind why did she ever want to come along on holiday with me?

'Is it really dangerous then Den?'

'Well yeah, of course, but you don't get shot at every day, the terrorists have to be careful not to get caught.'

'So what happens if you *do* get shot?'

'Bleed a lot I suppose,'

'No, you know what I mean, what happens to the lads who get killed over there, who notifies their families?'

'Oh I don't know, the Police I suppose, or the Army Padre, I don't think about it really, to tell you the truth,'

'Sorry, none of my business.'

'No that's fine Actually, Lofty has written letters to his family, he calls them his death letters and I'm holding them for him. If he gets killed he wants me to post them for him,'

'Ah ha,' nodding.

'Mm'm I'm not sure if I like the idea, I'll be indirectly involved and responsible for giving them bad news.'

'No, don't be silly, you're just honouring his wishes, I think it's inspired, allowing your family to know that they are loved, in such a permanent way.'

I was quite surprised to hear that from her. I had the letters in my bag at Camp. I suppose all I'd be doing is carrying out his instructions; I just hope I won't have to send them. We finished our meal and looked for a club. With only two nights left we promised ourselves a mad night out on the town. We danced and drank until the early hours, and by the time we arrived back at the room I was hoarse with laughing and shouting.

'Thanks Den that was the best day I've had for ages,'

'You're very welcome young lady.'

'Cheeky boy, I'm older than you,'

'Friends ...right,' I held out my hand and we shook.

I don't know how it happened; I didn't pull her arm, and I couldn't feel her pull me. My feet were firmly on the ground and I didn't move but *we* did. Her eyes sparkled and her mouth turned up at one edge as she smiled. She was turning into my best friend, a person I could tell anything without shame and I knew she wouldn't criticise me in return. We'd argued and laughed and talked and talked; we were linked now. I'd never needed someone to confide in or to know me totally, although being with Peanuts made me feel happy. I hoped in return that she held me in the same light and, looking back at her, we were two good friends, having a brilliant time with no one to tell us what to do. I wanted her. I could have had her but I didn't want to ... sometimes it's like that.

Chapter Sixteen

Fort Whiterock is a grey dismal place situated just outside the Turf Lodge Estate in West Belfast. It was my home for the next six months, although describing it as such might indicate that it was comfortable. On the contrary, prison is comfortable; Fort Whiterock was about as well located as an ants' nest in an anteater's enclosure. The room that I was sharing with Lofty, Eddie and Mick was small and dark and didn't have a window and it smelt of Lofty's feet. We had bunk beds and being the last into the room (remember Lofty had arrived the week before), they had left me the top bunk. That meant I had the least storage. There were no lockers to hang clothing in, just a wooden trunk called a bed-box that slid under the bunks and all my personal possessions were crammed into it.

The lads had established their routine living and working in The Fort; a set pattern that for the next six months would change little. I'd begun on patrolling for two days, and then I'd move to guard duties; after that I'd man the quick reaction force and then have a rest day. Things were different to battalion life and for the first week or so, as I changed from shift to shift, I found it confusing. I was expected to get on with my job and be at locations without anyone chasing me. It was difficult with no one instructing me. However, I was back with my team and I had missed them, which surprised me; it was good to return to work. Lofty had told me to listen and watch the more experienced guys when I talked to him. I thought he would have asked about the trip, but he's clearly still smarting from events so I didn't volunteer any information; I'll wait until he asks.

Patrolling around the estates wasn't like training had suggested; most of the people I met were cordial and not at all abusive. The kids gave us a bit of verbal and when we drove past in the armoured vehicles they'd chuck stones at us, but on the whole it was quiet. I had taken an interest in the hoods or terrorists and started learning about them from the Intelligence Officer; he lived in the barracks collecting information and giving briefings before we went out on patrol. I soon knew where most of the hoods lived, what car they drove; their wife's name, kids, pets, younameit and I knew it. Everyone knew a few of them but it didn't take me long to get a reputation for myself in the Company as The Spotter. I was even loaned out on occasions to other patrols to explain and show where people lived and tell them about their routines, I could name nearly forty different individuals within three weeks of first going out on the streets. It took as long for the first letter to turn up.

I arrived back to the room after having patrolled most of the night in Anderson Town and the letter was sitting on my bed. Lofty and Eddie had a letter too and Mick had a bank statement. We shed our kit and sat opening the post as we stripped our rifles down to clean them.

'Fuckin' Aida! The cat's dead.' Lofty was grinning, 'I bloody hate that cat. Mind you it was mutual. Amazing, isn't it lads? That another living thing, especially female, could actually resist me? It pissed on my coat once so I launched it across the room and it never came back in the house.' He pretended to kick something as he told us of his heroics. 'Anyway the little fucker's dead now. Oh my God! Mum's buried it in the back garden.' He looked dismayed and folded the letter and put it in the envelope.

'Another bank statement sad boy?' Lofty had finished his mail so now he occupied himself mocking everyone else's correspondence. Mick looked at him over the letter.

'Yeah 'fraid so, no one loves me, but at least I can afford a tart when we get back.'

The banter between the lads had changed noticeably in a short space of time; we always spoke like this now. Living and working together, the constant sarcasm and disrespect served as prevention for getting on each other's nerves. I needed to raise my game because it was bound to be my turn soon. Eddie sat reading his letter and chuckled to himself as he turned the pages; it was a bad move, as Lofty homed in on him.

'So how's the boyfriend then?'

First rule of carping sarcasm. Never show a weakness.

'Shut up stupid.' Even Eddie had descended to our level and wasn't putting on his superior airs; the atmosphere in the room was calm but funny and I felt relaxed with the situation ... until Lofty started.

'Who's written to you Den?'

'Oh Peanuts, I think. You know the girl from the ...'

'The chick you took to Amsterdam, am I right?'

'Yeah, she went, she's going to give you some money for it.'

'So why a letter? You must have got on well, nudge nudge, wink wink.' He'd done this before, gone into some clichéd Monty Python sketch about women and photography. It didn't annoy me but it was a twice-told tale and I was dying to read her letter.

'So is it a sports page then mate? Two's up.'

A sports page is when a girl writes very explicitly, a sort of soft porn letter. I'd never had one but I'd seen other lads receiving them and pass them around; and therefore it's called two's up or second reader if you like. I'm sure Peanuts wouldn't have written anything like that; I wish I had five minutes to myself to read the damn thing. There was no way I'd get any peace so I stowed the letter away in my jacket for later. It was the first letter I'd had from anyone excluding Mum since I'd joined, and it was cheering realising that she was back in Winchester thinking of me. Lofty hounded me through tea about the letter and in the end I decided to seek the solitude of the toilet.

Dear Den,

I've got to get this first letter to you and it's been difficult to decide what I'm actually gonna write ... Firstly I would like to thank you for inviting me to Amsterdam, I had a great time, we really should do it again. Which leads me on to the second thing I want to discuss; we are friends aren't we? It is such a tricky subject. Look, I'm going around the houses here Den. I miss you. This is coming out appallingly I don't know what to say.

I'm fine and leaving the halls of residence at the end of this term; three of us are going to rent a house, yippee! I'll send the address later. The cheque is for Lofty, I left the top blank cause I can't remember his name, would you pass it on? Take care of yourself.

Love K. a.k.a. Peanuts

What does 'I'm fine' mean? After all the entire letter couldn't be any shorter! Or the other classic phrase of letter writing 'all is well at this end.' It's not guaranteed when I receive the letter that they are fine. They might not be fine and things may not be well and by the time I write back, things may be worse. It's like that old chestnut when sending a postcard from holiday of 'wish you were here'. Well, if you wanted them there, why didn't they get an invite? They might be skint and haven't had a holiday in years so let's rub their noses in it. Hey, the next one I write will be phrased 'wish I'd have given you an invite, but you might be poorer than a church mouse and I didn't want to embarrass you.' Anyhow, I'm not writing back 'things are well here' because they might not be when she gets the return letter. I can't write 'things are well here at the moment but by the time you get this they might not be'. Just thoughts before I write back. I've got nothing to say really apart from life is a treadmill, but then again it might not be in a few days so why put that? I could tell her about the lads I suppose or how much I enjoyed my time in Amsterdam, but she knows that already. Oh this replying malarkey is tricky.

Time ticked by with the same-old, same-old routine that had been established. Had I been in England I'd be buying Christmas presents now and waiting for the baby to be born. Peanuts and I wrote nearly every week; she exposed the minutiae of her course and, more interestingly, the parties at college; and I related what I'd been up to, which was becoming dreary after the third time of writing exactly identical weeks. Marc's baby came along and they called him Dhillon, yes Dhillon! I had to send a card and say how novel the name was. Which was a blatant lie, as I thought it sounded absurd. They sent a picture of a baby; I assume it was him, it had its eyes shut and was wrapped in a blanket; and Debbie had put a sticker on the picture in a speech bubble saying 'Hi Uncle Den!' Very funny.

Lance Sergeant Chant raised a question. When did we want our leave? I hadn't expected any time off during the tour but we had six days called R&R or rest and recuperation. I took one of the later dates that would leave just a few weeks to serve in Belfast before we went home at the end of the tour.

Christmas was pretty much a non-starter as I was on foot patrol that day. New Year was much the same, sober and working. I received cards and presents from home and a personal card from the Company Commander, Major Bell. Nothing happened and it seemed like it would be that way for the next three months.

Early one Saturday morning in January, our team was escorting the Police to serve a summons on some scrote who'd been caught nicking cars in the city. We travelled in a convoy of three vehicles, two police Land Rovers and our armoured Land Rover bringing up the rear. The streets were quiet. Lofty and I chatted about our leave; he was going home the week after me to his Mum's house. Our convoy travelled through Anderson Town and turned left I knew the street names in my patch. There's a junior school on the corner, its fence line runs uphill towards a row of houses about one hundred metres away, mostly semi-detached with garages, lawns and fences. As our vehicle approached the junction Lofty said.

'Quiet isn't it?'

'Yeah, it's a Saturday mate, there's no school.'

'No, I mean there's no kids playing, no bikes out, no cars in drives,' I was looking backwards as we turned the corner, scanning the houses, with the windows open and the curtains closed, Lofty was right, it was too quiet. A hooded head appeared on top of a garage behind, then another person and then a rocket launcher. A millisecond later crack, crack, crack of rifle fire sound reverberated in my ear. We had been on a live firing demonstration during training and the instructors taught us about 'crack and thump'. This describes the supersonic crack from the bullet passing and then the thump as it hits its target. You're meant to be able to judge which direction the round has travelled from, but enclosed by the houses surrounding us the sound echoed and bounced, and it was impossible to evaluate where we were being attacked from. I was aware that something was occurring and that it could have fatal implications, but it felt like a scene from a film or a picture from a book. I felt detached. I could see everything around me being acted out as it was in our training; but then I heard Eddie bellow into his radio, the scene turned real and I was scared.

'All stations this is Foxtrot One One. CONTACT, wait out.'

The words terrified me. My throat dried like I'd swallowed a bucket of sawdust and I could hear my pulse in my ears. My brain filtered the information and was demanding me to do something, do *anything* but I was stationary, like a spectator in a football match waiting for the ball to cross the line in the final second.

BOOM! the rocket left its launcher, it juddered as it passed our vehicle and then stabilised in its flight towards the police vehicle in front of us. No one could have yelled a warning in time; the missile struck the Land Rover from behind. I looked back at the garage roof but the hoods were gone. The rear doors of the smoking Land Rover opened and a copper fell out, dazed and bloody faced. I wondered how many were inside injured. What had I witnessed? In an instant a quiet convoy routinely policing the streets had turned into cataclysm.

Eddie was screaming at us to run in the direction of the garage where the hoods had been standing as he exited the vehicle. Lofty and I ducked out of the rear doors and sprinted towards the adjoining house; my wits told me to stay put in the Rover but I had to go; this is what I had trained for. The apprehension of what I might encounter pushed adrenalin around my body. I didn't feel the weight of my kit and I ran so fast that when I reached a small surround hedge my momentum allowed me to leap over it in one bound, landing in the front garden feet away from the firing-point.

'Stop, Den. Stop.' Lofty's hand grabbed my shoulder and pulled me to a halt. In the disorder I'd forgotten everything that we'd been taught about protecting the area from where the missile had been fired. Forensic evidence was vital to the Police for prosecution, and beside that there may have been a booby trap left for us. We moved around to the other side of the house and made our way through an alley and onto a street that ran parallel to our patrol vehicle location. Nothing. They'd made a getaway and the street was deserted. I stood in the road looking up and down for any movement; Lofty and Eddie checked the gardens for concealed persons or discarded objects. I was beckoned to move up to the side of the house to take a fire position.

Sirens announced the arrival of Police and Army backup vehicles and as I kneeled in position, I had time to reflect on the policeman with his injuries and fervently hoped that no one had died in the attack. We had been taught during an attack the priority was to catch the terrorist and leave the injured for the medics. It had made me feel inhuman leaving a man in pain because of protocol but as I considered what had happened this morning I grew immensely angry towards those who'd tried to kill us. As if on cue, people started emerging from their houses and walking towards us.

'Fucking rent-a-crowd, that's all we need!' Eddie pointed at the plastic bullet gun on my back, I needed no more prompting. They swarmed on our position, shouting and laughing at the damaged police vehicle and cautioning us to go home. A small boy about the same age as Callum approached where I was now stood and spat at me. I was incensed at their mentality and pulled the baton gun up to the aim. More troops arrived and filtered into riot positions around us with shields at the ready. Half a house brick flew through the air, smashing against the door behind me making me jump. The crowd laughed at my alarm. There was now in excess of a hundred people shouting and throwing things as Eddie pointed out my first target, a man with a bright blue tracksuit top. I took my aim and the crowd instinctively ducked, moving back behind walls and hedges. All of the practice training at Longmoor paid off as the guy fell to the ground clutching his thigh. The mob had dispersed.

'Come on. Let's go.' One of the Sergeants from 2 Platoon had taken charge of the soldiers on the street and decided that we should extract our patrol back to where the incident had started. By the time we returned to our original location, the injured policeman had been taken away in an ambulance. I enquired after him and any further casualties and was told that only one bloke was harmed after hitting his head on the inside of the vehicle.

We were driven back to Fort Whiterock to enter statements

with the Police, describing what we had seen, recording my eyewitness of time. My thoughts returned to the injured guy and his face covered in blood. This single event altered my attitude towards this tour. I had considered it dull stationed at The Fort, seeing and doing nothing much day after day, but now I had total concentration with everything I did. I kept my rifle cleaner than I'd ever before, listened to Eddie with more interest, and studied the names and lives of the terrorists until I knew sixty of them by name and face.

Chapter Seventeen

Dhillon is an adorable baby with bright blue eyes like mine, although not quite as handsome yet. I gave him a cuddly toy and bought Callum another Action Man; he'd soon have more troops than the British Army if his collection continued. Mum did her usual roast dinner. It was great to be there again but somehow regressive being back at home and it felt like I've never been away. Everything was in the same place as when I left and daily routine continued; even my models where exactly as I'd left them, predictable and reassuring. However, I *had* been away and as comfortable as home was – I was different.

Marc and I went to the pub on the second night for a couple of beers.

'You look tense mate – is everything all right?' Marc said as we sat down.

It's the marrow of all families how their sibling relationships develop. I hadn't depended on Marc when we were younger and he hadn't bothered about me; not in a uncaring way; I was his brother and there wasn't anything he could do about it. We just accepted each other and that's where the idiosyncrasy comes in, I suppose. Siblings get on and like each other or they don't. Here we were, two brothers, both adults who hadn't seen each other for a few months yet he could still pickup on my feelings. I was tense; I had been working hard for so long and thinking about getting home. Thinking about setting eyes on the family, drinking alcohol, having a normal time. I felt like I wanted to do everything I'd missed out on in six days. I suppose I was overexcited, and I began to feel covetous of Marc's routine life at home with his kids and wife and three-bedroom house. I wanted that, but I wasn't ready to surrender my freedom. My line of business was becoming far too interesting now, but I couldn't see when I'd be able to get the happy family.

'I'm fine mate, just tired.'

I hadn't told them about the incident either, to save myself a lecture from Mum, mainly. So we sat and wet the baby's head and chatted. Marc was trying to get into vice and was taking some exams for promotion. It would bring more money, naturally, but downside was possibly a change of station and therefore relocation.

"Ello, 'ello, look what's just walked in.' Marc nudged me and nodded his head towards the door as two girls came through and sat at the bar.

'Oi you, you're married! I'm the single stud around here.' I was appalled at Marc ogling other women.

'Only window shopping mate, you can have a look as long as you don't try them on.'

I stared because one looked familiar; I definitely knew her from somewhere. If I could only remember where. I couldn't pull my gaze away in time. Without warning her head turned and our eyes met. There's no avoiding these situations; being caught gawping at a woman is bad enough, but mentally undressing her while she's watching is dangerous, especially with those great tits. Unbelievably, she smiled and turned to her companion to say something before getting up and walking towards our seats.

'Hi you! Long time no see.' The penny dropped. I hadn't recognised Julie because she'd dyed her hair blonde and was wearing far too much more makeup than can be healthy.

'Crikey! Hi Julie, how are you? Sorry I didn't recognise you, it's just you look so ...' Say something spectacular Den – don't screw this up '...blonde.' Oh you divvy, goodbye Julie.

'Ha, ha. You are funny, can we join you?' Marc looked at me as if I'd grown another head as she went to get her drink and collect her friend.

'How did you get away with that? And who the hell is she?' Marc was speaking out of the side of his mouth as he took a sip of his beer.

'Oh, you know, mate. All the girls love a soldier.'

Julie's friend was married. Phew! She couldn't stay as she was on an early shift in the morning so she had one drink and said goodbye, leaving us three in an awkward silence. I could see Marc looking surreptitiously at Julie and then back at me between sips of beer like he was trying to work out who we were. I'm sure it's just a copper thing.

'Who wants another drink then?' Julie stood up and rattled the ice in her glass; she was a stunner and smiled as she looked down at me.

'I'll have another beer please, but Marc's just going home now so he'll be fine.'

'No I'm ...' my foot struck his shin full on and he jumped out of his seat trying to hide his wince of pain.

'Yes I was just off. Lovely to have met you Julie.' The word *Julie* came out far too loud as if he was letting me know that he registered her name for some sort of bribe later. It felt like the old days when he'd cross-examine me about girls I was seeing, in a childish tease. He grabbed his coat from the back of the chair and shook Julie's hand before patting me on the head.

'Remember Denis, be home by ten, you've got school in the morning.' With a triumphant smile as if to say, 'Ha! I've got the last word in, you lucky dog, I hope you can't get it up'.

Julie returned and smiled again as she sat down this time next to me.

'So what are you up to then?' I told her about joining up and going to Ireland, which seemed to impress her and I asked if she was still seeing the doctor she'd introduced me to at the hospital fête.

'That's why I was out for a drink, consoling myself. We've just split up.' I listened and nodded sympathetically as she told me how he's gone off with another nurse from work. Not quite every tiny detail but why he would dump Julie is anyone's guess.

'So anyway, enough about my troubles. Do you fancy a drink somewhere else?'

'Yeah sure. Where do you want to go?'

'I was thinking we could go back to mine if you like, I've bought a place around the corner.' Without jumping up both arms raised and shouting 'Yes!', I casually nodded,

'Yeah fine, sounds good.' We drank up and left.

Sex, in my mind falls into categories.

Poor: It is embarrassing and over before things get going. This normally results in eternal silence.

Fair: Both people get humped and a cigarette after with no hard feelings but not completely fulfilled.

Good: Much bouncing around between the sheets happy that bodily fluids are exchanged in a very enjoyable manner. This usually leads to a period of dating.

Mind Blowing No Holds Barred (Somewhat Illegal In Some Countries) Raunchy, Filthy, Rogering: A loss of all inhibition, very selfish but extremely satisfying. This always leads to the bloke boasting how satisfying he is in the sack and that she'd never had such a good lover. Also leads to poor sex next time around.

As I left Julie at her front door next morning I kissed her and asked what she was doing that night. She said that we could meet again.

With two days before my return to work I was in a hole (excuse the expression). Should I go to Winchester or just bum around Dunstable and shag Julie? It's a tough decision, but I go for the sure-fire thing and stay to spread a few more seeds. Mum wanted to go to the shops so we catch the bus into town. It felt like I hadn't spent any time with Mum since I'd been back, even though I'd been in and around the house – well, getting my meals there mostly. It was refreshing to walk with her and look in shop windows. I was feeling relaxed not having to keep an attentive eye on Lofty and be watchful of the surrounding area.

We had a coffee and she nattered about the boys. Mum was doting on her grandchildren saying how good they are, just like Marc and I were. I sensed as if she was trying to draw a parallel between the families, but Marc's family didn't compare to our household. She was a single parent, struggling to get by the way I remember it, and Marc's family seem comfortable and stable and there's a father at his house. I listened and looked at Mum as she reflected on her memories, and from nowhere I saw her as an old woman, lonely and wanting her sons around to help with the shopping and give her a lift to the bingo. I would do that, of course, if I was living at home but I'm not. I had my career to look after now and anyway I'd always come back to visit.

I carried her bags of groceries along the High Street towards the bus stop, conscious of her gratification in the proud way she related to us; and then... an almighty bang rang out. A car backfiring? A door slamming? I have no idea what it was. I crouched in the doorway of the newsagents, looking for the contact point, for a hooded figure to run across the street or the people scattering as the noise resonated down the street.

'Denis, what are you doing? Get up, you're making a scene.' Mum looked down at me. People stared; a small boy laughed and told his mummy that the man had been frightened. I was frightened, terrified, and alert, in another place for those few seconds. I was back in Belfast. Mum had bent down and put her hand on my shoulder.

'Denis, please get up, you're worrying me.' I felt the sweat drip down my back, the shopping was scattered across the pavement with tins rolling into the road. An older man had picked some stuff up and started putting it back in the bag. He looked over at me, crouched down in the cover, his brow furrowed and concerned. I stood and hastily gathered the rest of the shopping, shoving it in less neatly than I'd done in the supermarket. I thanked him for his help.

'It's finished son, give it time.' He needed to say no more and it made me feel better, Mum was staring in disbelief at what she'd just seen and I was gaping back in utter embarrassment at what I'd just done. We travelled home in silence, and I put the groceries away before the unavoidable questioning started.

'Ok, I think you need to tell me what's been going on.' She put a cup of tea in front of me, and an ashtray, as I lit a cigarette. This must have been a serious grilling if she let me smoke in the house. So I told her about the RPG attack.

It's the first time I'd felt weak. Nothing normally bothers me; I can sort things out on my own, I don't need help, especially from my Mum. My account to her made me realise the gravity of my experience as my Mum listened in horror as I told her of how the policeman staggered out of the Land Rover. I could see the whole scene as if it were yesterday. I didn't know if telling her was the right thing to do but I had to rationalise my behaviour.

Julie could tell something was up as we sat in the pub, and things didn't improve from the moment I arrived. She looked at me for an explanation but didn't request it, which I was grateful for. I wanted to get drunk and laid, so I could think about something else. I was struggling with the conversation and replying with one-word answers. Gone without trace was the funny, charismatic Den I could always muster; and in his place was a person I'd never known before. I left Julie's house early that morning, having put in a terrible performance but not caring, just wanting to get back to the lads in Belfast.

Lofty lowered his newspaper as I dumped my kit on the bed.

'Wotcha! So how many poor young women are there in hospital with scorch marks then?' It was good to be back. I stuck two fingers up at him and drank the rest of his tea before snatching the paper from his hand and slumping into the chair.

'Well, there were these two lesbians who did me a show and ...'

'WHAT? You're fuckin' kidding!'

'No honestly, then their Mum joined in.'

'You didn't get any did you? Ha, ha. Oi! Mick. Den's still a virgin!'

It didn't take long to resume the ritual mickey-taking. I'd missed this banter. Mick and Lofty jumped around the room, pointing and chanting, 'Virgin, virgin.'

'So have you heard about the move then?' Lofty had stopped for the moment and sat back down.

'Move?'

'Yeah the Battalion are going to Catterick in December.'

'Where's that?'

'North Yorkshire I think, for three years.' My heart sank, I didn't want to shift from Winchester, and I liked it there. Lofty went on saying that we were taking over from the training battalion who were posted to Germany. A bit like musical armies, everybody gets to sit in another seat. Our new role would be Armoured Infantry, meaning that we drive and man small tanks. Lance Sergeant Chant came in to see us later that evening and I pressed him for more details. The new post for our battalion meant that we might get a tour in Bosnia, which sounded good, but he couldn't confirm that until the Commanding Officer had been told. He also mentioned that when we returned, individuals would be selected to go on a course in preparation for a thing called Junior Brecon. Only the best lads on the Company would be chosen to go on it, and passing both courses would mean promotion to Lance Corporal. I'd heard Eddie talk about Junior Brecon: a six- week course consisting of learning and teaching tactics and leadership. I thought if he could pass it then anyone could, plus I could do with the extra cash; it sounded very appealing.

'So you and Lofty think about it then, and I'll see you before we go back.' I didn't even consider that he would have thought of *me* as Lance Corporal material but I wouldn't look a gift horse in the mouth.

'Child's play those courses, you've just got to keep your mouth shut and listen.' Lofty announced after he'd left. 'Yeah, I'll do it.'

The last month in Ireland was quiet, the only exception being that the Battalion who were going to take over our jobs sent a group of officers on a recce of the place, and we had to show them our patch. They looked young and apprehensive, like we did. I started to think more and more about the promotion course; I could do this. Lance Sergeant Chant interviewed everyone. I was very pleased to learn that he held me in high regard and, being the Company Spotter, showed great potential.

'So have you thought about going on the promotion cadre, Yarwood?'

'Yes, I'd like to have a go for it.'

'Good that's what I like to hear there's only you and Lofty who I was going to recommend anyway, you've both got off to a great start.'

Me and Lofty? He had said that there was only going to be one space for our Platoon so how would he choose?

'When we're back I'll decide who it is, I won't keep you in suspense.'

'I don't think Lofty's interested, to tell the truth.' The words were out before I'd even considered the consequences.

'Oh! What makes you say that? He seems keen enough. Is he a DS watcher then?'

I shuddered, knowing that I had not just stepped over the

mark; this was a world record long jump over it. A DS watcher in the Military's eyes is another term for a creep, he who waits for the Directing Staff to appear and then performs so that they see what is needed to be seen. That's not Lofty at all; he just gets on with life and tells it how it is, regardless of rank and stature.

'When you're not about he reckons that promotion is too much hassle.'

Chapter Eighteen

Andy the barman was as good as his word, and there was a welcome-home party planned for the following Saturday. He'd mentioned it to one of the other regular lads from 'B' Company who told a mate, who told ... yeah, you know how it goes; so the evening of our return, Lofty and I thought we had better go and confirm arrangements in the Nelson. On my way I'd checked my bank account; it was looking very healthy. I had saved loads of money while I was away by default; there just wasn't any time to spend it and we weren't really allowed in the pubs. Unlikely as it seems I can't smoke that many fags or eat Mars Bars by the dozen. So I remarked to Lofty that I might buy myself a car.

'What do you want to do that for? There's plenty of better things to buy than that.'

'Oh yeah? Go on then, like what?'

'Alcohol.'

'Very good. I take it you'll be squandering your wages on booze and have nothing to show for it in a couple of weeks.'

'Mercy! you can talk, as a matter of fact I'll blow ninety per cent of my money on beer and fags ... and just waste the rest! Ha ha!'

There was no reasoning with him. Mind you, after nearly six months away I felt like doing the same thing.

'Ah, the heroes return.' Andy was stood in exactly the same place as we'd left him in November, and it looked like the same shirt as well! He poured two pints and as I took a fiver out of my wallet he signalled with his hand indicating they were on the house. I think it's the first free drink I've ever had out of the Nelson. Andy had a reputation for being tight; in fact it was said that he'd begrudge breathing out.

'So Squire, how was it then? Rid the world of all known evil, did we?' Andy had been in the Army when he was younger, but it turned out that he spent two weeks in training before asking his mum to get him home. He was a likeable chap but what I call a frustrated soldier. One of those who know loads about it but hasn't actually managed to last the course.

'Yeah, right. Give us another pint and I'll tell you about it.' Lofty had sunk a pint in seconds and rattled his glass on the counter.

'No chance squire, I've got two kids and a budgie to feed. Keep your gallant stories, that'll be three quid this time please.' It was like we'd never been away same place, same chat, and the same beer.

'Den, your associate with the funny tights said she'd be in later.'

'Peanuts?'

'Salted or dry roasted?'

'What?'

'Peanuts, what flavour?'

The penny dropped.

'No, sorry my friend, she's called, well I call her ... look, it doesn't matter, what time did she say?'

'She didn't, her and her fella normally tip up around nine, sweet couple.'

Lofty had disappeared to the other side of the pub to chat to some women and in his usual style had them laughing in seconds, I thought about going over and chancing my arm with stories of RPG attack but I was tiring of the story myself and right now, beer was more important.

I was surprised that Peanuts hadn't told me about a bloke in her letters. On the other hand I didn't say anything about Julie. No, it was fine, I just wanted to see her again and after all she's a mate.

The lads from the Company drifted in, in groups of twos and threes and soon the pub looked more like the restroom on Camp.

I could see Andy on the phone behind the bar desperately calling bar staff.

'Do you want a hand, Andy?' I had nothing better to do and the thought of serving the guys and getting a few free pints seemed like a good idea.

'Yeah I can't get Caroline to come in. She's washing her hair or something. Have you done bar work before?'

'Yeah, loads.' Liar, Den; you'll go to hell, but hopefully pickled.

Andy demonstrated the till, which didn't take the brains of an Archbishop to work out, and showed me the price list behind glass on the wall. Funny I'd never noticed it before. It wasn't very useful to be honest; nobody actually asks for Campari shots or stout. He stated no free drinks, as if I would! The lads were leaning over the bar waving glasses and money with tongues hanging out; cries of 'me first' rang out ubiquitously and I scanned the crowd before choosing one of the familiar faces to serve first. The lads were getting rowdy as the beer flowed, six pent-up months and all of a sudden they had been given a long leash.

'One for yourself Den.' It seemed that everyone I served wanted to buy me a drink. Brilliant, I liked bar work. Once the mad rush had finished I took up a perch where Andy normally sits and lit a fag. I must have had about five or six pints and felt heady and in a completely elated mood with my new-found vocation.

'You paid for that?' Andy appeared red-faced, holding a barrel of beer that he'd fetched from the cellar.

'Erm ...excuse me. Are you serving or just drinking?'

I spun around and there was Peanuts grinning from ear to ear. She looked much shorter than I'd remembered, but that may have been due to the fact that she was standing the other side of the bar and I was drunk.

'Are you eighteen young lady?' I said as I poured a pint of cider, spilling some on the floor.

'Why, are you some sick pervy who hopes I'm younger? Oh and a gin and tonic for Danny please.'

Over her shoulder stood the skinniest, four-eyed, greasy haired student I'd ever set eyes on. He was wearing a suit jacket and T-shirt which hung off his shoulders as he waved/saluted in my direction. As I put both drinks on the counter I leaned across to give her a small welcome kiss and whispered 'Who's the hunk?'

'Oh, sorry. Danny, this is Den, the guy I've been boring you about. Den, this is Danny, he's ('a complete prick' I thought) doing applied maths.'

I shook his bendy hand and gave him his G & T as I stifled a grin.

'Pleased to meet you, Sir.'

'Oh no, call me Danny, please.'

Peanuts was glaring over her glass at me.

'Shall we sit down Kerry?'

If ever a girl needed rescuing it was she. I couldn't believe her taste, and she must be going through one of those mental-pause things that women suffer. Mind you, he must have some balls to walk into a squaddie pub looking like that; either that or he's got no common sense whatsoever. Andy said that he could cope now, so I poured myself a cheeky pint for my efforts and sat down with Peanuts and the super-nerd. We exchanged the usual 'How are you's?' and talked about what we'd been up to for the past half a year, with Danny sitting there sipping his drink and listening politely. They had met in the Student Union about a month ago and she found him intriguing. Well, his mind was fascinating, according to her, to which I nearly replied 'unlikely if you rub his lamp a genie will appear,'; but held my tongue, as she seemed happy enough. Lofty had for once been unsuccessful with the girls and spotted me sitting with the unlikely couple. He made his way over, staggering slightly and slapped Danny on the back.

'You're one of the new 'A' Company lads by the look of you.' He looked Danny square on with a huge smile on his face.

'Erm, no ... I think you're mistaken, sorry.' Danny looked astonished at the big man who had his arm around his shoulder, cuddling him like an old lost mate.

'Don't I get a hello then?' Peanuts elbowed him in the ribs as he released his grip.

'Oh yeah! Hi there, remarkable tights. More beer, boys and girls?' Lofty swayed as he looked around the table, winking at Danny before picking his glass up.

'Could I have some crisps please Lofty?' Peanuts asked.

'Yeah, what flavour? Salt and vinegar, cheese and onion or kryptonite?'

The comment went to no avail so I joined him at the bar.

'Who's the superman Den?'

'It's Peanuts' new boyfriend, at least I think it's her boyfriend. He could be a mercy date.'

'I've seen more meat on a butcher's pencil, does she need glasses?'

'Don't know mate, maybe he's hung like Trigger.'

'Let's have a bit of fun with him then. Andy, large gin and tonic mate, and stick a vodka in it as well.'

'No Lofty, leave him alone.'

'Ah come on mate he looks like he could do with a couple of beers inside him, it's probably the only real food he's had in ages.'

I begrudgingly gave the unfortunate student his drink and we sat and chatted some more. I bought another round and filled Danny's drink as well, he was starting to giggle at our stories and be given some strange looks from Peanuts.

'So tell me Clark, what do you do then, are you a journalist?'

'No. I study applied mathematics and my name is Danny.' Peanuts slapped her forehead with her hand as he answered

Lofty's taunting. I thought she was going to tell him that we were unsubtly pulling his leg but as she opened her mouth he announced

'Kerry, I'm going to have to go back. I don't feel very well, excuse me. Are you coming?'

'No, it's just the way she's sitting!' There was no stopping Lofty when he was on a roll. 'Do you want me to call a taxi or are you going to fly, there's a phone box around the corner.'

Peanuts had stood up and was supporting Danny to the door, one arm around his shoulder and one arm in the air with two fingers pointing in our direction.

'Something I said?' Lofty and I burst into laughter.

Amazingly, Peanuts returned and sat back down with a smiley scowl on her face.

'You so-and-sos, he's just thrown up everywhere.'

'Not going back with Superman, Lois?'

'Shut up Lofty!'

He stood up sniggering and headed back to the bar.

'So come on tell me, what's the score?'

'You've got him all wrong. He's a good bloke, really intelligent and ...'

'Go on, and what?'

'And nothing actually, he seemed like a good idea at the time.'

'Like me, ha ha.'

'Look Den ...'

'Tell ya what, the party on Saturday, there's bound to be one of the lads you'll fancy, dump super-nerd and I'll fix you up.'

Lofty returned with more drinks. I must have had eight pints and was feeling decidedly pissed; I lit a fag and gagged immediately as I sucked on the wrong end.

'So has Den told you about the move?'

'No, what move?'

My heart sank and I felt myself sobering up, Peanuts' voice sounded surprised. I hadn't mentioned that in my letters either; some mate I was turning out to be.

'Shit ... sorry, I meant to tell you, we're going to Catterick.'

'When?'

'After Christmas for a couple of years, but I think we manage to get a Bosnia tour in.'

'Bloody hell Den ... why didn't you tell me?' Peanuts put her drink down with a slam.

'Hey – calm down, I'm sorry, what's the big deal?' I just can't get my head around women when they fly off the handle. I looked across at her and her eyes had pricked with tears. She held them back and lifted her head to keep them from spilling down her cheeks.

'I'll see you on Saturday.' She stood up and grabbed her coat from the chair.

'Peanuts ...'

She walked out of the pub and didn't look back, leaving the door to flap on its hinges.

'Blimey mate, I think you've put her back up,' Lofty said as we stared at the door.

'I only forgot to tell her. Lordy! Oh well, she'll come round.'

The parade was a farce; even Lance Sergeant Chant looked rough. He called the roll and told us to get our running kit, as we needed some exercise. It was the first run I'd done in ages, and despite the alcohol misuse last night, my body felt great. We ran about six miles with loads of the lads strewn behind in a trailing rabble and Lance Sergeant Chant shouting at them. I could see Lofty heaving away in the slow crowd, red-faced and sweaty. We turned into Camp and were met by the Officer Commanding and Sergeant Major.

'Well done lads,' the OC shouted as we ran past to our

accommodation, 'I'm looking for some in the leading group for the inter-company boxing team this year.'

Boxing! I was still waiting for the motorbike display team, but boxing sounded immense. Once we'd stretched off and finished for the morning I approached Lance Sergeant Chant to ask him more.

'Want to fight then Yarwood?'

'Well I'd like a go, yes.'

'Look you either want to fight or you don't. I'm afraid there's no "having a bit of a go" in boxing, son.'

'Yeah, I want to fight.' He smiled, turned and walked away without giving me an answer so I returned to get a shower with Lofty in tow.

'You gonna box Den?'

'Yeah, sounds like fun.'

'FUN! Drinking and shagging are fun ... volunteering to get your head kicked in isn't.'

'Topple might be there.'

'How do you know?'

'Come on Lofty, he's bound to want to a pop and I'm about the same size as he is.'

'Sold to the handsome bastard, count me in then.'

'You'll have to see Sarge about that mate.' And he turned on his toes to find Lance Sergeant Chant.

Though I don't keep a written record of everything I do, my mental diary for the year was fast filling up. After the party on Saturday I have some leave, then the boxing and after that the promotion cadre and Junior Brecon, by then we would be ready for Christmas and the move to Catterick. I was pretty pleased with myself and kept thinking back to the bad old days in Luton where I would be struggling to fill an afternoon unless I had a snooker match to go to, and now I was planning a whole year at a time!

Saturday was nearly a complete failure; the pub was empty, as many of the lads had gone home for the weekend to see their families. I sat with Andy and Lofty trying to consume my own body weight in ale until Peanuts walked in, alone.

'Hi you lot!' she announced happily. I looked around to greet her.

'Blimey, what happened to you?' She wasn't wearing her normal miniskirt, crazy tights and T-shirt. She'd had her hair cut and her fringe curled under at her eyebrows, and the rest of her hair tied in a ponytail at the nape of her neck. The black dress she was wearing clung to her body and stopped just above the knee, showing her calves and a hip pair of stilettos.

'You on the pull?' Lofty was gawping at her and winked as he spoke.

'I could be. Is that an offer?' she replied.

'It might be, but you'll have to buy me a beer first before I agree to anything.' I was frankly taken aback at Lofty trying to chat her up.

We must have looked like the three wise monkeys sat there as Andy filled a pint of cider.

'Okay Den, where's these hunky guys you promised?'

'Right here.' Lofty had slipped back into normal, sporting comment mode as he stood up and flung his arms wide.

'H'm, I was hoping for a better specimen but as you've bought me a drink I'll have to reconsider.'

Peanuts had surprised and confused me; she'd plainly dumped Danny and was at liberty, but the sudden change in appearance threw me. She looked, well, out of character. I needed to get to the bottom of this.

'What's with the camouflage Peanuts? Last time I saw you, you walked out and now this.'

'Do you like it? I thought I would re-vamp my wardrobe and

try a new look. You know, a fresh approach, different bait as they say.'

'Yeah. I should have mentioned posting before, sorry; but it's not as if we're going to lose touch.' She'd sat down and lit a fag, blowing the smoke at me.

'I absolve you Den. Now can we drink somewhere a touch more seedy? How about the Student Union Bar?'

'No way, if I walk in with you and super-nerd sees us, he'll think we're going out together and beat me up! Ha ha, let's hit a club.'

She mumbled something and then agreed, before the three of us set out to the town centre.

2 am, and I'm stuck outside a club with an intoxicated newt and a ravenous giant. I know that Lofty can look after himself but the newt will need taking home, so I wander off with Peanuts draped over my arm as Lofty forays for the nearest chippy van before walking back to Camp. As I plonk Peanuts on her bed, she laughs, pulling me on top of her. She licks her finger and wipes it on my shirt.

'Now then Den, let's get you out of these wet clothes.'

Chapter Nineteen

Training to fight means lots and lots of running; perversely, perhaps for a quick getaway I don't know. Still, it suited me. Lofty needed encouragement to keep up with the amount of physical exercise being dished out by our instructor, however. Corporal Chris Newton had boxed for the Company and the Army before getting an injury, and now passed on his wisdom as a coach making me ache like I'd never known before. We had been weighed on the first day of the training and allotted fighting classes; I was welter and Lofty unsurprisingly enough superheavy. He protested about that, saying that the scales must be faulty. We had to endure six weeks of punishing early morning schedules as well as working during the day. Chris had told us that 'B' Company hadn't lost the title for two years and he'd make it his business to ensure we'd hang on to the Cup for another year yet. If it wasn't for the fact that we were going to fight 'A' Company, Lofty would have thrown the towel in on the first day, as Chris stated that there would be no drinking for the duration; but I managed to persuade him that it would do us both good and he might even lose enough weight to fight at heavyweight instead. I also had Lance Sergeant Chant hounding me about the promotion course, which was starting the day after the boxing match. I was, therefore, getting up at 5.30, running for an hour, or sparring, and then going into work after breakfast to brush up on my leadership skills. I was getting back to my room a physical and mental wreck but I felt alive and stimulated. Going back into a busy routine is just what I needed after a mundane leave period, after hanging around the house and playing snooker with Marc in his spare time. I hadn't seen anyone and only managed a snog behind the pub with a girl whose name escapes me, which left me feeling a little unloved, I suppose.

In the Headquarters building there are military clerks who are responsible for pay and personnel documentation, something I ordinarily don't worry about, but there was a report that a new girl clerk had been recently posted to our Company. Lo and behold, only two days later I needed to ask a question about my wages so I thought I'd check out the new subject matter expert. As I swanned into the HQ wearing my boxing top, shorts and a combination of fitness, raging libido and self-confidence I was slightly dismayed to be stopped in my tracks by the Office Sergeant, a bloke called Dirkin. Sergeant Dirkin is an angry man for no apparent reason; he barks at junior soldiers and his breath stinks like the inside of a shit smuggler's duffle bag.

'Who are you?' He stood in front of me with his hands on his hips trying to make himself as big as possible.

'Yarwood, Sarge.'

'SARGE? What do you mean sarge? Sausage, massage, anal passage?' Oh and he was the archetypal derisive bully. Sarge is actually an accepted abbreviation. I wasn't being insolent.

'Sorry Sergeant.'

'What do you want?'

'I needed to ask a question about my pay please Sergeant.'

'Ask.'

Oh Ace! I hadn't even thought of a decent question. I just wanted to steal a look at the new girl and see if she was receptive. I could see a figure bending over in a filing cabinet at the end of the room; My first impression was pleasing but it didn't help my immediate problem.

'Well ... I'm waiting.'

'Erm ... I wanted to ask about my tax.' I was struggling now. Damn it Den, cut and run. She's probably a BOBFOC anyway; this is one of Lofty's particularly apt descriptive phrases when a woman looks like a hotty from behind but not so attractive face on. Body off Baywatch, face off Crimewatch. Yeah, I know, base, but a good illustration before wandering into an unwanted encounter.

'Tax eh? CLARKE!' he bellowed over his shoulder, and the small figure turned around from her filing.

'Deal with this, and make it quick. I need a brew.' She looked at him uneasily and put the files on her desk before walking over to me. She wasn't a BOBFOC – in fact she was a slim little thing, and cut me a smile before asking me to sit down.

'Are you really called Clarke?'

'Yes. Now what can I do for you?' I could tell she was under pressure from Mr Dirkin; his tea was more important than any of our troubles, without a doubt.

'Erm – I wanted to ask about my tax.' My transparent query in retrospect is probably the worst thing I could have asked; the Army's tax is pre-calculated and never wrong. On my pitiful salary I had no reason to ask anything about the subject. This wasn't quite how I'd envisaged our conversation and had I thought about it beforehand I would have made a more believable request. She sat with a large folder, looking through the payslips, and didn't ask my name.

'No you don't.' She kept scanning and flipping the pages of her ledger and making notes on a piece of paper.

'Pardon?'

'You haven't a clue about your taxable income. I do hope it was worth telling stories to get into this office for an assessment.' Blimey! Pretty, clever and sharp. I'm exposed. I need to think of something witty and articulate to spur her into conversation.

'I'm a boxer.' Oh my God! Where did that come from?

'Well done you, make sure you keep your guard up. Now you'll need this before you go. Goodbye.' She handed me a piece of paper and stood up.

'Thanks ...'bye.' I stood there for a moment and watched her return to her filing, feeling a complete fool. I must have been as red as a freshly smacked arse. I walked out of the building back to my lines. As I moved away I glanced back and saw her smiling at me through the window. Oh if only the ground would open up. I'm going to have to spend the remainder of my time avoiding the place like the plague. I took the scrap of paper out of my pocket and looked at it before I threw it in the bin.

Chat up line C-

Looks B+

Potential B

Likelihood of taking me out for a drink tonight at 8 by the guardroom A

I looked back into the window and she was sat opposite Sergeant Dirkin taking notes. I waved the piece of paper in the air to attract her attention and she looked up over the top of her glasses. I smiled my best ever-winning smile and she looked away again as Dirkin looked out. I ducked.

'How are you mate?' Mick was stood over me.

'Yeah fine thanks.' I stood up abruptly 'I was just...'

'Lecherously looking at Tina, lush isn't she?'

'Yeah she's a ... how do you know?'

'Blimey Den you're slow off the mark. The office hasn't been that in demand for years. Let's have a look at your score then.'

'What?'

'She's been getting that much attention that she's started scoring the lads, the sauce-box gave me a C- for looks.'

I hid the piece of paper behind my back like a small boy hiding top secret classified information.

'Oh average, I knew she was having a laugh.'

'Yeah right,.' Mick held out his hand, 'Come on then let's have a look, or didn't you do too well?'

I pushed past and started jogging across the parade square, 'Sorry mate, busy day today, must dash.'

Mick shouted something derogatory about being ungraded as I hurried off. Stone the crows, she's giving scores out! So I spent the rest of the day oblivious to the lessons on how to plan an attack with eight guys and pondered the note, should I or shouldn't I? Well – I had nothing to lose by it and she was a real looker.

I stood in the shadows of the guardroom half expecting to be blown out by the enigmatic Tina for what seemed like ages, and then she was there.

'Hiya Tina.' She jumped and looked around.

'Oh, hi! I didn't think you'd turn up, none of the others have.' Freak out, she's a serial dater. She was lean with long blonde hair and great body; I couldn't let this one go despite the tiny voice in my brain screaming a warning to me.

'Right, shall we go somewhere then ... for a drink I mean.' I was stumbling over my words already.

'Yes.' Pause. 'What's your name, boxer guy? You already know mine.' Goodness me, she was a knockout.

'Den.'

'Did you have somewhere in mind? For a drink then?' We started walking along the canal towards the town.

'Look Tina, I don't mean to be rude but why the note?'

'Well I've been hit on by nearly the whole Company since last week and when I saw you getting a hard time from Dirkin, I thought why not? At least you've got some nerve, the rest normally run a mile after coming across him.'

'Oh.'

'Look – I'm not a tease, but when there's the choice of so many blokes surely it's ungracious not to give them each a little attention.' She winked, and strutted on with me scurrying behind like some lapdog. We hit town and went into the Prince Regent. I knew that not many of the lads drank in there, as it had a reputation for being a gay pub, but I thankfully couldn't verify that. We sat by the window and she drank vodka and coke as we chatted. Tina had only been in the Army for six months and this was her first job from training; she was eighteen and had wanted to be in the Army since she was a kid. But because she was so small, she couldn't join any of the jobs she would have liked, so became a clerk. I liked her; she was witty and easy to chat to and getting squiffy.

We walked back to Camp talking about music, films and other trivia; it was cold and dark and looked like it was about to rain when she turned to me.

'You're lovely Den.'

'Thanks. So are you. Can I kiss you?'

She nearly leapt on me and flung her arms around my neck, pushing me off balance and into a small clearing in the trees on the bank of the canal. We kissed and hands wandered and next thing I knew my hand had found itself up her dress with no resistance at all. This was risky, but the thought of getting away with it excited me and I wanted to go further. Tina walked further into the clearing and slipped her dress over her head; she must have been freezing but I joined her. And that's when I found out that the most sensitive part of my body when nearly naked outdoors is my ears, as I heard a rustling in the bush behind me and proceedings came to a halt. I put my finger over her lips as I listened, and it was there again, branches moving and getting closer. I could hear something but I could not see what it was; then the biggest shock of my life. A wet, cold nose made contact with me and I must have made a reactionary thrust.

'Oh yes Den ...' Oh no Den, I thought, I didn't do that for effect, and pulled back to see a small Jack Russell sniffing my nether regions.

'Shoo,' I hissed at the small dog as it wagged its tail and looked very pleased with itself. A more terrifying noise followed.

'Digby!'

I'll Digby you, I thought as the owner looked in the bushes for the lost canine.

'What have you found, boy?' The woman's voice asked. I was panic stricken and Tina had started rummaging around for her clothes.

'Den. Where's my dress?' She was checking the ground where we lay.

'I don't know,' I whispered back.

'Oh Digby, what have you got there boy?' I could see the woman grab the dog by the collar and throw the unwanted present behind her into the canal.

'I think Digby knows where your dress is.' For a small girl she could sure pack a punch, and I reeled as her open hand made contact with my face. As situations go, this wasn't the best. Tina viewed me, mouth open, and shaking her head. The woman and dog walked away down the towpath and I waited until they were out of sight before looking in the water.

'You ... you ... beast!'

'What?' I couldn't stifle my chuckle. 'What did you call me?' I'd taken a slap for no reason so I wasn't going to put up with her feeble attempt at abuse. I pulled the dripping material from the water and wrung it out as best I could.

'Come on, let's get back.' I pulled my jumper on and reached for my jeans.

'What about me Den?'

'What about you Tina?' We needed to get back to Camp, and the romance was completely spent for me after having my arse sniffed by Digby.

'My dress – it's soaking.' She held up the bundle as she stood shivering in her knickers and bra..

Why women breathe fire and fury is anyone's guess, I'd retrieved her dress from the canal. 'It's not that bad, I've wrung it out. Come on, I've got an early start, it's late.' She thrust the dress into my chest and grabbed my leather jacket from the floor. It was a quiet walk back; I tried to spark some conversation, telling her about Ireland and the boxing team but I was blanked. As we walked through the Camp gates she turned and said.

'You can get your jacket back in the morning, once you've put that dress in the dry cleaners.' And she was gone.

Hum. I wondered what grade I'd get for entertainment?

Chapter Twenty

I'd broken my vow of abstinence during the first week of the boxing training and Chris noticed instantly. I was given an extra session of physical exercise that evening to make sure all of the booze was out of my system and to teach me a lesson. Chris demanded that I run up and down one of the hills near Camp wearing my jogging suit with a bin liner on underneath. It was hell and I poured with sweat for nearly an hour. He left me on my knees outside my block with a pat on the head and condescending; 'Now you'll not have another snifter nipper until it's over.' My jacket was still in Tina's possession and my pride in tatters so I was looking forward to the weekend and having a regular life for a couple of days.

Being bright-eyed and bushy tailed on a Saturday morning is the pits and I felt stir-crazy in my room. Lofty had gone home and Tina wasn't speaking to me, not that that bothered me. I needed some company and a time-honoured chat so I got dressed and walked across town to the college. The students must have been partying the night before as the halls of residence were deserted and had beer cans on the floor. I could hear ELO through the door and had to knock hard before I got an answer.

'Hello stranger!' She beamed at me and it felt good to see a happy and friendly face, even though it was partly covered in some chemical compound gunk. She had a towel around her middle and one on her head in a turban.

'Come in, I'll make some tea. How are you?'

'I was a bit bored.' If there was a prize for speaking before thinking it was heading my way.

'Oh! Thanks Den, I feel flattered.'

'Erm whoops! I didn't mean that, I just fancied a chat and a walk around the shops or something.' I am lucky that Peanuts understands and makes allowances as she poured two cups of tea and joining me sitting on her bed.

'So what's going on? You seem rather vacant.' I complained about the fitness regime and about Tina. The incident had bothered me more than I'd realised. I'm young and don't want the settling down thing yet but just to have a everyday relationship would be cushty, it was just finding the right girl. I told her about Marc's boys and how Mum was looking old.

'Den, you sound like you're having a mid-life crisis. Perhaps you should consider learning to play the guitar?' I gave no response.

'I'm only kidding. Now what does a young man like you need to cheer him up then I wonder, pub ... scrabble challenge ... pictures?'

I sat staring at my cup and swishing the contents around, as she got dressed carefully under her towel.

'Come on Den, you mustn't let your tea get cold over this.'

I slurped my brew. 'Oh sorry, I'll be fine.'

'No, it's a phrase my Nan used to say when things weren't worth worrying about. She meant that if things were really important you'd drop everything and sort them out, my Nan loved her cup of tea and it took a real problem for her to put it down and leave it. Hence, don't let your tea go cold, get it?'

'Yeah. Pictures sounds good.'

She stood by the open door waving me out like a VIP.

'There's a problem though.'

'What?' She put her hands on her hips. 'You've forgotten your glasses?'

'No it's not that, you haven't wiped that muck off your face!'

Winchester in spring is picturesque; the town is promising to burst with colour on every corner and the cherry trees shed pink blossom over the pavements making it look like it has been snowing. The canal was buzzing with bees and small flies and the towpath was beginning to narrow with growing grass. Peanuts interlinked my arm as we walked, leaving my other hand free to force a burger into her mouth that I'd had to buy her after much pleading of 'I'm only a poor student.'

I wanted to see Braveheart but on the contrary I ended up watching something about a bloke going up a hill and coming down a mountain or something like that because it had Hugh Grant in it, longhaired idiot. However, it did the trick and I came out of the pictures with a different attitude. We went for lunch. I chose this time so it was Italian and lots of pasta. Peanuts appears to eat anything and everything in huge quantities so I didn't feel guilty about my decision. And besides I'd had to watch a Hugh Grant film against my will.

Between mouthfuls Peanuts asked

'Where's Catterick anyway?'

'Yorkshire somewhere.'

'Oh, I could catch a train and visit you then?'

'Yeah sure. Cripes Peanuts you make it sound like I'm going down.'

'At least we get to spend the summer together.' She was steering the conversation to somewhere, I could tell.

'Yeah, go on?'

'Well, I wondered if you'd be keen on another expedition, if you have some free time?'

I thought back to Amsterdam; it was a good trip despite the disagreement.

'Well I've got a promotion course after the boxing tournament for three weeks and then there's another course in July but I could get some leave after that, I suppose.'

She smiled again, 'Great, August it is then. Where do you fancy?' That was it. She was in full organising mode,. I hadn't decided what I wanted for pudding yet!

As the training progressed I felt stronger and faster. Chris said that I had great potential. A week before the fight I was sparring daily and we looked pretty ominous as a team. 'A' Company hadn't released their team list; it made the whole thing more exciting as I had no idea who I would be in the ring with until the night. For the last six days I didn't have to go to work either and was allowed to sit in my room during the day, which sounded heavenly, but in practice was the doldrums. Chris gave encouraging talks and declared this was the most formidable team he'd ever seen and that we'd walk over 'A' Company.

The Saturday morning I opened my eyes and the butterflies started. My mind was filled with scenarios: getting ready to step into the ring and hearing the bell. I imagined myself dancing around, picking off my opponent with left jabs, avoiding his feeble attempts to hit me and finishing him with a massive right hook, all in round one. Lofty and I had to be at the gymnasium by mid-day for a final weigh-in and to meet the 'A' Company team, so we walked over together. He'd achieved his goal of getting down to heavyweight and the big man looked fierce. The six demanding weeks had toned the flab on his body and he stood, a giant mass of muscle. An entourage of Officers from the Battalion received us at ringside; the gym had been transformed, powerful overhead strip-lights illuminated the ring. Seating stands had been erected around the ring in blue and red seats to represent the relevant corners and VIP seats had been neatly placed feet away from the skirt; the place looked magnificent. Chris beckoned us into the changing room where the rest of the team sat.

'I've got a present for you boys.' He opened a sports bag and pulled out a brand new tracksuit. It was blue with white piping and a white 'B' on the chest logo; he held it to his body so that we could see the front.

'Well, what do you think?' We nodded in approval.

'That's not all lads,' and he turned the top around so we could read the back.

'B' COY

THE POWDER TO THE PUNCH

'Who made them Chris?'

Everyone was silent and forced themselves to smile, apart from Lofty.

'My wife's got herself a printing machine. Great, aren't they?'

'Did she finish them all?' I added.

'Oh yes. Mine says Coach on the front.'

'Wasn't her solar powered torch working?'

The door opened and the Sergeant Major put his head around the door.

'Corporal Newton, everybody's waiting, get the lads out ... now.'

'Yes Sir. Right lads, get your kit on and let's go.' He threw a packet containing a new tracksuit at each of us. Lofty looked across at me and shook his head; the other lads said nothing and stripped.

'Maybe no one will notice,' I whispered to Lofty as we dressed. Chris was preoccupied admiring his outfit in the mirror and stroking the embroidered Coach on his chest.

We sidled out of the dressing room into the gym trying to keep our backs to the wall and lined up opposite our competitors. Topple was nowhere in sight. The Commanding Officer, Colonel Dilks, stood between the two groups and in front of the scales; next to him stood the Sergeant who was in charge of the physical training for the unit. I could hear whispered comments from some of the Officers behind us.

'Powder?'

The CO explained that the weigh-in was to verify boxers' size before tonight and to make sure there would be no mismatched fights and called the first boxers forward. Our lightest guy Bruce stepped up to the Colonel and turned to move onto the scales.

'A' Company crowed. Howling and whooping spread around the room; even the CO snorted. Chris looked baffled and grabbed my trackie jacket to read it again before putting his head in his hands and mumbled something chagrined into them. In unison we took our tops off and rolled them up. This would take some living down.

I waited in the changing room for my call; the two boys who'd fought first had both won their bouts and it was me up next. Chris stood up and made me go through some moves with him, constantly talking as I swung my punches.

'He's going to knock your head off Den, you know that.' The words meant nothing.

'I heard him say that you were a short work, you're going to get hammered in that ring tonight in front of your mates.'

I swung harder, seeing my opponent smiling at me as I swung.

'His mate Topple said that you and your mate Lofty needed a good kicking.'

The suggestion of him knowing Topple enraged me.

'But he said that you wouldn't be standing for long enough to get one.'

That was it, this pleb is going to get it tonight. I heard the door open and from the ringside microphone the Regimental Sergeant Major called, 'BOXERS!'

I was jogging but not moving fast, covering small amounts of ground with many steps, looking at the ground and hearing the cheers as I left the changing room. A drummer led me to my corner past the VIP seating where Lance Sergeant Chant sat with the Sergeant Major,

'COME ON YARWOOD!'

The shouts rang in my head as I neared the red corner and I

looked up to see my Company in its entirety stood on their seats yelling and cheering ... for me. Everybody knew who I was, everybody respected me, wanted me to win. Whether it is for their self-gratification, the good of the Army or what, it just didn't matter. I was the man they wanted to win and I had nine minutes to prove to my supporters that I was the daddy. No way was my opponent as mentally or physically as tuned as me, I hated him ... but who was it?

The drum struck up again as I lifted my leg over the ropes and in waltzed the 'A' Company soldier to a cheer from his corner. The preceding two defeats must have taken the wind out of their sails, as his reception wasn't half as loud or passionate as mine.

We stood in our corners, while the shaking our legs and nodding our heads at each other, posturing and staring, while the MC announced us. The noise of the crowd became secondary to my thoughts and focus as we were beckoned into the centre of the ring for our briefing; at last, a good look at him.

'Right lads, I want a good clean fight, no rabbit punches, nothing below the belt and listen to my instructions at all times.' I loosely recognised the guy from around Camp but it was of no consequence now as I stared through his gaze and deep into his eyes, not blinking, focusing on his fear of me. We returned to our corners and Chris patted me on the back.

'When that bell sounds Den ... unleash hell.'

DING DING: 'Round one.'

I was terrified and bounced forward on my toes towards him with my muscles feeling like coiled springs. There were nearly two hundred people in that gym, but only me and him in the ring. The dance started, I landed a few preliminary jabs to his gloves and he returned the compliment, moving around the ring in unison. For every threatened attack I'd put in a counter attack and he the same, there was no way in for me. I waited, ducked and dived, looking for the moment. Soon there would be a millimetre of space that he'd forget to cover and I'd be in. Seconds ticked away and nothing was happening, no noise from the crowd. A punch made my head jolt backwards and I could see stars. It took my breath away, leaving me confused. The next hurt like hell and my nose cracked, the noise rattling around my head as the blood poured into my mouth. Stop it, stop hitting me. It came again, this time to my chest and I felt the ropes of the ring on my back as I staggered backwards. There was nowhere to hide now, I had no time to think of what Chris had told me about keeping up my guard The punches were coming far too quickly, leather making contact with my skin. They stopped and I had time to orientate myself as the referee looked at me square on. He counted the eight seconds. I realised what was going on; this bloke was taking liberties, and I was losing. If I got another standing eight count that would be it, all over in round one.

'BOX.' The ref swung his arms together to indicate that we should continue, and we linked again, no time for sizing up. I had to launch now or it was going to be all over. My right glove steamed through his guard and struck his face below the right eye and he staggered backwards looking shocked. I had to pin him down quickly but he was too fast and came back with another crippling strike to the side of my head.

DING: three minutes had gone and a cheer erupted from 'A' Company as I walked towards Chris in my corner.

'Excellent Den, fucking excellent, you've hurt him. Now this round you've got to finish him.'

What was he talking about? I'd just taken the beating of my life and he thinks I'm winning. Has he been watching the same fight? I looked around and our crowd was sat in near silence, talking to each other and shaking their heads, I felt desperately lonely.

I've heard people talking about inner strength before but never understood it those men before the bout regarding me as their Goliath and now writing me off turned my stomach. I looked at my opponent who was being patted on the back as he left his corner. He was fresh and determined, bouncing and circling his hands in front of himself like a professional boxer. I moved away from the shelter of my corner a broken man, bloody and sore with a busted nose; and then he did something I'll never forgive. He smiled at me. A knowing smile that said he was the winner and that made me a loser. Rage came from my toes, moved up my legs, into my chest, arms, fists and I hurt him. My arms striking out at my target the resistance of his head lessened, he tried to hit back but couldn't reach me. The more he tried, the more gaps in his armour appeared. As his flailing arms started to miss altogether I saw the chance I needed as he left his face exposed. It was over as he fell backwards onto the canvas, and the referee pulled me back and pointed to my corner. Chris was performing what could only be described as amateur gymnastics outside the ring and my supporters were back from the dead, jumping and down and pointing at the felled soldier. I could hear chanting, 'Yarwood! Yarwood!'

The bell sounded and I turned to see him sat back in his corner being treated by his Seconds who were busy mopping him down as he shook his head. The sight of him compos mentis shocked me slightly; I thought I'd finished him. Last round and three minutes left to get this over and done with.

We met in the middle of the ring and touched gloves before the final joust. I had the upper hand and I wasn't prepared to lose it. The first clash began as a mêlée of fists from both sides, similar to windmills turning in synchronicity; the forced energy was draining my strength and as I hit out I could feel the ferocity of my punches becoming less of a threat. He was losing momentum too and soon we were slumped in each other's arms with the referee pulling us apart. The crowd didn't like it and booing started as we crashed into each other again slower than molasses. It was unachievable to muster the strength for a decent punch and I missed my target again; sweat had filled my eyes and I was flailing my fists in vain, as was he.

'Come on! ... you look like a pair of fighting cocks!' The only voice I heard from the crowd was my Platoon Commander, Lieutenant Graves. The abuse took a few seconds to register. The fight had deteriorated into a scrap, no honour could be gained from this now, and we were exhausted, going through the motions of what looked like a drunken brawl. More abuse from the crowd followed as we faltered and lunged at each other with no will whatsoever to win, just hoping to hear the final bell.

'Good effort mate.' Chris didn't sound convincing and he pulled my gloves off and spun me around to face the ref, who was calling me back into the centre of the ring. The other guy was already there holding the ref's hand in anticipation of the result, I joined them, scanning the crowd and waiting for my hand to be thrust in the air as the victor. The judges had put their results on a piece of paper and handed them into the ring. The ref took a glance at them and waited for the MC to call the winner. I had the best of the fight; it wasn't me who had been on the canvas.

The crowd fell silent as the Regimental Sergeant Major scaled the ropes and dusted himself down. My ears were ringing from the punches and crowd noise and I could taste blood in my mouth, aches started to take their effect after previously being kept at bay by adrenalin. My left eye was closing with a swelling and I couldn't focus properly.

'Blue, winner.'

'A' Company went wild.

Chapter Twenty-one

Christmas got complicated very quickly; Marc had invited Mum to stay for the week like last year, even though she only lives four miles away but when I announced I was coming home for the holidays this year she got herself in a fluster. I'm a big boy and have had my own key for years but she'd got it into her head that she should stay at home with me. Anyway, it became convoluted and to defuse any further concerns or problems I'd decided to spend Christmas away for the second year and return to home for the New Year.

Though I needed another plan. It didn't take me long to call the new number Peanuts had sent me. She was sharing a rented house and her housemates were going home for the holiday, so she suggested that I stay a few days; it might be a wheeze. And that was my plan. As a result, the day before Christmas Eve I drove to Winchester. I was looking forward to seeing her as we had missed going away in the summer and after moving with the Battalion to Catterick I'd only phoned a few times and written to her once. She greeted me at the door as if I'd only been gone a week, in her usual guise swinging a bottle of wine in one hand and two glasses in the other a big smile stretched across her face.

'Hello Santa!' She leant forward and kissed my cheek as I pushed my bag through the door.

'Hello you ...new tights then.'

Peanuts giggled and showed me inside. We sat and she poured the wine, chatting about the holidays and the drama students' production she had become involved in and whom she'd seen and so on until she suddenly stopped.

'Guess what?' Now if there's one thing that bugs me it's being asked a pointless question.

'Dunno, Luton Town have won the first division? No, hang on, someone has discovered penicillin? No, let me think. The world isn't flat?'

'No silly – I've got a work placement for next year.'

'Oh great, so you're gonna have to work for a living?'

'You know my course. I've been studying for the past twenty-four months and now I'm on work experience.'

'Oh yeah, sorry, well done you then.' She was waving a hand in front of her mouth as she drank before speaking.

'It's in York ... well?'

'Brilliant.' I didn't have a clue what she was getting at so I offered her a fag and finished my glass. What she was trying to say was that we could see each other more when she was there. I could take her to see the delights of Darlington.

The temptation to run along the canal was too much for me to keep away; even in freezing December, the air was still and crisp. I enjoyed watching the billowing steam clouds I made as I tracked the towpath into the town. Lights and decorations filled the High Street and the shops had snow sprayed into the corners of their windows. It was then I realised I ought to buy Peanuts a present or at least a Christmas card and I'd need to be sharp about it. When I arrived back Peanuts was still in bed so I showered and took her a cup of tea, nearly breaking my neck on the pile of clothes on the floor. I could see her quilt moving vaguely. I put the brew down and nudged the lump.

'Wakey, wakey. I'm going out to do some shopping.' A hand appeared from under the covers and waved as she grunted in response.

'There's a cup of tea on the side for you. See ya.'

As I left the room I watched the hand carefully pick up the hot cup and negotiate its way back into the abyss of the quilt without spilling a drop.

Shopping is a skill that is passed from female to female; men cannot mimic the enthusiasm or delight in the event that is the shopping trip. I had bought everyone a present; well, I'd bought the boys' presents; they are easy to please and you'll never go wrong with an Action Man and a Beano Annual. But I was now faced with the dilemma of choosing an appropriate gift for a friend, a female friend. Dicey – especially when I knew zilch about her taste in things. I knew what she liked to wear, but that's a very personal gift to buy and I didn't suppose that opening a pair of tights on Christmas morning would be altogether thrilling. Makeup was completely out of the question, as I knew about as much about cosmetics as she about rifles or cars, I assume. So I wandered and pondered, scanning the shop windows for … things.

I popped into a fast food bar for lunch empty handed and sat down to munch my burger. As I stared out of the window I noticed a pair of stripy tights pass by and my dilemma was solved. I pushed the remainder of the burger into my mouth and shadowed her up the High Street, far enough behind to observe the shops she was looking into. I couldn't make out what she was looking at for the first two windows as they were on my side of the road and I couldn't get a proper view, but as she made a beeline for the Oxfam shop I had full vision of the window display. She was peering inside at an old clock on display; she nodded her head and moved on. Brilliant Den, you're a genius! She's got a new house and no clock. Four pounds later and I was off to buy the mandatory card and some wrapping paper.

She was still out when I arrived back which gave me enough time to wrap the clock and stuff it behind the couch. I scrawled inside the card and placed it by the kettle and sat down to watch some television, happy with myself. Peanuts came back to the house about an hour later laden with shopping bags from the supermarket, one clearly filled with bottles as it clanked onto the kitchen floor. She turned to put the kettle on and picked up my envelope.

'Oh! I wonder who this could be from?' She opened it and tilted her head in mock curiosity.

'Lovely words Den, thank you.'

I'd written, *To Peanuts, from Den.* Well, these cards have already got a poem or a Happy Christmas in them so I see no point in writing it over again for the sake of it. She placed it on the side with a pile of other cards and started unpacking. Some mince, wine, broccoli, more wine and a plastic moulded Christmas tree.

'Great, that's the decorations done!' she said, as she put it on the dining table and stood back to admire it. 'I wasn't going to bother this year but as I have a house guest I thought I'd go to town.' We both laughed at the pathetic little tree. I'm not the biggest fan of tinsel and holly so for our purposes it would do fine.

'Okay, the proposal is to eat, get tarted up and hit the Nelly. I told Andy you were coming and some of the crowd will be there. Then we could go to midnight mass.'

'That's a better plan than mine.'

'And yours was?'

'To see what you wanted to do.'

She gave me an indulgent smile and started chopping an onion. By seven o'clock we were dressed and ready to go. We had put to rest a bottle of wine during our preparations and made a healthy dent in a second. Even though the house was foreign territory I felt quite at home as I shouted at her from the bedroom to the bathroom. It was lovely to be in her company after so long. It started to feel like Amsterdam all over again.

Andy welcomed me with a handshake and a pint of bitter.

'Good to see you Squire, that'll be three quid with the cider.' Some things never change I thought, I bet the prodigal son didn't have to give his dad rent as soon as he returned. Andy went on to complain that since the Battalions switched there had been lots of trouble. Apparently the Green Jackets wanted to put their mark on the town, and had started by inciting a riot in the first week they were there, claiming that the Nelson was no longer a Guardsman's pub. They were on leave now so the locals could return downtown without fear of a drunken soldier trying to punch them or chat their girlfriends up, for the holidays at least. Anyway, tonight was going to be a cracker; he'd got a karaoke disco and some nibbles on the tables and I was starting to feel festive for the first time. Peanuts had gone to sit with some people from the university, some of whom I recognised. The pub filled within an hour, and the noise of laughing and chatter made it hard to hear anybody singing; which was good because my version of Blue Jeans would have put Neil Diamond in his grave. By chucking-out time I was completely sloshed and grabbed hold of an equally plastered Peanuts. We headed for the cathedral, to be met by a very sober and not too amused deacon.

This was the first time I'd been to church in quite a while; of course Mum had taken me when I was younger, much to my displeasure. We were steered into a pew beside an elderly couple who smiled warmly at us. The organ played reverently in the background. My head was spinning with the beer and fresh air and I started to think that this wasn't the best idea she'd ever had. I looked over at Peanuts perusing the service sheet and humming a carol; she nodded at me and returned to her reading. All of a sudden we were on our feet as a procession of choirboys and churchy people filed through the congregation in a solemn mood. I thought they'd be happier seeing as it was Christmas Eve; maybe they had missed last orders.

'I hate to say it, but I feel a bit odd, Den.'

'Okay, let's get you out of here before you're sick.'

As the music died away, she began to whisper.

'No, not like that! Sort of melancholy, it's my first Christmas I've been away from my family.'

'Yeah, second one in a row for me, at least I'm not on my own this time.' We sat back down as the carol ended and the priest started to speak. I had completely lost any interest in the service and wanted to chat.

'I'm glad we're spending Christmas together Den.'

'Yeah, I've had a good laugh tonight. I'd only be stuck around Marc's house waiting for the boys to wake up. It's for kids really isn't it?'

'Yes. I'd like to have children one day.'

'Me too I suppose, but not for a while.'

She turned to face me. 'Have you wondered what our kids would look like?'

'Pardon?' I exclaimed, a bit too loudly, and the couple beside me looked over disapproving and then returned to listen to the mass.

'If we had kids, hypothetically speaking, dipped our toes in the gene pool together?'

'Bloody handsome if they looked anything like me!'

She slapped my thigh.

'Denis! don't swear in church.' She had a grin appearing in the corner of her mouth,

'I imagine she'd have your blue eyes and my mousy brown hair.'

I couldn't envisage being a father as in having a baby; the concept of breeding hadn't occurred to me but it was destined to happen sooner or later. Marc and I look kind of similar when I come to think about it, we both have blue eyes and brown hair and roughly the same height but what would a baby look like if it was mine? She'd got me thinking now.

'If we had a boy, he'd be a nice big lad.' She indicated a height in the air with her hand above the crowd and again brought attention to our drunken state as I dragged her hand down. For a second time everyone sprang to their feet and began 'While Shepherds Watched Their Flocks by Night'.

I knew that one from school so I joined in. Peanuts jabbed me.

'Would you like a boy or a girl Den?'

'A boy' I said, between verses.

'Why a boy? I'd like a boy.'

'So he can take me for a pint when he's old enough.'

Another dig from her elbow followed.

'What if it's a girl then? You can't have her dragging you down the pub.'

'No, she could cook when I got home, ha ha!'

We had started giggling again, this time I couldn't control myself and tears welled up in my eyes, Peanuts had a hand over her mouth and once again hush fell as the congregation sat down.

'When were you thinking of getting started?"

'What! And lose my freedom for ever?'

We were getting out of hand; people in the row in front turned around as we teased each other.

'Will you and your wife please show some restraint?' A woman dressed in a tweed suit clucked at us from behind, looking over a pair of half moon glasses.

'There see? We don't need to bother now, we look like a pair of sad old marrieds as it is, that'll save me a hangover!'

Peanuts flung her hand to her forehead and pretended to weep. For the next half an hour we were up and down, singing and chanting along with the crowd before at last the priest announced we could Go In Peace.

'Alleluia, let's get some chips.'

I grabbed her hand and we ran out of the cathedral and into the rain. Amazingly at half- past twelve on Christmas morning there was nowhere open, so we walked home.

I woke to the sound of Slade ringing out downstairs and gingerly descended to the living room, stopped by a cup of tea and a small wrapped present from a rather jaded looking Peanuts in her dressing gown.

'Merry Christmas!' She gave me a peck on the cheek and then slumped onto the couch.

'Did the *Ghost Of Christmas Present* overdo the spirit?'

She did look pale. I bent over Peanuts to retrieve my carefully wrapped present from behind the sofa and put it in her lap as I joined her on the couch. We sat and looked at our gifts and then at each other, I wondered if I looked as rough as she did with her red half-open eyes.

'You first Den.'

'No, you first,' I replied, thinking if she asks me again I'm going for it or we'll be here all day.

'Let's just open them together, eh?'

Brilliant idea. I wish I'd thought of it.

As the paper fell from my hands I saw a shiny new brass-coloured Zippo lighter.

'Oh Peanuts, thanks!' I flipped it in my hand and engraved on the front was:

My Hero

KPB

'Bloody hell, it's gorgeous, thank you.'

I felt immediately guilty about the clock but it was too late; she was holding it up in front of her.

'It's nearly eleven o'clock Den, thank you!'

Was that meant to be funny, sarcastic or what? I was just about to ask her when the phone rang and she reached over to pick it up.

'Hello? Happy Christmas to you too … no…yeah … me and Den … wine, yeah …okay see you in an hour. 'Bye.'

She put the receiver down and stood up rubbing her eyes and stretching.

'Right, that's lunch sorted. We're going to Jayne's.'

'Whose?'

'Oh, just a friend of mine, you might remember her, she's invited us and any other lost souls around for Christmas dinner. Isn't she kind?'

'Yes, very congenial.'

I hadn't a clue that she was, I continuously seemed to meet new acquaintances every time we had gone out. Still, a dinner sounded good.

I asked if I could give Marc and Mum a bell and wished them a Happy Christmas. It sounded like bedlam in the background on the phone and I could hear Debbie shouting at Callum, or it might have been the other one, as she cooked dinner. Mum asked when she'd see me but I couldn't think straight with my headache, so I said 'before I finish my leave', and left it at that.

Jayne's house was only two minutes' walk away, which was a good thing, as we had overestimated our requirements against our carrying abilities, and staggered around with five bottles of wine and any beer we could find in the house. The shower that I had before we left had cleared my head. There was no hot water; in fact, if the sprinkling had been any colder snowflakes would have been coming out of the showerhead. I realised that I'd met Jayne once before in the pub and as I was introduced I noticed another face that feebly rang a bell. It was the guy I had punched at a party. He stood up and walked straight towards me with his hand out.

'Hi Kes! Hello ... sorry I can't remember your name. I'm Marcus; I think you dropped me a while back. I was out of order anyway. Merry Christmas to you, fancy a beer?' Well, that was a good start. I didn't need any agro today, so in the spirit of goodwill to all men or however it goes I accepted as he handed me a bottle.

It was a better Christmas than last year. We sat and drank and chatted before Jayne paraded a dreadfully overcooked turkey around the room much to everyone's delight and we ate a very amateur dinner. Afterwards we played charades and drank even more until it was decided that music and singing was fitting late in the night. I woke up in the darkness, slumped on the sofa wearing my jeans and socks oddly. I was totally disorientated with my bladder near to bursting, and began stepping over bodies strewn across the floor in various states of collapse in search of the bathroom. I'd visited the comfort station a few times during the day but my weakened judgment and direction took me into every room except the one I needed so desperately.

There was nothing for it. Silently opening the front door, I stepped into the cold night to find a suitable bush. Now blokes make a few noises to notify anyone close that they are in pleasure and relieving an overburdened bladder triggers a sort of near orgasmic groan that to many could easily be mistaken for being in pain. I let my exhilaration be heard at a volume that was evidently too loud and a light came on in the house behind me.

'Who's there?' I heard a male voice ask with his silhouetted head poking around the open front door.

'It's Den.'

I whispered my reply so not to make any more noise than needed. The sleepy head looked around and squinted for a few seconds before retreating into the warmth, closing the door behind him. I couldn't move as I was still in mid- flow; I watched the door click shut and the light extinguish. My feet were getting cold from the damp ground and I hadn't seen the need for my shirt, which I now remembered I had hung over the back of a chair. I was up a certain creek without a certain item. I could knock and wake up the rest of the reprobates but I didn't think it would be greatly appreciated so I jogged on the spot rubbing my sides with my hands while I thought of an alternative.

I walked around to the back of the house hoping to find another way inside, peering through the glass of the kitchen window. I looked up and saw one of those small push out ones ajar with a metal arm holding it open. By now, shivering had taken full control of my body and I needed to get in quickly so I grabbed the bottom of the window ledge and hoisted myself up until my head was poking through the gap. It was tight so I put my arms out first to make a diving shape and with my feet on the bottom ledge I launched myself through the window. Then my hips caught. The warm air was good and I felt partially relieved; however, I was now stuck in the kitchen window with my arse exposed by moonlight and my legs kicking away. The sink was full of plates from dinner and glasses littered the other surfaces; we must have drunk a serious amount. Someone flicked the light on and I was temporarily blinded as my eyes adjusted to the light. It was Marcus, peering back at me as he walked through to the sink. He rubbed his eyes and picked up a glass, emptying it and filled it with cold water, his eyes bloodshot and breath like something out of a horror film.

'G'morning, 'scuse me.' As if we always met at this time of day. No amazement or inquiring why I was hanging out of the window half-naked, more a polite questioning.

'What are you doing?'

Daft and clearly very observable questions as always deserve a stupid answer in my book, especially when the answer is quite obvious.

'I'm stuck in the window, you fucking idiot!'

He frowned and tilted his head before sipping from his glass and taking a step back.

'Erm ... you're stuck in the window ... right?'

'Right Marcus ...'

'And I'm the fucking idiot ... ?' He turned and tripped the switch again, plunging me into darkness as he retreated into the front room and shut the door. I beckoned him back, actually I was pleading for him to come back, but nothing. As I contemplated my next feat, which wasn't going to be anything spectacular, I heard more movement from the front room and another figure appeared. With nothing left to lose now apart from the use of my legs, I gave a cry.

'Oi! You there.'

The figure stopped briefly and then continued on to climb the stairs, I hear the flush of the karzy and then who ever it was approached the kitchen. For the second time the light flipped on.

'Peanuts, thank goodness, that's my shirt!'

She stood as Marcus had, rubbing her eyes into focus.

'Before you start realising how foolish I look, I locked myself out ... I wanted a slash and got lost; look it's a long story, just help me out please.'

By this time my pleading had turned to whingeing as I beckoned her over to me. She stopped, looked and started to giggle.

'Hang on a minute,' she said before turning and running into the living room. Where was she going? Was she going to wake up the rest of the house? If only I could get myself free. The window frame was beginning to slice me in two. Then she appeared, fiddling with her camera and smirking to herself as she lined up for the shot.

'Denis Yarwood, you silly boy.' I couldn't believe what was happening as she clicked away, pausing only to relieve an itch on her leg.

'Happy now? Any chance of liberating me?'

Finally she put the camera down on the table and lent over the sink to grab my hands.

'No, that's not helping, you're going to have to lift my legs.'

My middle, which had been bearing my whole body weight, was now throbbing from the sharp metal frame digging into my hipbone and my legs had gone numb. She began to open the back door and nearly fell over laughing.

'What ... what's so funny?'

'The door's on the latch!' She was holding her sides and tears started rolling down her cheeks.

'Do you always attempt the most complicated entry?'

She came outside and lifted my legs as I slithered through the window, crawling over the sink and onto the work surface, knocking a cup off the side and smashing it on the floor. As I stood up and looked down at myself I could see that I had scratch marks all down the front of my body from my chest to my thighs, my legs were shaking and my feet were covered in dirt.

'Tea, Den?'

'Please, you are a darling.'

We sat and chatted and laughed as we drank our tea and warmed up. It was nearly dawn and the excitement of the last hour had worn me out and I needed somewhere comfortable to sleep. Peanuts suggested we went back to her house, so I grabbed my clothes, we left a note of thanks to our hosts and headed home.

I left Peanuts on the day after Boxing Day, once I'd nursed my hangover away and I could function properly; then made my way to Luton to spend the rest of the holiday with Mum and co. New Year was quiet and I did the Duty Uncle thing, taking the kids to the zoo and out for walks before returning to Camp on the first Monday of the New Year, a few pounds heavier around the stomach and a few pounds lighter in the bank.

Chapter Twenty-two

My days seemed to pass from the sublime to the ridiculous; on one side there was the calm and structured life in Camp with its reassuring routine and fairly predictable training. Erstwhile my manic time on leave with Peanuts, living by the seat of my pants and loving every minute of it. I'm not whingeing, I wouldn't have it any other way; the two seemed to balance themselves out nicely. I was reflecting on my holiday as I unpacked my bags and placed my clothes away in my locker when a familiar voice came from outside the door.

'Den, are you in there?'

'Come in, Lofty.'

Before I could enquire him how his leave had been he thrust a photo towards me, nearly hitting me on the nose and far too close to actually focus on.

'Got myself a new bird mate.'

I pulled away and studied the Instamatic photo of a much older woman; she looked to be in her thirties and had two children at her side. To say she was a babe would have been a lie, but she had a curvy figure.

'She's a right dirty cow mate, she let me ...'

'Yeah okay, thanks, but I'd rather not know the details,' but I had little choice as he described in great animation how he'd tonked, as he put it, this latest and rather liberated lass, well – woman. If there were awards for miming, he'd win an Oscar and by the time he'd finished, I felt queasy.

'Right ... great, thanks for that mate. I look forward to meeting her.'

'Not for a couple of weeks Den, she won't be able to walk until then.'

He slapped me hard on my back and without asking how I was, left and walked to his room studying the picture and humming a tune. Welcome back Den, I thought.

On parade the next morning Lance Sergeant Chant told us more of our forthcoming tour, we had been made aware before our leave that the Battalion was going to deploy but not the dates. Now we knew: April until September. It wasn't far away, and some of the married lads began to complain, saying that we'd not long come back from Ireland; however, their protest was soon dismissed.

'Look lads *you* signed the dotted line, so *you* should have explained that when *you* got married.'

It didn't seem too harsh coming from a married man himself and as difficult as it may have seemed for the Pads, as they are known, Lance Sergeant Chant was right. It was part of the job, no more moaning. We would be away in the Balkans all summer; I couldn't see a problem myself.

We were back in training before the week was finished; another round of weapon handling followed by practice at the ranges, which I was getting better at every time. Corporal Tupp gave me the Light Support Weapon as a promotion; it's basically a machine gun on a bipod and can fire about thirty per cent more ammunition than the rest of the section put together, so I was pretty pleased with myself. Our training was different to the Ireland preparation because we would be working in correct infantry sections this time, which are made up of eight men. Dave Tupp, the Corporal leading us and Eddie the Lance Corporal his second in command; the rest of us made up two fire-teams of three men, called Charlie and Delta. I was in Delta Fire-Team with Lofty and Mick. The programme for the next three months was learning to drive the Warrior Armoured vehicle, an awesome piece of equipment that could travel at over fifty miles per hour and fire huge thirty millimetre bullets whilst at full speed. We would be taught how to maintain it during the extreme weather, how to change the tracks that it ran on and how to fire the Raden Cannon. I was seriously up for this tour.

Three weeks into it we ended up in another purpose-built village on the edge of Salisbury Plain. It was a replica of a settlement in Bosnia, and our task was to keep the peace between the warring factions, which actually meant patrolling on foot and in the vehicles again. It seemed familiar, with incidents happening daily, but this time we were not the main target and spent more time in a policing role. To add realism as only the Army can do, an interpreter was assigned on every patrol and their job was to translate and explain what had been said; also to advise the commanders of the likely reactions of the local population. Our battalion's interpreter was Glad. She became involved as an interpreter for the UN forces when the conflict began in Yugoslavia, and was promoted from her post in Bosnia to a more senior advisory job in the UK when it was found necessary to have better knowledge of the resident community. Glad, as she was called due to no one being able to pronounce her given name, and that she was always smiling, was assigned to accompany our patrols and even dressed in Army fatigues, looked amazing and was very popular with the lads. She had picked up on our wit and joked with us about how young we looked. Bosnia must be full of old men, I thought; all the same, she fitted in. Lofty, needless to say, wanted to tonk her as he so descriptively put it. In contrast I was just happy to be in her company and glean as much knowledge from her as possible.

We were given lectures and talks about the Rules of Engagement similar to the policy we had learnt in Ireland about when we could open fire. Every conflict has different rules and every soldier has to be fully aware and recite the law verbatim. We were also given a small handbook which Dave Tupp took pleasure in testing us on at every opportunity. Inside it were road traffic signs, maps, and religious information; and on the back page was a list of useful phrases, translated into English. Dave would read in his best Mediterranean accent from the book and we had to guess the phrase. Most of them were quite useful in the right situation but one puzzled me: *Stavino, mino stanoo?* Translated it meant: Where are the mines buried? Call me Mr Picky, but when in a war zone and faced with the enemy, I wasn't particularly convinced that they would be likely to share that information. And in any case, since the book didn't have the phrase for 'over there you English prat' it didn't seem the most bright thing to ask, or maybe I was just thinking too deeply.

Our mine-clearing lessons added another dimension to the meaning of being unenjoyable and stating the bloody obvious. The instructor from the Royal Engineers showed us various types of mines scattered around the Bosnian hills. I was beginning to wonder if there was anywhere left to stand. He went into graphic detail regarding the sorts of injuries received from standing on a mine and subsequent infections such as gastric gangrene. I thought that the typical procedure was to jump two hundred feet in the air and widely spread 'soldier' over the position. Anyway, he went on to explain a method for clearing a way out of a minefield, and to make matters worse, this bloke sounded exactly like Bill, my first employer.

'Raa' lads, if ye fahn' yeself int' middle o' eur minfield . . . '

Surely I would have been blown up on the way in, I found myself thinking

'Ye 'ev eur gran' skeg roun' ye feet te mek sure theear aren't enny mines ye goin' te step on.' Blimey, this man is a genius! I do love being patronised.

'Next, ye pur ya 'an' daahn an feel aroun' ye feet fa enny funny lumps.'

I think he meant on the ground but I was having visions of someone like Lofty shouting that he'd found a verruca on his foot.

'An once ya'appy 'a' there's nowt nasty daahn theear ye can gerr ya prodda art.'

It was too much, it's not possible to lecture like this and not expect a smart remark.

'We're not going to fuck 'em are we?'

Mick doesn't often come out with one-liners but this was his moment, and the section roared. It took Dave Tupp five minutes to calm us down before the bewildered Corporal could continue. Apparently, the next stage after realising that there is a chance you've stumbled into a minefield (this happens when you actually eyeball a mine) is to stop in your tracks and scan the ground, looking for any obvious earth disturbances and brush your fingers over the surface to ensure there were no other mines around you, in an area big enough to lie down in. Your objective now is to find a clear way back to the last known safe place like a metalled road. So spread your body weight and disturb the topsoil carefully with what's known as a prodder. This is a highly classified piece of equipment used at a 45 degree angle that allows a person to dig around them slowly, feeling any major resistance in the soil, like a jolly great mine. The prodder is a dual use device in plentiful supply that might easily be mistaken for a tent peg.

I was pleasantly surprised when Lofty said that he'd come running with me that night Since the boxing training he'd kept himself fairly fit and we must have covered about eight miles together. I like running on my own; it helps me collect my thoughts, although the company of the big guy made the time pass quickly, and between his laboured breaths we chatted about leave.

'So what's this new girlfriend called, Lofty?'

'Donna.'

I thought I'd keep the questions simple, as he was unlikely to provide more long-winded answers.

'Where did you meet her?'

'Pub.'

'Are those her kids in the picture?'

'Yeah.'

'Have you met them then?'

'Yeah.' I've never known him this muted and thought that we should go running together more often; then he came out with something I hadn't banked on.

'Gonna marry her.'

We were at the Camp gates and I started to walk, giving him time to catch his breath before I grilled him.

'Lofty, how long have you known Donna?'

'Crikey! you sound like my Mum!'

'Well, I thought you only met her on leave so that would mean you've only known her about five weeks.'

'So – she's a good girl, mate and I can't hang around, besides she bangs like a shit house door in the wind.'

That's more like it I thought, good old base Lofty, never a man to judge women on their beauty or companionship. I left it at that, sure that he'd mature out of it or that she'd see sense before it was too late. We showered and changed into tracksuits ready to head for the bar.

We returned to Catterick for the driving phase of our training, taking rotation in commanding and operating the Warrior. It was important that we could do each others' jobs in the event of an emergency. Early Friday morning and we were ready to go out manoeuvring before knocking off for the weekend, I love Fridays, since it's the weekend and I can do my own thing and we normally finished work around mid-day. POETS day, as Mick called it: Piss Off Early, Tomorrow's Saturday. As we prepared the vehicle, Lance Sergeant Chant approached and waved me towards him.

'Go and see the Sergeant Major, Yarwood.'

'Why, Sarge?'

'I don't know, he's just asked for you, best get a wriggle on. He doesn't seem too happy.'

I told Dave where I was going and he said he'd wait for me so I walked across Camp to the Company Offices, slightly confused and worried. There are only a few circumstances where a soldier is summoned to see the Sergeant Major; he runs the discipline in the Company so consequently if I'd been in a punch-up downtown (which I hadn't) I'd see him for a bollocking; or if he wanted me for a company sport (which there wasn't any going on at the moment) he'd be telling me not to lose or I'd get a bollocking. Apart from that I couldn't think of any other grounds to be called.

Outside his office there were four other guys from the Company who I'd met briefly on courses. We were barked at to enter one at a time while he took details, number, name and initials and were then made to wait outside Major Bell's, the Officer Commanding room. I was terrified, it was the first time since the boxing I'd had to face the OC and that was for congratulations, even though I lost.

One by one the boys were marched in at quick time and I could hear the Sergeant Major shouting commands as they marched in and halted, then marched out and away from me up the corridor to a conference room at the end.

'YARWOOD!'

I jumped to attention and followed his commands until within seconds I was stood bolt upright and shaking in front of the boss.

'Private Yarwood, do you know why I have asked to see you this morning?'

'No sir.' My throat had dried and was croaky.

'Well it's my duty to inform you that you are incorrectly dressed.'

He looked at me for a reaction but the statement left me expressionless. Since training I'd worked hard on my kit and never been picked up for being scruffy. I felt confused and angry that the Officer Commanding should bother about something so trivial; Dave Tupp could have dealt with this sort of business.

'What have you got to say for yourself then?'

'Erm ... Sir ... I ... don't really ...'

A grin spread across his face and he stood up with his arm outstretched to shake my hand.

'Yarwood, you have been promoted to Lance Corporal. Congratulations!'

I took his hand and let him lead the shake, my arm useless with the shock. They have promoted me, and I'm as good as Eddie. Cor blimey!

'All right Corporal Yarwood, leave the OC alone, he doesn't want to kiss you.'

As soon as the Sergeant Major brought me back to reality, I let my grip release.

'March him out Company Sergeant Major please.'

I was moved at speed down to where the other guys were sitting, chatting and slapping each other on the back.

'Right, my turn.' The Sergeant Major's statement stopped all the conversation.

'Now, you boys have been selected by whatever reason to lead men. This is the hardest promotion to gain ... and the easiest to lose. Mess up once with a stripe on your arm gentlemen and I'll take it off you. Set an example for me and to the rest and you'll be all right. You get a pay rise with this so take the responsibility seriously and use the power that comes with it sensibly and fairly, be consistent and the lads will follow you, weakness will lead to disarray and lack of respect. Lead from the front and have the moral courage to make unpopular decisions. And finally, be in the

Company bar at two this afternoon. The beers are on you lot, got it?'

I wandered back across the square still bemused that I was actually good enough to gain promotion. I had thought about it when I was on the cadre but didn't imagine it would lead to anything. I was going to be the second in command of a section, telling men what to do and give them advice; I started to wonder if I was really up for this. Dave Tupp had been forewarned and slapped my back as I arrived back, saying it was 'bloody well deserved' and was joined by the rest of the lads. Ideas of what I was going to do swished around my head, mixed with partial elation, pride and slight doubt. I wouldn't know until I did the job if I was that man. I looked at Eddie as he taught the other lads about the gun on the Warrior Vehicle and tried to see myself in his task; he looked different now. I'd proved that I could teach, but never done it for real, I mean real stuff like returning fire; I'd just been the good guy who got most things right and didn't make dumb mistakes. It was going to be my advice and guidance they'd be listening to now ... Holy Joe.

The morning flew by, so by the time we arrived back in Camp I'd not managed to get to the bank. The Company bar is an old store that used to house spare parts for vehicles and smelt oily. We had arranged some plastic chairs and painted the walls; it only had one window, two six-foot tables covered in Union flags and that was the bar. Ron, one of the lads from 3 Platoon, was appointed the barman because his dad ran a pub; a bit tenuous I thought as he'd told me that he'd never been behind the bar before. Calling him barman is a play on words because all we sold were tins of bitter and lager, no wines or spirit, crisps, nuts or anything else actually, so he was more of a guy who opened cans. The whole Company seemed to be crammed into the place by the time we arrived and a cheer went up as I was thrust towards the bar by Lofty.

'Come on Corporal Yarwood, get 'em in,' Lance Sergeant Chant shouted at me.

'Lofty, I need a favour mate,' He looked at me and pulled his wallet out, pre-empting my request.

'How much?'

'Twenty should do it for now, thanks.'

He opened a can and was sucking the contents out as if it were the last beer he'd ever have. I handed the money straight over to Ron who winked at me and gave me a can of bitter. As the sun went down Lance Sergeant Chant told us to get changed and meet him at the guardroom in ten minutes, as he'd been given a leave pass from his wife, which I assume meant that he didn't get out much. I'd never seen him downtown before. It was turning out to be a cracking night.

The Colburn Inn's staff were running around like headless chickens as the lads piled in. I'd managed to get some money on the way down and once Lofty had paid for his first round I gave him his money back.

'About bloody time.'

Always the grateful one I thought, as I sipped my pint. Lance Sergeant Chant was by this stage swaying as he hung onto the bar, lecturing the lads on his career.

'Blimey Lofty, is he scrounging money already? Bit of a cheek on his wages, mind you, it could have been you if you'd been up for the course.'

The hair on the back of my neck stood up.

'What? Who the fuck told you that then?'

Lofty had slammed his pint on the counter, spilling the contents. My face must have told him the whole story without me having to mutter a word. Lance Sergeant Chant glanced at me, confirming that it was me who'd betrayed him. Two years' friendship flushed down the pan and I hit the floor as his fist connected with my chin. Before anyone could stop him he was on top of me and landed two more punches in quick succession, one square in my mouth and one on my forehead.

'You bastard Den,' he screamed as arms wrapped around him and dragged him to the door.

I lay there bleeding while the lads looked on in disbelief at what must have seemed the two closest guys in the Company battle. I deserved that, he trusted me and I him. It wouldn't ever be the same between us, other than I was still a Lance Corporal.

Chapter Twenty-three

Lance Sergeant Chant is a decent man. He could have reported Lofty and me for the scuffle; but instead, the following Monday, I was moved to a different section, which meant I was still in the same Platoon but I wouldn't have to work with Lofty directly. I think that Lance Sergeant Chant may have reasoned this solution out of his own guilt, because it was his blabbing after a few beers had brought the situation to a head; anyway, it was arranged now. This left me to concentrate on the job; we were going back to Salisbury for further patrol training and a final test exercise to make certain all of the drills were correct.

I went out on foot patrol with my new section. I was second in command under a guy called Decker, a Corporal with a fierce reputation for mullering anyone who didn't do as he said. Glad, the interpreter, came along and we chatted as the patrol moved from house to house, checking to see if the locals had seen any militia in the area. My mind kept drifting back to the fight in the pub and I must have seemed distracted.

'Your mouth is sore, yes?' Glad was walking beside me with her hand stuffed in her pockets, looking concerned.

'No, not really, its fine, thanks.'

I wasn't in the mood to talk, and was more curious about where we were going and what the place was going to be like. She had told me that she was from a small town called Prozor on the edge of a lake. Her family owned a butchers shop there until the war started. Her mother became ill after having her fourth child so they decided to move into a relative's house in the port city of Split. That's where she became involved with the UN. One of the officers who patrolled in her area had picked up her ability and asked her to become his interpreter. I'm sure it doesn't happen that easily and there is more red tape but that's the way she recounted it. She sent some of her wages home to her family; nevertheless, she liked England and her life with the Army, and meeting new people. I think it gave her a sense of importance and the feeling that she was helping in some way with the crisis.

'But you have a big bruise Denis, I hear about your fight.'

'What? Oh, that ... never mind, eh. I'm not going to let my tea go cold over it.'

She laughed and asked me what I had meant, so I tried to explain that I'd heard it somewhere before and we left it at that. The days drifted by and I settled in with my new section; Decker seemed content and if that was good enough to stop me getting another slap, I was happy. Glad had relayed a very good picture of the tour and what I was to expect. She'd told me that I must go and see Prozor Lake as it was the most beautiful lake in the world, and a statue of Tito's Fist, a defiant structure on a mountaintop signifying his rule. I said that I would try but in reality couldn't see us going on cultural days out.

I packed my possessions and put them into the stores for safekeeping; then I wrote to everyone to give them my new address. I'd received two cards congratulating me on my promotion: a home-made one from Peanuts, which I thought was cool, and Mum's card said 'Well Done on becoming a Lance Colonel!' I need to speak more clearly on the phone, I thought. After doing a tour away from Camp before, the routine was quite simple. After our training has finished, we would have a drinking session, then a couple of days' leave and then divide our belongings between the stores or to be taken on tour. I felt sad that I could fit my worldly possessions into a box, but hey, I only had to clothe myself well enough to pull.

After being in the air for a couple of hours the last thing I needed was to sit on the back of a rickety Army truck that leaked for ten more hours along meandering half-built road. But that's what I did, along with the rest of our Platoon. We arrived at Vites Camp in the dark, tired, confused and very bashed about from the journey, only to find that my torture wasn't over yet since we were made to sleep on the gymnasium floor for the night.

The Camp was an old school that had been commandeered by the British that year; it was bombed and nearly falling down in places. Some of the better classrooms on the ground floor were now offices and on the first floor became living accommodation. We ate in the school canteen, and the gym was supposed to be left clear for those who wanted to do physical exercise but was mainly used to bed down transiting troops. Around the outside of the building, the Royal Engineers had erected a blast- proof wall of old shipping containers filled with aggregate, and shelters dug into the ground in case of a mortar attack. Due to the lack of roads and parking spaces, all of the Warrior vehicles were parked on the playing field, which was now a quagmire as it rained most of the time and made going to work a hazard. One wrong step and you were covered in mud for the day. Every piece of redundant space had been used to erect Portacabins for other agencies, such as UNHCR (United Nations High Command for Refugees), and their Land Rovers littered the roads, badly parked. I saw a BBC vehicle on the first morning parked by the guardroom with aerials poking out from the roof and wondered if I'd get my face on the telly. Mum would love that.

As we took over from the outgoing troops I realised that this was going to be a much more intense tour than Ireland. I had been told of our lads seeing quite a bit of fighting between warring factions and having to open fire on more than one occasion. The guys who were going home looked tired and in some ways older than their years. Their kit was dishevelled and manky and I felt an enormous sense of pride in relieving them of their duties.

When an outgoing unit exits, sometimes they dress or paint one of the vehicles as a leaving present but not this time; these lads were just relieved to be getting out of there. The last of their trucks rolled out of the Camp a week after we had arrived for their long trip home with exhausted smiles and shouts of 'Have a good one!'

So the routine started, and I was appointed the commander of one of two Warriors who would patrol together. Decker was in the first vehicle with his three lads and I in the second with Tom, who drove, Ian the gunner, and Jack, who alternated between the two as a relief when we were on long patrols. Jack wasn't his real name; his surname was Frost. Yeah, very original. They seemed like good blokes and we got on well; not as close as my previous comrades but we had time as we would be stuck in these vehicles for the best part of six months. Our main job was to patrol around Vites ensuring that the front line between the two sides wasn't moving. There had been a stalemate and that's how the UN wanted to keep it until they could stabilise the country, so the factions had dug into defensive positions and took random pot shots at each other. From time to time, one side would mount a futile offensive that would be abandoned after losing a few men and things calmed down again for a week; that's where we would try and step in to calm the situation. It sounded simple but I was quick to learn that when the troops came to the front line, not only did they bring enough ammo and food to sustain them; they also packed enough Slivenedich a local potato whisky, and amphetamines, stolen from chemists to keep them high as kites and drunk for their stay. This explained the rather disastrous attacks on each other and their aggressive nature when we tipped up. Another of our jobs was to watch for any signs of ethnic cleansing; I'd never heard of it before. Any burning houses had to be investigated or families of refugees that suddenly emerged and began walking down the road carrying their life's possessions. The more I learnt the less I liked the situation.

Letters began arriving that boosted my morale no end; two from Peanuts, one from Mum, one from Marc, which was a surprise, and then came one that I didn't recognise. The handwriting was beautiful and had a postmark from Guildford.

Dear Denis,

I hope this find you well and settled into my beautiful country. I got your address from the Quartermaster.

I am working now in Aldershot, I don't like it so much; the soldiers are vulgar and asking for a drink. You are nice during our time together in Salisbury, I enjoyed our discussion, you make me smile and feel welcome.

I hope that you write back to me Denis I would like to hear from you and please tell me how you like my homeland? May be I come back one day? Who knows? Take care please Denis.

With my love

Segmedina Dizdarevic (Glad)

Wow! ... a letter from Glad ... I was glad too!

The next day I witnessed something I'd rather not have seen. We had been patrolling around the town for a couple of hours and all was quiet as it had been for a few days. The front-line troops were about to change over, which meant sitting and watching rickety buses full of drunken troops drive away, and then the same bus return with other men in an equally intoxicated state but slightly dirtier, pass back. It was going smoothly; we took the usual abuse and a few bottles were thrown at us, but nothing unusual. Then we moved back to Camp and traversed along a hillside road that was cut into the face of the rise, so we doubled back on ourselves every few hundred metres. I stood out of a hatch in the top of the vehicle to keep look out and get some fresh air, and as I took in the terrain I could see a car in front of us swerving along the track. At the next bend it pulled over and two men got out, shouting and waving hands at each other. I couldn't hear what they were saying, as we were about fifty metres away but as we approached the argument quickly transformed into a punch-up. The stockier of the two men, who had got out of the driver's side, ran around the bonnet of the car and punched his taller and skinnier passenger, sending him reeling backwards onto the ground. They were both dressed in what looked like military officers uniforms; well, they were smarter than the normal soldiers and wore hats which led me to that, and they seemed to be travelling alone. The downed man rubbed his chin as the fat guy turned and casually walked back around the car; but the downed man wasn't finished fighting. From his waist belt a pistol appeared and he stretched out his arm to take aim from his position on the ground. The driver, unaware of the gun, turned to give more abuse but the words never left his mouth. As the gun recoiled, the driver jerked back on his feet, taking the shot and looked panicked as he glanced down at the entry point in his chest. We gained speed as the man on the ground stood and took aim for a second time. This time the wounded man's head exploded with the impact of the bullet as it tore his skull open, spilling brains and blood in every direction. He fell where he stood. Our vehicle was now only ten metres away and I could see the full devastation of the situation. My gaze was transfixed onto the dead man, his life spreading into a pool around him. The car pulled away, not at speed but quite casually, as if it had just dropped someone at their house, except it hadn't – a man had been murdered right there.

Tom, the driver of our Warrior, the lead vehicle of two, had stopped just short of the corpse, and Decker had drawn up behind us. He was out before me and ran to the body, stopping as he reached it and looking down at the mess.

'Get on the radio Den,' he shouted as he knelt down to inspect the man to see if there was a scrap of life left.

'Shouldn't we go after the other guy?' I was confused and saddened; it was so final and just there in the dirt of a shitty Bosnian roadside.

'Just get on the radio and get an ambulance up here now,' his voice was sharp and direct.

What was the point of getting an ambulance? The guy was dead, but how could we catch the killer? He could easily outrun the Warrior on these roads. Decker shouted again at my lack of response.

'Yarwood, get on that fucking radio, get an ambulance and tell them you need a road block in town to stop the car.'

Of course, yes – a roadblock. I sent the message back to headquarters.

'Hello, Oscar one one, send a description of the car…over,' was the reply I received almost instantly.

'Hello Zero, I'm not sure, a small car, maybe a Peugeot, red I think…over.'

This was poor; I couldn't even remember what colour it was. My credibility was going down the pan fast.

'Oscar one one, I need more information … over.'

I haven't got any more information; what do you want me to say? It had four wheels and a murderer inside; I don't want to be here.

'Zero, no more information on the car, red Peugeot, one occupant, travelling towards town…over.'

We waited by the dead man with our radio buzzing messages about cars and suspects but it was futile. A while later an ambulance arrived under escort from another two Warriors, one carrying the OC and Sergeant Major. I stayed away from the crowd of soldiers rumour-mongering on the incident as the bosses asked

Decker questions and took notes. It was a lovely day and the sun beamed down on my face with a slight breeze, drying the sweat that ran down from under my helmet onto my face. As I looked around I could see a woman walking up the hill herding a single cow with a long stick. The cow seemed to know where it was going and didn't protest at the continual prodding on its hind by the old lady. Her head was down as she walked; I imagined that this was her daily routine to take the cow for grazing into the meadow. What an uncomplicated and enviable life. She crossed to the opposite side as she approached, not bothering to look up at the fracas on my side of the road.

'Dobra dan,' I said, nodding to her as she glanced over to where I stood. It means 'Good day' and she strained a toothless smile and replied with a dip of her head before continuing on her journey. It was completely surreal. Only feet away from a dead body the world had already moved on.

As soon as I had cleaned my rifle for the day and made myself a brew I sat on my bed and took out my writing kit. That could have been me lying in the road this afternoon, no farewell to my friends or family, only the account of another explaining how I'd lost my life. I was going to write my death letters.

Chapter Twenty-four

Coincidences unnerve me; they have done since I first learned what they were. So a week later, when a letter arrived from Peanuts asking after Tony I had goosebumps. She didn't sound like she was particularly interested in getting back together with him; it was just a general enquiry after his well-being, but as I'd been chatting to him for the first time in ages the day before in the medical centre it was one of those freaky moments.

I'd felt a verruca on the ball of my foot for a day or so; it didn't hurt at first but after wearing boots constantly it soon became sore and difficult to walk on. I thought I'd probably picked it up from one of the lazy buggers who hadn't brought any flip-flops with them on the tour and had been walking around the showers barefoot. Whatever the cause, it really hurt, so I took myself to see the Army Doctor. Tony was next to me in the queue and we exchanged pleasantries as we waited; though he didn't ask about Peanuts, I remember now. He worked in 'A' Company with Topple and heard about the fighting during riot training all that time ago. It was amazing how gossip went around the Battalion, and the story had developed from Lofty and Topple having a clash into something near attempted murder. Very amusing.

Anyway, I went in to see the doctor before him, expecting to be greeted by a grumpy old Colonel; but instead found myself staring open- mouthed at a tall, photogenic, brunette Captain who smiled as I sat down and looked at me over her half glasses. She was charming and friendly; she was the first woman I'd seen in a couple of months with all of her own teeth! As I came out of the treatment room, much happier and visually stimulated, I wandered over to Tony who had his head buried in a copy of National Geographic. Well, you'll read any old rubbish if you haven't seen a copy of the Sun for long enough.

'You're next mate, what are you going in for?'

'My knee, I whacked it getting out of the Warrior yesterday and it's come up like a melon.'

'Well take my advice Tony and tell her you're having problems with your old fella as well, you won't be disappointed.'

He looked at me quizzically as he stood up.

'Den, what room are you in? We should catch up some time.'

'Top floor room ten, I'm in the bed space on the right, yeah ... that would be good.'

I left him to keep his appointment, happy that we would catch up later. It hadn't been that we were avoiding each other; our paths just hadn't crossed. Since moving sections I didn't have a mate; Decker was a loner, which the guys said was subtly connected to him going to attend SAS selection later in the year, and the other lads looked at me as the Lance Corporal in charge so held their distance. They must have been waiting to get to know me, I suppose. My second letter of the week came from Glad, by return of post; it was much longer this time, telling me about her family and how she thinks I would like them. I thought that strange as I don't think I'd ever meet them.

Tony came and saw me the night after we had been in the medical centre together. He sat on my bed and we talked about our time in the Battalion. I think he was jealous of me getting promotion, though he didn't say it directly but kept referring to my pay rise.

'I'd give the doctor one, wouldn't you Tony?'

I changed the subject as there is only a certain amount of military talk I can sustain before Regimental rigor mortis sets in. Sex seemed to be an appropriate subject, as no one was getting any; it's strange how males in a pack think when they are deprived of a basic human need. Most of the lads had a girlfriend or wife waiting back at home but even the raunchiest of letters couldn't replace the fulfilment of a physical act with a woman. By the second month, the girls back home must have been feeling flirtatious, as the letters that had been pinned on the notice- board were getting decidedly more adventurous and descriptive.

There was a competition in 3 Platoon to see who could get various items of clothing sent through the post; it started with one of the lads receiving a pair of knickers from his girlfriend in a parcel; then a bra appeared and a pair of stockings. Two weeks later the notice-board in 3 Platoon's lines was looking like a Chinese laundry. One girl had even sent a shoe – sick. Porn magazines had become currency; I could swap a decent European monthly for two hundred fags. A British magazine, being tamer, only fetched a packet of twenty but a decent collection of readers' wives would bring untold wealth. The readers' wives publications became extremely popular; it was a fascination; were these women real? They weren't models getting in the buff for cash. I wondered if women like that really existed or it was a cruel trick. Could I find a girl who would fulfil my every smutty fantasy? The dream kept me going and I'd lie in bed at night visualizing a chick that would strip for me on request. The dreams became more vivid as time went on and the Army doctor appeared in them from time to time. It transpired that I wasn't the only one with a healthy interest in her.

A couple of weeks later I attended sick parade again to get my feet checked by the lovely senior medical officer. My verruca had cleared up and I was disappointed that I wouldn't be going back. Having said that, I have never been one for whingeing about minor ailments, and in the Battalion there were a few lads who were looked on as malingerers; any excuse getting a sick note and skiving off a run or some hard work. I didn't want to fall into that category.

When I arrived, the medical orderly told me I'd have to wait, as she was busy with another patient. so I took a seat in the waiting room and read yet another letter from Glad that had arrived that morning. She was a voracious writer and though I was happy to receive mail, the content of her letters seemed to be getting more personal every time. In this one she said that she missed me and when I came back to England she would like to go for a drink and catch up! I'd already told her my news and she wrote back in great detail about her every waking hour. I'd sussed that she fancied me; I was flattered with the attention; clearly, she was a woman of taste. The door opened after I had finished her letter and the patient walked out fixing his uniform and putting his beret back onto his head as he walked past me.

'Hi Tony! I didn't expect to see you back here; I hope you're not turning into a sickie.' (The term used for malingerers.) He looked flustered at seeing me and I felt awkward about the adverse comment.

'Er ... hi Den, no ... just getting my arm checked.' He rubbed his elbow as he spoke and gave me a tight-lipped smile. I thought it was his leg?

The Bosnian summer faded into a harsh autumn with winds that buffeted against the buildings and rain like I'd never seen before, lashing down and turning the playing field where we parked our vehicles into a small muddy lake. Getting to and from work got more challenging by the day. We'd park in different positions around drier parts of the field and find a way through the mire to the accommodation, only to find that in the morning we were forced to wade back through a foot of mud. Tony and I had visited each other on regular occasions when we weren't working and I'd shown him the now daily letters from Glad. Peanuts had said 'hi' by post to him, after I told her that we were talking. My main concern was Glad's letters; well, the constant

213

compliments and longing. As each one arrived I got more anxious, thinking that any more encouragement and she'd never go away. Sports pages started to come through and the basic quick snog on return had progressed to afternoons spent in cornfields writhing around in ecstasy with yours truly. I had a stalker. The decision was made, with Tony, to stop writing; not that I was going to get any prizes for literature as I'd only managed to return four of her letters, but nevertheless I had to stop egging her on and thinking that *I* was going to be a *We* on my return from the tour. We had discussed a letter from Tony telling her that I'd been horribly killed in a surprise attack but she was employed by the military and would hear that I was faking; so no smoke screen, no more letters was the way ahead.

One of my new duties in my section was to file a post patrol report to the Operations room, every time we came in from our tour of the city. I would wait until Decker had written up the report, which was made up of our route, sightings of troops and any unusual occurrences, and then hand it in to the radio room to be sent later to the Ops Officer who would log it down. We came in just before lunch, having started patrolling at four in the morning. Nothing significant had happened; we had escorted the logistic convoy through the town and seen a couple of T-55 tanks, so the report only took an hour to complete. As I walked into headquarters I could see a row of people lined up next to the Sergeant Major's office; the OC's voice was reverberating through his office door, and he sounded fierce. As my destination was past the people stood in line, I thought I'd have a quick nosey at what was going on and listen to whoever was being tornoff a strip by the boss. There was Tony, not in the office, but stood outside with his head down; next to him was one of the Regimental Police Staff, a Corporal whose job it was to lock any offenders in the makeshift gaol. We'd had no bad boys during the tour so far, mainly because of the lack of alcohol, so he was probably feeling redundant. The OC's door flew open and the tasty doctor came running out, wiping tears from her face. Tony's hand came up to stop her as she passed but was brushed away by the RP Corporal, and she carried on, pushing past me, now in floods of tears.

'All right Tony? What's occurring mate, she botched up your arm?'

I assumed that the doc had been given a ticking off for keeping one of our troops away from the patrol programme for too long, or had been taken for a ride by Tony who was maybe posing as a malingerer; he *had* been spending a lot of time in the medical centre. Before I could get a reply the CSM's booming voice summonsed him into the office and the corridor was empty again.

I handed in my report and went to eat my dinner; I sat with my section, tucking in to pie and chips. Decker had an audience and seemed to be telling a joke, as every time he stopped the lads would laugh.

'The report is in, Decks.'

I sat next to him and ate my lunch; he always wanted to know that the reports had made their way safely to Ops or he'd be in trouble himself.

'Your mate Den, the one that comes to see you, Tony something ... '

'Yeah, I've just seen him outside the CSM's office, what's that all about?'

As I said, news travels fast around the Battalion so I wasn't surprised that someone would know what was going on.

'He's only been caught giving the doctor one, red-handed by the Padre.'

Laughter started around the table as Decker explained that the Padre, who was having a casual look around the medical centre, a good place for a chat sometimes, blundered into the treatment room, only to find young Tony, giving the doctor an injection of his own!

'Lucky bastard,' he exclaimed, just before shovelling a huge forkful of chips into his mouth.

Blimey, I didn't know he had it in him. I sat and pondered the circumstances back in my room as I disassembled my rifle for its daily scrub. There's me thinking that he was throwing a sickie when he was actually throwing a length into the doc, the lovely polite, university- educated doctor. Same old fantasy about nurses and doctors was forming; I'd always wanted to have a posh bird or an officer; sex knows no bounds. You're either attracted to someone or you're not, regardless of class or status. Four or five years at medical school on Daddy's money but one sniff of a bit of rough and knickers fall, it's as simple as that. Good old Tony, I wondered what would happen to him? I wondered if, given the chance, I'd do the same? I was at present surviving by way of self-manipulation, if you know what I mean. I would prefer the feel of feminine softness next to me; trying to cuddle my own hand just isn't the same. There's absolutely no romance whatsoever in cubicle two of the toilets on my own, my company being a well-thumbed porn mag and a roll of tissue. It keeps me sane, I suppose. I went to see Tony for an explanation.

'A' Company's lines were buzzing with the scandal and Tony was nowhere to be seen. One of his mates told me that he'd been shipped back to face disciplinary action and the doctor had got the sack from the General Officer Commanding for abusing her rank. I wish she'd have abused me.

So Tony was a celebrity in the Battalion and will always be known as the one who dicked the doc on tour and broke the monotony. He wasn't disciplined as such when he was sent back, just put on the guard shift. It was overkill in my books to charge a guy for doing what comes naturally.

We were going home in a couple of months and, as had happened in Ireland, the next unit sent representatives over for a look at the place; they were indeed a sight for sore eyes. The ploy of not writing to Glad had paid off as well; I hadn't had a letter for days from her. Peanuts and I had loosely arranged to meet up while I was on leave; she was going back to Luton for a while and gave me her mum's phone number. Right now I could do with taking her out and getting completely plastered. Living, eating, and breathing Army for six months was a necessity and I got well paid for it, but I now understood why the last lot of blokes left with such a relieved look on their faces. Every morning I'd look at myself in the mirror and inspect my face for tell tale-aging lines; it would be a travesty to age such a handsome face, I thought.

Decker handed me his patrol report and asked if I wanted a brew after it had been delivered. We had a well-established routine now and I had the feeling that he had begun to trust me. I said yes, and made my way to the radio room. The other lads had some maintenance work to do on the vehicle, as it took a bashing every time we ventured out, so I'd told them that I would do an inspection on my return from Ops. It wasn't uncommon to see strange new faces in and around Company headquarters from time to time; visitors from other units and agencies that we supported would come and ask us questions. Sometimes an officer would be visiting with a wide-eyed bunch of press reporters who would want to know how the unit was faring in such terrible conditions. They would be from local papers; the Luton Herald & Post newspaper guy came over to chat to lads from the town. It must have been the first time he'd been away from home as his personal administration was awful; it made me feel like a veteran, living away and coping with change, as after only two days he had developed an odour and a rather scruffy beard. Our section had to look after him, which Decker wasn't exactly chuffed about, so we tossed a coin to see which Warrior he *wouldn't* travel in. I won after going from the best of three to the best of nine and so on, until the game was completely futile and Decks gave in. Steve, or Stig as we renamed him because he smelt so bad, was like a schoolboy being shown around a toy factory; frustrated wannabe or a bloke who always had dreams of joining up but never found the grit but now was his chance to go home and tell his mates in the pub about his bravery in Bosnia. He wasn't a bad bloke, but I can see him in my mind's eye, perched on the edge of the girl he could never pull's desk, wooing her with his anecdotes of war-torn Vites and the danger he faced; then walking off with an unusual swagger in his step and her gazing at him with adoring eyes thinking he was Rambo ... pathetic. Stig lasted just under twenty-four hours with Decks; the CSM caught him giving the young reporter a fatherly chat behind the vehicle lines that went something like this:

Decks: 'Steve, your personal admin leaves a lot to be desired.'

Stig: 'Can I have a go on the gun please Decks?'

Decks: 'Steve, you're not listening, you can have a go on the gun when you have had a go in the shower.'

Stig: 'Yeah sure later, but if I could get a picture of you and the lads by the gun with you pointing to that house ...'

Decks: 'Look there's no nice way of putting this ...'

Stig: (now talking to the lads like he's in charge) Right men let's have you here, and you stand over here, take your helmet off ...'

Decks: (now with his hand grasped firmly around Steve's shirt collar) You smell so bad your shit is glad to escape, go and get a shower before I ...'

CSM: 'Corporal Bright, please put Steve down, he's got to catch his plane home tonight and we don't need to be sending him back injured now do we?'

Decker released Steve and that was the last we saw of him. I just pitied whoever had to sit next to him on the plane.

So I was back in the Ops room, report in hand and waiting for someone to take it from me, normally without so much as a hello. I considered most of the guys who worked in there as prima donnas, not wanting to get their hands dirty but taking the credit for making everything go smoothly. I'd have loved to take some of them out to see what we had to face one day. I was looking down reading my notebook whilst waiting for one of the rushed-off-their-feet-*not* staff to see to me. A hand reached out from across the desk. Just as I lent forward to offer the report I saw that the hand had beautifully painted and manicured fingernails, slender and clean, and then came the voice.

'Hello Denis, I come to see you.'

I was bolted to the spot as I looked up and met Glad's gaze; she was beaming from ear to ear. She continued,

'Well actually I have to come to see the intelligence officer but now I'm thinking I come and do business and pleasure.'

She had my hand in hers now, stroking it. I needed someone else to interrupt so I could make good my escape but there wasn't a soul around. This had to stop quickly; the woman had come over to trap me. This was my entire fault; I shouldn't have encouraged her by returning her letters. Now what do I do? I'm stood there as gormless as you like, trying to think of a way out. Okay – my options are: telling her to go away, I never want to see her again; arranging to meet her on my return and not following it through; or just saying to hell with it and giving her one, it would sort my frustration out in the short term but would probably have a few repercussions, like marriage.

'Denis, are you all right, you look as white as the sheet?'

She had her head tilted slightly and one eye closed, she smelt divine; her bright red lips framed that knowing smile. Do it Den, get rid of her, the voice rang out in my head; no Den, just give it a go and to hell with it. I don't think I'd ever had an argument with my conscience before and I couldn't figure out if I was going to win or lose. In fact I couldn't work out which one was right or wrong, or either was right or ... oh, this is tricky. If she could come to see me in Bosnia, where else would she be prepared to hunt me down? We stood staring at each other, hand in hand, though not voluntarily on my part, and she looked and waited for an answer.

'I am here for two weeks Denis, that is good, yes?'

Stop asking me questions and go away you crazy woman, just leave me to my porn mags and cubicle two. Grit my teeth and smile.

'Glad ... we need to talk.' Oh Den, I've heard that so many times on the telly.

'Good, I miss our discussions, how do you like my country?'

'No Glad, not like that, about us.' I can't say that I was handling this particularly well; it sounded like I was talking about us as a couple already.

'Ok that's good, I thought you would, we need to arrange when you come back to England.'

'No Glad, we don't, in fact we're not meeting when I go back. The thing is, I do like you, your letters were great but I think you might have read me wrong, I, er, don't want a girlfriend Glad, though you are very agreeable and if I were to want a girlfriend then I might, well, you know, ask you out, but I don't at the moment, so I'm sorry Glad. Look this isn't a good time for me, my, er, mum is ill and I need to go home to look after her and I have this sort of, well, disease, you know, downstairs so you might not want to see me again.'

Lies upon lies spewed out of my mouth as I tried in desperation to dump this woman. I felt her hand withdraw and looked up expecting to see tears streaming down her face.

'Denis, it's okay, I know you are tired, I'll see you later.'

She smiled again and disappeared into the Ops room, from where one of the staff came out and snatched the patrol report out of my hand. I was dumbfounded; not only had I told her that I didn't want to see her again, quite clearly, I had made up some cock and bull story about my mum and VD. She wasn't having any of it; in fact the tone in her voice made me think she felt sorry for me. Within a minute I'd rushed around to the OC's office and without thinking rapped my knuckles on the wood.

'Come.'

How did I get myself into this? No one is going to believe me. I marched smartly up to the desk and saluted the boss.

'Ah, Corporal Yarwood, what can I do for you?' He was reading through some papers as I'd approached but he put them down and sipped a cup of coffee.

'Sir, I'm in trouble and I don't know who else to go to.'

'Can't your Platoon Sergeant be of assistance? You should go to him first.'

I knew that, but Lance Sergeant Chant would probably laugh and tell me to sort it out myself, so I needed the boss to deal with this. I relayed the whole story from the first letter to the meeting in the Ops room moments earlier in about ten seconds, pausing only to catch my breath. He smiled and sat back in his chair.

'So it's you this time is it?'

'Pardon Sir?' I didn't understand the response.

'Well she was pursuing one of the Officers from the last unit, so you're not alone, young man. I'll have a word.'

'Yeah, I mean yes please Sir.' The relief flooded over me.

'She's only after a British passport you know, I'll tell her to leave you alone.'

He picked his papers up, shuffled them on the desk and carried on reading.

'Thanks.'

I saluted again, without a response and marched out. Old Dart was home and more than ever before I wanted to be there among familiar faces with a cold pint. Was it just me or was life getting more complicated?

Chapter Twenty-five

Oh my God I've got wrinkles; well, crows' feet. It must be a warning. I don't feel old, but things are different now; time moves on and so have I. For instance, there's a guy that I've known for years called Glyn, who I went to junior school with and he's getting married. Even though I've had nothing to do with him since I was about fourteen, Mum keeps in touch with his parents and she's been given an invite to his wedding and she has asked me to go with her. I've not regretted much I've done in my life and I've made some rash decisions and suffered the consequences along the way but the past couple of years have been a cosmic leap to the man I am now. I don't have any responsibility for anyone, only the guys in my section. I've got some money in the bank, a passport and friends but when I think of Glyn getting hitched I wonder that he might be a bit hasty? I don't feel that old.

In the years before I joined the Army, I thought it was all mapped out for me, bumming around playing snooker, drinking and smoking., getting an occasional job for a few quid, wheeling and dealing, leading to a couple of kids maybe, living on an estate where everybody knows everyone else's business. It might not have turned out like that I suppose, when I think of Marc and his family settled in suburbia, looking at chances of promotion, for more money and a bigger mortgage ...

Anyway, it never stops, I know that; but I can tell that things are different now. For a case in point: I look at the charts and I feel uptodate if I recognise two artists in the top ten. You can't count Phil Collins or Cliff because they are a part of our heritage and will always have a place in British music – though not in my collections, may I add. I don't understand the rap stuff either. Where did Pink Floyd and the Police go? Another thing: my car insurance premium has gone down; I've reached an age where I'm grown up and sensible, allegedly. I might think like a twenty-something delinquent and drive as recklessly as I did when I was nineteen. Does that mean that the policy gets progressively cheaper until it's free? By the time I'm ninety and dementia has kicked in, I'll be able to drive around, bashing into everyone without a care in the world. Isn't there a regulation ensuring that OAPs drive slowly on country roads delaying the twenty-something delinquents? There's a secret pact between semi-senile drivers and farmers; they convey messages on their ear-pieces, informing each other where the roads are clear, and then they slow it down to ten miles per hour. The farmers' tactic is to turn into a field, lulling the unsuspecting and frustrated driver into a mad dash, only to be met a few miles down the road by the elderly roadblock, chuckling to themselves. Goodness – I sound like an old git. And why is being politically correct such a virtue? Calling a spade a spade will land me in court. I'm not a racist, sexist or whatever label-ist but I am reminded that some comments are just not PC. So when do I get a bit of this PC protection? I can't tell jokes about the Englishman, Scotsman and Irishman, jam labels are different, and the fear of offending anyone rules. Well, I'm offended by PC-ism, so stick that in the pipe and smoke it! Perhaps I am changing. I didn't wake up one morning thinking I should grow up; but I have. The incidents in Ireland and Bosnia have made me see the world differently.

I see lots of guys leaving the service as a consequence of their girlfriends or wives demanding that they get a job that doesn't take them away from home. Why do they do that? What kind of person are they? I love my work. When I saw those soldiers on the motorbikes, the prospects of travel and adventure was the pull. I'm not trying to look back on my original motives for signing on the dotted line with rose coloured spectacles, but why would a man leave for domesticity? I bet the cavemen didn't have the pressure of gaining employment closer to home, with Mrs Cavewoman saying that slaying ferocious dinosaurs may put food on the table but inventing the wheel would ensure that he came home every night fully limbed.

The job is fun and rewarding; even though only a few people understand the lifestyle nowadays, that doesn't mean it's out-dated. Mum is proud of me; she has one son in the British Army and one in the Police. It must be quite a coup at coffee mornings and I'm not going to burst her bubble. I'm sure Marc's job can be as tedious as mine but between us she knows that she has brought up two well-balanced men who offer society something.

My grandad was a soldier in the Second World War; he died before I was born, but in his day every household in the country knew someone or had a family member in the military, and understood the Armed Forces. The only image the public have now is a fading Falklands conflict with Marines hoisting the Union Jack above Port Stanley after defeating an enemy three times their number.

So at the moment, my independence is important to me, for reasons that are partially to do with pride but also a self-fulfilment that clearly I get from being a small cog in an impressive historic institution like the Army. Glyn obviously leads a life aeons away from mine and I'm not going to criticise him; each to their own, and good luck to him. Which reminds me, I should buy a suit for his wedding. Blimey, my first proper suit, I must be getting old! I hope it works out for Glyn and his intended; I hear so many horror stories of the statistics on divorce. It must be virtually impossible to find your soul mate, whatever that is. I don't know if I have finalised my criteria; at the moment it consists of 'must have huge tits and shag a lot!' Hair colour isn't important, looks are; and they must have a job and something interesting to say for themselves, as I don't want to be leading the conversation every time. She mustn't get jealous or be too demanding, a kind mum and if her dad owned a brewery that would be a bonus; so all I have to do when the time comes for me to settle down is to move to Venus and take my pick.

Shit – this is my turn off.

Stig was not only the world's smelliest individual, he was dense as well; he'd written quite an exciting account of his time with our unit and the local lads from Luton, 'Dereck Yarwood'...Dereck! Mum was appalled, but she kept the paper clippings and as I browsed the write-up she told me that we had to be at the Catholic Church in Dunstable for mid-day on Saturday for the wedding.

I parked in the supermarket car park so as not to be ashamed of my rusting transport, and we walked together to the church. Mum held my arm; she looked amazing. I hadn't seen her madeup for ages and it knocked years off her. The groom's parents I sort of recognised and we took up seats on their side. I'd noticed Glyn, who hadn't really changed, just more rotund and going thin on top and I wondered what his wife would look like. This was the first wedding (family dos excepted) that I'd been to, so I watched with interest as the organ struck up and the bride made her way past us, followed by a couple of small girls in long dresses and a not-so- small girl who I couldn't take my eyes off, who I assumed was the chief bridesmaid. In true Catholic tradition the service took ages and we were up and down like a pair of whore's knickers until the newlyweds made their way past us once more, smiling and nodding at everyone as they went. The chief bridesmaid came level with our pew and I had a chance to have a good look at her and her rather ample assets.

'Ah, don't they look sweet?' Mum cooed as they passed. I don't think she meant the breasts of the bridesmaid, but my reply could have passed as a compliment for the bride and groom anyway. The reception was at the plastic factory club around the corner and as we filed along to congratulate Glyn and his wife I saw her again standing guard over a bowl of punch by the bar, alone.

I had a preconceived idea that speeches were meant to be funny, or maybe it was just a few miles away from my sense of humour, but the best man seemed insistent on pointing out Glyn's faults, much to the embarrassment of his family. I wasn't the only one who was only just bearing up to the tedium of the speech as Mum tried to stifle a yawn.

'Are you tired, Mum?'

She nodded and I said I'd take her home before the disco kicked in and she break-danced on the table. No sooner had I got through the door, I was on the phone to the taxi company, giving me enough time to replenish my aftershave and grab some cash out of my bag before heading back to where the party had begun. I thought it was a good start to try and get a word in with Glyn as I hadn't had a chance to talk to him; I didn't know if he'd even remember me. Despite his office worker appearance he was cheery, and his new wife Janet was charming. This was indeed a brilliant move, because as we sat and chatted the bridesmaid came and joined us.

'Den, this is Mary, Janet's sister.'

'Hi, I'm just about to get a round in, would you like a drink?'

She smiled and asked for a vodka and coke. I stood waiting in the bar queue along with about ten thirsty customers when I felt a tap on my shoulder.

'Can I be cheeky and ask for a double please?' Mary looked stressed as she asked me.

'Sure, so have you had a good day then?'

'Yeah, apart from that wanker of a best man who seems to think that it's part of his job to get my knickers off, whoops sorry, you didn't need to know that. It's just that since this morning he's been creeping around me like some smarmy lecherous pest asking when do we get to dance. He's a bloody dog and not even offered to buy me a drink, erm – whoops no, not that I'd get my draws ... oh dear ... sorry.' By the time she'd finished her oration I'd been served and turned to her with her glass.

'There you go, one large v. and c. and you don't have to strip either.'

Her embarrassment was obvious as she led me back to the table where the best man was now sat.

'Good health to you then.'

I raised my glass and then took a seat between Mary and her pursuer.

'I'm Rich, pleased to meet you.'

A hand stretched out. 'Glyn tells me you're a squaddie. I'm in the Territorials.'

I looked over at Mary, who was glaring at him as she gulped her drink. He was a pillock, I could tell; his words were slurred and he slapped me on the back like a long-lost friend.

'So what unit are you with Den?'

'Guards.'

'Oh, Infantry, I'm in the Signals, you're cannon fodder.'

He let out a hearty laugh and looked around for a supporting chorus. An urgent tap on my thigh.

'Do you want a dance Den?'

As I've said before, I'm no Fred Astaire. But the chance of getting away from the table was irresistible.

'Sure, let's go.'

I almost dragged Mary across the hall to where people were gigging around to the music.

'He's a real catch, what's up with you?' I asked sarcastically and grinned at her.

'Are you really in the Army Den?'

'Yep, I've just come back from Bosnia, what do you do then?'

'Was it scary?'

'What?'

'Were you scared in Bosnia?'

'Naa, so come on, what do you do?'

'Oh, I work in a travel agents.'

'So you're good for a cheap holiday then?'

'You'll have to marry me first.'

She laughed and winked at me; I liked her sense of humour. From where we were I could see Rich staring across at us larking about to Boney M, the party was in full swing, and as alcohol was consumed more folk took to the dance floor. It was getting near to closing, and Mary and I had danced for most of the night; she'd been showing me some moves and I thought I looked good, but maybe that could have been due to the seven or so pints I'd consumed.

I'd been observing that at a wedding there needs to be a few fundamental elements to distinguish it from a normal party, and as we danced we made a list of essentials. The list is as follows:

A spinster auntie, an example of which Mary pointed out to me, flitting from table to table, sweet sherry in hand.

A man in a kilt; she didn't know who he was but thought it was one of Glyn's friends from work.

One very drunk, single individual who makes a complete arse of themselves; this of course could be combined with the spinster auntie. But on this occasion was Rich.

A girl crying in either the women's toilets or kitchen. Dependent on location. One of these hadn't been found yet, though the spinster auntie had a weep during the speeches, they nearly had me going too.

Someone whose sense of dress had completely left them for the day, who normally presents themselves quite reasonably but for the sake of a wedding, wears an article of clothing that leaves everyone speechless. A lady in a pink mini dress had outclassed everyone by a mile. Due to her rather unique shape we decided that either the dress was made of Lycra or had a breaking strain greater than the Aswan Dam.

A fight, though this would normally occur at a northern wedding, we decided.

A man who tries to teach children how to dance. Uncle Brian won that prize.

Finally someone who can't dance, but tries all night. That would be me.

I excused myself and ventured to the toilet, only to open the door to the most horrendous retching noise. The cubicle door swung open and I could see the heels of Rich as he staggered to his feet. He wiped his mouth on his suit sleeve and with a sick smirk on his face approached me with outstretched arms.

'Dan, did ja give 'er one then?'

I definitely have matured, as behaviour like this would normally warrant a slap.

'No, look I need to use the bog.'

'Well are you gonna let me 'ave a go then?'

The tone of my first reply should have told him that I wasn't in the mood for conversation. I disregarded his last comment and made my way to the urinal.

'Come on Grunt, let's go and shag 'er,'

The combination of being regarded as a grunt (a derogatory nickname for an Infanteer) and Rich talking about a woman as if she were a slag left me no option ... so I flattened him with one punch, not that I would have been given much of a fight. I left him slumped against the cubicle door, used the toilet and washed my hands before returning to Mary, who was bidding the honeymooners farewell. I waved as they drove away and felt her hand slip into mine, then a tug, and we were off too.

A taxi took us to her parents' house and we slipped in through the back door, creeping up the stairs.

I whispered, 'Aren't your mum and dad at the reception still?'

'No, I saw them leave just before us so they will be tucked up in bed now and that's precisely where you're going to be in a minute.'

After six months away and a belly full of beer I needed no more encouragement and my kit was off before she could finish undoing her dress.

'Blimey, you're keen.' She looked apprehensive at my ... well-excited state, so to say.

Mary was very eager, and willing, and dirty, which suited my needs; it was the best sex I'd had for six months, surprisingly enough.

'Are you sure your parents won't have heard us?' I whispered as we lay there in the dark.

'No, Dad sleeps like a baby since he came out, especially after a few beers.'

'After he came out?'

Now either her dad has just announced that he's gay or there was something the delightful Mary had forgotten to tell me. She went on to explain.

'Dad came out of nick on Thursday, just in time for the wedding, Mum was delighted.'

'Erm – what for?'

'Oh, my last boyfriend was a player, you know the type, and Dad sort of sorted him out.'

That changed things slightly, to say the least, from there on; and to say I was psyched by Mary's statement was very conservative. I pounced up like I'd been stung on the arse by a wasp and groped around for my trousers and shirt.

'Den, it sounds worse than it actually was.'

I didn't have time to listen to her explanation; I'd managed to have a look at her dad at the reception and he wasn't what I'd consider a small guy. I don't want to die like this, torn limb from limb by a mad axe-murdering father for tampering with his daughter. When I do die it needs to be quick; an explosion or a well-aimed shot would do me. No pain, and unless Mary's dad had a hoard of Semtex under his bed and a cleverly constructed initiating device that he strapped onto fleeing freshly laid young men, I wasn't prepared to hang about for the consequences. If he was the big bad wolf, I didn't want to be the prince who woke him up!

'Den, let me explain.'

Mary sounded panicked as she tried to stop me evacuating quicker than wartime London.

'The guy knocked me about, and when I came home with a black eye, well he went around to his house and returned the compliment, I didn't tell him to ... honestly.'

I was fully dressed and waiting by the bedroom door, listening for my assassin sneaking up on me. She grabbed my arm and led me back to the bed.

'I shouldn't have said anything, he's a really bang-on bloke Den, he was only inside for two months.'

I wasn't mad at her, just mildly shit-scared and sat back on her bed.

'Mary, it's been lovely, I've had a great time but I've got to go, no offence and maybe I'll see you around.'

I'd been in the papers once this month and didn't fancy

reaching the front page this time. I'd heard what Mary had said and yes, I suppose that's acceptable; I'd not long ago launched the intolerable Rich for a lesser crime in my books. Mary let go of my arm and slipped her dressing- gown on. She did have a great body.

'Okay, I'll show you out, will you be all right getting home?'

'Yes, fine thanks. I don't live far from here,' I lied.

We kissed on the doorstep, she with her eyes closed and me scanning the hallway for any signs of movement.

'See you again then Den?'

'Yeah sure will, 'bye.' I'll get myself to confession on Sunday.

Chapter Twenty-six

It was time to call Peanuts; I needed a good night out with no drama. I'd only been home a week and I was looking for something to do. Marc was on night shift, so he was no good for a drink.

'Hello?' a rather shaky voice answered.

'Ah, hello, is that Mrs Brady?'

Why do I always start with 'Ah' as if I'm surprised that anyone will pick up the phone? Mum would say something now like: 'sorry to disturb you,' or 'I know it's getting on.' I think she shouldn't bother to call if she feels that awkward about it. Once when she picked up and the caller must have said to her something along the lines, 'sorry to call so late,' she replied, 'It was ringing anyway!' She couldn't understand why Marc and me rolled around the floor laughing.

'Yes. If you're selling I'm not interested.'

'No, no I was wondering if Kerry was in?'

'Yes, she's upstairs.'

Now I don't know Peanuts' mum at all, but I reckon she must have grown up with mine or at least they went to the same school. I wanted to ask her if she could guess what I was gonna say next. Maybe I'll just say that I was pleased and put the phone down? Either way it was bringing out the worst in me.

'Could I talk to her please?'

'Yes, who shall I say is calling?'

'Denis.'

Flip! No it's Den, not Denis; why have I gone into polite overdrive? I feel like a complete snob now, but she sounds very nice, just as a mum should. I heard the slow ascent of the stairs and then a rapid banging of wood and then what sounded like a small crash of rhinos storming towards the phone.

'Hello Denis!'

'Hi, long time no see, do you fancy a drinky with Den?'

'Mmm, now let me see, I'm washing my hair tonight, doing my legs tomorrow, then there's my piano lessons, how does a week on Friday sound?'

Sarcastic missie.

'No can do, I'm going to brass rubbing class, shall we leave it another six months?'

I could hear her Mum asking who it was and the receiver went dead for a few seconds.

'Okay. Where are we going?'

Why is it always the blokes who have to choose?

'Into town. London.'

'LONDON?'

'Yeah, it's only half an hour away, come on it'll be a laugh.'

'Hang on a minute, let me think.' The line goes quiet again I greet her with a big hug and then we argue over the window seat on the train like a couple of school kids, so I gallantly give in but only after declaring that it was mine on the way back.

'So Peaches, is there a plot to this adventure, or is it an ad hoc arrangement?'

'Erm, not really, I thought we'd find a pub somewhere.'

She tutted and then giggled at my lack of forethought, but hey, living by the seat of my pants is fun.

'Where to?'

The taxi driver was a stereotype of London cabbies, a large happy fellow in a tank top who played golf this morning.

'Camden Town please,' Peanuts said, in a confident voice.

'You know London?'

She knew bloody everywhere!

We pulled up along a busy high street that I assumed was

Camden, and she gestured towards a pub called The Castle. We walked in and it was plainly obvious why she'd chosen this place; it was full of students. However, these outclassed any students I'd ever encountered before in their dress and weirdness. And then I saw it.

'I love it here; I'll get the first ones in. What are you drinking? Den ... are you still with me?'

'Uh?'

'Denis!'

'What? Sorry, this is mega, look.'

I pointed with outstretched arm at the poster above the bar, like a trainspotter in front of the Orient Express, and sighed.

'Madness ... Madness were here.'

The poster had been signed by the entire group; it was, apart from maybe my model Stuka, one of the most brilliant things I've ever seen.

'I thought you'd like it, this is where they were discovered. The bands play in the back bar.'

And she handed me a pint.

The bar at the back cost a few quid to get in and was dark and begrimed, covered in promotional posters and a sticky floor sort of cellar affair. The stage was a quarter circle in one corner with a few ceiling lights to illuminate the performers and a black background of hessian; the air was heavy with smoke from a machine on stage mixed with drugs and sweat. A thick atmosphere as the people crowded near to the stage front as a M*t*rhead tribute band blasted out Ace of Spades. M*torbrain, which in true tradition was a very cheesy name, didn't exactly emulate the great Lemmy and Co., but they could knock out great sounds. The lead singer had drawn a mole on his face and had the gravelly voice that I'd heard so many times on my LPs. It was very cool, I loved it. We stayed until Deep Vermilion struck up, a true bunch of wannabes, who struggled to make an audible tune from their din; the front girl screamed some obscenities into the mike before breaking into what I assumed to be a cover of Dear Prudence but sounded more like she was being assaulted. Peanuts found a seat in an open alcove with a bunch of vagabonds.

'So,' she said. 'How was it really Den?'

We had no privacy and I could tell that one of the blokes was earwigging our conversation. I relayed the events of the tour and mentioned the murder, waiting to hear her stance on it. She'd normally think things over for a while and then return with a theory or view, but she sat there dumbfounded by the whole thing.

'Oh, and I had a stalker.'

I thought that the statement would snap her back to my universe.

'Why? I mean what? Yeah, right Den.'

'This girl, well, woman, called Glad, she's an interpreter. She started writing to me, at first just once a week then she wrote daily and then bugger me she turned up at the Camp.'

'Desperate was she?'

'Well ... I ...'

'Oh Den, I feel privileged to be here.'

'Cheeky minx.'

We laughed together and I offered her another cider.

'Just a coke please.'

I almost fell of my chair.

'Come on, this is our big night out, I'll pay.'

'No, honestly I'm fine with a coke, you have a pint.'

When I returned she was browsing through her handbag, but suddenly stowed it away as I sat down.

'Do you want to go somewhere else?' I asked, thinking that the cider pump must have been dodgy.

'We're going to have to head back in a minute or we'll miss the last train, Den,'

'No we won't. Let's find a club.'

'Den, we'll have these and go back, or we'll be on the milk train if we're not careful.'

'Okay, let's find a club when we get back then.' I was determined to make a night of it.

'There won't be any open by the time we get home.'

'So come for a drink at my house, I've got some beer in.'

'No, I'm going home.'

I gave Peanuts my best 'pleeeeease' look (something like looking through my eyebrows at her) with the hope she'd change her mind, but it didn't work, as she emptied her glass and stood up. I felt a little chastised by her sensibleness, so I followed her outside, where a taxi was waiting to whisk us to the station.

I walked her to her front door and silently agreed that it was late and we'd had a great night.

'What are you doing tomorrow then, do you fancy a coffee in town? I need to do some shopping.'

She turned and yawned, before replying.

'Yeah sure, what time?'

'About ten?'

'Yeah ... no, afternoon is better for me, I've got an, er, a meeting first thing,'

'Oh! What for?'

'Just college stuff, you know.'

I walked slowly through town, hoping to find a club open or a party I could crash but the place was like a ghost town. I crossed the park and headed up the hill to Mum's house when I heard a car pull up behind and the door slam. Before I could turn to see who it was my arms were taken out of my pockets by a firm grip and shoved unceremoniously behind my back. I pulled away but they wouldn't let go and I found myself frog-marched to the waiting car and pushed onto the bonnet.

'What the bloody he...'

'Quiet ducky.' The voice was stern and panicked me. 'You're nicked.'

A hand was placed on the top of my head as I was pushed into the car; now bound with handcuffs, I landed face down on the seat.

'But I haven't done anything, I'm in the Army, my identification is in my wallet,' I pleaded with the officer as the car pulled away.

'Are you Denis Yarwood?'

'Yes, what's this all about?'

'You're under arrest.'

'What for I haven't bleedin' done anything!'

'Having an offensive shirt on, you little knob.' Marc's voice from the driver's seat made me realise what was going on.

'At least when you used to borrow mine they made you look good, your taste hasn't changed then?'

The guy in the back seat released my cuffs and let me sit up.

'This is police harassment, don't you know?'

'Yeah, I take pride in my work. So to the station for a coffee or home to Mummy? It's well past your bedtime!'

'You're rushed off your feet then Marc?'

He still knew how to wind me up. Being in the company of one of his colleagues he knew I wouldn't retaliate too much. I agreed to come for a brew with him, as we hadn't had a chance to talk since I'd come home, so we headed to the station. We sat in the custody suite drinking our coffee and having a fag; there were a couple of drunks perching on their seats and a girl dressed quite inappropriately for the inclement weather.

'So how's things?'

'Great thanks, the boys are growing up fast, little sprogs, they are itching to see you, it's Uncle Den this and Uncle Den that, makes me feel a bit second rate.'

'Well, kids know don't they?'

We had an old familiar conversation and it felt like we hadn't been apart.

'Do you want to take Mum out for a meal or something soon?'

'Yeah, good idea, how about we go out as a family on Sunday. Have you found yourself a woman yet?'

I hear a laugh; the girl who had been silently waiting to be charged struck up in a northern accent,

'Twenty quid and yew tinnie 'uv me darl'n.'

Marc warned her to shut up as she sniggered into her hand. Before taking me home we arranged lunch. However, Sunday came and Peanuts declined my offer, saying that she'd organised something with her mum. There'd be another time.

Chapter Twenty-seven

I had a choice; I could either spend the winter in the north of England, or volunteer for a six-month stint in the Caribbean. When a notice was posted in Headquarters no one put their hand up, I thought it was incredible; the travel bug had bitten me and I couldn't let an opportunity like this go by. I just needed to find out where Belize was and what the job entailed. The description read:

One Junior Rank required to serve with the Second Battalion for six months in Belize. All volunteers to present their name to the CSM by close of work Friday. Anyone putting his name forward will need to be fully fit and own a driving licence.

Our sister Battalion had been in Ireland for two years on a residential tour, and this was the Army's peculiar way of giving some respite between operational tours. The task was lower key, mainly training the Belizean Defence Force and acting as a deterrent against the Guatemalan Army, who shared a western border. I was to join them insitu, as they had already deployed, but had later found out that they needed extra men; it wasn't an uncommon occurrence, as soldiers were swapped to meet a shortfall on a fairly regular basis. A couple of others had gone over as well, one of them being Dave Tupp, who had been given the acting rank of Sergeant for the tour, as he was just about to be promoted in our Battalion.

Peanuts and I set off for the station; I'd just been to her house to drop my car off. I asked her to sell it and send the money on. I could trust Peanuts; if I'd asked one of the blokes, they'd rip me off. She had given me a book to read. I don't know why; the last book I read was a Gerald Durrell story at school. We found the platform and waited, smoking my cigarettes and drinking what might have been tea before the announcement that the train was arriving. As it slowed to a halt, we carried my bags to the nearest door and let the passengers off before letting some rather rude and impatient ones on. They needed that window seat or their journey would be ruined, I assumed; or maybe the train only stopped for a few short seconds and if they hadn't pushed past they would have been left forlorn on the platform or running down the track trying to hop onto the last carriage. For whatever reason, we let them have their moment of glory and put my bags into the door space between seats. I slammed the door behind me with a heavy clunk and pulled down on the metal window frame. I hung out of the window and looked down on her as she swayed from one foot to the other with her hands behind her back.

'Right next stop the Caribbean then.' I joked.

'You jammy bugger.'

'Oh that's nice, I was gonna send you a postcard as well!'

'You'll be wanting a kiss goodbye next.'

I pointed to my cheek as the conductor, who was stood behind her, blew his whistle.

'Take care Den ...'

'You too, love the tights.'

She smiled and turned away.

The flight from Brize Norton took seven hours to reach Washington, where we were unceremoniously plonked into a segregated lounge; we waited four hours for the plane to refuel, and then continued for another six-hour leg of the journey to Belize City Airport. By the time we were low enough to see the coast my head was spinning with fatigue and my stomach ached. I wasn't aware of this system, but the RAF have a policy of offering a meal every few hours and I'd stuffed the first three servings away; by the fifth sitting I'd had enough, and slumped back into my chair and ploughed my way through Peanuts' book instead.

I stared out of the window at the turquoise sea and golden

sands until a Harrier Jump Jet appeared at our wing tip; this caused a flutter of excitement as another flanked our other side, escorting us in to the airstrip. The coastline disappeared and I could see swampland surrounding small villages.

The pilot announced that we would be landing in a few minutes and banked hard right displaying the runway, which seemed a little on the short side, to say the least. I could see trucks lined up at the side of the airstrip and men perched on top of the canopies waving at the plane as we turned and descended. I'm no expert but I've been on enough planes to know what a landing should be like; either our pilot was late for his tea or he was dared in a mad competition to scare the shit out of his passengers, and having flown for free, I thought it was probably the latter. We dropped out of the sky after a sharp turn, and the ground rushed towards us at an unnerving rate as the engines laboured to keep us in the air. The bloke next to me, who hadn't muttered a single word, took a sharp intake of breath and asked if this seemed right to be plummeting at such a rate. I fibbed openly that it was fine. The undercarriage clunked and the wheels locked into position, which made my colleague turn religious and give a poor rendition of a Hail Mary. With a bump that shook my eyeballs we were on the tarmac and the reverse thrust drowned my obscene comments about the pilot being fatherless; terra firma hadn't felt this good for ages. The doors opened to a wave of hot, humid air that filled the plane and I stepped out into the scorching sunlight, feeling rather overdressed.

No sooner than I had collected my bags I was bundled onto a bus with the other passengers, destination Airport Camp along another unsealed road. I wonder if the Army only deploy to places with particularly poor highways; it's part of the decisive factor for a deployment with a senior officer enquiring,

'I say, where in blazes is that? Naturally, we'll be requiring somewhere rather remote.'

'Yes Sir.'

'And are the roads poorly maintained?'

'Indeed they are Sir.'

'Super! That's settled then. When does the cricket start?'

As we passed through the gates of the Camp the driver gave a running commentary, he'd been here for a while with his deep tan and casual attitude and took great pains to highlight the local attractions.

'That's the sweet water canal over there.'

He pointed to a small stream running parallel with the fencing. "More than thirty diseases in that, only twenty-two are known to man, fall in that dyke and you're on a plane to Miami with a tube up your arse! That's the guardroom,' a hut with a couple of tanned men sitting outside, 'you get your johnnys there, never shag without a raincoat lads, or you'll be down the dick doctors getting a needle in your arse.'

He seemed intent on telling us that any action would result in some sort of derrière invasion.

'NAAFI on the right, don't eat the malaria burgers or you'll be shitting through the eye of a needle.'

I do love friendly advice, but I couldn't make sense of a word of it. There was more to come as we pulled over next to the Royal Military Police station.

'Monkeys,' (the derogatory name for RMPs). 'Get caught in Raoul's and your arse is theirs!'

Blimey, it was like he was talking in tongues. I looked over to the guy who had sat next to me on the plane and we both shrugged and got off the bus saying 'thanks' to our guide. After a rather depressing salad lunch we reported to the main briefing room for a series of lectures about Belize and its idiosyncrasies; for the first time in my life I'd appreciated air conditioning. The

Commanding Officer introduced himself and welcomed us, requesting that we pay heed to the briefings as there were a few things out here that were in our interest to learn. No way; one of them was studying a new language, I thought. He handed over to a tall Major, who told us he was the Forces Health Protection Officer; I didn't think I'd need protecting against my health.

A slide show offered some explanation and it transpired that the bus driver wasn't far from the truth. The sweet water canal was an open sewer and to be avoided at all costs. Snakes and beasties came next; a beastie is generally anything that can bite, sting or lay eggs in you, of which there seemed an endless list. Most disturbing was the screw worm, a fly that stung and simultaneously laid a maggot under the skin, which would eat its way around the body until matured and then appear like an alien and fly away, leaving a nasty disease behind.

'Raoul's Rose Garden ....' The Major's voice made my ears prick up; another comment that I hadn't understood on the coach. ' ... is out of bounds to all ranks and anyone caught in there will face immediate disciplinary action.' But what was it? Ah it must be a guessing game, but a cruel one; a tease to make me want something more than ever because of the mystery that lies behind the secret. I had no more time to ponder as another slide show began, and a Sergeant in a white coat allowed a few pictures to be shown before introducing himself. They were of diseased male genitalia with captions like 'Gonorrhoea' and 'Genital Warts'. Lovely.

'I'm the bloke no one wants to visit.'

With slides like that I'm not surprised.

'Why, are they your holiday snaps Sarge?'

The crowed gave a nervous laugh as he shot the heckler a stern stare.

'No young man, I'm the Genito-Urinary Disease Nurse, the Dick

Doctor, Blobby Knob Bloke, whatever you want to call me. If I see you at my surgery, call me Sergeant Weaver.'

He had our undivided attention as he listed different ailments and their cures, all of which involved lots of injections. The national sport must be knitting or something. Being presumptuous, I'd not been in a unit with a GU Nurse before. What's that old saying? Make love not war.

It gets dark very quickly in Belize; one minute it's dusk and then the lights go out, just like that; so it took Gus, the guy I'd shared the flight with, and me, ages to find our billet. The other thing they do just to make life more interesting is to dig storm drains in random places around the Camp. After finding more than one, much to Gus's amusement, we arrived in our Nissen hut.

'Fancy checkin' it th' toon tonecht?' Gus asked as he dried himself from the shower. He came from Glasgow and I found him difficult to understand.

'Yeah, I'll give it a go, how are we getting there?'

'Git yer kit ain big cheil, ther's transport fe th' guardroom.'

I don't know why it's called the Happy Bus; it was in sad repair but we arrived in Belize City and followed a crowd of soldiers towards what I assumed was a pub. So the Caribbean wasn't quite what I'd visualised. I'd travelled on two dusty roads, one in the dark, and not seen anything that resembled paradise; maybe there was better to come.

The Upstairs Café wasn't one of those beach bar idylls that I wanted to be in; it was a retro sixties bar with a balcony overlooking the main strip running through the town. I was forced to drink rum and coke from a plastic cup, and what made it worse was the girl put the smallest childlike straw in it that resembled a flamboyant gesture, for which I should be grateful. We found seats on the balcony and sat sipping our drinks and me trying to comprehend a single word he said. He was a good laugh and had volunteered for the same reasons as me; we still didn't know what jobs we were doing so were determined to make the most of the two days acclimatisation just in case we were given a really bum job.

'What's this Raoul's Rose Garden do you think Gus?'

'A whoor' hoose mucker.'

A mate of his was here last year and used to visit the place on a regular basis. The only drawback was he'd given his girlfriend an unwanted present care of the Rose Garden. It intrigued me, though I wasn't quite ready to go and get myself into that kind of trouble.

The humidity was stifling as we sat on the balcony. I could feel myself sweating at a steady rate. The air wasn't acrid but mildly smelly, and breathing was an effort; every expected gulp of fresh air turned out to be a lungful of hot sweaty fumes. The café was obviously the place to go as most of the British Army was there. A group of blokes who were sat on a table near the railings caught my attention as they laughed and looked over into the street. A small boy was trying to pick up a coin that had been tossed over the side but every time he touched it he dropped it again. Another coin hit the floor and more children came, juggling the coin in their hands, which incited more laughter from the men.

'Gimme dollar man!' they shouted, dodging the cars. One of the men sat at the table, balanced a coin on the edge of the railing and then held a lighter under it. He aimed the flame on the underside for a couple of minutes and then flicked it up into the air and towards the shouting kids, to a hail of laughter from his mates.

'Ye boak bastards.' Gus shook his head and gave a grin as the next disk of hot metal hit the floor. 'They're only wee kiddies.'

The man who had heated the coins looked across.

'Git off. We're aidin' the local economy an' givin' wor a laugh,' came the casual answer, prompting us to finish our drinks and walk back to the bus.

So first impressions weren't good. If I were to survive out here with my sanity intact and without resorting to sadism for entertainment I'd need to find something to do. The last day of the induction briefings described the cultural history, which I found interesting, and there were lots of fishing and snorkelling opportunities; but what I wanted most of all was to see the country itself, meet some locals and maybe visit a Mayan ruin. It was an experience too good to pass over.

Gus was first into the Garrison Sergeant Major's office; he was the man I was working with. The Battalion had deployed without bringing enough men to cover the driving duties for the GSM and CO. Because the Battalion was going to be resident for six months, the Regimental Sergeant Major was in charge of the whole Garrison, hence the change of his title. He told me that I'd be driving him and that I was to report to the Military Transport section and win a Land Rover that had been assigned to him. GSM Bailey seemed a good bloke, quietly spoken with an air of authority that gave him immense respect within his unit. He was in the last year of his service and when he retired he wanted to be a plumber. I suppose after twenty-two years, he didn't want any more drips.

He told me that we would be visiting Companies who had deployed in different areas in Belize; it sounded right up my street. Gus was working for the Commanding Officer who, according to the GSM, was a barking mad jock; they would make a good pair.

Mum's and Peanuts' letters arrived on the same day. Mum had been away for a few days with her friend from the Women's Institute to Blackpool, and Peanuts had gone back home for a week or so during breaks from her placement. Both letters were pretty nondescript, so I decided not to reply until I had something to say.

At last I was going to get to see something; we were going to drive to Belmopan, the capital. Our medics had set up a surgical unit in the town hall as a public relations exercise and held a free clinic for minor surgery. The GSM wanted a nosey, so we set off at first light along the dusty roads. To see the Belize City in daylight was a vision; the Haulover Creek split the main town west to east with wooden shacks constructed on each side. Some looked as if they were about to fall off the banks, and some had. The road passed a commercial centre with a few purpose-built, air-conditioned shiny office blocks with tinted windows, overlooking the riverside wooden huts, in stark contrast. I couldn't imagine the inhabitants of these timber buildings opening their doors – I mean big sheet of plywood – and ambling towards to one of the office blocks after saying a cheery goodbye to the wife and kids every morning. I might be wrong, but somehow the structures looked starkly incongruous. No sooner had we entered the city we were out of it again and heading up the Belmopan highway. 'A tarred road' might be a better description.

'Right Corporal Yarwood, I'm going to get my head down, when we reach JB's give me a shout'

'Yes Sir, no probs. What's JBs?' I asked shyly.

'It's a watering hole, you can't miss it, just drive for an hour and you'll see it.'

And so I did, metalled road to dust track and back again. This bloke could sleep for England; his head bounced on the window as we remounted the tarred road. After looking at palm trees and ramshackle houses for just under an hour, JB's Sunset Bar appeared from nowhere like a mirage at the side of the road. I needed a drink to refresh myself. As I pulled the handbrake on, the GSM woke and immediately stepped out of the vehicle.

'Blimey, that was a strap hanger of a drive.' He stretched and walked off through the main doors. I followed in disbelief;

steering was torture and I had to do it again later. How could he moan about having to sleep for an hour? Immediately he was forgiven, as an ice-cold coke was thrust into one hand and the fattest burger I'd ever seen into the other.

We continued and reached Belmopan, which was more substantial than Belize City with tower blocks and paved streets. I was directed to the town hall, the biggest building in the capital, and we parked under a veranda next to an Army ambulance. I still wasn't quite sure what to expect, as a medical officer in combat uniform met the GSM at the door.

'Come on then Corporal Y, let's get scrubbed up, they're cutting in a minute.'

The Officer who I now recognised from the briefings introduced himself, and told me that as a gesture of good favour, the locals could have some minor surgery done on them by our team in a safe and clean environment. He explained that the local hospital was in a terrible condition and any treatment had to be paid for in cash; no wonga, no treatment. So the British Army's free clinic was a phenomenon.

We followed him into what looked like a conference room, where the medics had set out a temporary operating theatre. They had brought a six-foot table and dressing packs, gowns and a hand scrub; it didn't look particularly state of the art. To my amazement an old man on crutches walked in from an adjoining room; he had a pair of Hawaiian shorts and shirt on and a full set of dreadlocks; it could have been Bob Marley's dad. He sat on the table and swung his legs up, pointing to his stomach and nodding at the doctor.

'It's me stomach man ... I tink I godda bad lump.'

'That's fine, just relax old bean, we'll give you something to go to sleep and it'll be fixed in a flash.'

'Iree man.'

The guy lay back and waited to be put out; they were going to operate on this bloke right now. This put a new meaning on the phrase 'Join the Army, visit exotic places, meet strange people and kill them!' I was transfixed as the surgeon and anaesthetist winked at each other.

'Just a tiny prick now.'

They were openly taking the piss as they put the injection in his hand.

'Okay, try and think of something jolly.'

The man's eyes started to glaze over as the drugs took effect. Just before he lost consciousness the surgeon, with a grin on his face, snapped his gloves on his wrists and announced,

'Left leg orf then is it?'

The hapless patient made a final struggle to run for it and then collapsed into unconsciousness as the two doctors howled at each other.

'Gets 'em every time, think that's hilarious, wait till the poor old bally wakes up.'

At that point I decided that I must never put myself under the knife of an Army surgeon. The poor man was having a small hernia repaired, but his last thought was that some mad English quack was going to slice his leg off. The GSM and I watched the procedure and then offered a wave at the surgeon, as we weren't allowed to talk, so we could leave before the panic-stricken Belizean woke up to find he was complete as per CES (that's a complete equipment schedule, when all the items issued by the quartermaster at the start of every operational tour are taken as a full complement of kit); in short, he still had his four limbs.

The drive back was as monotonous as the way out minus the stop at JB's. We arrived back in the darkness and I dropped him outside the Sergeants' Mess.

'Thanks Corporal Y, by the way, what do the lads call you?'

'Den, Sir.'

'Okay Den, see you in the morning,' and he was off, and I dumbfounded that the Garrison Sergeant Major was calling me by my first name.

I found more things to do as the weeks passed, and we spent a lot of our time on the road visiting the troops. One occasion took us on the Army ship that re-supplied the furthest of our stations. I was as sick as a dog for the four hours we were afloat, getting lots of smarmy comments from the boys of the Royal Logistic Corps who manned it. How delighted was I when on the return voyage one of their guys joined me head-over in a throwing-up competition. The other thing I discovered, much to my dismay, was that if you don't drink from bottled water, including ice cubes in bar drinks, you find yourself rapidly evacuating solids. After a night of quaffing my ritual rum and coke I awoke in the early hours to find the contents of my body trying to escape into my underpants. A night of running to the loo kept my roommate awake but much amused; he started timing me and broadcast a running commentary as I dashed for the door.

'An', he's aff, juss loook at 'at laddie gang, aiv ne'er seen heem rrrin se fest, nae he's at th' duir, canny git it oopen, och a wee pause te adjoost his undercarriage an he's aff again inte th' night ...'

I could hear his chuckles as I ran like a man possessed across to the ablutions. It seemed like the night would never end and the only thing left inside me were my vital organs, and my hand had a slight indentation from pulling the chain.

Tuesdays became a social event, as it was the day the flight from UK landed, and this meant mail and Moonies. A Moonie is an untanned person who has just deployed into the country. We would go to the airport and wait for two o'clock when the bird would appear on the horizon; some of the RAF guys stood on the pan and threw bread down, coaxing the plane into land, as if it wouldn't. The men and women who were departing would stand in anticipation for their escape, laughing and joking with us about how long we had left.

'How long? No one has that long left,' they would taunt. The thought of a cold shower and not being eaten alive by mosquitoes made them cocky.

One lad from our unit found out that a friend of his was replacing him; he was permitted to get onto the aircraft just after it had landed and stand in the aisle shouting his name. When his friend looked around he said

'You're in me sate skip, see yam in six months!'

Nearly every weekday became some sort of occasion, starting with Monday nights a Gozomie Bash, for the lads going home. Sunday is and will always be a day of rest, even for drunks. Then Tuesday was a Welcome The Moonie Party, Wednesday naturally was The Most Burnt New Arrival Competition, and there would always be a couple who had recklessly stripped off their shirts and the next day found themselves looking like a lobster. Thursdays were renamed Thirsty Thursday, because every bar downtown would have a happy hour, so instead of the rum and coke costing one dollar fifty, it was one dollar, a huge saving of about ten pence! Friday was the start of the weekend, and therefore we would head to town for a barbecue at one of the bars and then on to the Hard Rock Café, which had a sort of disco. I say disco, but they only played reggae very loudly all night. Then my favourite day of the week, and my self-indulgent Saturday.

On Saturday mornings I could run, get away from the Camp. I had a route that took me around a small town outside the Camp called Ladyville that was made up of more ramshackle huts. It was a great opportunity to lose myself, and even though the heat of the morning was stifling I felt brilliant. It also gave me a chance to rid my body of the alcohol that I'd consumed throughout the week. The pubs had their own characters in town; one man would be there every night selling black coral. Time and again he'd try and persuade the soldiers to part with their money without much success. I bought a few bits and pieces from him on occasion; a pair of earrings for Mum and a necklace for Peanuts. One particular Thursday I saw him sat in the Upstairs Café drinking on his own so I asked him why he wasn't selling.

'Me boat gatta problem man, de ting keep stallin' so I can't dive.'

'Dive?'

'Yah man how do ya tink I get it man? Ask de fishes to bring it?'

He grumbled a deep laugh and sucked his teeth. I was curious about his boat and the diving; Kirt owned his own boat and made what he could from gathering coral and making it into jewellery to sell. It didn't bring in much money and he told me that he lived on the fresh air most of the time unless he was lucky enough to get a group of people together for a fishing trip.

'You take guys fishing as well?'

'Used to man, but dey don't come any more.'

'How many?'

''Bout ten a day'

'How much?'

'Hundred dollar.'

I looked into my drink for a moment, trying to work out of there were any negatives in the plan forming in my head. Compute zero. Open mouth to speak.

'So Kirt, if I got you ten blokes would you put on a trip then?'

'Damn rite I's would man!'

I thought about it for a few minutes and went and bought Kirt another drink before propositioning him.

'I know some people who would like to go fishing; I have to make something on it myself though. How long would the trip last?'

'Ye man, 'bout six hours.'
'Okay Kirt let's go for it.'
I clunked my paper cup against his.

Chapter Twenty-eight

I was in business, and my outlay was the price of a rum and coke. Not bad; my own enterprise for twenty-five pence. The NAAFI seemed the best place to advertise for my customers, so I created a poster and stuck it above the bar. It took a few drafts before I got it completely spot on; I thought it would be good to put a picture of someone fishing and reeling in a huge catch. Unfortunately, I'm not great at drawing and after a few attempts that resembled mutant eels and another similar to the Loch Ness Monster, I gave up and risked it with words alone. By the end of the first week I had four takers, a good inauguration.

Kirt was waiting by his boat when we arrived. 'Iree Den how ya doin' man?' He held his hand above his head ready for me to slap a greeting.

'Iree bupa.'

We were like a couple of old-time buddies. The lads had no idea that I was winging it and that this was my first trip and, depending on our catch today, it might be my last. I'd liked Kirt; he had the most wonderful Creole accent. We'd agreed that we would split the money sixty:forty in my favour, as I was going to provide the transport and customers and he just had to tip up with his boat full of diesel. As I boarded with the others I could see another man sat holding onto the helm, in the shade of the cockpit.

'Kirt,' I enquired, without trying to make a fuss, 'who's this?'

'It's me uncle, man, he drives de t'ing.'

He introduced his Uncle Burt, who spun around on his seat, revealing both port and starboard absent.

'Erm ... hello Uncle Burt.'

The Creole had dropped out of me as I shook his hand, trying desperately not to stare at the stumps.

'Iree, you de boy, Kirt tell me about eh?'

'Yes, Den, pleased to meet you,.'

He looked completely non-fazed and showed a smile like a row of bombed houses. I couldn't think of anything to say. Fortunately, there was no time for pleasantries, as the engine coughed, a cloud of something carcinogenic was expelled and we were off. However, Uncle Burt and his missing legs crossed my mind, and I mulled over how the money might have to be split three ways. We chugged along the estuary out of town and reached the deep water in a few minutes. Kirt began assembling rods and reels, placing them into holders around the boat so the lines didn't cross. There were four rods fixed onto the roof housing and over the side and four off the stern. I was impressed and swanked to the lads that it was our usual set-up. I looked back to see the land disappearing and observed a blue horizon ahead; it was awesome and idyllic. This was the Caribbean I'd imagined and I was really here. I felt like pinching myself; it was difficult stopping myself from gushing when I was supposed to be mellow and practised and do this all the time.

'So Kirt, who gets the rod first then?' I asked, as if I did it every week, trying to lead him into actually explaining what was going on.

'Wait till dey bite man, whoever is quick enough.'

He let out a deep chuckle as he fiddled around with a rather large and dangerous-looking pole with a hook on the end.

'You'll know when you got a bite man' Burt added, and laughed to himself.

That made me feel uneasy; maybe my mutant eels weren't so far from the truth. Two chairs were positioned on the stern; they looked like the type from a dentist with comfy arms to seize onto as your teeth are being yanked out. In front, between the legs, were cylinders for the rods to slot into and a seat belt hung from their sides. The blokes who'd come for the trip had stripped to their shorts and handed out beers they had brought in a cool box; rather a lot of beer, actually, for four people. I gratefully guzzled one, as I'd neglected to pack any refreshments for myself; it was going to be beer or nothing! Burt and Kirt tucked in as well. It's the Caribbean way I thought; still, I'm not completely reckless. I had looked around the craft for life jackets or flares, or anything that resembled safety equipment, and not finding any, I decided that if we sank I'd want to be blotto and go down in style. When in Rome and all that.

A couple of hours and many beers passed and the rods hadn't moved, when I asked Kirt,

'Do you think we should have a look to see if we've had a bite yet?'

They howled with laughter.

'Den, we comin into prime cooda sea man, you'll see a bite soon, chill.'

'Cooda?'

'Barracuda man, when dem t'ings come, you gonna know man.'

As he finished his sentence the rod at the rear right of the boat snapped into action. The reel let out a whizz as fishing line tore from the spindle and the rod looked like it would snap at any moment.

'Come on man, get de reel.' Kirt gave me a nudge in his excited state and I grabbed the rod out of its fixing, nearly letting it pull me overboard.

'Get in de chair man, get in de chair.'

He was jumping around, and his voice rose as he pushed me back into the dentist chair and snapped the seat belt on. The engine cut out and Burt swung around to look. I was locked in and terrified.

'Right man, listen to me.'

Kirt leaned over, calming himself; as he talked. he placed one hand reassuringly on my shoulder.

'When cooda stop pullin' you gonna have to pull him in, slowly slowly man, you don't wanna tick him off right?'

'Yeah, right,.'

If the lads hadn't sussed me now they soon would. The reel stopped for a second, then whizzed again to the guys' delight. They crowded round to see whatever was on the end of the line. It was only then it occurred to me that I'd no idea what a barracuda looked like, how big it was or what they ate.

'Kirt.' I whispered.

'Yeah man.'

'Do these things bite?'

'Den, dey got teeth as big as you fingers man, and so sharp man, how de ya t'ink me uncle lost his legs man? Me don't gaff him quick enough one time and the fish took dem straight off.'

His arm had wrapped around my shoulder and he whispered in my ear in a dramatic voice.

'Really?'

I couldn't contain my squeaky petrified question at the thought of being wheelchair-bound for the rest of my life. I looked at him and could see a grin trailing across his face.

'Na, man, me only messin'.'

I felt a fool.

'It only took one leg man, de oder one fell off laita.'

He blasted a laugh into my ear and let go of his grip. I could hear Burt's deep chuckle behind me.

'Kirt, you scarin' dat boy ya bad t'ing.'

I'd been had; the lads joined in with the joke. At last the reel stopped spinning again and the boat fell silent.

'Okay man, reeeel him in.'

I was starting to feel like Captain Ahab. I could only imagine the most terrible creature attached to the hook, with humongous teeth waiting to take its revenge on whoever had dragged it from the deep. The rod snatched again and my seat belt tightened around my waist. The boat cheered each time I was pulled from one side to the other; it must be getting closer. My arms started to ache, as my prize got nearer and I was beginning to feel weak. Suddenly a can of beer was forced against my lips.

'Get this down you Den.'

He tipped the can but I wasn't ready, and the ice-cold liquid ran down my chest and into my lap.

'Dere he is man ... boy he's a big one.'

Kirt was leaning over the boat and signalling to me to wind the reel in as quickly as I could. He leaned backwards and grabbed the rather large pole.

'Okay Den hold him still I gotta gaff him.' What? Hold a fish still? What was I meant to do? Lean over and ask, 'look, you large thing with teeth, would you mind not thrashing around while my friend sticks a huge hook into your scaly flesh?'

I kept a fighting grip on the rod while Kirt swished away in the sea; the blokes on board were gawking and getting their cameras ready. With much relief to my tired limbs and a jerk of his shoulder Kirt announced,

'Got him man, one of you get me de stick.'

He frantically gestured at a baseball bat rolling around on the deck. He heaved with all his strength and the barracuda emerged, long and sleek, made for eating things bigger that itself. The hook was through its body just behind its head but rather than accept its fate the hook just seemed to annoy it. It must have been four foot long and as its tail slapped onto the floor, the blokes jumped onto the roof of the boat to avoid the new arrival. Two minutes ago they were hanging out of the boat trying to catch a glimpse. Kirt hammered the fish with the bat that came down with a sickening crunch, but with no effect; the last strike knocked the fish off the hook allowing the barracuda to thrash about without restraint. Kirt let out a scream and jumped up to join the lads.

So there I was, strapped into my seat, my legs on view to a vicious and angry fish that I had pissed off by pulling from its happy territory at the bottom of the ocean with a barbed hook, and aided by a limbless man in a hysterical laughing fit. It's all right for you uncle, I thought, you haven't got any bloody legs left for this bugger to chew on. The fish threw itself at me and it was difficult to hear who was making the most noise, Burt laughing or me screaming like a girl.

'Dat's a biiig fish man.' Kirt had his hands on his hips as he watched.

'Kill that sprat Kirt, quickly.'

My flip-flop came off as I attempted to kick the hungry jaws away from me. He tore it in his teeth and was distracted long enough for Kirt to jump from the roof and give him one almighty thwack on the head; the fish lay still at last. I'd landed my first ever catch, and it was something to talk about, not your three-pound carp that you throw back after the weigh in; this was a monster that could bite chunks out of flip-flops. As it lay there dead on the floor, I stood over it and looked up at the lads.

'Right lads, that's how you bring one in. Your turn next, but don't worry if you need a hand. Kirt and I are on call to assist.'

A small island appeared on the ocean horizon and we headed for it at full speed; there were two fish on the deck now, my leviathan and a much smaller one that Brian had pulled in with no real fight at all. Burt cut the engine again and a rusty anchor was thrown overboard.

'Let's eat boys.'

Kirt picked up my fish, slung it over his shoulder and jumped into the sea. We followed. Now this is what I see in my mind's eye when people talk about the Caribbean; there was a group of palm trees, golden sand and coconuts strewn on the beach. It was exotic, standing on the shoreline, feeling the warm breeze washing over my wet body; all I could hear was the quiet chatting of the boys and beer cans opening – Paradise! Kirt gave us a demonstration on how to gut a big fish with a small penknife, and then he slung the steaks on a barbecue that had been left on the island that he'd lit with husks from the coconuts. Nothing was too much bother for these guys. He waded out to his uncle with some of the char-grilled fish carried in a palm leaf.

If a story of this trip doesn't get around Camp like wildfire, I'll be stunned. I reckon that the next few Saturdays could turn out well for me. I was right, the next two weekends were full, and Kirt his uncle and I stuck to the same routine. It was a win:win situation, and the extra money had meant that I didn't have to break into my wages. One boat trip could fund my fags and beer for a whole week. Even the GSM came along after hearing about the excursion, and, to my relief, caught the biggest fish of the day, which grew in size every time he told the tale of pulling it in. By the time he'd related it to the CO, the catch was ten feet long and had half a car in its stomach. I think he'd seen too many Spielberg films.

My relationship with Kirt and his uncle was profitable and we had a good thing going. After a few outings I decided that I didn't need to go on any more fishing adventures as I'd pulled in more fish than Captain Bird's Eye, so I told Kirt that the sixty-forty deal could go his way as I was only doing the advertising.

The weeks flew by; my weekdays were busy driving and registering names for the next trip. Kirt never spoke badly of anyone; the worst insult that I heard from him was about one of the Officers, and he'd been trying to enlighten Kirt that though his methods were successful for catching fish, they were crude. In my opinion, if you're getting a good deal and having a great day out. you keep your mouth shut, but Officers are like that.

'Ya man's a blowfish,' Kirt had whispered to me on arriving back in town, which I suppose is a Creole insult of some sort. I was learning the language; they don't need to say much, and everything in their eyes is iree or good. In fact, iree has many meanings in Creole. It can mean hello, good, nice to look at; and, as Kirt explained one day, horny, after telling me., 'Can't wait te see me woman, I gat an iree feelin' man!' Lucky old Kirt.

Money comes to money, my mum says, like shooting fish in a barrel. That makes as much sense as life being like a box of chocolates, but when I read that Peanuts had sold my car, I felt that I was on a roll or at least a chocolate caramel (that's my first choice when offered chocs).

'And the buyer gave me an extra ten pounds because of the tools in the boot. I've written you a cheque, and sent off the paperwork to DVLC, I hope that's okay?'

My tools, she's sold them too. Is she brainless? Not only that but she sold the car for the price of a pair of jeans! Blimey, I shouldn't be so ungrateful; it was good of her to have the hassle. If it had been one of the lads they would have probably given me a tenner for the lot and told me that's all they could get for scrap. And what exactly am I going to do with a cheque in Central America?

I'd finished for the day and returned to the room to chill out. Gus was sat on his bed looking through a pile of cards.

'It's me bi'thdee Den, fancy a bevvy?'

'Yeah, sorry mate, I didn't know, happy birthday!'

He handed me a bottle with no label on it.

'What's this mate?' I enquired, as it obviously wasn't wine.

'Rum punch, it's greit!'

I took a swig and it *was* lovely.

'Gie it doon ye coopon, i've got anither three bottles, th' we're aff doon toon.'

Going out on a Monday night isn't any more happening in Belize City than anywhere else in the world but I couldn't let him down, so I grabbed a shower and got ready. By the time the bus was pulling up in the town we were both half cut. We toured all the pubs, trying a different tipple in each bar, before we landed at the Upstairs Café.

'Thus is crrap pal.'

Gus's drunken state made it nearly impossible to understand what he was saying, but I gathered that he wasn't over-impressed with the night life.

'Reit Den, av gat a greit idea.'

He was holding one finger in the air and waving it in front of my face as he sprayed me with spit.

'We'll gang te Raool's.'

I sort of knew this was coming; being in town was boring and the likelihood of getting caught was pretty slim, especially on a weekday.

'Okay Gus, I'm game, let's get a cab then.'

Raoul's Rose Garden is situated two miles from Camp on the main road; from the frontage it looks like an old barn with a sagging roof and no windows, with an everyday residential front door. I'd seen it open when I'd been in town and wondered what it was like inside. I imagined a seedy room, dimly lit with glass tables and steel stools against a shiny bar. The taxi pulled up sharply on the dusty lay-by that was the car park. The door opened before we had reached it and a huge guy loomed above us.

'Five dollar, RMP man.'

'What?'

'Five dollar man an' I tell ya whun da constalubury spitz to get ya.'

His arm rested protectively against the door and he stared over our heads into the bush; our taxi had gone and we were out of alternatives, so the only thing to do was to dig in my pocket and pull out ten dollars for Gus and me to enter. I thought it better to go in Raoul's than be observed waiting outside a brothel by the RMPs.

My visualization of a swish interior was shattered as the door opened; the barn-shaped building looked distinctly like a ... er ... barn from the inside too. One long rough wooden bar stretched down the wall. Garden benches littered the room and the dim lighting obviously set very low to disguise the poor state of the décor didn't enhance the atmosphere. For a place that was strictly out of bounds to all military personnel there were an awful lot of soldiers crammed around the bar drinking. We joined them and bought a couple of beers.

It appeared that the ladies approached the patrons in this venture; not that I frequent places like this, but it seemed unique. A short conversation, and then the pair would disappear through a door in the back to complete business. Some of the tarts were very busy and took bloke after bloke into their lair, spitting them out every ten to fifteen minutes with a grin on their faces; it was a shagging factory. I turned to talk to Gus but he was already in negotiations with one of the strumpets. It sounded as if he was attempting to get discount, as it was his birthday.

'Gus, come on mate, you don't need to...'

'Den it's mah birthdee an' aam gonnae treat me-self.'

He pushed me away and grasped the tart around her waist, pulling her towards the door.

'Iree darlin' how ya doin?'

I flinched at the sound of the female voice and felt a hand slide onto my thigh.

'Yeah, fine thanks, erm...'

'Thirty-one dollar gets ya an hour sweetheart, or ya could as me fe da night fe sixty one.'

Her hand was wandering over my crotch now and I could sense myself getting stirred up.

'Why the one dollar?'

'What darlin'?'

'You said thirty one and sixty one, so why the one dollar?'

'The one dollar goes to the church man, now do ya wanna party wit me?'

'Maybe another time. You're very nice but...'

She sucked through her teeth and shook her head.

'Ya don't like what ya see boy?'

As she spoke she lifted her flimsy dress and exposed herself.

'Erm ... yes ... I do but I just want to ... erm... have a drink for now.'

I felt myself cornered at her aggressive selling. More teeth sucking.

'Me t'ink ya want to look but too scared to touch man.'

She turned and strutted off to the next punter. Most of the other lads in the bar were in groups, chatting and laughing, but there were a few lost souls on their own doing the solitary drinking thing, waiting for the next available girl to offer her services. So I was now stuck on my own, in a whorehouse, waiting for my mate, feeling monadic.

'RMP!RMP!'

The man who had met us at the door screamed and waved his arms, sending the soldiers into panic as they hunted for somewhere to hide. Men ran through the secret door, pushing each other out of the way, and others leapt over the wooden bar. I'd just lit a fag and watched in wonderment as the crowded room emptied in seconds. Through the unfastened front door I saw a Land Rover pull up with its blue light flashing and doors open in readiness for the police to spring out. Then I realised I was the only guy still sat there. In one almighty bound I cleared the bar and ducked back underneath, where there was a shelf that should have had glasses stacked on it. I forced my body into the small space and held my breath. This shelf must have been ten metres long, and as I strained to look along it I could see the feet and heads of other men in a line hiding from the coppers. The barman stood with his legs at my midriff cleaning glasses and collecting bottles as footsteps of two, maybe three, monkeys approached across the wooden floor.

'Evening. Any soldiers from the Camp in here tonight?'

Now I'm not the world's most intuitive man, but if I had walked into a bar where bottles and drinks sat half full on tables, packets of cigarettes and lighters were strewn around the place I'd almost certainly assume that someone was around.

'No man not seun da single one tonight boss.' This guy could lie like a cheap watch. He bent down and tried to put a glass on the shelf that I was lying on. I took it from his hand and held onto it.

'So no soldiers at all then?'

'Look man I tell ya if I see dem right, dey not allowed to come in here man,'

It was a farce; the police weren't allowed to search the premises and had trust in what the barman said; he was doing a fine job of protecting his valuable customers. Then a door swung open and the rough Scottish voice I'd got so used to shouted,

'Den...av juus hud th' ride a me life meet...shite...coppers.'

It was too late; the triumphant Gus had been otherwise engaged during the chaos of the raid and had come to boast about his sexual exploits, only to find an empty bar and some RMP's waiting to arrest him. I could hear the scuffle as they pounced on him, informing him he was nicked for being in an out-of-bounds establishment against standing orders.

'It's me biirthdee ye fuckers, gimme a fuckin breek mon,' Gus protested as he was led through the door.

'All clear man,' the doorman announced, and I leapt back across the bar placing the glass down on the counter and rushed to see if the Land Rover had left. Outside, it was pitch black and the tail lights of the vehicle snaked off along the road towards Camp. There was nothing for it; I couldn't leave my mate to take the rap, and so I ran in the dark along the road, following the Rover.

The roads are pocked and the condition varies with the amount of rain; driving along can be tricky but running the length was a nightmare. I was tripping and stumbling all over the place. I'd run what I guessed was about a mile when I saw the tail lights again, this time stationary. I fell into a walk as it started to rain; I could hear the sound of the fat raindrops beating on the trees and the cricket choir singing in the background. It was definitely the RMP Land Rover; in the silhouette of the blue lights two men were looking at a wheel. Closer I crept, hugging the side of the road, which sloped into a swamp, soaking my feet. I paused to listen, about ten feet away from the vehicle.

'So why didn't you bring a spare?'

'Ah forgot tuh put it back on Boss, soz.'

'Give me strength! Forget to tie a knot in your handkerchief, dimwit? How far is it from Camp?'

'Abyeut a mile ah think, wuh cud radio back an' git the othor crew tuh brin yen yeut Sarge?'

'Not on your nelly, do I look like I'm gonna announce this to the entire Camp? I'd never live it down, I'd like you to remember that but I'm not sure you're capable. So keep your trap shut, as we are boldly going nowhere. This would be really funny if it wasn't happening to me. Bloody hell!'

'Sorry Sarge.'

This was it; they couldn't figure out what to do and were

staring at the flat tyre at the front of the Rover as if they could command it to inflate again. I reached out and tugged at the rear door handle; it wasn't locked and the door swung back with a creak.

'Gus,' I whispered.

'Den?' he replied louder than he needed to. I shushed him. The barney was continuing as Gus stumbled out of the back of the vehicle and I closed the door quietly and we made our way off into the night.

We retreated into the swamp as far as we dared and crouched down, giggling like a couple of schoolgirls at our jailbreak.

'Did they ask your name Gus?' I whispered.

'Nae, th' loons!' He was bouncing up and down on his haunches looking at me a little panicked.

'Den?'

'Yes mate.'

'Ah need a slash, aw 'at bumpin aroon in th' back o 'at lanny has dain me in.'

'Well go on then, I won't look,'

'Ah cannae.'

'Why not?'

'Whit if onna tham beasties bites me ol fella?'

'Gus you big ninny just have a piss, we need to get going in a minute.'

'Den?'

'What?'

'Ah can hear a snake.'

'Oh shut up for goodness' sake you'll be wanting me to hold your hand next.'

'De-en?'

'Gus.'

'Ah dinney lake snakes mucker.'

'Well I dinney like standing knee high in bloody swamps at two in the morning but it's either this or back in the Land Rover.'

'De-en,'

'Yes.' I was getting extremely annoyed now and my voice had risen.

'Ah dinney need te gang fe a pee anymair.'

He looked very sorry for himself now. We didn't have time to continue messing around and I shoved him in the direction of the Camp. We waded parallel to the Rover and out of sight until the headlights disappeared in the distance behind us, and we scrambled back onto the road to make it easier going.

As we walked along, another RMP Land Rover passed us on the way out. We looked at each other, smiled, and then waved as it passed us.

Chapter Twenty-nine

I've seen tarantulas on telly and at the zoo before but when I opened my locker to find one staring at me with its beady eyes and looking hairy and threatening, I wasn't quite so fascinated. Instead, I slammed my locker shut and called for back-up. Gus said to stamp on it but I thought I'd wait for it to leave voluntarily. The problem was that I needed to get my kit ready for the morning and the creature was blocking my way. I waited an hour and ventured back into my wardrobe only to find him still there, so I carefully grabbed my clothes and shut the door again; he'll have gone by the morning. Just in case, I moved my bed nearer the window and erected my mosquito net for the first time in three months. I mean, I didn't want him to stray onto my bed and then me roll over during the night, and damage him. After breakfast I checked again, and he was squatting there in exactly the same place. He must be resting after a long walk, or dead, but I decided to give him more time just in case he was lost and couldn't find his way home. I was driving to Belmopan with the boss and I told him of my arachnid visitor, much to his amusement. He said I should keep him as a pet; it wouldn't take much exercise and it would give me something to write home about.

Gus and I started on a suitable lodging as soon as tea had finished. We ripped off a chicken wire grille from the window and bent it into a box shape. For the floor I found a piece of wood, which fitted a treat, and in no time, hey presto! we were done.

'It's a wee bit boss Den, de ye hink we shoods pit some hin' inside te lit th' wee fella hide under?'

It was a good idea so I went to the bogs and unravelled a roll of toilet tissue and placed the tube inside.

'Stoatin, reit ye gie th' wee bugger?'

'What?'

'Weel ye foond it, ye gie it.'

'Why don't you get it Gus?'

'Cannae mucker, aam allergic tae spiders.'

'Get stuffed, that's a crap excuse, go on.'

We debated who was going to pick up the spider and decided that the fairest way, and my usual method, was to toss a coin, best of three, and so on until we had reached the best of twenty-five, and I lost.

'All right, you open the door and I'll ... Gus, how am I supposed to pick it up?'

'Jist grab th' bludy hin' it willnae bite ye.'

'Does the spider know that Gus?'

'Weel use th' dustpan 'en cheil.'

He was a genius, so I stood by as he swung the door open and retreated to the other side of the room.

'Gus, I think it's dead.'

'Whit? efter aw 'at?'

'Well it hasn't moved since I first saw it, I'm sure it's dead.'

'Weel poke it wi' th' dustpan 'en, make sure.'

As I gently prodded the spider's leg it sprang into action as if it had been waiting for two days for some clot; in unison, the spider and I jumped, he about two inches and I about four foot away onto my bed.

'Whoa Gus it nearly had me there.'

The shock had made me laugh and Gus joined me on the bed. Two grown soldiers, trained and professional against a small spider; it was humbling.

'Reit Den, scoop it up an' i'll hauld th' cage, ye flin' heem in.'

'Thanks Gus, you're such a pal.'

'Ahh that's nae problems mucker,.'

I went in again, this time sliding the tray until it touched the bottom of its feet; to my amazement it walked onto the dustpan without any drama. Slowly, lifting the pan, I walked towards Gus, who held the metal cage up from the wooden base, the spider riding on the dustpan. I carried my new pet like a welder's assistant, not looking just in case he tried any more funny business, and tiptoed along as my alleged friend watched.

'Den he's oan th' move.' Gus sounded excited.

'Where to?'

'Towards ye, he's walkin' towards yer hain, coorie up.'

I quickened my pace and lifted the pan higher so that I couldn't see what was going on.

'Den...git a feckin' move oan he's nearly oan yer hain.'

As I glanced up I could see a hairy leg looming over the handle and very close to me. There was nothing for it and I lunged forward shoving the spider and dustpan into the cage, which shut with a slam as soon as I released my grip.

'Got th' wee camel blower.'

We started to laugh in relief of our close brush with mortality and stared into the cage as the tarantula inspected his new home, complete with cardboard toilet roll and our dustpan. I could always go to the stores and get a new one.

'So what shall we call him then Gus?' I asked, as we sat down with a bottle of rum punch.

'Hoo de ye ken it's a fella?'

'I dunno, it just looks like a bloke that's all.'

'Den, as grait as yer logic is, a dorn think we can label th' puir bugger cos he looks lake a bloke, me lalatinkiepie looks lake a bloke, but she'd knock yer teeth it if ye called 'er Leslie!'

The bottle emptied and so did a couple more, as we disputed names for our new pet and the last thing I can remember was lying on my bed chortling at Gus's suggestion that we should name him after the GSM.

To have a hangover in a tropical country is an experience I'll never forget; as well as the thumping headache, the heat is so intense that dehydration sets in at a rapid rate. By morning I felt pruned, and could have drunk the contents of Lake Windermere. We cleared the empty bottles away, and I sat down for a morning fag and cup of tea while Gus went for a shower. The spider cage was designed so that we could watch our new friend from all angles; and apart from a dustpan, the only place for him to take shelter was inside the toilet roll holder, so when I initially glanced in the chummy and couldn't see him, I wasn't too worried. Gus returned with his towel around his waist and enquired after our pet, staring long and hard into the cage.

'De-en?'

'Yes mate, I'm just off for a shower.'

'De-en?'

'What?'

'Where's th' spider?'

A rhetorical question if ever I heard one.

'Den, th' spider's gain.'

'He's in the toilet tube.'

'It's nae.' His voice went up and down like they do in the theatre when they say *oh yes it is*. 'Ack it's not.' The last part is strung out in sarcasm.

I joined him to look; we looked from corner to corner, scanning to see where he was hiding. He was gone!

'How did he get out Gus?'

He stared in disbelief into the cage, scanning under the dustpan.

'He main hae hud a wee key Den.'

'Okay ... where do you think he's gone then?'

'Den fa th' buck dae ye hink Ah am man? David bludy Attenboroogh? Ah dinney ken.'

I was feeling vulnerable to say the least, dressed in only a towel with a huge man-eating spider on the loose. I needed a plan; no, I needed David Attenborough.

We scoured the floor, walls and roof for the spider, turning up boots and shaking clothes to see if it had taken up an ambush position but after some considerable time we had failed to spot him.

'He's gone mate,' I told Gus, as he was sifting through his wash bag at arm's length.

'Hoo dae ye know?'

'He's bound to have humped off back home Gus, leave it.'

Time was getting on and I needed to pick up the boss in half an hour so I started to get dressed, and flung open my locker to grab my kit.

'FUCK MY OLD BOOTS!'

'Whit cheil?'

Gus rushed over as I leapt backwards, pointing at the spider that was sitting in the same position as we had found him.

Gus let out a sigh. 'Phew, thenk God fur 'at.'

'What do you mean? He's back in my bloody locker.'

'Dornt fash yerse, it coods hae bin waur, it coods hae bin mah locker.'

He laughed and strolled off to his side of the room, whistling a tune to himself.

'Gus, you twat, what am I supposed to do now?'

'Och, jist lae heem, he looks braw.'

'Well what do you suggest I do then, move out?'

'Swatch Den am aff oan me R an' R in a coople ay days, use mah locker mucker till Ah come back, he'll suin gie fed up an' gang haem.'

Gus was going to Florida for a couple of weeks' leave, and as the spider had decided that an open cage was more fitting, I would make alternative arrangements and use Gus's locker and bed space until the little bugger moved out.

For the next two days I watched my new neighbour sat in the bottom of my locker; apparently they can squeeze themselves through all manner of small spaces and that's how he escaped. The day came for Gus to go on leave and I checked again.

'Gus, he's gone.'

'Ah tauld ye he'd gie fed up in thaur, an' in onie case fa coods stain mair than fower days wi' yer lowpin' socks, eh?'

'Ha ha very funny, so what time are you off?'

'Mah flight's at three sae i'll be gain by th' time ye gie back frae wark, dae ye want anythin' bringin' back mucker?'

'Er, yeah, a blonde would be welcome, thanks.' I left Gus packing a case for his holiday.

The GSM was in his office writing when I reported for work, so I made him a cup of tea and went to find out if we were going out anywhere.

'Morning Sir, made a brew for you.'

'Morning Corporal Yarwood, thank you. Did the CO's driver get away on his holiday?'

'He leaves at three Sir, who'll be driving the boss while he's away?'

'You'll have to double-hat young man, I'm not going anywhere this week,'

'Okay Sir, no probs,.' I turned to walk out.

'Hang on a moment, I haven't finished with you yet,'

'Right Sir,'

'You need to see the boss. Nothing to worry about, come on, he's expecting you.'

I followed in curiosity as the GSM led me to his office and knocked at the door; he marched in and saluted.

'Sir, Corporal Yarwood to see you Sir.'

'Thanks GSM, show him in would you?'

I entered as the GSM had done and stood to attention at his desk.

'Sit down Corporal Yarwood, I've got some news for you.'

As I'd only ever chatted to him a couple of times I couldn't read into any body language to tell me what sort of interview this was.

'This is in no way connected with you personally you savvy Yarwood; however, your Battalion has been having a few irritations recently and has been CDT'd, much to our dismay some of these tests have resulted positive. It seems that the men have been using the grass for more than playing rugby on. Anyway, I digress. Your CO back home and I have been chatting and he is light on full Corporals for the next tour of Belfast, and, well, to cut a long story short, he has promoted you to acting Corporal. Do you know what that means?'

'Well, erm, no Sir.'

'You are to be a full Corporal and paid as one from today, but on a probation. If, after a year, you perform well, the promotion will become substantive, well done, march out.'

And that was that, promoted on the spot, even if it was on trial. I walked back to see the GSM.

'So.' His hand was held out to shake mine. 'Full Corporal now Yarwood, well done son, I wish you were in my Battalion full time, you're a good lad.'

I was lost for words. I'd been a Lance Corporal just over a year and now I was expected to step up.

'So I suppose you'll be wanting the day off tomorrow to recover from your hangover?'

'Pardon Sir?'

'Come on lad, when I got promoted to Corporal I got so drunk the lads had to put me to bed. Go on, have a good night.'

'Cheers Sir.'

I ran back to the block to tell Gus, stunned but glowing with excitement. I wanted to tell the world. Gus wasn't in, so I sat on my bed and took my writing kit out to tell Mum and Peanuts. I thought a detailed letter to Mum was in order so that she didn't go telling her friends that I was now a General. Gus came in carrying a plastic bag and tipped out the contents onto the bed.

'Alrecht Den, nae wark the-day 'en?'

He carried on sifting through his shopping and held up his items one at a time to show me.

'Sin tan oil, Ah dornt use it ower haur but if am gonna pull Ah dornt want tae swatch lake a lobster. New swimmers, got some 'at shaw aff mah pooch, i'll need tae shove a coople ay socks doon th' front, ha ha...'

'Gus.'

'Och an' a huge pack a johnnys jist in case....'

'GUS.'

'Yeah whit pal?'

'I've just been promoted.'

'Bludy heel congratulations.Why didn't ye say?'

'I was trying to but I couldn't get a word in.'

'Ha ha sorry mucker stoatin we'll hae tae gang fur a bevve when Ah gie back, Den Ah got tae scit ur i'll miss mah plane.'

He shook my hand and threw his case out of the door.

'Crivvens, Ah nearly forgot.' he was reaching in his pocket.

'Ah picked th' post up, sorry they're a wee bit wrinkly,' and he threw me two scraggy letters; a bank statement and one from Peanuts, and let the door slam shut.

Chapter Thirty

It was dark when I awoke; I had no idea how long I'd been unconscious or how much alcohol I'd consumed. My stomach churned and head pounded as I tripped over bottles and cans to get to the light switch. I winced as the bulb blinked and staggered back to my bed. I tipped the wad of my wallet on the sheets and fingered through taxi rank cards and scraps of paper looking for a phone number. I needed to talk, but the number wasn't there, and I threw the pieces of paper into the corner. The GSM always left his office open; I'd been in there at night before when he'd forgotten his map and sent me to fetch it; there was no worry in my mind I was doing anything illegal by rummaging through his drawers but I couldn't care about that now. He must have a military phone book somewhere or some correspondence for my unit in Catterrick; it couldn't have been late as people were milling around outside the NAAFI, laughing and drinking; how could they be laughing now? I needed another drink so I went into the bar and pushed my way to the front of the queue.

'Whisky ... big one.'

'Please .' the woman sang at me.

'Whisky ... big one... PLEASE.' My flippant retort met with a disapproving look as she pushed the glass against the optic. I pushed a five-dollar note across the bar and gulped the drink down.

'Another one.'

'Are you all right dearie?'

'Please, just pour another one.'

The glass didn't touch the bar this time; I took it straight out of her hand and sank it. This time I gestured with the glass, demanding a refill.

'Goodness me, you may as well have the bottle if you're going to carry on like that.'

'Good idea, how much?'

'I was only joking, it looks like you've had enough anyway.'

'HOW MUCH?' I slapped another ten dollars on the counter, making her flinch, and I felt a hand on my shoulder.

'Look mate, don't be rude, she's doing her job.' I wanted to punch whoever was commenting on my manners; I wanted a drink, not a lecture in etiquette. The bottle appeared in front of me with some coins, so I took it and staggered out into the night. The ink on the paper was spotted as I tried to find the number; it must be here somewhere. My frustration grew into anger and I started to rip through the letters and then reached for a fag. It was then I saw it. Carefully tearing the number out I decided to go to the international phone booth by the guardroom. The walk back across Camp took ages as I lurched over drainage ditches and fell from the footpath; the whisky and tears had blurred my vision so that the lights from the windows had a halo around them.

When I arrived at the phone booth there was already someone making a call so I stood to one side and waited. To make it feel more like home, the Army had transported an old red phone-box over. It looked out of place, it had a broken window, and the paint had peeled in the Belizean heat so it was mostly pink. My pacing up and down had caught the attention of the caller, who turned his back on me time and again as I paraded around the booth chanting, *'come on'* to myself and looking at the number in my hand. What would I say?

'Yes my darling I'll be home in three weeks, give the munchkins a kiss for me.'

'I love you back honey, miss you ...'bye.'

The receiver went down and the man opened the door smiling; he held the door for me and I thanked him. I'd never had to use the international phone box before so it took me a few seconds to read the instructions on the wall.

'Hello International Operator, number rank and name please.' She sounded Belizean but spoke clearly and not in the usual Creole. I gave her my details.

'What country please?'

'Luton ... no ... England, what time is it?'

I'd realised that I had no idea what time it was at home; were we six hours ahead or behind? It wouldn't be any good to phone up in the middle of the night. What was I going to say?

'It's ten past six, Sir.'

'No, no I mean in England, what time is it in England?'

'About mid-day Sir, what number please?'

I read the number slowly; my focus was unsteady and the digits seemed to be moving across the paper on their own. Like ants. My heart started to race as I heard the clicking of the connection. It sounded like the video printer on Saturday Grandstand as it snapped out the football results, and then silence before the ringing.

I waited for an eternity before the Operator's voice came back online.

'No answer sir, can I try another number please?'

This can't be right, someone must be in.

'Sir, can I try and connect you to another number?'

The light was on in the GSM's office as I crashed through the door; on the wall hung lists of contact numbers for other units in Camp and at the bottom of one was a handwritten note saying, 'First Battalion, Catterick Guardroom.' I sat at his desk and dialled the number. Again, the noise of the connection took ages and then the ringing, but this time it was answered.

'Guardroom, Corporal Stevens Sir.'

The voice echoed through the distant connection and there

was a delay as it took its time to link up. I composed myself before answering.

'Hi, this is Corporal Den Yarwood, I'm in Belize with the Second Battalion. Look, I need to get hold of Guardsman Coleman.'

'Lofty?'

'Yes Lofty, I need to speak to him.'

'Lofty's a Lance Jack now mate.'

'Yeah, great. Look, can I speak to him?'

'He's in 'B' Company mate.'

'Yes, I know.'

'Well phone 'B' Company then.'

I could feel the anger swelling up inside me.

'Look, I haven't got the bleedin' number have I? Or I would have phoned them instead.'

The man's answer had made me well up; he had no idea of the gravity of the situation, not that it was his fault; but if I'd called for a casual chat about telephonics I'd have made it blatantly obvious from the start.

'Cor Blimey mate, don't get yourself in a Harvey Nichol, hang on I'll find the number for you. It's extension 3344.'

'Thank you.' I dialled again and got through to the Company offices and the delightful Tina, who I hadn't spoken to since our tussle by the riverbank in Winchester.

'Hello Tina, it's Den Yarwood.'

'Oh, long time no see, how's the Caribbean? That's where you are isn't it?'

'Tina, I need to speak to Lofty Coleman, is he around?'

'Why don't you talk to me? I've still got your jacket.'

'Tina look – it's great out here. I'll tell you all about it when I get back. I'm sorry but it's an emergency.'

'Maybe you could take me for another drink, we've got some unfinished business.'

'Tina please, where's Lofty?' I could hear my own voice breaking against the echo of the phone.

'He's not in today Den, 3 Platoon are on the ranges, can I take a message?'

'No, tell him I'll phone tomorrow, it's really important, will you do that for me please?'

'If I see him, I'll tell him.'

'Thanks.'

'Den, is everything all right?'

Everything was all wrong; it was terrible, I was empty and upset and tired and confused and I needed to hear a friendly voice, not some stupid slapper asking me if everything was all right when she didn't even know me. How dare she ask if I was all right? How the bloody hell could she have known how I was feeling?

'Yeah, just tell Lofty I called. 'Bye.'

I placed the receiver back and laid my head on the desk. There was a photo of the GSM with his wife and his children; they were younger then I imagined when I'd heard his talk about them; a boy of about ten and an older girl, who had her arm draped around his neck and was giving him a kiss on the cheek. She was wearing a denim top and stripy tights and my world fell apart as I sobbed. I remembered the first time Peanuts had kissed my cheek in the pub. It wasn't the kiss I remembered clearly, more the feel of her hand on the side of my face cupping my cheek. It was soft and warm and smooth and she'd moved it a little and touched my ear, sending shivers down my back; not in a sexual way, just something nice, it felt like home. It felt like the sort of hand that could make you better when you were ill. I closed my eyes and tried to feel it again with my own hand to see if I could take away the pain but it wouldn't. Just one small touch, it felt like she ... she loved me. Then I remembered our argument in Amsterdam, and how she barfed and we made up and went out for dinner, and when I rescued her at the party and her selling my car and sending me the money. This could be some stupid wind-up. The phonebox was empty and I dialled the Operator again, this time answering her questions straight off. The phone rang and a frail voice said 'Hello?'

'Mrs Brady?'

'Yes, who's calling?' She sounded tired and not as polite as I'd remembered. I kept calm and steady as I talked.

'I'm Denis.'

'Who? Sorry could you speak up please?'

'I'm Denis, a friend of Pea ... Kerry.'

'Oh ... hello Denis.'

I knew then; her voice fell away and the line went dead, then a fresh voice came on the line.

'Hello, who is this?'

'Erm, I'm Denis, a friend of Kerry.'

It was as if we were both too scared to ask what the phone call was about; my voice trembled as I spoke and I felt like hanging up.

'I'm her Auntie Brenda, did you know her?'

Did you know her? Past tense.

'Yes I knew her ... I know her well.'

'Are you her boyfriend?'

'No, well kind of ... I don't know what to say ... is she ... all right?'

'I'm sorry dear you must be one of the last to know. Kerry passed away last Thursday in hospital, it was all very peaceful, they made her very comfortable.'

The empty bottle smashed on the floor and I slid down the booth to join it, holding the receiver to my ear but unable to speak. This woman was telling me that Peanuts, my Peanuts. Had really died, no joke, dead.

'She wrote to me, how did she write to me?'

'Oh, are you the young man in America?'

'Belize.'

'Yes, that's right, Belize. My sister, Kerry's mother, posted a letter to you last week. Oh you poor dear, have you only just found out?'

'I got the letter today, why did she write to me like that?' I could hear my voice whining.

'Kerry asked her to post it, she said that it was important, I'm glad you got it.'

'Why she didn't tell me ...?' Someone tapped on the booth and pointed at their watch.

'FUCK OFF, sorry, not you.' I was still connected.

'I'm not sure I understand you Denis. The service is on Friday at two. Will you be coming?'

'No. I can't.'

'Well, call again if you want to chat. I'm so sorry you had to find out like this, it's been so hard for us to lose her. She was such a good girl.'

'Yeah ... I know ... I better go now.'

'Thank you for calling Denis.'

"Bye.'

Selfish cow. I can't believe she'd do that to me after we had talked about it as well. I thought I'd made myself clear that to receive a letter like this would devastate someone, and she carried on regardless, bloody well regardless. I don't give a toss if she did fancy me, she should have had the decency to tell me when she was alive not chicken out. I don't even think it would have taken her long to write the letter, probably an afterthought; it certainly didn't take much on her part, but it's not just me, is it? Her mum must feel awful now; she may not have seen the content of the letter but she damn well knew that the recipient would find out the hard way. It's just so underhand and deceitful. I ask you, what did she think I'd do if she had told me? I'm not a doctor but I could have given her some support. All of the secrets we swapped, and she kept the biggest one from her best friend. I don't think so, when it comes down to it blood is thicker than water and all that. I feel like a fool for crying over her; she knew when she wrote that, that I'd be stuck over here; well, maybe she was wrong and not so clever after all, maybe I didn't actually want to be with her, and our friendship meant nothing. That's it: nothing. I didn't feel a thing, that's why I bought her a clock for Christmas because that was all our friendship was worth, and this crappy lighter was just to keep me thinking that she really cared. I don't think she cared about anyone.

I scrabbled through the torn letters and found the last one she'd posted, two weeks ago, that seals it. That's why she posted me the bloody cheque – she didn't want the responsibility of my money. I must have been a real burden to her. Bitch!

The room was decimated when I returned. I couldn't remember making this mess. Bottles and letters thrown and kicked all over the place, the spider's cage smashed in the corner. My body was shutting down with the shock and I shivered for the first time in months. I lit my last cigarette and pulled her letter from my pocket. Auntie Brenda's words kept replaying on a loop in my head.

If Peanuts had told me I could have done something. I can't believe that no one could help her and they just let her die. She knew that she loved me and didn't say a word. I could have been her boyfriend, and instead I'm nothing, just a bloke in Belize that no one will listen to. I wonder if I was the only person she'd written to; no, Auntie Brenda definitely said letter and not letters. But I'm a no one, not quite a boyfriend, a could-have-been, and it *could have been*. I was happy as a single man, not ready to fall in love; but I didn't know then, I don't need to know now, we were good together, best friends, someone I could trust and laugh with and fuckety, fuck, shit, fuck ... Love, why didn't I see it? This is my fault. She died not knowing if I loved her back; I did love her, no I do love her, I would have been the best boyfriend ever, we would have eaten meals together and gone to the cinema and on holiday and I wouldn't have cheated on her or anything. Another conversation clouded my thoughts of what our children would have looked like. I buried my head in my hands in disbelief at missing the obvious, and she spelt it out to me. I visualised her lying in a hospital bed telling her mum about me and that I could have been her husband if things had been different.

I pulled open Gus's locker and there was another bottle of rum on the shelf and a packet of fags, I took a healthy swig, lit up and opened the letter again.

To my dear Denis,

I've got some explaining to do, I know. I meant to tell you about the leukaemia but I couldn't ever find the words and now all there is is this letter. I should make the most of your attention and use this chance to be utterly and completely honest – finally.

We made a sensational team Den. I wish that night in the cathedral had been different and we were married; I always regarded you as my better half. Please be strong, I think it is one of your most compelling traits, my knight in shining armour defending the nation and me. I have constantly adored you since we met but thought our relationship would only succeed without the 'love' complications. However, you are an admirable heart-throb and I treasure the times we spent together.

I understand that your art lessons have now come to an abrupt end. Would you accept one last class? There is a painting called 'The Kiss.' It is extraordinary and is a symbol of happiness. Countless flowers encircle a couple and spirals represent never-ending life. I want to be in love like the woman in the painting, but it is beyond me. Promise me that you will find a true love Den and make the picture real.

What I'm trying to say is please believe in yourself Den, you are such an amazing, sexy, sometimes bewildering but largely a breathtakingly rare and charming man whom I cherish, I love you Denis Yarwood. Please remember me fondly.

With all my affection forever
Kerry Petra Brady (nom de plume) KP Nuts

Chapter Thirty-one

The cold light of the morning arced through the window; I thought that expression would be more accurate in northern Europe. The weather hasn't changed; it's in spite of everything humid and hot now, easily about 28°C, but I felt chilly and bitter. It didn't take me long to fill a binbag with the debris I'd left from last night; the stench of fags and old bottles made me feel sick. I was still drunk, as I didn't feel like I had a hangover in the slightest. Anyway, I think skipping breakfast would be a good idea.

I picked up the letter and read it to make sure it wasn't a very bad dream. The words meant nothing to me, and I had no emotion left to pour out. It felt like I'd used up my grief in one go and I felt guilty; I should have been crying more, but I couldn't. Never having lost anyone before, I wasn't sure if I should be in more of a state. I didn't feel blame or gloom about the event, just my feelings of loss and guilt, and I needed to talk to Lofty. No one knew me here well enough and I hadn't mentioned Peanuts to anyone so I was lost for support. It had crossed my mind to phone Mum but she hadn't even met her. We weren't an item and I didn't know why I was now referring to her and me as one; it was like the letter now made us a couple.

I reported for work and was told by the GSM that we wouldn't be going out for a couple of days and I was to service the Land Rover, so I made my way to the Military Transport Section and got on with filling my mind with menial tasks until tea-time. Another wasted meal. I knew I should be eating but I just couldn't stomach it, so I returned to my room and opened a can of beer instead.

The office was open again and I dialled the number hoping that this time I wouldn't get some fool on the other end of the line.

"B' Company; Corporal Coleman Sir.'

'Lofty.' I could hear the relief in my own voice, so pleased to hear him.

'What is it Den?' He didn't sound surprised to hear from me.

'Lofty I need to chat mate.'

'Don't Den, don't call me mate, it took me months to get my promotion after you shat on me so just spare me the kindness.'

'I'm sorry Lofty, I ...'

'Look, just what do you want?'

'Remember Peanuts?'

'Yeah, the bird with the stupid tights and stupid mates'

'She's ... well ... Lofty she's...'

'Pregnant, big fucking deal, what do you want me to do about it? Are you coming to me for help? 'Cos if you are, I just can't let go what you did, if you're looking for sympathy, you'll find it between shit and syphilis in the dictionary...'

'Lofty, she's not pregnant, she died.' My voice finally broke and the tears came again. The phone went quiet for a long time.

'That's low Den.'

'What do you mean?'

'I mean that to try and get back, you pull a stunt like this,.'

'What?'

'Listen Yarwood, don't bother, you're a lying little cunt, you don't deserve any mates, now fuck off back to your pointless life and leave me to get on with mine.'

The phone crashed down on the end of the line and I was alone in the office, very very alone.

The friendship and trust was shattered and he even thought I could lie about Peanuts. I needed him to be there for me and he turned his back, just like she'd turned her back on me when she wrote that letter. The anger of betrayal took over and I threw the phone against the wall, shattering the glass of one of the GSM's pictures. I needed a drink.

Once again the NAAFI was packed. I wanted to be in a crowd, where someone would understand and talk to me. The lady behind the bar sold me another bottle of whisky and I set about trying to chat to the lads who loitered around the bar. After a while of trying desperately to break into different conversations I sat on my own, devouring the drink and chain smoking. It seemed a good thing to do, although I was starting to get strange looks from groups of blokes at different tables. My vision was starting to go but across the room I noticed a small group playing cards, so I staggered across to watch. The play was fast, and not knowing much about cards, I concentrated on the nearest bloke to me to see if I could pick up on anything of the game. It was poker; I figured it out after he'd gone broke a couple of times on seventeen and threw in his hand in disgust along with a handful of matchsticks that had been piled up in front of him. He stood reaching into his pocket and retrieving his wallet.

'I'm out lads, how much do I owe?'

One of the other lads raised his hand to stop him pulling cash out of his wallet.

'Not here, Dave you'll get us all shot, pay up in the morning, you owe fifty.'

The man said goodnight and walked off, leaving his seat free.

'You want a game?' a voice asked as I stood watching. I thought I'd picked up enough of the game to play now, but I wasn't sure about the matches.

'Sure,.'

I plonked myself down on the chair and poured another drink. A big lad with grey hair sitting opposite leaned over to talk to me. I'd seen him whilst servicing my vehicle earlier that day and I thought he was one of the Sergeants from the transport section.

'You're the GSM's driver, aren't you?'

'Yeah, Den.' I shook his hand.

'Right mate, it's fifty dollars to be in the game, we only play with matches in the bar, each match is worth ten, you pay what you owe or collect in the morning from me. Right?'

'Yeah, sure.' I could afford fifty dollars easily. He counted five matches out and slid them over to me; I mean, what did I have to lose? Lofty had thought I was lying about Peanuts, and she was getting buried in the morning; so I had nothing but my money and a bottle of whisky. I wasn't going to let my tea go cold over it. As someone so fittingly put it. The only thing with playing cards is that a lot of concentration is needed and seeing as I was now half-way through the bottle and kept getting flashes of Peanuts in my head it wasn't long before I was being asked if I wanted to stick or twist. Queen and a four; I shoved two matches into the middle and asked for a card. A three, that was ... seventeen, another, ten; bollocks, bust. Another two hands and my matches were all gone, so I sat and watched the game again until the big bloke asked,

'You still in mate?'

'No, I think I'll leave it.' which was a good plan as I could feel my stomach churning.

'Right you are, see me in the morning before ten and settle up then, remember I know who you work for.'

The statement left me indifferent but it was time to go and the bile was starting to make my mouth water.

'Yeah, see ya.'

I picked up my bottle and ran for the door, just making it to the outside before I was sick.

The room was in a mess; and I lay on my bed finishing the rest of the bottle, glancing at the letter from time to time. What did she mean about me being such a good bloke? We'd had a laugh but I couldn't recall doing anything that would be deemed as Bon Vivant. And wishing we were married ... why didn't she just ask me? I know it's a bloke's part but I didn't know, I just couldn't see it; or her – that's it, I couldn't see her. Like bloody leukaemia whatever that is, you just can't see it until it's too late; but just as she couldn't see the cancer until too late I couldn't see that she loved me until it was too late. I took a momentary look at my watch. It was ten o'clock; four in the afternoon in the UK, and they would be getting ready for the funeral. Peanuts would be in a coffin, dead, quiet and still, I wonder if she would be wearing tights, but that would mean that some stranger had dressed her, seen her naked. It's so impersonal being dead. I'd never see her again.

I woke with a start and looked at the time. Ten-thirty; not only was I late for work, I hadn't paid the cards bloke on time. Panic set in immediately and I rushed to get dressed and scraped my face with a blade.

'Good afternoon Corporal Yarwood.'

The GSM's sarcastic voice made me stop in my tracks outside his office but before I could speak he beckoned me in.

'I think we need a chat, don't you?'

He told me to sit down and I looked at him as he took a slurp of his coffee.

'Right, apart from being late and me having to cover for you with the boss, someone has been in my office and I want you to find out who it was.' The picture that I'd smashed the previous night lay on his floor next to the desk, with the glass missing and a dent in the front.

'See that.' He pointed at the picture,. 'That's me when I was an instructor at Sandhurst. Some wicked blighter has been in here and smashed it with my phone. I'm not very pleased.'

The realisation of what I'd done had sunk in and I stared open-mouthed at the picture, thinking that what I was doing was senseless. I thought that if I told him now he would take pity on me. I could get the picture repaired and that would be the end of it.

'Right S, I'll ask around,' and I stood up to leave.

'One more thing.'

'Yes Sir?'

'You stink of booze. I suggest that you disappear and go and clean yourself up.'

I left, and went straight round to the Transport Section, where the Sergeant was waiting for me. He warned me not to be late again as I gave him the fifty bucks, and I disappeared to my room once more to get a shower.

I've never been one to clock-watch, but today was the day that she would be cremated and I toiled over every minute. As tea-time grew closer my stomach rumbled and my body told me that alcohol wasn't going to sustain me for much longer, so I made my way to the cookhouse and ate for the first time in two days.

As I sat alone on my bed for the third night running with only a bottle of whisky and some fags as my companions, I let my emotions flood out. Somewhere there must be a handbook to tell me how to grieve; because I couldn't be doing it right. Sitting and sobbing felt good in a way but I should do something. Nine p.m.; in an hour she would be in church with her friends and family and I would be drunk and alone in Central America. I was the only one she wanted and I couldn't be there to say goodbye. At my stage in life I should be happy, married and happy, with a kiddie or two running around calling me Dad.

'I love you Denis Yarwood. Please remember me fondly.'

The killer line, it's all I could see. Peanuts, I do remember you fondly, I love you back. I want to hold you darling and be with you now, to keep you warm at night and feel you next to me. When you're down I'll be there to pick you up and make you laugh. When we get married you can wear your silly tights at our wedding, we'll dance to Madness and sing; everyone will eat fish and chips and drink cider. My dearest Peanuts, please don't ever leave me, don't let your memory be faded in my mind, I need it there with me. I feel flattered that out of all the blokes in the world who are cleverer, stronger, better looking, I was the one that you wanted to be with. We could have lots of children to look after us, a big strong boy to take me to the pub and some girls for you to go shopping with. I'll be the best-ever dad and when they grow up we'll have parties for them and take pictures of us smiling and laughing. Every day I'll tell you that I love you, and kiss you before I go to work, and when I come home you can cook me tea and I'll do the washing-up. We can go to midnight mass every year and wrap presents together and in the summer I'll take you for picnics to the countryside and we can read books together. You can show me The Kiss and we can be like that; my love for you will be always that sort of love that you can't see or touch; it will feel like a warm blanket on a cold day, like a hot-water bottle. Look at me Kerry; look at what I am now without you. There is half of me missing. Come and make me a full person so I can't see where I begin and you end ... ten o'clock.

Eleven o'clock ...

Midnight ... it would be done now.

A knock on the door. It was him again, the big Sergeant from the MT.

'You all right in there mate? It's just that I saw your light on and wondered if me and the lads could hold a school in your place tonight?'

I looked up at him; he was carrying another bottle and a pack of cards. I brushed myself down and wiped my eyes, not wanting to share the moment with anyone, but not wanting to be alone.

'Yeah, sure come in.'

'Gerry, yeah get the lads. He called over his shoulder and three more guys followed him into the room, each carrying their own supply of drink. Without any prompting they moved a table into the middle of the room and set chairs around it.

'Thanks mate.'

They shook my hand and introduced themselves by names that I instantly forgot.

'It was getting delicate in the NAAFI, someone dobbed us in for gambling, there's always some busybody waiting to spoil a bit of fun, eh Den?'

'Yeah, always someone.'

I took up a seat and gathered my cards.

'Right lads, now that we have a bit of privacy we can put money on the table, let's see...fifty to be in...that all right with everyone?'

I dug into my wallet again and pulled out my last fifty dollars. By two in the morning I was out; I'd been up a hundred and thirty at one stage but took some risks to get more. Oh well it's only fifty dollars and at least I didn't have to meet any deadlines to pay up in the morning.

Chapter Thirty-two

Whisky does unexpected things; it not only makes me drunk; on the contrary it stimulates me, makes me very aware of what I'm doing. I don't consider myself alcoholic but I like a drink, or two. I mean, most blokes do. It's a travesty when someone is labelled like that, although I suppose some pigeonholing is a good thing; they can warn when someone is dangerous, but having a passion for a few beers isn't a crime. No one has given smokers a name. Maybe I could have a fetish for whisky or be a whisky abuser instead? Anyway, the thing is, once I've started I can't stop myself from drinking the rest of the bottle and without sounding conceited, I can do a bottle in a night. However, this evening it's been put to me that I'm an alkie by one of the card school. I was horrified; it *was* asked in a half-joking way, but it caught me off balance. These guys have been my means of distraction for the past four nights; they drink like fish, but one of them has noticed me knocking back the golden medicine too frequently, and he just came out with it. I really wanted to talk and unburden my heart; that was why I was spending, or rather gambling, and drinking away vast amounts of money from nowhere but to reveal that it was over a girl who wasn't even my girlfriend who had just died would get little or no sympathy whatsoever. So when I had drained the last of the bottle, Geoff turned and looked at me and said half teasing,

'Blimey Den, knocking it back or what?'

The rest of the blokes laughed. I felt my skin flaring with embarrassment.

'Er, no not really, it's just ... erm ... well, my wife died the other week and ...'

In unison their mouths fell open and cards were placed face

up on the table, and it was then I realised I'd gone too far. I couldn't go back on what I'd said because that would make me look a mental case.

'Yeah, she got hit by a car and was killed, she was so badly disfigured that I refused the leave, just want to remember her as she was ... so ... yeah, I've had a few too many this week.' I gave a small laugh to Geoff who was trying to hide his clumsiness. The table was silent.

'I don't really like talking about it guys, sorry to drop it in on you like that, it's ... just ... we'd only been married a year and ...'

'Shit Den we didn't know.'

They started nodding and agreeing that it was time to go and offering condolences. The big sergeant from the MT leant over and asked if there was anything he could do, he thought it was outrageous that I hadn't been sent home.

'No thanks Sarge, I'm okay honestly.'

And with that the night was abruptly over, the guys collected their cards and cans of beer and sidled off through the door leaving me alone. That wasn't quite what I was hoping for and for the first time since I'd learned of her death I wept. I sat with my head in my hands and watched tears hit the floor, dripping from my nose; my involuntary sobs ebbed the flow slightly. As I lit another cigarette my eyes stung from the salt of my tears.

I arrived for work the next day and things had escalated. The GSM called me into Garrison Headquarters. The atmosphere in his office was formal and the scowl on his face said it all.

'Sit down Corporal Yarwood.'

He pulled up his chair and lent his elbows on the desk, cupping his face in his hands and then drawing them down to his chin as if he were at the end of a terribly long day.

I not only felt apprehensive of what he was going to say, I'd guessed that someone had a word in his ear; and I felt irritated that my personal life was now public. I'd seen it before with Tony and the lady doctor. Why do the Army feel it necessary to get involved? I wanted desperately to crack but at the same time I wanted keep this to myself. I say that – I needed to speak to someone about Peanuts but confidentially and to someone I had chosen. One of the lads from the previous night had obviously taken it on himself to tell the GSM that my *wife* had died and that I wasn't going home, so what? As a full Corporal I should be trusted to think for myself and make my own life decisions, no matter how irrational they are. When the Bosnia affair came to light I remember thinking how wide of the mark it was; the guy was having a fling and she was a consenting adult so what was the fuss about?

The Commanding Officer got involved straight away and passed judgement according to an archaic set of rules written by some moral prude who probably couldn't get his leg over. I bet as soon as they had been sent back to Blighty he never gave them another thought. He could have ruined two careers because they had sexual relations. That hadn't done Bill Clinton any harm and he was in charge of a whole super-power! I felt mistrusted, like I should go to my room and think very carefully about my naughty behaviour. The British Army do have a duty of care to their troops and this works at times. I recall one of the lads from 'C' Company losing his dad whilst out on patrol in Ireland; when the news came through to the Ops room he was off the streets and on a plane home within the hour. Yes, brilliant for circumstances like that I guess; but everyone knew his business, poor sod. We had a lecture on discipline; I can't remember what it was called but it seemed to be an umbrella of institutionalised regulations for how we are to conduct our lives. The only piece I can remember from a rather uninspiring and dull speaker was the statement that he made about The Service Test; it said that any action resulting in the

Operational Effectiveness of the Army being disrupted would result in administrative action being taken against the individual. My misdemeanour seemed not to fit into this, even if it was true, and I had a wife and she'd been killed horribly in a car crash and I didn't want to go home to see her – why would that disrupt Operational Effectiveness? Tony and the lady doctor appeared very comparable; no one was getting hurt, he was just boning someone of a different rank. That doesn't mean that the Unit was going to collapse. It just didn't make sense that grown men with immense responsibilities should be scrutinised at every level; surely to be able to make colossal personal choices was a good thing? For now, this didn't help my position. I was faced with my private affairs up for general gossip and my credibility under question and unlikely to be able to gloss over my own temerity.

'Go on then ...'

'What Sir?'

'You know exactly what I'm referring to, young man. Why have I had a visit from Sergeant Davies today then?'

Bastard, I knew who was the grass, then.

'Look Sir, I can explain, it doesn't have to go any further. I know I've screwed up but it was because I'd had a few beers and ...'

'You've been having a few beers every night, so it seems Corporal.'

'Yeah, well, thing is that my ...'

'Your wife maybe?'

I felt sick and dropped my head to avoid his gaze, it was also an acknowledgement.

'Who else knows?'

'No one, just me, and the lads you were drinking with last night, but they have been told to keep their mouths shut. Right, now listen to me; I've known you for a few months now, and you are a good bloke. Something has happened that you haven't told me and right now, you are in deep trouble. You're only an Acting Corporal and anything you do from this moment will jeopardise that and you will be demoted immediately and sent back to your unit under a cloud, so you have a couple of choices. One, tell me the truth and we see if I can stop this going to the top, or two, keep on your self-destruct mission you seem to have undertaken and you're on your own.'

The palms of my hands became cold and wet and the silence became palpable. I could just let this go right now, walk away and go home to Luton to see Mum. Ireland, Bosnia, promotion, just chuck it away and play snooker and drink myself paralytic. But that would be ... what was the point? I like it, I like the Army, I love the money and responsibility and when I go home I am the guy who has been shot at and done things that the others haven't. I chat to blokes in pubs and they have nothing to say for themselves, I want to talk about patrolling and boxing and fishing and this is my life, right here and right now. I'd never experienced the thrill of being truly scared before or representing my Regiment in a boxing ring, and the two occasions when I was told that I was good enough to gain promotion it made me so proud. I can lead men into battle, teach them new skills. In the few years of service I'd come a long way. The possibility of returning to unemployment and being broke wasn't a tempting idea, even less was the shame.

As I raised my head the GSM was looking at me and waiting for my answer. If I was going to remain I needed to bend completely, my private life, my outlook, everything. I felt like I was on the edge of a cliff, surrounded by a firing squad; step back and I would die. Step forward and put my trust in them and I would be live but be committed, they would save my life but I would be one of them. I stepped off the cliff edge.

Thirty minutes later and I was stood in the office of the same big Military Transport Sergeant facing the lads and telling them about Peanuts and not being her husband. The GSM banned me from the bar for the rest of my time in Belize and gave me to the MT Sergeant for extra work at night.

After my confession it was Sergeant Davies's turn to have a pop at me. He beckoned me in to one of the offices and shut the door behind him.

'You are a waste of rations Yarwood. I went into that office yesterday to help you, thinking that you'd just become a widower only to be told that you weren't even married. How much of a dick do you think that made me look?'

I opened my mouth to answer but was cut down.

'If I could get away with it I'd knock your bloody head off. Now a word of advice, you're a full Corporal, well – acting which is apt isn't it? Anyway you'd better keep your lying gob shut before I shut it for you.'

I nodded and left, thinking it couldn't get any worse than this. I had to make amends and do my time for being so thoughtless.

Gus returned from his holiday a few days later full of stories of American bars and women that he'd met. He seemed to have had a fine time in the States.

'Sae what's bin happenin' haur Den?'

I was sort of expecting and dreading the question as soon as I'd seen him and I wasn't sure whether to not mention the disaster I had made or just blurt the whole thing out.

'Sae is she a coosin ur someain?'

'No Gus a ...'

'Yer aunty 'en?'

'No she was my, well, girlfriend, sort of.'

'Sort ay, was she ur wasnae she?'

'She said in the letter that she wanted to marry me but didn't get around to it.'

Gus looked confused.

'Look Den, Ah dornt gie it? Thes lass wasnae yer quinie but she writes tae ye oan 'er death bed proposin' marriage, soonds a bit strange tae me.'

'Gus, we'd known each other for ages, oh this sounds pants, I just thought she was a good friend and that.'

'Sae whats th' big deal 'en Den. Ah know she was your friend but dornt ye hink yer makin' a sooch o things? Nae offence an aw 'at.'

It felt pointless going on to him but he'd learn soon enough about the extra work; so I thought I ought to fill him in on the details, so I continued to the card school and the fib. He slowly unpacked his kit and walked around the room listening before he gave me any answer, letting me rattle on.

'Den, ye hae got yerself in a spot thaur mucker,' he pointed out so obviously.' But Ah cannae see hoo Ah can help ye aam afraid, Ah am pure sorry abit yer friend but ye shooldnae hae lied lake 'at, it's a bit guff.'

'Yeah I know Gus, I just need time to get over her, she meant so much to me.'

He'd missed the point and I couldn't claw back the original story.

'Den Ah didne e'en ken th' lass existed afair Ah left, dae ye nae see wa nae a body is interested?' He had raised his voice and sounded frustrated at my devastation.

'Gus I just ...'

'Jist lookin' fur sympathy, but ye lied an' no-ain likes a liar dae they?'

I felt myself losing grip again. Gus was my last hope of someone who could listen to me, we'd had some great times together and I thought I could trust him. I'd finally been honest but he wasn't prepared to see it my way.

'Gus, look it's not like that ...'

'Den, Ah am wabbit cheil frae th' flecht, sae it till later.'

He grabbed his wash-kit and a towel and left me alone in the room.

Time started to drag in the two-man bunk; I was working from first light to dusk doing my extra work in the MT shed and carrying out my normal duties in silence with the GSM. I would return to the room and Gus would leave as if he had taken it upon himself to punish me for lying; it wasn't even to him. I felt livid to be left so stranded by a bloke who used to call me a mate. I'd tried to make small talk but always ended up returning to Peanuts, I couldn't help myself. The sobriety was becoming a problem and day after day my body and mind craved a drink and some welcome distraction; the weekends became a nightmare as there wasn't enough work to keep me occupied and I relished the weekdays when I could busy myself. Letters from Mum arrived and sat on my bed unanswered. What could I say to her?

At night I could hear the laughter from the bar and hear Gus stagger in and throw himself onto his bed in a stupor. I felt like smuggling in a bottle of whisky just to keep me sane. The letter looked dog-eared, as I'd read it over again, the words pricking my eyes every time I saw them. I ran, a long way, I kept running until my thighs burnt with lactic acid and my chest felt like it was about to collapse. The new running routes gave me freedom again for a while; I was out of the Camp that I'd made a prison and I didn't have to speak to anyone for a while, just me and my Walkman playing the same old Ska tape I'd had for an eternity. Sometimes I'd run and watch my feet hitting the soil and wonder where they were taking me; it didn't feel like I had the energy to make the decision for myself any more, I'd just follow my feet; at least they weren't taking it in turns to go in my mouth. I'd work in the MT shed and one of the guys would pass a comment about my *wife*, or

I'd be sat in the cookhouse eating and Gus would walk in and sit on another table. In my silence I put a chuff chart on the inside of my locker door, a small calendar telling me that I only had to suffer another few weeks in this state of torture.

My mind was so tired of thoughts that I couldn't get rid of, they haunted me at night and reminded me during the day. I could feel myself slipping into a dark corridor with no light at the end of it. Before, the glass would be half full; now it was half empty. What was the point? Just get these few weeks over and things would improve – or would they? One day a letter turned up from Marc asking why I'd been incommunicado for so long and that I should be writing to Mum, so I jotted him a note saying I'd be home in a month and was really busy. I'd explain everything then.

The last three weeks passed and I finally boarded the VC10 home. As we took off and circled the Camp I studied the country that held so many bad memories for me; leaving the dark swamp, the jungle and the tropical heat behind, a place that I'd loved only a few months before. And of course McStick. Somehow my existence had changed and I was unsure if I would ever be the same again.

Chapter Thirty-three

Please make the noise stop. I'm going to have to get the damn thing within striking distance. Another day, another hangover, and as if I wasn't feeling bad enough I've got to go and see Miss Rawlinson at the bank. It appears that I'm a tad overspent. Surely if I'm overdrawn they will make the money back in interest from the extortionate charges. The letters are threatening, as if I'm the scum of the earth, and to make sure I've got the message I've got to return my cards and cheque book this morning. I know when I get in there I'm getting a lecture from some haggard old spinster about how a couple of years ago my balance was very healthy and has steadily got worse until the bank can't accept my amount of spending. They have no faith whatsoever that I could win it all back tonight if I'm lucky, the law of averages and all that; so if they can give me another few days I'll pay them their precious money back, and some. One day I'm going to win so big that they will come running to me for a change – which reminds me, I must get my running kit on if I could find my trainers. There they are, outside the door. What fool put them there?

Aldershot is such a dislikeable, loveless place to be stuck in. I'm surrounded by everything I've learned to hate, and the regime of the military is all around me. I'm not allowed out of Camp into the town with my uniform on and this is a Garrison town. How absurd! but the coppers would like nothing more than to arrest a Guardsman, especially a Corporal. It's times like these that I wish I'd got out of the Army back in Belize; committing myself just seems to have prolonged the inevitable and I'm surprised to have hung on to my rank this long. When the Commanding Officer told me that I was no longer acting and now substantive I nearly fell off my chair. So what's stopping my just signing off now and handing in my notice? Well, the debt I suppose, but four grand isn't such a big deal really. I'll get Miss Rawlinson the debt manager her money back. God, it's not as if I'm Nick Leeson.

By the time I've had a shower and changed into a pair of jeans and T-shirt I'm in a foul mood. I can't put my finger on what I find more enraging: the fact that they think I need help managing my debt, the letter, or the twenty quid they have fined me for the pleasure of her correspondence. Why do they do that? Twenty quid for a letter is ridiculous, especially when they are telling me that I'm in debt already. I made my way across town and up the High Street to the bank; I needed to be there at mid-day so I had time for a nifty pint in the Trafalgar with Tom the landlord.

'You in tonight Den?' he asked, as a pint was placed down in front of me.

'Yep.'

'Are you up for a game?'

'Nope.'

'Why not, there's gonna be a few of us, could be a good game Den.'

'Tom, I've got the big one tonight mate, I'll be walking away with a couple of grand.'

'Oh yeah.'

'Yeah Tom, believe it, all or nothing tonight, someone's getting fleeced.'

'So who you playing with?'

'Tom, don't be silly, look I'll pop in tomorrow to buy you a drink with my winnings, then I think I'll book myself a little holiday somewhere.'

I finished my pint and slid my glass over the bar into the hands of the ever-expectant Tom. He's been a good mate over the past couple of years and set me up with some of the most lucrative card games I've had. Once I walked out of his pub with nearly a grand in my pocket, only to give it to someone else about a week later, but that's not the point. He would set up a school with different people from the resident regiments; the best games were when he had a new guy posted in who thought he could play. Tom would chat him up to see if he was game enough to put some money on the table and then invite a couple of us in to set a school going in the upstairs room. All being well the poor sod would walk away skint but a lot wiser.

Once there was this big bloke, a loggie or Royal Logistic Corps (I think I've mentioned them before) and we took two hundred quid off him in one sitting; he'd only been in town a couple of nights. When Tom asked him to pay up he went ballistic and started throwing the table around the room, so I had to jump in and clobber him. I smacked him square on the chin and he just stood there, didn't even acknowledge I'd hit him, and when I'd finished nursing my sore fist I looked up and Tom had vanished rather quickly leaving me alone with this monster. I had to make a dash for it as he'd turned his attention on me, so I ducked under one colossal punch and scooted out of the door, thinking he could go ahead and smash the whole room up if he likes. He did.

So I walk into the bank at five to twelve and take a seat by the customer services till, trying to spot Miss Rawlinson, the dragon debt manager who was about to ruin my life. An elderly lady with half-moon glasses coughed to gain my attention; she was sat in the till area and had stood up to make herself more prominent through the glass-covered hatchway.

'Yes?' I enquired, as she glared at me.

This must be her in her knitted twin set and floral blouse, gesturing with painted nails for me to come over and not getting her head too near to the glass so that her perfectly set blue rinse hair doesn't get messed up.

'Can I help you young man?'

There, what a giveaway. 'Young man'; the bank must specially train these people in belittling.

'Erm ...I have an appointment with Miss Rawlinson at twelve.'

I expected her to tell me to come through and that she'd been expecting me.

'Oh well, please have a seat. I'll see if she's free. Who shall I say is asking for her?'

Blimey, they have someone else far more terrifying to interrogate me; this woman must have failed the selection for slipping into niceness.

'Den, no, Mr Den, no I mean ... sorry, Yarwood, Mr Yarwood.'

'Are you sure?'

I had no idea why I was bumbling, I felt small. The bank was busy as it was most people's lunchtime; I saw a couple of guys from the Battalion getting money over the counter. That sort of thing had passed for me, once they had withdrawn my cards; I was forced to play the post-dated cheque game. I used to do that in the NAAFI until they had one that I mistimed and it bounced, causing a drama at the pay office. Since then I'd found a shop in North Camp who would turn the paper into cash for a small fee. Near the end of the month I'd phone the bank and extend my overdraft by a few quid each time just to keep ahead of the cheques. The trick with that was to make sure I got a different person to do it or they would have stopped that as well. It's not as if I'm trying to rip anyone off; as soon as I get this next game out of the way I can say goodbye to all of this nonsense. It's only a matter of time.

'Mr Yarwood?'

A young lady poked her head around the security door and announced my name to the whole bank.

'Yes,' I said, just loud enough to be heard, knowing that it was too late and everyone would now know that I was up to my eyeballs. They'd be whispering to each other 'that's the debt counsellor', then they would tell their friends; then they would wait until I'd been released and stare and laugh at me as I walked out.

So in I go to the financial lion's den with Miss Rawlinson's clerk, a small back office with one table, a computer and two chairs. The window has a blind covering the view and the only thing missing is a security camera to record my every move. She indicates to me to take the seat on the outside of the desk so that I won't be able to see the screen, and shuts the door behind me. I can only assume now that Miss Rawlinson is limbering up for the inevitable battle, rehearsing her lines in the manager's office and plotting my demise. Her clerk will now go into announce 'he's ready' and her boss'll wish her the best of luck and she'll be told to return with a suitable result. The door swings open again and in walks the clerk with a bundle of paperwork under one arm and a cup of tea in the other. To my amazement the clerk reaches out her hand and introduces herself.

'Mr Yarwood, I'm glad you could make it.' Cripes, she's Miss Rawlinson! This is a turn-up for the books; she's young and looks harmless, this should be a piece of cake. Some charm here and I'll be out of here and back in the pub in half an hour.

'Now you understand from our letters that the bank is having an issue with your spending and it's my job to see if we can sort this out without too much fuss. It's apparent from your last five statements that your overdraft is increasing by an average of fifty pounds a month; currently you have a limit of four thousand pounds, which you have already exceeded. I know you are in the Army so the payments come in on the last working day of each month but I'm assuming now that your wages won't even cover your overdraft. Is that correct?'

'Erm ...'

'Now the bank have been more than lenient and sent you proposals for a loan to clear the debt that you haven't responded to, so now we have to take action to recompense this.'

'Hang on a minute.'

'What I think is best for the shortterm is to take out a loan, clear your overdraft and draw up a spending plan so that we avoid this sort of mess again. I have some forms to fill in and I can seek approval through Head Office to process this within the week. Until then I must take your cheque book and cash card.'

'Just stop for a second please.'

'Yes?'

'What if I don't want a loan?'

'Well I don't see any other alternatives. We have been exceptionally patient Mr Yarwood, and you have done nothing to resolve your situation.'

'All right so I'm a little short for cash at the moment, but I don't see how bullying me into permanent debt is going to resolve things. Why don't you give me a couple of days and I'll give you your money back.'

'What – four thousand two hundred and twenty- three pounds? We have reminded you three times now.'

'Threatened more like.'

'We are trying to accommodate your ...'

'Yeah, help me make a never-never debt to your bank.'

'Please Mr Yarwood, if you would just read the facts.'

'What the letters? They weren't any help,'

'Mr Yarwood, if you keep taking this attitude I'm going to call this interview off and ...'

'Oh it's a bloody interview now! well, I'm the one co-operating by coming in, in the first place, you're the one being pushy.'

'Please don't swear at me or I'll get my manager. Now are you willing to accept my proposal?'

'I don't need your help thank you very much.'

'Well, you leave me no choice I'm afraid. I'm suspending your account and withdrawing your cheque book and cards,' and with a few taps on the computer keyboard she had ceased my spending.

I stood up and threw down the book and card. her face was bright red as she nearly snatched them from me and stood to meet my gaze.

'You'll be hearing from us by post Mr Yarwood.'

'Yeah, whatever.'

I pushed the door and stormed back to the pub.

My wallet had twenty pounds in it and with the change in my pocket it came to twenty-eight pounds and seventy-two pence, not enough for tonight's game. Tom looked across as I sank my first pint and asked what was wrong.

'Oh, just a bit of hassle with the bank Tom, you know what they're like.'

I explained my brief encounter with the woman and how I felt absolutely disgusted at the way they were treating me.

'Den ... ?'

'Yes mate.'

'Don't you think you're being hasty, telling them to stick it?'

'Why? It was them that started it all.'

'Well, it sounds like you've just cut your nose off to spite your face.'

'Oh don't you start Tom.'

'No Den listen, you're in a hole financially – 'scuse the witticism – and they have offered you a loan. Believe me Den, they don't do that for everyone.'

'Yeah but ...'

'Just hear me out. If you are that stuck for cash and they are offering to bail you out I wouldn't be so quick. You've now got no means of getting any cash whatsoever, so what are you going to do about that then?'

'I'll borrow some.'

'From who exactly?'

'Well, I was going to ask you if you'd ...'

'No way mate, sorry.'

'Come on Tom, it's only for a couple of days until ...'

'Until you blow it all on another card game, don't take me for a fool. I've seen more money pass through your hands than comes over my bar. I say, and this is only friendly advice, you go back to see this Miss what's-her-name and say you're sorry and take the loan. Or you can just piss the rest of your money against my wall.'

'But Tom, I've never had a loan in my life.'

'Think about it Den. I've been around longer than you, if someone is telling you that you have a problem then they are probably right.'

Tom walked off and served another guy stood across the bar as I pondered on what he'd said. I wasn't going to get anywhere without money and if I did take the loan I suppose I could get back on my feet again. Besides, I needed two hundred quid to be in the school tonight. She wouldn't let me take that loan after the way I talked to her; I suppose she was only doing her job. Cornered again. I nodded at Tom and made my way back to the bank.

As I approached the doors I could imagine her sitting typing a letter about me to my CO telling him how irresponsible I'd been; it would finish my career for sure. I knew they did this as one of the lads from 'A' Company had been hauled over the coals by the same bank for not paying a direct debit. I walked straight past the door and into the flower shop next door, buying a bunch of rather uninspiring chrysanthemums before making my way back in and up to the customer services counter.

The same old lady I'd seen not an hour ago met me.

'Excuse me, can I speak to Miss Rawlinson please?'

She glared at me and at the flowers before giving me her answer.

'Wait here please, I'll see if she wishes to see you Mr Yarwood.'

The fact that she knew my name sent a shiver down my spine. I sat and waited, passing the bunch of flowers from one hand to another before I heard her voice again.

'Mr Yarwood, come through.'

She was much more formal this time and led me to the same room, opening the door to let me go first. Before she'd even closed the door I spun around and offered her the flowers.

'I'm really sorry, I was out of order earlier. It's just that I'm not used to banks, I've never been in trouble before and I didn't know what I was saying. I didn't mean to swear at you and I know that you are trying to help and it's just your job and ...'

'Please sit down.'

I obediently sat as she took the bouquet from me.

'Well, it's the first time I've ever been bought flowers by a customer, thank you. I assume this is an apology and you'd like to start again?'

I could feel myself slumping, defeated into my chair as if she had won a victory over me, and worn me down into submission.

'Yes I suppose so, I'm so sorry.'

'Okay, I've been looking at your track record with us over the past few years and it seems that you are just going through a glitch, shall we say. The last couple years haven't been your best have they?'

'I know, I've been having a bit of trouble since ... since I came back from Belize and I just keep getting it wrong you see...'

'Yes I can see that, Mr Yarwood'

'Den, please.'

'Den, let's get this loan arranged. The only reason you're

accepted is because your credit rating was good for a long time and we can sometimes find ways to help quality customers.'

'It's not because I'm cute then, ha ha?'

As far as pathetic lines go to lighten up a conversation, this was a poor one. She looked at me for a while and then back to her screen without any comment. Her voice had softened and through her grey-suited exterior and neatly plaited hair she was quite attractive, very trim but pretty.

'Okay, I'm getting the forms printed for you to sign. I'll allow you a five thousand pound loan to clear the debt and give you a head start to get back on track.'

'Yes thanks that's great, well I mean that's good. When can I have it?'

'Well, the money will appear in your account today if I can get clearance. Why, do you need some cash in a hurry?'

'Yeah, about two hundred quid.'

'I see. I'll need a couple of moments for the funds to transfer.'

As she left to get the paperwork I sneaked a look at her; she had a good figure. She returned a few minutes later with the forms for me to sign and after a lengthy explanation about interest rates I put my mark down and the deed was done.

'Right then Mr, I mean Den, that's gone through. You can use your card again now. I've booked you in for another appointment with me next Tuesday so that we can talk about a savings strategy'

'Yeah that's fine.'

I wasn't going to upset her as she'd just taken a huge weight off my shoulders and given me enough money for tonight's game.

Chapter Thirty-four

It turned out to be the fastest two hundred pounds I'd ever run through. They were a bunch of sharks and I'm fairly sure they played together. Still, technically I hadn't lost anything, as the money from the bank had saved my life for the time being. I know I've got to stop this; it's got out of control. I can't go on being so incautious and ignoring the consequences. It's not as if I've been a hermit though; the opposite, actually, but throwing myself into drinking and gambling wears thin after a while.

I think one of the saddest things is that Marc and I have grown apart; my mistake, he told me to grow up and face my responsibilities and I nearly sparked him out in the pub. He wasn't to know. Women have become brief flings I've had, only lasting a few weeks at the most; as soon as they start to invade my privacy by asking about my past I can't help myself going into one. I want someone to know but I'll choose who I tell and nosey girls don't get a good response. It's just self-gratifying sex for the time being, which is short term, and I feel that I want more but I can't understand why I keep pushing them away. I do try to talk but I just cringe at the thought of all that sympathy that would be shoved down my throat. Right, after this next game I'll give it up and start saving again. There's still the chance that I could recoup some of this week's money. I'll just be less quick with my bets.

Another week and another loss. I'm not in the best of moods to be in the bank yet again for my counselling. Miss Rawlinson keeps me waiting for an age until her head appears again to call me in. This time we're in a different office, bigger with comfy chairs. She sits down and from behind those rather official glasses she has lovely eyes.

'So Den, here we are again. We are having an expensive time, aren't we?'

She flips through my statement as she speaks, looking up only to tap into her keyboard.

'I've had a couple of rather big bills to sort out, yes.'

Or perhaps I should just go for it and say, 'Well it's two hundred quid a time to join the table.'

Maybe not, I'll listen to what she has to say.

'It really doesn't help, continually withdrawing cash from your account like this; there is a limit to the generosity of the bank. I can see that ...'

'Yeah, enough of the lectures thanks.'

'Den, I'm trying to help, can't you see that?'

'Sorry, I ...'

'I've drawn up a budgeting plan. In this column we list all the outgoing like rent, utility bills, council tax, hire purchase of cars, credit cards, etcetera. You'll have to be honest and frank.'

She stared with pen at the ready to jot down my response.

'Well, what?'

'Your outgoings. What regular payments do you make?'

'Erm ... none.'

'But you're drawing two hundred pounds out at a time, so you're either a heavy drinker or a ...'

'Gambler.'

The word just flew out of my mouth before I could stop it. It was as if I needed to admit it to someone and I cursed under my breath.

'Ah, I see.'

She stopped sounding like a bank person and started talking like some sort of psychologist. I was waiting for her to ask about my childhood and how I got on at school or if I had bed-wetting problems but she didn't; she leaned back in her chair and waited for me to continue.

'Look Miss Rawl ...'

'Leanne, please.'

'Look Leanne, I've had a few problems over the last couple of years and things have got a little out of control. I've tried to sort them out but every time I think I'm getting a grip of things it just spirals all over again.'

'So what is it, cards, horses, dogs?'

'Cards.'

'How often?'

'Couple of times a week.'

'And how much do you win?'

'Dunno, 'bout half I suppose.'

'And you take two hundred pounds every time?'

'No, not every time, it only started as fifty quid but if I want to win big I've got to put down a bit more.'

'You have to?'

'Of course, how else am I going to sort this mess out?'

'Stop.'

'Stop!?'

'Yes Den. Stop playing cards and find something else to do with your time. Don't you have a girlfriend?'

'Right Leanne, I didn't come in here for a lecture. I only agreed to this because I thought you were going to help.'

'It is my job to assist, you're right; but in the bank's interests, not your pastimes. My responsibility as your account manager is partly to ensure that there are funds to meet the loan being repaid. You apparently are on a course of recklessness, and think that the bank will turn a blind eye. '

'What I do to myself is my business, thanks.'

'Okay, I'll sort out another loan. Couple of hundred to keep you at the table for another week and don't tell me you'll win it all back eventually. Will that keep you happy Den? Well ... will it?'

I was numb, I'd never been spoken to like this before, especially by a girl. I didn't want to admit that I couldn't handle my money, but the truth was, she was right. A couple of hundred quid wouldn't solve anything. We had stopped talking and sat there staring at each other. I couldn't work out why she had said those things; banks don't normally bother with the face-to-face problem solving. It's normally done in letter form, much safer than having a living breathing person in the building. I mean they might be able to argue back and actually be justified.

'Look. I see people like you in here all of the time. I want to help you out. Now, you can accept my suggestion and offer of a drink later or I can withdraw my proposal and you can wait for the post.'

'Pardon?'

'Well, it's stilted in here and we could chat over a drink if you like.'

'Is that normal policy then?'

'No, not really, but it's been a heavy week and I could do with company, but if you're not interested in talking somewhere ...'

'No, no, that would be good, when?'

'Tomorrow, it's always nice to start the weekend with a beer after work, but not around here. I can't stand Aldershot on a Friday night. We'll go to Camberley or somewhere.'

'Yep, that sounds good. I knock off at four on a Friday. What time is good for you?'

'Erm, lets say six, I'll meet you by the cinema.'

'Great, there's a bookies next door. I could ...'

'Den ...'

'Just kidding, seeing if you were paying attention. I'll see you there,.'

I gathered my papers and left, slightly bemused at the impromptu date that we had arranged, but she seemed sweet so I thought 'well, in for a penny, in for a pound' – so to speak.

The boys had a big night out on Fridays and I was getting hassled to join them on their tour of the pubs followed by a curry and game of cards. I'd have normally been the first one out of the gates with my civvies on, but as I had spare time I put on my running gear and went for a few miles down by the canal. As I started to run I could feel my body responding to the exercise, the gentle patting rhythm of my feet and breathing in and out was like a tune to me. I knew from the start that it was going to be a good run because I'd hit my pace within metres of leaving the Camp gates. As I ran along I caught up with and overtook others out for their early evening jog; for the first time in ages I felt like communicating, saying a quick hello as I glided past.

Leanne was taking a huge risk going for a drink; we hardly knew each other and the only time we'd talked it had turned into a slanging duel. I wasn't sure if I was going to be an excuse; I mean she already knew my financial state, which was more than I'd tell anyone normally, so I couldn't be what would be considered a catch. Maybe she just fancied the pants off me; she was a girl after all, but that was far too smug. Well, I'd find out soon enough. As I ran back into Camp, the Company stragglers were heading out with their best clothes on. Then I saw someone who put my jovial mood back into its box and before I could avoid him, Lofty was stood right in front of me in the guardroom booking out of Camp.

'All right.'

I had my head down as I waited for a response. I couldn't meet his eyes and just felt him push past and out of the door. I'll never fix that.

Pulling out my shirts from my locker was bringing back memories of better times; I hadn't worn some of these clothes for ages, before ... well ... a long time ago. In truth I'd had no one to wear them for, and I'd normally go out in what the lads used to refer to as CEFO or Civilian Equipment Fighting Order: that consisted of a pair of desert boots, T- shirt, blue jeans and a bomber jacket. Not very inspiring when there are another hundred or so blokes wearing exactly the same stuff less the T-shirt and haircut. We looked more like the National Front than members of the British Army. It felt strange leaving the Camp in moleskin trousers and shoes but I did feel smart and good about myself. I'd put on one of my favourite shirts and my leather jacket and caught myself in the mirror as I left the block, smoothing down a rogue hair as I passed.

I waited until six-fifteen giving her the obligatory time to be late, and then headed up the road towards the pub where I knew the lads would be. I was just about to push the door when I heard my name from further down the road. I spun around to see Leanne running towards me; she looked flustered as she called

'I'm so sorry Den my lift was late.'

'Okay, fine, so where are we going then?'

'Not in there, it's full of trashed squaddies. Oh sorry that came out wrong, I mean ...'

'Ha, that's fine, you're right, the lads would be in full flow by now, come on – you said something about Camberley.'

We headed back to the taxi rank and jumped into a cab. She was looking very chic indeed, wearing a silk skirt and white long-sleeved jumper; her hair was loose and covered her face slightly, making her look shy as our eyes met. It was the first time I'd noticed a woman for ages, I mean really seen what they are wearing; I suppose I'd just got into the habit of taking them for granted. But Leanne was different, she looked well dressed, like she knew exactly what to dress in, a more mature but foxy image. I was so glad that I hadn't worn my black pulling shirt. She stopped the cab before we had reached the town centre, at an ivy-covered pub with garden furniture on a lawn outside and hanging baskets, well tended, lining the windows and door. I hopped out of the taxi and reached for my wallet.

'No Den, my treat.'

'Erm, I can afford it, I'm not a charity case you know.'

I smiled at her.

'And I'm paying for the cab, you get the drinks.'

'Oh so that's your game, first out of the cab and last to the bar.'

She giggled and rolled her eyes at the taxi driver. I'd made a joke!

The pub was homely and quiet, which probably isn't very good for the landlord but it was just what I needed as I'd spent for ever in rowdy boozers shouting over the din of a jukebox and drunken conversations. I bought her a Bacardi and coke and myself a pint and we sat by the open fire.

'Right come on then let's get this over with Leanne, what have you got in mind for me and my money?'

'Den, I didn't drag you out to talk about money. Wasn't that obvious?'

'Oh so what did you drag me out for then?'

'To talk about stuff, share some time, have a laugh, whatever.'

She was sipping her drink and trying to flick a cigarette from a packet as she spoke. I leant over and pulled it out for her.

'Ta, so go on then.'

I couldn't help but feel that I was still in an interview and I couldn't work out why she had asked me out in the first place. I started to ramble about Mum and the Army, where I'd been and what I'd done. Not the full version of course but more of a making-conversation list of things achieved. Leanne sat and listened, nodding and raising her eyebrows occasionally at my stories of Ireland.

'So come on then, your turn.'

I was getting tired of talking and came close to telling her about Peanuts on one occasion, so I thought it better to pause.

Leanne was a Hampshire girl, the sort that hadn't been north of the Watford Gap. She had grown up, lived and worked in a ten-mile radius and talked about her life in a very relaxed secure way that I couldn't really relate to. She had been at college on day release from the bank and had worked since the day she left school. She told me about her house that she was decorating and her disasters in the garden. Leanne was a great storyteller; she had bought some hedging from the garden centre at great expense and then forgot to water it, and by the middle of the summer it looked like a row of twigs planted in the lawn. However, she was more accomplished in the kitchen; she told me about a prize she had won for cooking once, when she was eleven. I suppose it was then, after about an hour of sitting listening to each other that I realised that I was on a date, a real date, and quite enjoying myself!

She giggled and looked up over her glass.

'Right ... top-up for you then?'

'Yes please.'

I strode to the bar, feeling much better all round; she was a good-looking girl and easy to chat to. I felt at ease and didn't want to jump straight into bed with her, which was a good thing; not that I wouldn't of course but, well, I was just having a fine time as it was and didn't wish to spoil it for myself or her. We sat and chatted until the pub was closing up for the night, and I walked her back to the taxi rank.

'Leanne, can I see you again?'

'Yes that would be lovely. Look, phone me, have you got a pen?'

'Erm.'

I searched my empty pockets for no reason. I didn't have a pen so what was I expecting? Something to appear like a genie from a lamp? She scrabbled in her handbag and brought out an eye pencil thing.

'Got any ... '

'Paper? Not a chance.'

She leant over and grabbed my hand and scrawled her phone number on it. I was surprised how much it scratched and couldn't imagine how painful it must be to drag over her eyes.

'Thanks for a lovely night Den.'

She was beaming a smile and leant over to kiss me.

'No thank you Leanne, I wouldn't have asked you out.'

Her eyes raised. 'Oh thanks.'

'No, erm, no I didn't mean it like that, I meant, oh bloody hell, what do I mean?'

She laughed again at my awkward face and kissed my cheek.

'See ya soon.'

Chapter Thirty-five

As guard commander I get a lot of time to think, especially in the small hours alone at my desk. Last night's date was good; Leanne doesn't seem like a lunatic. She's attractive and talks about funny domestic stuff like the last video she watched and how her mum lives just around the corner and lets her borrow the car, and supermarkets. Far away from the sort of nights I'd become used to, where the conversation normally follows the lines of 'do you have a boyfriend?' and closely followed by an invitation indoors. I actually found it extremely refreshing and could imagine my brother having a similar chat with his wife. When I had got back to my room I wrote her phone number down on a scrap of paper and stuffed it into my wallet. She must have liked me to give me her number.

But when exactly do I call her? She said something along the lines of she was in every evening, which I'd sort of guessed because she works all day. But I didn't want to call her today because that would be too soon and might make me seem desperate, which I am most definitely not. I could call her on Sunday but she might be at her mum's house I suppose; I mean, what do you do when you live around the corner and you don't have a car? I'd be straight around for a Sunday lunch that's for sure. On the other hand, if I don't give her a bell soon she's going to think that I'm not interested and I most definitely am. I'll call her on Monday night and set up a date for Tuesday.

There was a local rag on the guardroom desk so I flipped to the entertainment page to see what was on at the cinema; then I closed it. No, I'll take her for a meal. Because she made the first move it was now up to me to sort out something inspirational. Maybe I could take her for a meal and then go to the pictures; I opened the paper again and glanced at the films. No. What if she thinks I'm going to try and seduce her in the back row? Plus neither of us can chat in the cinema and she seems like the chatty sort; so the paper ended up in the bin. How about a meal out and bowling after? We can chat and bowl at the same time; that sounds good, but she might think I'm the competitive type and if I beat her she'll feel bad; or I could let her win, but that would make me look like I can't bowl and I can. I know, a walk in the park, followed by dinner and then a pub; except I don't know any quiet pubs in Aldershot; but I do know one in Farnham; but I haven't got a car any more, I sold that one. I could borrow a car, I get on quite well with Nev who lives in the next room and he doesn't go out often. Right; I'll get a car on Sunday, call Leanne on Monday and take her out on Tuesday.

I'm sure that dating girls a few years ago wasn't quite this staged; it more or less involved as much alcohol as I could afford and a few condoms. The difference is the meaningless sex that satisfied me then seems shallow now, and from the conversation last night I definitely want more. I could at last have a girlfriend. As I pondered my rendezvous I felt quite sophisticated and retrieved the paper once again from the bin to look for a restaurant to take Leanne to. I wonder what time I should phone? Not too late but giving her enough time to get in from work; about seven sounds right. I don't know why this whole situation is getting me so stressed out; it's only a date for goodness' sake. It feels like the old assured and cocky Den has gone. Subconsciously, it must be not wanting to feel that sort of hurt again but if I'm going to get through this I've got to get on with life or it's going to wreck me.

Sunday came too quickly and I was back in my room, organising my kit for the next week. I felt the bosses in the Company weren't giving me the responsibilities that the other

Corporals were getting. The pressure of gambling and hard living had taken its toll and I knew that I wasn't putting as much effort into work as I could have been, mainly because I was either hung over or scamming a way to get a few extra quid for my next game. The Battalion were going to be here for a couple of years after moving from Catterick and there was no sign of us deploying anywhere, so now was probably as good a time as any to get my arse back in gear and sort my career out, as well as my social life.

My existence was a mix of solitary confinement in my shabby room or mass entertaining with the lads. Most of the blokes had managed to find a girl to go home to; even if they didn't commit to marriage they had somewhere outside of the barracks to relax in. There is something missing in my life. So I sat down and wrote myself a list of Things To Do in order of priority. I'd used them at work on a daily basis and managed to get my jobs done so I thought why the hell not use it for me?

Get a career course

Get girlfriend

Pay back my overdraft/loan

Buy car

Make more time for Mum

Make it up with Lofty

I pinned it on my locker so that when I shut the door no one wandering in could see it; not that I had many visitors; and got on with my tasks for the next week. We were going away to Salisbury Plain in a couple of weeks on manoeuvres, which would give me an ideal opportunity to shine in front of the Company bosses and regain some of my professional credibility. The last occasion I made a drongo of myself my mind was on the weekend, and being the end of the month I was playing the cheque-cashing-game at the pawn shop to ensure it didn't bounce. Because I couldn't get back to check on my balance I had to pray that I would have enough money for the table. Whilst doing this, my section was supposed to be giving fire support for the Company to attack an enemy base. Basically, we were meant to fire like billy-o in the general direction for a few minutes so that the Company could get close enough to rush them. Due to me trying to ring my bank on one of the lad's mobile phones, I missed it, and the whole attack had to be cancelled. I wasn't favourite, to say the least. So first thing in the morning I'll get myself on a course, something challenging, maybe as an instructor.

Monday morning and I was stood in the clerk's office going through the list of courses available. Not much being offered, it turned out, so I took a photocopy and went to see the Sergeant Major.

'Come.'

Sergeant Major Duffy had taken the post on my return from Belize when the last one left the Army; before he'd taken this job he was an instructor at Brecon where the Infantry courses are run. He had a reputation for being tickety-boo. He'd only seen me in a bad light unfortunately so I had much to prove to him.

'Corporal Yarwood, what is it?'

He was well aware of me after my mistake on the last exercise, so I wasn't shaken at his impatient attitude.

'Sir, I want a course, and was wondering if you had any vacancies that you can't fill?'

'For you?'

He sat back in his chair with one of those 'why should I give you anything?' looks.

'Yes Sir, for me.'

He stared long and hard before answering, making me feel like I shouldn't be asking in the first place.

'Why, Corporal Yarwood, should I give you anything? You came back from Belize under a cloud and frankly haven't done anything to impress since you returned. The clouds seem to be gathering when I remember that incident and it's underlining your lack of motivation towards the job. Younger men in the promotion ladder are overtaking you and it appears that the sun can't get through. Meteorologically speaking.'

'Yes I know Sir, that's why I need a course; I've been in a rut recently and need to kick-start my way out of it ...'

My sentence petered out, as that's all I had to say for myself. He took a clipboard from a hook on the wall and flipped over the first page, running his finger down the list.

'Okay, just the ticket. NBC instructor, how does that grab you? We need one in the Company and there is a vacancy on the course next month.'

Nuclear, Biological and Chemical Warfare Instructor. I couldn't have dreamt it; I'd rather push rusty pins in my eyeball than do that.

'Love to Sir, sounds great, thank you.'

Whether my cringing was visible or not, the CSM gave me a wry smile, knowing that it was the worst course out there and he always had difficulties trying to get people to go on them. The NBC instructors that we had were deemed to be no-life swats who could quote the instructor's manual from memory and who got particularly purposeful if you couldn't put your gas mask on in the allotted time. Soon to be me then. I needed to show that I'd do anything to get back on track; at least if I passed I'd have some clout in the Battalion because once a year, everybody from the Commanding Officer down had to take a mandatory test and go into the gas chamber. So back in my room I put a tick next to task one and rummaged around in my wallet for Leanne's phone number.

The phone in the block wasn't private enough, so I walked into town loaded with coins to use the one outside the chip shop.

It rang for ages until a stressed voice answered.

'Hello.'

'Hi Leanne?'

'Yes.'

'It's Den, have I called at a bad time?'

It sounded like the poll tax riot in the background; there was crashing and banging and someone crying.

'Erm, no, hi, no I've erm ... it's the telly ... hang on I'll turn it down ... hang on.'

I heard a door shut and then she was back on the line.

'Hiya Den, sorry about that, I'm always forgetting.'

'That's all right, anyway I was calling to see if you'd like to come out with me on a ... well ... date I suppose, you know last Friday was, well, ...'

'Yeah love to.'

'Great, how about tomorrow night?' The line went dead for a second.

'Oh, I can't do tomorrow sorry, I've got something on.'

'Oh, well Wednesday then?'

'Erm, I'm busy this week, you know work and that and I'm not much fun during the week, how about Friday? Sorry Den.'

'No, don't apologise, that's fine, so how's work going?'

'Yeah I turn up in the mornings. How about you?'

'Oh fine, I've got myself on a course, I'm gonna learn how to survive a nuclear explosion.'

'Oo, that'll come in handy.'

'Yeah, ha ha.'

She sounded distracted so I thought I'd end the conversation as I'd achieved my aim.

'Look Leanne, shall I call you on Thursday? Or maybe I'll call into the bank during the week?'

'Call me Thursday about seven as I'll be busy until then, okay?'

'Okay, take care, 'bye.'

"Bye,' and number two on the list was getting a tick ... soon.

I was quite pleased with myself; not only had I done two positive things in a row, I hadn't arranged any more card games. It had been noted that I wasn't playing. I'd been asked a couple of times so my standard answer of 'I'm skint at the moment' was holding up well. My cash flow was poor but at least the bank was off my back. I'd started on another project: to tidy up my act, my room to start with, as I'd been hiding clothes in my locker for the past couple of years. I would take them out of their corner and see if they could pass as fashion and if not, I would get rid of them. I couldn't let some items go though, like my favourite black shirt which still looked in good nick; so those items I'd wash and press and hang back up. My box, however, sat in the bottom of the wardrobe, covered with dust and looking ominous. No way could I muster the strength to lift the lid, as I knew that the letter would be the first thing I saw. I remembered the days where I'd read it two or three times and sob before going out and getting blind drunk and throwing hundreds of pounds away. I'd use the letter as an excuse and justification for doing so. It had done the rounds, been thrown away and later retrieved; and on one occasion even taken to the pub in my pocket. It was like a talisman that would control me. I'd find myself talking to it like a demented idiot, cursing the ink on the paper and the words that to me would be taunting me into another drunken rage.

So the box stayed where it was. I was moving forward but not that fast; it could wait. The only thing that hadn't suffered was my fitness; I could run like the wind but, I thought, if I am going to do this radical life laundry I may as well try living more healthily. I'll give up the zig and zags and do one of those detox things. So I went downtown, straight to the chemist, as I didn't think I could just stub out a ciggy without any help.

'Hello, can I help you?'

The pharmacist stood behind the counter with his clinical white coat on and his hands behind his back.

'I'd like to give up smoking and wanted some chewing gum or something.'

'Yes, we have gum.'

He reached down and produced four different packets. 'Which flavour?'

'Erm, I don't know ... what have you got?'

'Mint, fruity or regular.'

'Mints please.'

'What strength do you need?'

'I don't know, the strongest you've got I expect.'

He then went through a list of questions about how and why I smoke and we decided that the two-milligram would be best. Next I walked around to the supermarket and bought four cartons of grapefruit juice and a bag of apples. I'd read about this detox thing in a magazine and it sounded easy; and after a well executed shopping expedition I was fully armed and headed back to Camp smoking my last-ever fag.

Two hours later and one carton of juice left I felt sick as a dog; I had the start of a huge ulcer on the inside of my mouth where I'd bitten it and I was gagging for a smoke! I lasted until midnight before heading back to town to the garage to buy twenty cigarettes; and it was in the middle of Aldershot High Street that the grapefruit juice kicked in. I stood bolt still as I felt the liquid try to escape from my body and my stomach cramped; there was nowhere to go, not even a night club would be open to use their toilet. The garage should have one, I thought, so slowly I started to shuffle up the pavement towards the lights of the forecourt. The fifty metres took me an age and with every shuffle my stomach protested and rumbled, moving their contents nearer to the floor.

I started to sweat and as I rounded the sign for 'Open 24 Hrs' I could see the unmanned hatch of the night service till. There was no one in sight and I was getting desperate. My tap on the window alerted a rather slow moving older man who sidled up to his seat and insisted on brushing it with his hand before taking a seat and leaning over to address me. He gave me a sideways look and asked

'Yes please?'

'Can I please have twenty Marlboro Lights and use your toilet?'

He threw the cigarettes under the counter and replied, 'Toilet's broke, mate.'

'Do you have a staff toilet I can use please, I'm caught short.'

'Got a disabled toilet I suppose.'

Why didn't he say that in the first place? I'm sure I look desperate; it must have been apparent but now wasn't the time to start an argument.

'Yes please.'

He passed a key under the glass with a huge piece of plastic attached to it as a fob. I thanked him and he pointed to the end of the building, so I set off shuffling. Just out of sight of the desk the disabled toilet door swung open and there in front of me was the most beautiful loo I'd ever clapped eyes on. It was like a mental trigger to my bowels as they murmured a sound that told me I needed to speed up. Oh the relief! it was fantastic and I lit a fag to celebrate. As I relaxed with the smoke billowing out of my mouth I glanced around the room and shat to my heart's content. There was something missing but I couldn't put my finger on it what it was. Paper, there was no bloody paper. The old sod in the office was probably howling to himself thinking I'd be sitting here paperless. There was nothing I could use; no towels, old newspaper, nothing; so I sifted through my wallet to see if I'd inadvertently left a roll of bog paper in there. Again, to my dismay, I had nothing but a twenty-pound note. I cleaned myself up and not for the first time, flushed the money down the pan. When I returned to the desk the old man was reading.

'There's no loo paper in there,' I stated.

'I know mate you have to ask for that.'

He took the key back and put his head back into his book, signalling me to shut up and go home. It was the most expensive crap I'd ever had.

Chapter Thirty-six

I hate 'passing-in' tests, so on the first day of my NBC course my heart sank. We sat in the classroom in syndicates of thirty men and were handed a paper of one hundred questions. I'd tolerate being taught, working on the theory that if I ever needed it, my subconscious recall would kick in and I'd be able to save my own life. But faced with an hour of torture by paperwork I couldn't remember my own name; the questions were mostly about describing the symptoms of different types of poisoning, so I took a wild stab and put Death, to all apart from Blister Agent, to which I put the obvious answer. Then after having been told to put our pens away, like at school, we met outside to compare what we had written. From listening to the others, it was quite apparent that I wasn't the only one not to have done any pre-course reading; thankfully, some of the other lads were as clueless as me, and I was relieved. Momentarily that was, until the instructor came out and told us that the practical test started straight away. Practical! What? 'Are they actually going to gas us?' I thought as our group headed over to a playing field, where another gang of instructors stood waiting along with the other four assemblies of men. As we walked, a guy next to me introduced himself as Shuggy; he was in the Cheshire Regiment and spoke with a thick Manc accent.

'Let's boldly bowl whuz nah squaddie's beun before,' he stated as we grew nearer.

'What, have you done this before then?'

'Yis, got kicked off de last cose fe fuck'n about.'

The statement didn't fill me with confidence because, as a struggling student, the last thing I needed was to be associated with the course-trouble-maker, so I left it at that and listened to the briefing.

'Right gents, you'll be split into groups and sent to different stands. Once you have completed each stand and been given your mark, the instructor will move you on to the next location and so on, until you have completed all five. Any questions?'

As there were none we were broken down and sent on our way. Shuggy tagged on behind me adding, 'This is bonza, lah!'

The sign at our first stand said NUCLEAR and my brain strained trying to remember my reaction to seeing the light of an explosion. I was sure that it was to drop flat on to my stomach and hide my hands under my body until the blast wave had passed by. Sounds simple I thought, in the calm of a spring afternoon in Wiltshire where the threat of an actual nuclear detonation was remote. The instructor didn't make eye contact with anyone; instead he bellowed the mandatory practice warning of a nuke going off by shouting, 'FLASH!'

As I dropped to the ground I could see a pair of boots stood in front of me and I cringed as the now familiar voice of Shuggy sang out

'AH, ahhha.... Saviour of the Universe!' to a ripple of giggles from the rest of the group, sending the instructor off into his own explosion.

From there on I decided to distance myself from Shuggy and took every opportunity to talk to the nearest person about any subject that sprang to mind instead of letting him cement any friendship. The day passed without any other hitches and to my surprise I passed with surprisingly good marks. Most of the other blokes on the course were Corporals who were training to become instructors at the Army Training Depots around the country; the rest were Sergeants who had to complete the course to become eligible to train officers at The Royal Military Academy in Sandhurst. That sort of thing had never appealed to me; from talking to some of the guys who had served there before; they told me that they would be working from six in the morning until nine at night. I have a social life to consider after all.

I was seeing Leanne depending on what time I got back. It was becoming a regular thing; well, in my books anyway, if I do something more than three times then it's regular. We had been seeing each other for a month and it was going okay, even if I hadn't slept with her. In a way it was cool not to have that pressure; we could talk freely and I thought I knew her better because of it. This week though she had said that we could go back to her place for a drink after the pub if I wanted.

And in other spheres I was doing fine. I hadn't gambled for ages, the course was giving me back my confidence and my bank balance was recovering from the pounding it had been subjected to. I hadn't thought of Peanuts either; it was like the cloud was lifting. Okay, so I did think of her a bit at night when I'd finished my studying for the next day, but it wasn't to regret what I hadn't done or crying over the way her letter had hurt me, just pondering thoughts of what we had done. I could see how bloody miserable I'd been and that did make me cringe a little. I can remember the days when I'd wake up and as soon as my eyes opened I felt malevolent, sometimes for no reason that I could pinpoint. If I woke up like that then the whole day would be ruined until I could get myself into a bar and drunk or a game of cards. Simple things would set me on a downhill spiral and I would notice that people around me would be walking on eggshells so as not to start me off.

One day I hit one of the young Private soldiers for making me a cup of tea without sugar in it; no one said a word to me, probably thinking that they would get the same treatment if they opened their mouths. As compensation, I took him out that night and got him blind drunk, resulting in him getting into a fight with some Parachute Regiment guys who beat him to a pulp. He never spoke to me again!

Things were different and I could only put it down to my meeting Leanne. Was she a guardian angel sent to save me? That's what it felt like; I didn't, however, feel in her debt, because you either fancy someone or you don't. She could have let me walk away from the bank that day and let me sabotage my own life, but she insisted on the night in the pub and I accepted. And I did not ask for help; I would have eventually got myself out of the mess, so I'll take it for what it looks like and just admit that she likes me and I like her, the by-product of this being that I am on the mend.

I'd managed to organise a lift for the weekend with a bloke called Sid in 'A' Company who was on the course too; that saved me the rigmarole of public transport. He didn't even seem to mind that I slept as soon as I'd got into the car. So on Friday lunchtime I packed a bag ready to go back and slogged my way through the afternoon lectures and end of week test before we were, made to parade and then be stood down. The week had been spent in the classroom looking at view foils or acetates and writing like mad about nuclear weapons and their capabilities; it was repetitive but must have done the trick as I scored 80% in my first test.

Leanne looked great as she stood in the doorway of the pub scanning. I waved her over to the table and handed her a glass of gin and tonic before she kissed me and sat down.

'Hiya, you look lovely.'

'Thank you Den! How was your course? Did it go well?'

She offered me a cigarette and took a gulp from her glass as she slumped back into her chair.

'Really well thanks, and how was your week at the bank?'

'I turned up.'

'Oh, not so good then?'

'Teething problems with the new computer system, it's meant to make life easier, except it keeps crashing and then we have to hand write everything, just like we used in the first place. That's progress for you!'

'Yeah, I'm glad I don't have to deal with those things.'

She took another swig and her glass was empty so I offered to fill it again. She smiled with interest as I chatted about my week, even though I thought that it was unamusing but the story about Shuggy made her laugh. For the first time though I didn't know where the night was going. Before it seemed quite straightforward; we'd have a few beers and a laugh and then I'd take her back to the bus stop and we'd snog until her bus arrived. But tonight we'd be going back to her place; well, that's if she remembered that we were; she hadn't mentioned it and I didn't want to be so presumptuous as to ask.

'Do you want to go somewhere to eat?' I enquired.

'Yes that would be nice, where did you have in mind?'

True to form I hadn't thought of that, so I sat there scratching my chin and trying to look as though I had a list of restaurants in my head that I was sifting through. She leant across the table and put her hand on mine.

'Do you like shepherd's pie?'

'Yes I do.'

'Come on then, I've got some at home if you'd like to come around?'

'Like to? I'd love to.'

I sounded far too pleased so I went onto auto correct. 'I mean I'm really hungry ... for some food ... you know ... just food ...well ... '

She laughed out loud and stopped me before I dug myself completely in.

'So am I, come on.'

We finished our drinks and walked the short distance to the bus stop hand in hand.

As we sat on the bus Leanne turned to me and before she spoke I could see that she was about to announce something monumental. She took a sharp intake of breath and pushed herself upwards in her seat.

'Den, I've got something to tell you.'

I knew it: she's a transsexual. I thought but stopped myself from making a jokey comment, just in case she was. Then again she couldn't have been because her hands were too dinky; well, if she was, she was a good one. But that would have meant I kissed a bloke! I cleared my head.

'I haven't exactly lied to you but I have omitted to tell you something, I didn't want to until I got to know you better, but as you're coming home, I'll tell you now. I know you might run a mile but I can't keep this from you 'cos its very important to me.'

Bloody hell I thought, she is a tranny!

'I've got a daughter ...'

She looked at me with expectation.

'Thank God for that, I thought you were going to tell me that you are a bloke.'

For a second she seemed deflated and then giggled.

'A what?'

I had a think. No, I didn't mind, I was actually quite flattered that she had told me. It's quite normal for women to have children; I mean you don't have to be married nowadays.

'She's called Demmi and she's eighteen months old, you won't meet her tonight because Mum has her on a Friday.' She'd gone into turbo-blurbal.

'That's an interesting name.'

It was the only thing I could think to say as Leanne spouted off about how she and Demmi's dad had been seeing each other for five years and then she fell pregnant. That was his cue to make a hasty exit from their lives and they have seen neither hide nor hair of him since. 'So you see I have to work because he doesn't pay me any maintenance.'

'Can't you make him?' I was asking about stuff that was well out of my remit.

'Not if I can't find him, no.'

She stood up and rang the bell to ask for the next stop, and we both staggered down the staircase to the doors. We walked the short distance onto the estate and started to weave our way around the maze of houses that looked the same, and then she announced 'Sorry about the mess.' She reached for the keys in her pocket. What did she expect me to say? Look Leanne, I don't mind about you not telling me about your child but if the house is chaotic then we're finished! As far as untidiness goes it wasn't shocking, a couple of small toys lying on the floor and a half-full teacup on the kitchen surface.

'What would you like to drink Den, I've got some beer or wine or ...'

'Beer thanks.'

She seemed nervous as I looked around the kitchen at her collection of pictures pinned onto a board.

'That's Demmi at her first birthday, Mum and Dad bought her a car but the wheel fell off.'

She was leaning over my shoulder pointing and I couldn't resist her exposed neck just there waiting to be kissed. She took a breath and pushed closer as I snaked my mouth up to her earlobe.

'I've got another confession.'

She stepped back into reality as I stopped my seduction.

'Blimey Leanne, what does it take to shut you up?'

More giggles and she took my hand and led me into the adjoining room where a table was laid for two with unlit candles and wine glasses. There was a small bunch of flowers in the middle and it looked charming.

'Well, I knew that you wouldn't have eaten so I thought we could have supper together.'

The room was small and she had her briefcase balanced on some laundry in the corner; music went on in the kitchen, hiding the clanking of plates as Leanne served up. I could almost be at home with Mum fussing over me.

Soon Leanne appeared with two plates loaded with shepherd's pie and peas and placed one in front of me before putting hers down and disappearing, only to return a few seconds later with a can of bitter. This was luxury at its finest, the food smelt fabulous and the can had just come out of the fridge.

'Is it all right for you Den?'

'It's heaven ... I mean yeah, lovely thank you.' She sat and tucked in, looking very pleased with herself and so she should be.

It's incredible, I wouldn't have thought to do this for someone but then again I don't have the resources, like a house. But it was unexpected and the more I ate the happier I felt. We didn't speak as we ate, partly due to the sound of the radio but mainly as the food was so flippin' tasty, they just can't do this in the Army cookhouse. I kept glancing up to find Leanne checking on my progress and I felt like she was fishing for some approval so as I placed my cutlery down I leant back, rubbed my stomach and said, 'Perfect, thank you.'

We cleared the debris together and she told me to leave the washing-up so we sat down in the living room; actually, we slumped on her tatty sofa together.

'I've got a film for us to watch.'

She pounced to her feet again, just as I was about to pounce on her.

'Great, what is it?'

'A romantic comedy, haven't seen it, have you? It's got Hugh Grant in it!'

The over-animated emphasising his name made a reply in the negative particularly difficult to impart.

'Oh ... good.'

Actually it was a clever film and my guffaws must have sounded convincing. I didn't mention that the best part was the fight, because it might spoil things and there were times during the movie when I became distracted and looked around me. I was sat with a can of beer, a sweet girl and in a home watching a crappy love film on a Friday night. I thought of the lads trekking from pub to pub looking for either a fight or an easy lay, and I wondered if I could go back to that. Marc has this every night and looks well on it; I've just had the one night and felt brilliant. Maybe brilliant was too strong a word; I might be sent packing in a minute, back to the cold barrack block and my lonely single bed. But from the way Leanne was snuggling up to my shoulder and refilling her wine I could sense that I wasn't going anywhere tonight. I hadn't even packed my toothbrush!

As I opened my eyes I could see Leanne's smiling face next to me, her hair was bedraggled but it didn't spoil her looks. I was incredibly tired and the bed so warm with her skin touching mine but I couldn't drift off again.

'What time is it?'

'Nearly ten, I've brought you a cup of tea, it's next to you.'

She was half sat up with her hand resting on her chin. I almost sensed that she was admiring me but that would be vain. I picked my tea up and noticed a pair of stockings on the floor, reminding me that it wasn't such a quiet night and I smiled to myself as I took a sip of tea. I obviously hadn't had time to have a look at the décor last night and noticed something that I can only describe as a bra tree. It was in fact a nail that had been hammered rather amateurishly into the wall with ten or so different coloured bras hanging from it; it deserved a comment.

'Do you collect them or do they have a practical use?' I nodded at the artwork and she looked over her shoulder.

'Oh, my bras? I need them all.'

'Zoiks doll! Please don't tell me you have a shoe collection to match.' My confidence was spilling over and I felt rightly placed to be as cheeky as I liked.

'Do you want to wear that tea?'

She had more pictures on the wall of her bedroom which looked out of place; why have photos of kids and family in your bedroom? They only lived around the corner, you could pop out and see them at any time, but I said nothing.

'What are your plans after you've made my breakfast?

"scuse you! I have to pick Demmi up from Mum's, you could come with me if you like.' The thought panicked me slightly and I realised that through all of the relationships I'd had I'd only met a couple of parents. Did it mean that we were a couple or would she say I was just a friend? I had nothing planned, the idea of returning to the barracks after breakfast felt cheap, and I was interested in her.

'Yes, fine of course I will.'

She smiled over her shoulder and started putting clothes on; she obviously had a couple of different wardrobes for different occasions. The skirt and blouse from last night were thrown in the corner and she now had a pair of black trousers and jumper on, very Mummy. I dragged the same stuff that I had on from the day before and we headed downstairs.

Leanne was obsessed with photographs; they were everywhere. I hadn't noticed them but I did feel watched as I tucked into a bowl of cereal and another cuppa. Cereal was unusual to my day; I hadn't had it for ages, only at home with Mum. I normally have a fry-up and it reminded me of an advert that I'd seen on telly where a dad is trying to convince his child that the cornflakes he has prepared for his kids are tasty. He takes a mouthful, saying 'Look, it tastes really good' and then realises that it does actually taste delicious, and eats the lot without letting the kids have a look-in. I had another bowl.

After sitting through another photo album I thought I could recognise every member of her family on sight and I felt more prepared to meet Leanne's parents. As it was, when she said it was just around the corner I didn't think she meant so literally; in fact, it was so close that I was beginning to get worried that they might have heard me ravishing their daughter last night! Leanne let herself in and shouted a hello; Demmi toddled around the corner with a shriek of delight and held her arms aloft. Soon after her mum appeared and as Leanne was fussing over Demmi I took it upon myself to greet her.

'Hello, I'm Den'

'Oh, nice to meet you at last. I've heard all about you, would you like a cup of tea?'

My insides were sloshing but I couldn't refuse. She wasn't like my mum; she didn't look a day over fifty. I was shown into the front room where a man sat propped in front of the Grand Prix on telly; Leanne's mum gave him a slap on the shoulder.

'This is Den.'

She turned to me and gestured that I should sit down; as I did so, the man straightened himself and held out a hand.

'Hello Sport, I'm Vince; do you like racing?' No, I absolutely hated racing or any other sport for that matter which involved men chasing each other around a circuit for hours and hours in machines.

'Yeah, it's great.'

I sat in the chair next to him and was brought a brew by her mum.

'Now Den, I'm not sure how you take your tea sweetheart, I

hope this isn't a fortnight?'

I must have looked slow.

'Too weak!' she tittered, as he started to report how well some driver was doing considering the conditions. Her dad went on for a while until Leanne appeared again with Demmi on her hip.

'Dad, switch that off, Den doesn't want to be bored by you going on about motor racing.'

He begrudgingly sat forward and switched the button.

'So Den, you're in the Army are you?'

'Yes, been in about ten years now.'

'I was in for a while: Paras.'

Leanne interrupted him before he could continue.

'Dad, you were in for six weeks and then you were chucked out for a dodgy knee.'

She laughed, and he scowled at her.

'If I hadn't had a bad knee I'd still have been in. I loved it, so what are you in, Den?'

'Guards, I'm a Corporal,'

'Oh very good, I could have been a Sergeant Major I reckon, I was fitter then.'

'Demmi needs some lunch, I'm just going to feed her.'

Leanne winked at me and went through to the kitchen, where I guessed her and her mum were in fierce conference about the new man she'd brought home.

'Right Den, I'm off for a pint, do you want to join me or have you got to check with the missus first?'

He chuckled and got his coat. I didn't quite know how I felt about Leanne being referred to as my missus so I said that I'd love a pint.

Vince was in his early fifties and worked at the paper mill as a supervisor; he enjoyed his job, as it was steady and paid well. He had opinions and advice about things, which made me think that maybe his job and life were a bit too routine. Everybody in the pub knew him and he kept introducing me as 'Leanne's new bloke'. It felt like I'd become part of the family overnight; they were extremely trusting, or maybe they had seen this before and just paid lip service. We had another pint with his mates, who quizzed me like they had never met a soldier before, which I thought strange coming from a garrison town.

'Do you like a bet Den?' Vince asked.

'No, never done it,' I lied. 'Just seems like a waste of money to me.'

'Ah, you shouldn't knock something unless you've tried it once, except for homosexuality and incest … right lads?'

His mates laughed and carried on supping their pints. It was a funny thing to say and I smiled to myself before replying.

'Well that's a good job, my brother would probably knock me out.'

The retort was met with a hail of approving chuckles from all and I swelled with confidence as I had been officially accepted into the fold. I couldn't help but let a thought drift into my head: if it were only incest and homosexuality, then were necrophilia and bestiality all right then?

'Come on, let's go and have a look at the nags.' Vince tipped the remainder of his pint into his mouth and led me into the bookies a few doors along. I didn't feel comfortable stood in a place where temptation was so great to throw the odd fifty quid down the pan; I'm sure Leanne wouldn't have been so pleased if I had told her about it. He put three bets on and we went home to drink more tea. This family wouldn't dehydrate in a hurry, that's for sure.

Chapter Thirty-seven

I passed the course with flying colours and was even asked to return as an instructor, but declined politely rather than the 'I'd rather slide down a razor using my balls as the brake' answer that sprang to mind. It set me back into Battalion life rather well, and as the months passed and I began to teach the troops I regained my reputation. I'd even started running for the Company in the cross-country team. Leanne and I were getting on well and any spare time I had I would catch the bus to her house and stay overnight. We celebrated Demmi's second birthday, inviting some of her friends around for a tea-party and I met Leanne's friends, most of whom were single girls.

I had time to reflect on the military as a whole way of life and as I achieved and overtook my peers in the unspoken batting order for promotion, my memories of the previous years faded. Basically, I was being rewarded for my hard work; any jobs that arose were directed my way. So after laying off the booze and cards I had paid my debt to the bank and had enough money to buy a leaky old car; my only outlay were fags and condoms, which are really expensive, even when you buy them in twelve packs. This was me, I was back and stronger and more thoughtful than ever before. I could see my future in the Army blossoming into something worthwhile.

Then, a few events in quick succession opened my eyes wider than they had been before.

I had a half day for sport, as only the Army can do; it's such a ritual that if ever the IRA found out then surely they would attack us on a Wednesday afternoon! Leanne was held up at work and she phoned me on my recently acquired mobile asking if I would pick Demmi up from crèche. I agreed, and arrived outside a brightly decorated establishment and duly rang the bell. A lady opened the door and on a table in the entrance were some soggy paintings of ... something, with the child's name on the corner, nothing I was keen to risk my clothes or car interior with, hoping secretly that Demmi hadn't done any painting today. As I stepped forward and said that I'd come to collect Demmi the woman cheerfully declared,

'Demmi ... your dad's here to get you.'

I stared in horror, not knowing whether to put her straight by telling her that I was only her mum's boyfriend or just keep quiet and hope for the best; so I froze and watched as Demmi turned with the same excited look that I'd seen on her face the first time I had been to Leanne's mum's house, and ran at me with her arms out. Did this child know how silly it would make me feel to explain or ... she thought I *was* her dad! She wasn't my child, but I couldn't help hug her with a mixture of relief and joy at being called a dad. I mean I had done a lot of the dad things I suppose, and I was on the scene quite a lot. God, I was confused; I wasn't a dad at all, but the woman saw me as a father figure, responsible enough to carry a kid in my car and feed her and sing songs and ... oh, it was overwhelming. I didn't tell Leanne.

The second thing was the weekend I took Leanne to meet my mum, another first. Demmi was staying with her grandparents, so as not to give my mum a heart attack when I waltzed in with woman *and* child. We went out for dinner, the whole family; Leanne and Debbie got on like a house on fire and Demmi was mentioned casually in the conversation, that to my surprise was met with acceptance by Mum. We stayed overnight, and Leanne slept in my room while I was given the sofa to kip on. She stood in amazement looking at my model aircraft and then started to tease me as I hurriedly shifted them to make way for her case. Anyway, during the night, I stealthily crept upstairs to check that Leanne was sleeping soundly, and if she might need a drink; and completely by accident I tripped and ended up on top of her in bed! After much struggling to get away we ended up under the covers, and later we lay together with the curtains open looking at the sky. It was like something out of a Mills and Boon paperback.

'I love you Den.'

The word pierced the silence and I could tell by her tone that she now needed me instead of just liking me. I had become half-a-dad and half-of-a-couple, but even though she had said it out loud and the words were with us in the room, it was far too late in the day to do anything about it.

'Same here,' and I didn't know if I'd answered or just tagged along with the game.

It took me a long time thinking if I, I mean we, were serious; Leanne was definitely serious and I was definitely seriously in a relationship; it just meant that everything was going well I suppose, until the next morning when we drove back to Aldershot.

'Would you ever leave the Army Den?' she asked, without even looking at me, and kept her gaze firmly out of the window.

'Yeah, well I'll have to one day ... why?'

'No, I mean do you have to do the full stint, however long it is?'

'Not if I don't want to, but I have to give a year's notice; what are you getting at?'

'Oh nothing I was just wondering.'

There was silence again for a few miles.

'Are you going to have to go back to Ireland again?'

'I suppose so, but no one has said anything to us yet. Sorry Leanne are you trying to ask me something?'

I could feel myself getting irritated by the questions and had no idea where she was leading.

'It's just that if you do go away, Demmi and me will miss you so much, she's come on leaps and bounds with a man around the house, and I love having you to stay, it would be a terrible shame.'

'It would only be for six months, not a lifetime Leanne, I told you that our Battalion is going to move next year. As it is, I don't know what you're so worried about.'

'Let's hope it's not too far then.'

With that the conversation tailed off and she switched the radio on for the last few miles. I did really like Leanne, she was easy going and dressed nicely and she could cook and we laughed together. Her insecurity stemmed from her boyfriend who left the scene when she was pregnant I guessed, but I couldn't do anything about that; she needed to work through it herself.

I learned in Belize that my Battalion had taken part in the Queen's Birthday Parade, an occasion that I'd been unlucky enough to miss. So when it appeared on Company Orders for volunteers to help the second Battalion, I thought that it was a way I could raise my profile. The fact that I as a guardsman hadn't done the birthday parade thing was always looked down upon by the seniors as bad form. Apparently, it was one of the events that made us stand out from all of the other Infantry units, but what with tours to Bosnia and Belize I just hadn't got around to it.

Leanne didn't seem too sunny when I told her; I was only going to London for goodness' sake; six weeks, and not a lifetime and I would be back at the weekends, apart from the rehearsals that she could come and watch. The decision was made and as far as I was concerned it would do me far more good than harm, so once I'd spoken to the Sergeant Major and got the thumbs up, I started to get my ceremonial dress kit ready; bearskin and boots mainly as they took the most looking after.

Stan was the other lad who was going. I liked Stan; he was a quiet bloke who had a habit of drawing unwanted attention to himself. He didn't want much out of life, just his pay and weekends off, it seemed; but every time he attempted to merge into the background he'd do something that everyone in the Battalion would hear about.

His most famous goof was on the ranges in Wales where he was on the back of a truck practising ambush drills with live ammunition. The idea was that he lay at the rear of a flatbed lorry so that he could cover an area to the far right hand side; next to him lay three more men who had different areas to fire at should the enemy appear. As the vehicle drove along the road, targets would appear in various places to simulate enemy and if they popped up in the area that was being covered by him then he could shoot at them until they dropped. These targets are remotely operated by a Range Warden, who sits in a small hut on the edge of the range and flicks switches to make the six-foot metal men shaped targets appear; if a bullet strikes them they fall backwards and disappear from view. So the truck moved off at a crawl and the blokes started to shoot at their targets; all except Stan, who because of a mechanical problem had no targets in his area. Unbeknown to him, the Range Warden, a civilian employed by the military to ensure all of the training went smoothly, had decided to go out to the first target to fix it. Stan then sees a target on his far right, takes aim and squeezes his trigger; much to his delight, on his first shot the target falls. The Warden, now with Stan's bullet lodged in his shoulder, realises that he is in a predicament as he is in open ground with little or no cover, and not thinking straight, as he is the proud new owner of a piece of fast moving lead decides to get up and run back to the safety of his hut. Stan's second shot, on the appearance of his target, is true and he is lying there grinning at his accuracy from a moving target at one hundred metres when a boot from behind and a screaming 'STOP!' tells him that there may be something up.

'You've shot the ruddy Range Warden!' the instructor shouts at Stan.

'Blimey, I thought the targets looked realistic,' he replied.

Luckily for both parties, the guy got away with shoulder injuries, and because of his stupidity in getting up to fix the target when firing was in progress, Stan didn't get disciplined for his actions.

So we arrived in London and assigned to the Company that we would be parading with to start the practising. It was a drill overload and by the end of the first day my feet were pounding from marching up and down the parade square. I had to play catch up with the other lads who were veterans of the QBP, as it is known. My evenings were spent polishing my boots so that I could see my face in them and shampooing and conditioning and brushing down my bearskin hat. I'd never looked so well turned out. The days progressed and the drill got steadily more complicated; we would march with rifles and carry out different moves with them. First stood still, and then marching, slowly at first and then faster as the Regimental Sergeant Major and drill Sergeants shouted at us. Kit inspections became a morning routine and we were going to be on display to the public and more importantly HRH, so we would be ordered to show ourselves in different forms of the dress uniform, looking gleaming. One day we would be wearing the bearskins to ensure that they fitted correctly and that an onlooker couldn't see our eyes, and the next day we would carry them and wear our peaked caps to show the top of the hats were brushed.

Soon the whole Battalion looked gleaming, according to the RSM, and things were coming together with the rifle and foot drill. Once again I found myself being praised for my performance on the parade square. I was given one of the most important jobs in the Company whilst on parade for my hard work. There is a drill movement called a left form, which is done by the whole Company when marching along in ranks of three. The idea is to change our direction by ninety degrees to the left while marching, without changing our formation, so that the three long lines could turn a corner without doing something resembling Frank Spencer in an ice rink. My job was to let our Company Commander know the precise location that we had to start the turn by counting the paces in my head as we marched. When he gave the precautionary words of command,

'Change direction left,'

I would count to myself, and at the precise time shout,

'RIGHT, SIR!' on consecutive paces, so that he could tell us to start the turn by yelling

'LEFT FORM!' immediately after. It was easier said than done. To ensure that this was trickier, we would have to change the position of our rifles whilst doing the direction change and just to make it completely unfeasible we would do it in slow-march and quick-march. Any lapse in concentration would mean our lot crashing into the next Company.

I didn't feel like I was gelling with the other lads and they looked on at me as the Corporal from the other Battalion. Stan and I spent most of our evenings in the local pub when we weren't polishing our kit. Well, when I say evenings, it was the last hour before the hoards of tourists turned drunks were tipped into the street. He wanted to go on to somewhere else to see if he could pull, but the fact that Leanne and I are an item made me decline. In the mornings, I'd be told of the women that he'd managed to coerce into some seedy liaison in a park. I was quite pleased of the security I felt with being part of a couple.

This made the weekends feel better when I'd go straight to her house and relax. *Her* house was becoming my home, I suppose. I'd notice things that needed doing and just get on with them, cutting the grass and mending one of the cupboards. It hadn't occurred to me before that it would ever happen, me becoming in charge of a lawn; although sometimes I felt like a handyman who stayed overnight. And yet Leanne made the important decisions about Demmi and the household. She did however start letting me go shopping for food; another novel task that gave me a sense of well-being as I trawled though the supermarket finding the buy-onegetonefree items, or landing on the reductions counter just at the moment a shop assistant put a packet of steak down with a pound saving. I felt like a shopping-demon as I scanned my receipt to see if I'd been a supersaver. She'd even given up a drawer in her wardrobe for me to put my clothes in.

It was the Saturday morning of the first big rehearsal, called The Major General's Review, and the first time we would be on display to the public. I was up and about at six, and took myself for a run around London before having breakfast and getting ready to fall in on parade. Everyone was on a buzz, and the morning flew by and before I knew it we were lining up with our rifles ready to go. I could hear a commotion from the line and tried to earwig on the fume that the Sergeant Major was having. It seemed that someone had not turned up; a cardinal sin on such an auspicious occasion and whoever it was surely would be dealt with severely. Suddenly the Sergeant Major was in front of me, barking about the mate of mine who was missing. It was Stan; the bloody fool had taken today of all days to have a lie-in, and I was getting it in the neck.

'Go and tell him I'd like a word in his shell-like.'

The Sergeant Major spoke calmly but with a determination that didn't bode well. I didn't even answer. I just handed my rifle to the bloke next to me and ran.

I rapped on the door and shouted his name through the keyhole. Either he had gone AWOL or pulled last night and was still in bed with some poor unfortunate. My heart started to pound as I peered through the keyhole and saw that the key was in the lock from the other side; he must have been severely on the piss last night. But I knew he could get up and at 'em after a skinfull, so perhaps he wasn't there after all but why was the key was in the lock? I banged and shouted, this time much louder. I looked and listened but nothing; he could have fallen over and hit his head or something. The Sergeant Major wasn't impressed that I had returned without him.

'Get his spare key from the Quartermaster.'

'But Sir, I ...'

'Just do it Corporal Yarwood.'

'Sir, he's locked himself in!'

I had to shout to be heard over his bellowing and as I did his face changed and he hailed the Provost Sergeant, who was stood at the rear of the parade. After a few words out of my earshot he turned to me.

'Right; you're off the practice, go with the Provost and get into his room, tell Private Stanley to report to my office once he's sobered up.'

Bloody hell, this parade wasn't to be for me. I was going to miss the rehearsal, just as I was getting the hang of it as well. I fumed as I got the spare key and returned to Stan's to find the Provost Sergeant shoulder barging the door down and falling into his room.

'Got the key Sarge.'

'Don't worry abaht that, Corporal, 'e's brahn bread!'

I didn't hear him the first time. I peered around at the broken door that had swung open to reveal Stan, with a noose around his neck and strung up from the light fixing in the ceiling; a stool lay on the floor under him. It took a minute for my brain to absorb the information it was receiving. He was nearly naked apart from a pair of stockings and suspender belt.

'Oh my ... Go...'

I rushed in and grabbed his cold legs, trying to lift him up, but the wetness that his body had released made them too slippery to get any purchase. A hand grasped my shoulder and I was pulled away.

'Leave him.' the Provost said. 'Listen Corporal Yarwood, stay here and I'll go and get the duty officer.'

I didn't have time to reply before he was off on his heels down the corridor, leaving me in Stan's room staring at a body. The light was on and curtains shut. I pulled them open until light streamed in and I could see the parade marching out of the gates. It seemed like an age before anyone came and I wasn't sure what to do. I was going to tidy up, then thought that the police would want everything left as it is; so I sat on his bed and flipped through the magazine that was lying on the floor. I'd heard of it before, blokes asphyxiating whilst they get off on porn. At least he'd gone out with a bang I suppose and looked at the mag. There was something strange about it; I turned the pages looking for scantily clad girls but there were none, only blokes, blokes in leather uniforms, exposed!

'Oh hells bells Stan ...'

I threw it down and walked out into the corridor as the Provost returned with a very young Officer who had been lumbered with weekend duty as he was injured and couldn't march.

'Okay Provost where is he?'

The Provost pointed into the room and the Officer and looked around before coming back into the corridor.

'He's dead, Provost.'

'Fuck me Sherlock, of course he's dead,' I blurted out.

'Enough of that Corporal. Go to the Guardroom and call the police.'

The investigation took several days and I was called in for interview so that they could build up a picture of what happened, because I had associated myself with him; I had to protest rather loudly that I had a girlfriend and she was enough for me.

'They are just routine questions Mr Yarwood,' they would say, but it didn't take long for the rumours to start that led to a couple of sly comments from the numskulls about my boyfriend snuffing it.

His family buried Stan the day before the final rehearsal, and I declined the invitation to attend. I needed to distance myself from the situation. I didn't feel anything for Stan, no sadness; it was baffling and I suppose I felt guilty about it, but hey, he died doing something he enjoyed, and not a sad lonely man who had nothing left to live for.

The parade was a welcome distraction, and before I knew it my Company was marching onto Horse Guards parade square with thousands of people watching as well as television cameras. I swelled with pride, knowing that Mum had invited her WI friends around to watch it. It was a scorching day, and the dust from the gravel filled my nose and stuck to trails of sweat on my face and neck. The Life Guards on horseback had formed up behind us, bringing more clouds of dust and the massed bands quietened in readiness for the arrival of the Queen. This was what being British was about, the pomp and circumstance of men in uniform parading though the capital with bayonets flashing in the summer sunlight and boots shining. But it was bloody hot, and after the half-mile march down my tunic was damp and the pints of water I had consumed after breakfast had been absorbed into my clothing. I could see a child straight in front of me guzzling a bottle of, well it didn't matter actually; it could have been Umbongo for all I cared. It looked cold and wet.

'Wiggle your toes and keep your tiny minds active', the Drill

Sergeant would say to us. 'Think of the last time you had sex, or if it was too distant a memory for some of you ugly bastards, then think of the next time you'll have sex and how much you're going to pay for it!' He had a way with words.

'Let your minds go blank and the next thing you'll know is the ground rush as you faint, and if you pass out on Horse Guards then have the decency to land on your bayonet, it'll be less painful that what you're going to get in the nick!'

I pulsed my muscles as the royal carriage came onto the square and we started our drill movements. My mind flashed to Mum's front room, where six or seven elderly women sat with their tea swishing in best china cups as they remarked how lovely the Queen looks for her age. I smiled to myself as we turned to the right and formed up for the march past. It was indeed the finest day I'd had and through the sweat and dust I felt like a real soldier once more.

Chapter Thirty-eight

Another birthday; well, actually a fairly big one. Thirty years old; I'm not sure if this is a turning point, it doesn't feel like it. I'd missed the Millennium last year due to Leanne not getting a babysitter, which didn't really spoil anything as we had some of her single friends around instead, and they complimented us on how well we looked as a couple. A kind thing to say, but clichéd. I mean, you don't go around to someone's house and say 'Goodness you two are a right mismatch aren't you?'

Anyway, her mum took Demmi as we headed out for a delicious celebratory meal followed by copious amounts of wine and wild monkey sex; and then the child who had turned into the spawn of Beelzebub overnight was delivered home by her grandad.

'It's all downhill from here Den. Have a good time last night sport? Demmi's been lively since we gave her a Coca-cola, well, we didn't want her to feel like she was missing out on your birthday.'

'Great, thanks, oh and thanks for looking after her.'

He released her arm and she tore through the house like a Tasmanian Devil, knocking over cups of tea and plant pots until Leanne managed to snare her in the kitchen and discipline her, resulting in a high-pitched wail of tears that sliced through me like a knife.

Our normal Saturday routine would have been a day trawling the shops but I just couldn't handle that in my current state, so I slumped back in front of the telly and switched the News on. We didn't have cable or any of that new-angled technology, mainly because we didn't have the spare cash, but also because I was rapidly becoming technophobic. The idea of having to figure out how to switch the telly on and off was a challenge; I mean what do I want with fifty million channels anyway? Half of them are in Swedish or German and the sports ones aren't going to show Luton getting their weekly thrashing. Leanne brought me a cup of tea and gave me a kiss on the forehead that had become her hello when she didn't want to speak, and sat next to me, slumping her legs over mine.

'And the main headlines today:

British Troops to be sent into Afghanistan as America announces that the Taliban must relinquish power:

The Millennium Dome could be turned into a multi-screen cinema after the exhibition closes:

Tony Blair faces criticism over...'

'So that's it then, when are you going Den?'

Leanne had sat bolt upright in her chair and was leaning to look me in the eyes.

'What are you on about?'

'The News. What's going on? Are you going?'

'No, I would have told you wouldn't I?'

'Will you have to go?'

'Leanne, I don't know, I won't know until somebody tells me and as no one has said anything I...'

'Den, I don't want you to go over there, it's dangerous and Demmi will think that you've left us, and what will I do?'

'Hold on a minute, you know it's my job and if I get told to pack my kit then I go,. I did tell you that when we first started. What do you expect me to do, say sorry, my girlfriend doesn't want me to leave?'

'Don't be flippant Den, I mean it, you're going to have to get out of the Army.'

The exchange had turned into a row within minutes and that statement had added fuel to the fire.

'I fucking well won't be getting out of the Army, what do you think we'd do for money? I've got a pension and everything.'

'Don't swear, Demmi will hear you and it's all about money with you isn't it?'

'How the hell can you say that Leanne? You work in a flippin' bank, do you want me to get some dead end job instead? We're not minted sweetheart.'

She was on the back foot and she knew it. I was appalled at the suggestion of me getting out, she knew that over the past year I had been doing really well and if I kept on going as I was then the future would be bright.

'Well I won't be happy Den, just think of what you'll be doing to the family.'

Change of tactics from money to guilt; so I leave the argument and let her settle down, a practice that I had perfected over time. I used to stay and see if I could reason with her but my habit of waiting quietly would stir her into a frenzy and then the argument would be about me being quiet and trying to appease her. Then I would lose my temper, but my vocabulary deteriorated into a long string of swear words so now I use the leave-the-room strategy. It works well and I can go for a short walk or a beer and when I return Leanne will be playing with Demmi and we can start again.

I sat in the Trafalgar slowly sipping my beer and pondering the prospect of getting a chance to put my soldiering skills to the test for the first time when a fresh pint appeared next to me.

'Lofty!'

'All right Den, solitary drinking?'

'Yeah, sad ain't it?'

'Me too.'

He took a seat at my table; we sat in silence for a second or so.

'Lofty, I'm sorry about the ...'

'Yeah, mate me too, I heard about it.'

Another long pause and we looked at each other over the table.

'You gonna to put your hand up for the tour Den?'

'Yes … you?'

'Not sure yet. I'm supposed to be getting married this summer, gutted that this has come up now, anyhow I thought you were shacked up with some bird from town?'

He hadn't lost his touch of the human language.

'Yes, I'm living with Leanne and her daughter.'

'Blimey Den, she all right with you going on tour?'

'Oh yes, she's been fine about it. Fancy another pint?'

'Does a bear shit in the woods?'

He grinned a toothless grin and threw the remains of his drink down his neck before letting out an earth-shattering belch. I think Lofty and I were back on track and it felt good to smile at something stupid for a change.

When I returned, Leanne and Demmi were in the kitchen with a jigsaw puzzle.

'Fancy a cup of tea Leanne?'

'Yes please.'

'Me too Dad.'

Demmi always asked for a cuppa and it made me laugh so I poured her a glass of chocolate milk and sat down to help the girls.

'Den, we do need to talk about this.'

'Leanne, just leave it, the Battalion might not go, noone might go, it's only on the telly.'

'Den I'll miss you.'

'Where's Dad going?'

Demmi wasn't looking at Leanne; she was trying to force a piece of puzzle into the wrong hole with great determination.

'Nowhere,' I butted in.

'Yet,' Leanne added under her breath.

That night we lay awake after making love and she held me

tight, tighter than she had for ages; I did love her. We got on, which was most of the time; it was lovely having a home and a family, even if it wasn't mine.

I couldn't stop thinking about the News; it had been suggesting the British Army would be going on a new tour.

'I love you Den.'

'Same here.'

'No I really love you babe, what are we going to do?'

'What do you mean?'

'You know us, Den, are we going to stay like this?'

'Leanne, you're losing me ...'

'You know, just boyfriend and girlfriend, Demmi calls you Dad as it is'

'Leanne, we're okay as we are ... listen I'm not going to volunteer for anything stupid, right?'

'Forget it,' and she released her grip and rolled away.

The next morning the Camp was buzzing with Afghan talk; I was the most senior Corporal in the Company and well trusted by my peers and seniors alike, so I was often invited to attend important Company briefings. The Sergeant Major called us in at ten and the briefing room filled with all of the Platoon Commanders, Sergeants and me. The OC came in and we stood in silence and he thanked us before telling us to take our seats. He started immediately without any fuss.

'Gentlemen, good morning. It will be of no surprise that many units have been warned regarding deployment to Afghanistan. To quell any rumours that may be in circulation I have further detail today. Our Battalion will not be deploying immediately; we are second line reserve to bolster any operations. The second Battalion are deploying on January the 5th equipped and trained for full war fighting; that isn't to say they will definitely be involved in any hostilities, as no statement has been issued to indicate this. We will be filling gaps in the second Battalion and subsequently be asking for volunteers when we know the numbers and ranks involved. I have been instructed to prepare everyone for deployment and therefore we will be starting a full range and training programme next week. Sergeant Muir.'

'Sir.'

'Sort out a range package, book Ash Ranges for Monday through to Friday so we can kick start this off on the right foot. Corporal Yarwood.'

'Sir.'

'I want a full NBC training package to run concurrently with the ranges, everyone will be tested and you have the final say, right?'

'Right Sir.'

I swelled again; not only had I been mentioned by name at the conference, I had the full say about the training; this was the most responsible thing I had been given and I was going to make sure I did a superb job. The meeting finished with a question and answer session and we broke to go on a Company run.

That night at home was quiet, especially as we watched the News and saw the American troops getting ready to go. A reporter would stand outside one of the Camps in London and speculated which Regiment would go. I assumed that a blanket press ban had been put on them so it was hardly journalism. I thought about what I was going to do in silence, planning my training for the boys, whilst Leanne looked at the screen and planned our next meal; 'well at least,' I think 'that's what women think about.'

The training took full flight; we spent days shooting as we had done so many times before and the physical exercise got harder to prepare hearts and lungs for high altitudes. Train hard fight easy was the PTI's motto, and he stuck by it, making us carry stretchers around the football field and running with packs on for miles and miles. The more I prepared to go the more I wanted to deploy; I had done the manoeuvres time and again but for what? Some pretend war that would never happen against a fictitious enemy who wore their jackets inside out. No; this time I wanted to go, I'd have a story to tell about heroic events; this was history in the making.

We trained in the administration of morphine and finding a vein to put a drip into someone's arm. I felt green to the gills but didn't show the lads. Briefing upon briefing about the landscape and terrain, mountain sickness, water intake, everything anyone would need to know about fighting at 6000 metres. I listened intently and was able to confirm any questions; I even gave them a re-demonstration of the drip after a disaster by one of the younger guys in front of the OC.

Then the new kit arrived in Camp just after the Christmas break and one section at a time we reported to the quartermaster for issues. I was given two sets of sandy coloured combat suits along with a jacket called a smock; the SAS adopted the smock years ago after suffering in the jungle of Borneo. Next was a set of desert boots, much lighter than my normal ones and three pairs of woolly socks that I viewed with dismay until the Sergeant barked that they were designed for hot climates. The mosquito net went straight to the bottom of my new Bergen when I saw the lightweight sleeping bag lying on the counter; and lastly a bivvy bag. The bivvy bag is made out of Goretex that, in theory, lets out the body's natural moisture, like sweat, and repels any water from entering. It's shaped like a huge condom with a tie at the neck-end, and this one was sandy coloured as well. I had borrowed one for Senior Brecon and it saved my life on the top of the Brecon Beacons when we were caught in a downpour and I could feel myself getting colder and colder. One of the other guys noticed me suffering and shoved me, kit and all, inside it until I had warmed up; awesome bit of gear.

I signed my name on the issue slip and returned to my room to stow the new stuff; it was like Christmas had come again. When I reached the block some of the men had put everything on and were admiring themselves in the mirror; bloody posers I thought, but I was dying to get mine on too.

'You're very quiet,' I remarked, as I put Leanne's tea down.

'I'm fine, actually,' and she sprang to her feet. 'I've got something to show you.'

She dashed off into the kitchen and returned with three brochures, flinging them into my lap and nearly knocking my brew over.

'What are these then?'

'Holidays ... we haven't been away, so I was thinking that we could save up and go somewhere. Nowhere too extravagant, Spain is quite cheap you know!'

'Oh so you've had a look then,' I exclaimed.

'Just a glance,' and she sat watching as I flicked though the brochures. 'Come on Den, you're working really hard at the moment, surely we're entitled to a break after all of this training or whatever you are doing is finished.'

'Yeah, looks lovely.'

'So shall we book something then for the Easter holidays?'

'Yeah, okay.'

She snatched the one I was looking at out of my hand and fingered through the pages until she found what she was looking for, presenting it to my face.

'This looks really good, we could fly into Alicante, book a transfer so we don't need to drive, they've got kids' activities on and evening entertainment for Demmi, it's perfect.'

I stared at the monstrous grey tower block behind a swimming pool that was strewn with gorgeously tanned, beautiful families, laughing at something. God knows what, probably last night's entertainment or the state of the food or the fact that the German family who always got to the pool before anyone else had gone down with dysentery. The write-up said that the Hotel Del Grand Freaking Monstrosity was only five minutes from the beach (by jet-bike I imagined). I could feel my reactions being studied as I read on in horror.

'M'm.'

'M'm?'

'I can put a deposit down tomorrow, I've got enough in my account,' Leanne rubbed my arm as she spoke.

'Okay.' I handed back the brochure and switched the telly on.

My routine was getting more complicated day by day; I'd wake up in the house and put my green gear on before driving to the barracks and running to my room in time to change into my desert kit for the first parade. It stopped any arguments at home. I'd go without breakfast and have a packed lunch that I had prepared the night before, then change back into my other uniform before going home again and having tea. I was teaching the day after the holiday conversation when the OC and Sergeant Major walked in on my lesson; they did this to everyone who taught to ensure not only that the lesson was being conducted correctly but that everyone attended, as some of the more junior officers would take it upon themselves to make an excuse not to bother going. If they were caught out it meant a month of weekends on extra duties. I halted the lesson after twenty minutes to let the lads have a fag and the Sergeant Major collared me.

'How's it going Corporal Y?'

'Good Sir, lads are doing well, I've only got about twenty to get through and then I'm finished.'

'Nice one, you're doing a fine job, it hasn't gone unnoticed'

'Sir?'

'Yes Corporal Yarwood?'

'Has the OC found out if any of our lads are going with 2 Batt?'

'No, not yet. Why, you interested then?'

'Yeah, I mean yes, Sir, if anything comes up could you put in a word please?'

'I'll see, but it's first come in this case, so you'll need to keep your eye on Orders.'

I must have looked disappointed when I replied 'Right Sir,' so he tipped me a wink as he left the room, and as we walked to the smoking area he offered me one of his cigarettes; I was in there, like swimwear!

I got home late and my tea was covered over on the hob so I put it in the microwave and sat down in the living-room. Leanne came in and gave me the obligatory peck on the forehead.

'Good day babe?' she asked.

'Yeah, fine, bit tired now though.'

'I put the deposit in today for the holiday.'

'That's sorted then.'

'Well you could sound more enthusiastic Den.'

'Sorry, I've just had a long day.'

'Well you don't seem very keen.'

'No I'm fine, I'm pleased. Leanne, I've been asked out for a beer tonight with some of the lads, do you mind? I'll only be an hour or so.' 'No that's fine, I've got to bath Demmi anyway.'

I bolted my dinner and had a quick shower before leaving the house for a pint and a chat with Lofty.

Chapter Thirty-nine

Demmi doesn't resemble Leanne and she's nothing like me, she's got a sort of ginger look about her. Leanne says its strawberry blonde but in the light there is a definite hue. So I bought her a hat, which sorted it out. She's an endearing little girl and I'm constantly amazed as I suppose every dad in the world is at how she learns. We have jokes between us that Leanne can't, or won't, get, like when she asks for a cup of tea or running after buses.

The bus chasing started one day when we were shopping on our own. I'm a runner and I've been getting Demmi to race me whenever I can; it makes her giggle and I let her win occasionally. So we are in town heading to the park when the man who is walking in front of us breaks into a jog; Demmi shouts 'race ya' and heads off after him, much to my amusement. I'm walking behind with a couple of bags of shopping, so I let her tear off, thinking that as long as she's in my sight she will be fine and the exercise will do her good. As I watch I realise the man is chasing his bus which kindly slows down and stops a few metres after the bus stop; he was in a hell of a rush and didn't notice Demmi tailing him and gaining ground. He hops on, standing at the doorway catching his breath and lo and behold, so does Demmi, thinking the race is over! The number 14 goes to Farnborough, which of course doesn't matter to a small child who's just run a race; and she looked back and waved as I threw the groceries down and sprinted as fast as I could towards her. It was lucky that the man she had pursued didn't have the correct change and the driver was delayed enough for me to leap onto the bus and drag her off,. It was enlivening; I was howling with delight at not seeing her disappear on the number 59. So from then on, whenever we saw a bus leaving the stop we would run after it. Leanne said it was a silly thing to do, but what does she know about chasing buses anyway?

I know lots about Demmi; she likes princesses and I tell her stories at night sometimes about a beautiful princess called Kerry, who is kind and looks after people and grants special wishes. And we go to the café on a Saturday morning for a chocolate fudge cake that we call a Scrumdiddlyumscious, and when she grows up she wants to be a soldier but not like the ones on the telly who have to fight, only like the ones who help people. And she finds lots of dead things, wherever we go, like the time I took her out to Portsmouth and she found a dead pigeon; or the time next door's cat had a mouse and she retrieved it and asked if I could fix it for her (I would have done if I could have found the head); so instead we buried it in the back garden and called it Twitcher. Anyway, we get on pretty well and no one would ever guess that she wasn't mine; she's my little mate, my conscience sometimes.

So we sit in the café with our slice of Scrumdiddlyumscious, me with a cup of tea and her with a glass of milk and make stories up about people passing the window, until she tells me that she can see a giant staring in at her. I look up from my paper and there is Lofty with his nose pressed up at the window, pulling a funny face.

'I know that giant, Demmi.'

'Do you Dad? What's his name?'

'Lofty.'

'That's a funny name, was he born in the loft?'

I laugh and beckon him in.

'All right Den, got yourself a new bird then?' He came in and sat next to Demmi, towering above her, her little face a picture as she stared up at the big man

'My dad says he knows you.'

'Your dad! Blimey Den I didn't know you had it in you, I mean yes, we were, m'm are mates, and what's your name darlin'?'

'I'm Demmi and you're Lofty.'

'Yes, that's right.'

'Were you born in a loft, Lofty?'

'Ha ha close, no it's because … oh sod it! Yep, I was born in the loft, ha ha.Cute kid Den.'

'You swore.'

'Pardon?'

'You said sod, that's swearing,' and she cupped her hand to Lofty's ear so that he had to bend down. She whispered, 'but I heard Dad say bum once!'

'Did you?'

'Yeah, he said to my mum that she had a n…'

'Demmi, that's enough.'

'Sorry Dad.'

Lofty's eyes were glistening and he pointed at her cake.

'M'm what's that?'

'Scrumdiddlyumscious.'

'Ooh it looks lovely, can I have a piece please?'

'Dad can buy you some,' and Lofty let loose a loud guffaw.

'Da'ad, can I have a piece of Scrum'de'dum'dumscious ple'ease?'

He had his head turned to one side and tears streamed down his face with delight. I couldn't believe that I'd been left out of the conversation and those two were getting on like a house on fire. So I mouthed 'piss off', and bought him a brew instead. Demmi watched him in awe as he slurped his tea.

'You see Orders on Friday Den?'

'No!'

'They want blokes to go out with 2 Batt, names in on Monday.'

I didn't want Demmi to repeat this so I gave him a weary look and zipped my finger across my mouth. He looked puzzled and then down at Demmi, who had returned to her cake.

'Oh, got ya,' he winked, and started chatting about the training, trying his hardest not to swear.

'Demmi and I come here every Saturday for a walk.'

She looked up and gave Lofty a 'yes we do' smile. Our chats in the pub had resolved our differences and we put everything behind us. Despite my disloyalty, we were back on track, and friends. We finished our tea and cake and said our goodbyes to Lofty. Demmi and I headed for the park to play on the swings.

I like the park in Aldershot; it is busy with kids and mums, never too many dads around so I didn't have to show off and I had a chance to admire the scenery as we play. I love this fragment of my life, just me and a kid mucking around with no responsibilities. We can do anything we want within reason, so after a swing I built a shelter for us from the branches of an old tree in the corner of the field and we sat under it. I never felt self-conscious in her company and she didn't criticise me; when we were doing something daring, she'd look into my eyes and I could tell that she trusted me, completely.

A lovely day all around, only broken by my mobile phone breaking the silence of our hiding hole. It was Leanne asking if we'd like to come home for tea so we took a vote and unanimously agreed that we were hungry; so I told her that we would be back soon. Leanne had cooked us the most delicious cottage pie and bought some beer for me that had been put in the fridge.

'I met Dad's friend today, he's called Lofty, and he was born in a loft.'

'Pardon darling?'

'Oh, we met an old mate of mine. Have I not told you about him?'

'No, you haven't mentioned him before Den.'

'Just somebody I know, haven't seen him for years.'

All weekend I had Lofty's suggestion of something on Part One Orders on my mind, so first thing on Monday I rushed in and got into my desert kit. Company Headquarters hadn't started work when I found the board displaying the list of requirements: nothing, all Private soldiers; I was gutted. The Sergeant Major appeared behind me en route to his office.

'Morning Corporal Yarwood, are you still looking for a slot on the tour?'

'Yes Sir, but they only want privates.'

'Well I wouldn't bank on them needing too much, I'll let you know if anything comes up.'

I thanked him and skulked off to start the day teaching.

As the weeks passed into March, Leanne planned the holiday down to the last pair of socks; we were flying out of Gatwick to Alicante and the hotel bus would pick us up at midnight. Nothing was said about Afghanistan in the house; but at work, as men were called forward a couple at a time, expectation grew.

The second Battalion had been put straight onto the streets of Kabul and were doing an outstanding job by all accounts, getting a name for themselves as a no nonsense yet fair force, carrying out their duties with the utmost professionalism. I looked at what seemed dozens of sets of bikinis tried on, lots of pairs of sunglasses and fired thousands of rounds. We went for inoculations at work, and Leanne and Demmi bought sun cream and whilst I was checking and re-checking the men's kit, Leanne was slowly and methodically packing our suitcases.

I really wanted my home-life, Leanne, Demmi; they gave me love and stability. A family holiday would be just the ticket and I could indulge myself in them like when we first met, and I would rush back to the hotel at every opportunity. We could drink wine in the evening sunlight and lollop by the pool; I might even try and teach Demmi how to dive.

I went straight home that night and helped sort the cases out; four weeks and we would be jetting off into the sun for a fortnight of Spanish bliss. It was late-night shopping on Thursday, so I took myself off and returned with *Spanish for Beginners* phrase book; and we sat over tea and asked each other our names and said 'thank you' and 'hello'. Demmi said that it sounded silly, especially when I found what I thought was 'This is my girlfriend', which sounded like 'knobio', much to my amusement. That was until Leanne pointed out to me that it meant 'this is my boyfriend', and I was the knobio!

When Demmi's passport came through the post we both laughed; she didn't find it so amusing. So I showed her mine, which was up for exchange next year; and the image of me as a twenty-year-old cheered her up, with my outdated sideburns.

'Corporal Yarwood, the Sergeant Major wants to see you.'

Sergeant Muir and I had never got on, so he took great pleasure in thinking that I was in trouble.

'Thanks Sarge.'

I knew I hadn't done anything wrong, so I took myself off to Company Headquarters with the paperwork results for the NBC training that I had conducted under my arm, in case he wanted to see the figures. I knocked and waited until I was called.

'Come!'

'You wanted to see me Sir; I've got the Company's NBC results.'

'Shut the door.'

I obliged.

'You asked me to keep an eye out for any jobs with 2 Batt.'

'Yes Sir.'

'Well there's one come up.'

'Oh!'

'But ... and you need to think about this before you give me an answer, you would have to deploy on Friday, that's the next flight.

The bonus is, it's for a Sergeant and as none of the spineless herberts from this Company wants to go, it would mean you get the acting rank for the tour. I've passed it by the OC and he thinks that you are up for the job.'

'Well Sir...'

'The thing is, I've seen that you have put a leave pass in for later on in the month; did you have anything important planned?'

'No Sir.'

'But it says that you are going to Spain.'

'Its fine Sir, honestly, nothing's booked.'

'And your family would be all right if you were to go straight out to Afghanistan, even with three days' notice?'

'Yes Sir.'

'Okay, well I'll need an answer by tom...'

'I'll go Sir.'

'...orrow, close of work.'

'Sir, I'll go.'

'Corporal Yarwood, I know you live out, though not officially, but you have a long-term girlfriend.'

'She'll be fine Sir; we have talked about it.'

'Right ... I'm not going to say anything to the boss today; come and see me in the morning and I can tell the admin office to start the paperwork. If you do a good job over there, you know when you come back in November you're likely to take over 3 Platoon and keep your Sergeant Stripes?'

'Hola,' Leanne had been practising.

'Hola to you too.'

I gave her a kiss as she placed my tea down; steak chips and mushrooms, my ultimate meal; all that was missing was a cold beer.

'Beer?' she asked as she stood holding the fridge door open.

'Ah, gratsi, ma knobio.'

'Don't push your luck.'

She joined me at the table.

'Demmi's asleep, she was shattered after preschool so I gave her a bath and put her down early, you know what she's like if she gets herself too tired.'

'Yeah, little miss Grumpy Knickers.'

'So how was work, anything exciting happen today?'

Leanne watched me eat, with her hands cupping her chin and her elbows on the table.

'Naa, not much, you know, usual stuff.'

'Oh, I meant to ask you Den, have you got your passport? I can't find it.'

'Yeah it's at work.'

'Why?'

'Oh I just had to show it to them; I'll bring it home tomorrow.'

'Mm'm, have they not seen it before?'

'Yes, but they have to check it to make sure it's in date.'

'Why Den, are you not responsible enough to make sure it's up to date yourself?'

'No, nothing like that, it's just that some of the lads forget theirs. Leanne, you know I said that I might have to go away?'

I looked up and she was staring intently at me.

'Den, we have got a holiday booked.'

'Yes, look – I haven't volunteered for anything, it's just that there is a chance that I could get promoted.'

Silence and Leanne's hands wrung around the cup of tea she was holding.

'I could get my Sergeant Stripes, it's a once in a lifetime opportunity.'

'What are you trying to tell me? Or are you seeking some approval? Do you remember not so long ago how you said that this was what you wanted out of life, do you recall that Den?'

'Yes, I haven't said ...'

'Well what are you saying? Because it sounds to me like you're just about to drop a bombshell.'

'No Leanne, listen to me, please, I love you, and Demmi, and this is all I want, but what if we had more money ...'

'Den, I want you, we want you I don't care about the money, I'm not thick you know. I know that this is about Afghanistan, isn't it?'

'I've been asked to fill a place over there for a short while.'

'And what exactly is a 'short while'?'

'Until November, but Leanne I haven't said yes.'

'Den, you have got some serious choices to make and you had better think long and hard about what you actually want. I've invested everything in you, left myself wide open. Demmi thinks the world of you Den, she thinks you're her Daddy for Christ's sake, you are, Den.'

'Leanne please I haven't said that I'd go, honestly.'

I could see the tears welling up in her eyes and she stood and left the table. I heard her feet hitting the stairs and then tramp into the bedroom. Then it was quiet; so I sat thinking about my dilemma. I had less than twelve hours to give my decision and three days before the plane left. Leanne was right, she and Demmi were my everything.

Chapter Forty

The heat on the tarmac was intense as we got off the plane and there was a buzz of excitement as we waited for the bus. Even at night it was much hotter than Blighty in summertime and I could feel myself breaking into a sweat as I carried the bags. At least the trip on the bus was short and it had air conditioning. I started to feel drowsy and as I stared out of the window I thought about putting my head on a pillow, until I felt a sting on my neck and had my blood sucked by some foreign dipterans. I'd be surprised if the little bugger survived as my body oozed booze; even the girl sat next to me sniffed the air in disgust when she realised she had to endure the journey with a partially pissed man.

We travelled through the town, which in the moonlight looked beautiful; there were people on the streets even at this late hour making their way home after a long night.

I awoke early as the sunlight scorched through the window, and got dressed for breakfast. I know some people can't eat in a hot climate, but I was ravenous, so I opted for the full English with a cup of tea and some toast. It's relaxing not having to cook or wash up yourself; I was planning my day ahead and getting orientated. I'd just finished writing to a sixteen-year-old Demmi; she wouldn't be able to read my letter until then.

I didn't notice her until she was stood right in front of me; I looked up and she was smiling; she was much prettier in the early morning sunlight.

'Hello Tina.'

'I heard you were coming out. Ooh, Lance Sergeant now eh! You've done well for yourself.'

'Thanks.'

'The Sergeant Major wants to see you as soon as you've

finished breakfast.'

'Okay, I'll be along shortly; I'm not going to let my tea go cold over it.'

Glossary

AWOL	Absent Without Leave
BOBFOC	Body off Baywatch, Face off Crimewatch
CEFO	Combat Equipment Fighting Order
CES	Complete Equipment Schedule
COY	Company
CO	Commanding Officer, appointment not rank
CSM	Company Sergeant Major
DS	Directing Staff
GSM	Garrison Sergeant Major
HQ	Headquarters
ICP	Incident Control Point
IRA	Irish Republican Army
LSW	Light Support Weapon
MT	Military Transport
MONG	Man of no grounding
NAAFI	Navy Army and Air Forces Institute
NIG	New in green kit
NBC	Nuclear Biological and Chemical Warfare
OC	Officer Commanding, appointment not rank
Ops Room	Operations Room
PTI	Physical Training Instructor
QBP	Queen's Birthday Parade
QRF	Quick Reaction Force
RAF	Royal Air Force
RHIP	Rank has its privileges
RHQ	Regimental Headquarters
RLC	Royal Logistic Corps
RPG	Rocket Propelled Grenade
RSM	Regimental Sergeant Major

RUC	Royal Ulster Constabulary
R&R	Rest and recuperation
SWEAT	Soldier with experience and training
UN	United Nations
UNHCR	United Nations High Command for Refugees
VIP	Very Important Person

Lightning Source UK Ltd.
Milton Keynes UK
175224UK00001B/1/P